PRAISE FOR *JERUSALEM POKER*

D0851070

"Whittemore presents himself as one of the last, best arguments against television. He's an author of extraordinary talents, albeit one who eludes comparison with other writers . . . . The milieu is one which readers of espionage novels may think themselves familiar, and yet it's totally transformed—by the writer's wild humour, his mystical bent, and his bicameral perception of history and time . . . . If Whittemore were no more than an 'entertainer' his novels would be worth their price. But he does something more difficult than intellectual vaudeville. He assassinates the banal, revealing the authentic current of madness that courses through human affairs, reminding us that the fantastic is ubiquitous, invisible only because we've shut our eyes to it."
Harper's

PRAISE FOR THE JERUSALEM QUARTET

"Whittemore's colorful characters wrestle fitfully with meaninglessness, time, and the grim realities of war. Sinai Tapestry ends with a portrait of the Turks' 1922 genocidal assault on Smyrna that sobers up the reader like a jackboot at a sock-hop. As the Quartet progresses, the novels become less playful, their earlier flights of fantasy increasingly tempered by failure and pain into a resigned yet mystic melancholy . . . . Though the geopolitics of the Middle East always loom in the background, Whittemore is constantly probing for the gaps and loops in time. As in Gabriel Garcia Marquez's *One Hundred Years of Solitude*, characters return in name and shape through their progeny, while people, events,

and certain phrases are regularly reintroduced, giving you the feeling that you are wandering through a labyrinth of memory. The Jerusalem Quartet is rich with homegrown theology, and leaves you with a mystic taste for the empty network of all things: 'All lives are secret tapestries that swirl and sweep through the years with souls and strivings as the colors, the threads. And there may be little knots of tangled meaning everywhere beneath the surface, tying the colors and threads together, but the little knots aren't important finally, only the sweep itself, the tapestry as a whole.'"
The Voice Literary Supplement

"The four books which make up the Jerusalem Quartet are among the richest and most profound in imaginative literature. . . and also among the most obscure, out of print for more than ten years. Whittemore has been . . . unfairly neglected and it can only be hoped that his star will rise again in another decade or so. Such a superlative body of work cannot be overlooked forever."
Jeff VanderMeer, *Literature of the Fantastic Newsletter*

SINAI TAPESTRY

"The Sinai tapestry of 'lives that had raged through vast secret wars and been struck dumb by equally vast silences, textures harsh and soft in their guise of colors, a cloak of life' is a work of literature, a 'chaotic' book of life . . . . Whittemore is a deceptively lucid stylist. Were his syntax as cluttered as Pynchon's or as grand as Nabokov's or Fuentes's, his virtually ignored recent novel might have received the attention it deserves, for his imagination of present and alternative worlds is comparable to theirs . . . ."
Anthony Heilbut, *The Nation*

"An epic hashish dream . . . . cosmic . . . . fabulous . . . . droll and moving"
The New York Times Book Review

achievements in 20th-century literature. . . . Without illusion, but with supreme intelligence and a generous heart, Whittemore shows us just how painful, beautiful, and surprising . . . life's reversals can be, and how our struggles with ourselves and others can ultimately seem to change time itself."
The Philadelphia Inquirer

Jerusalem Poker

BY EDWARD WHITTEMORE

Quin's Shanghai Circus (1974)
Sinai Tapestry (1977)
Jerusalem Poker (1978)
Nile Shadows (1983)
Jericho Mosaic (1987)

Jerusalem Poker

by Edward Whittemore

Introduction by Lesley Hazleton

With a Foreword by Tom Wallace
and an Afterword by Judy Karasik

OLD EARTH BOOKS
Baltimore, Maryland
2002

JERUSALEM POKER

ACKNOWLEDGEMENTS

The essay, "An Editorial Relationship" also appeared in AGNI 55, Spring 2002

Published by
Old Earth Books
Post Office Box 19951
Baltimore, Maryland 21211
www.oldearthbooks.com

Original Interior Book Design by Kathy Peck

Book Production: Old Earth Books Edition
Garcia Publishing Services
Post Office Box 1059
Woodstock, Illinois 60098
www.american-fantasy.com

10 9 8 7 6 5 4 3 2

ISBN: 1-882968-23-9

PRINTED IN THE UNITED STATES OF AMERICA
By Thomson-Shore
Dexter, Michigan

For
Abby and Sarah

Contents

Photo by Helen Bar-Lev

Edward Whittemore (1933-1995)

"Some twenty years after the end of the war with Japan a freighter arrived in Brooklyn with the largest collection of Japanese pornography ever assembled in a Western tongue. The owner of the collection, a huge, smiling fat man named Geraty, presented a passport to customs officials that showed that he was a native-born American about as old as the century, an exile who had left the United States four decades before." Thus begins *Quin's Shanghai Circus;* it ends with the largest funeral procession held in Asia since the thirteenth century.

The year was 1974, the author Edward Whittemore, a forty-one year-old former American intelligence agent; he and I had been undergraduates at Yale back in the 1950s, but then we had gone our separate ways, he to the CIA and I to a career in book publishing in New York City. Needless to say, I was pleased that my old Yale friend had brought his novel to me and the publishing house of Holt, Rinehart and Winston where I was editor-in-chief of the Trade Department. I was even more delighted when the reviews, mostly favorable, started coming in, capped by Jerome Charyn in *The New York Times Book Review*: *"Quin* was a profoundly nutty book full of mysteries, truths, untruths, idiot savants, necrophiliacs, magicians, dwarfs, circus masters, secret agents . . . a marvelous recasting of history in our century."

In the next fifteen years Whittemore went on to write four more wildly imaginative novels, his Jerusalem Quartet: *Sinai*

Tapestry, Jerusalem Poker, Nile Shadows, and *Jericho Mosaic.*
Reviewers and critics compared his work to the novels of Carlos
Fuentes, Thomas Pynchon, and Kurt Vonnegut. *Publishers Weekly*
called him "our best unknown novelist." Jim Hougan, writing in
Harper's Magazine, said Whittemore was "one of the last, best arguments against television.... He is an author of extraordinary talents.
. . . The milieu is one in which readers of espionage novels may
think themselves familiar, and yet it is totally transformed by the
writer's wild humor, his mystical bent, and his bicameral perception
of time and history."

Edward Whittemore died from prostate cancer in the summer
of 1995 at the age of sixty-two, not much better known than when
he began his short, astonishing writing career in the early 1970s.
His novels never sold more than 5000 copies in hard covers, three
were briefly available in mass market paperback editions. But the
Quartet was published in Great Britain, Holland, and Germany
where Whittemore was described on its jacket as the "master
American storyteller." The jacket on the Polish edition of *Quin's
Shanghai Circus* was a marvelous example of Japanese erotica.

*

Whittemore graduated from Deering High School, Portland,
Maine in June 1951 and entered Yale that fall, a member of the
Class of 1955. Another Yale classmate, the novelist Ric Frede,
labeled Yale undergraduates of the 1950s "members of the Silent
Generation." The Fifties were also the "Eisenhower Years," that
comfortable period between the Second World War and the radi-
calism and the campus unrest of the 1960s. Ivy League universities
were still dominated by the graduates of New England prep
schools. Sons of the East Coast "establishment," they were closer to
the Princeton of F. Scott Fitzgerald and the Harvard of John P.
Marquand then the worlds of Jack Kerouac and Allen Ginsberg.
They were "gentlemen" and athletes but not necessarily scholars.
Often after receiving "gentlemanly C's" at Yale and the other Ivys,
they went on to careers on Wall Street or in Washington; to the
practice of law medicine or journalism. They entertained their families and friends on the playing fields of Yale as well as at Mory's.

They ran *The Yale Daily News*, WYBC (the campus radio station), *The Yale Record* (the humor magazine), *The Yale Banner* (the year book), and sang in various Yale music groups. They were usually members of a fraternity and were "tapped" by one of the six secret Senior Societies.

By the Yale standards of the day, Whittemore was a great success, a "high school boy" who made it. Affable, good-looking and trim, he presented a quizzical smile to the world. He casually wore the uniform that was "in": herringbone tweed jacket, preferably with patches at the elbow, rep tie, chinos and scruffy white buck shoes. In a word, he was "shoe" (short for "white shoe," a term of social approval). He was not much of an athlete, but he was a member of Zeta Psi, a fraternity of hard-drinking, socially well-connected undergraduates. At the end of Junior year he was tapped for Scroll and Key.

But his real distinction was that he was the Managing Editor of the 1955 *Yale News* Board at a time when *News* chairmen and managing editors were as popular as football team captains and the leading scholar of the class. During the immediate postwar years and the 1950s the *Yale News* produced such prominent writer-journalists as William F. Buckley, James Claude Thomson, Richard Valeriani, David McCullough, Roger Stone, M. Stanton Evans, Henry S.F. Cooper, Calvin Trillin, Gerald Jonas, Harold Gulliver, Scott Sullivan, and Robert Semple. They would make their mark at *The New York Times*, *The New Yorker*, *Time*, *Newsweek*, *The National Review*, *Harper's*, and the television networks, and go on to write many books.

*

I met Ted early in the spring of Freshman year. We were both "heeling" the first *News* "comp," and as was usually the case with survivors of that fierce "competition" to make the *News*, we remained friends throughout our years at Yale. It was assumed by many of us on the *News* that Ted would head for Wall Street and Brown Brothers Harriman, a blue-chip investment firm where Old Blues from Scroll and Key were more than welcome and where Ted's older brother later worked. Or at the very least, he would get on the journalistic fast-track somewhere in the *Time-Life* empire founded by an earlier *News* worthy, Henry Luce.

But we were wrong. Whittemore, after a tour of duty as an officer in the Marines in Japan, was approached there by the CIA, given a crash course in Japanese, and spent more than a decade working for the Agency in the Far East, Europe and the Middle East.

During those years Whittemore would periodically return to New York. "What are you up to?" one would ask. For a while he was running a newspaper in Greece. Then there was the shoe company in Italy and some sort of think-tank in Jerusalem. Even a stint with the New York City drug administration when John Lindsay was mayor. Later, there were rumors that he had a drinking "problem" and that he was taking drugs.

He married and divorced twice while he was with the Marines and the Agency. He and his first wife had two daughters, but under the terms of the divorce agreement he was not permitted to see them. And then there were the women he lived with after the second divorce. There were many; they all seemed to be talented— painters, photographers, sculptors, and dancers, but never writers.

There were more rumors. He had left the Agency, he was living on Crete, he had no money, he was writing. Then silence. Clearly, the "fair-haired" undergraduate had not gone on to fame and glory.

*

It was not until 1972 or 1973 that Ted surfaced in my life. He was back in New York on a visit. On the surface he appeared to be the old Ted. He was a little rumpled, but the wit, the humor, the boyish charm were still there. Yet he seemed more thoughtful, more reflective, and there was Carol, a woman with whom Ted had become involved while in Crete and with whom he seemed to be living. He was more secretive now. And he had the manuscript of a novel he wanted me to read. I thought the novel was wonderful, full of fabulous and exotic characters, brimming with life, history, and the mysteries of the Orient. The novel that came to be called *Quin's Shanghai Circus* went through three more drafts before we published it in 1974. Set in Japan and China before and during the Second World War, two drafts even began in the South Bronx in the 1920s and involved three young Irish brothers named Quin. By the time the novel came out only one Quin remained and the Bronx interlude had shrunk from eighty pages to a couple of paragraphs.

As mentioned, *Quin* was a bigger success with the critics than it was in the bookstores. Readers loved the novel, even though there were not nearly enough of them. But Whittemore was not deterred. Less than two years later he appeared in my office with an even more ambitious novel, *Sinai Tapestry*, the first volume of his Jerusalem Quartet. Set in the heyday of the British Empire, it takes place in Palestine during the middle of the nineteenth century. Foremost among the larger-than-life characters were a tall English aristocrat, the greatest swordsman, botanist, and explorer of Victorian England; a fanatical trappist monk who found the original Sinai Bible, which "denies every religious truth every held by anyone;" and an Irish radical who had fled to Palestine disguised as a nun. My favorite was (and still is) Haj Harun, born three thousand years earlier, an ethereal wanderer through history: now an antiquities dealer dressed in a faded yellow cloak and sporting a Crusaders' rusty helmet while pursuing his mission as defender of the Holy City. He had several previous incarnations: as a stone carver of winged lions during the Assyrian occupation, proprietor of an all-night grocery store under the Greeks, a waiter when the Romans were in power, and a distributor of hashish and goats for the Turks. Before I first went to Israel in 1977, Whittemore, who was then writing in New York, gave me the names of several people in Jerusalem. One was named Mohammed, the owner of an antiquities gallery. When I finally tracked him down in the Old City I saw before me a fey character who, if he had been wearing a faded yellow cloak and a rusty helmet, would have been a dead ringer for Haj Harun.

Clearly Ted had been caught up in a new life in Jerusalem. The immediately preceding years in Crete where he had been living on a modest pension in the early 70s were behind him. He had been sharing a house with friends in Khania, the second largest city on Crete. In its long history it had been occupied by the Romans, conquered by the Arabs, Byzantines, and Venetians before becoming part of the Ottoman Empire in the seventeenth century. Now it was a sprawling Greek City. Athens without the Parthenon, but with an even richer history. In other words, a perfect place for a former intelligence agent to take stock and decide what history was all about, to re-examine what he had learned as a Yale undergraduate.

*

While in Japan in the 1960s Whittemore had written two unpublished novels, one about the Japanese game of Go, the other about a young American expatriate living in Tokyo. In Crete he began to write again, slowly, awkwardly, experimenting with voice, style,and subject matter, distilling his experience in the Agency into that sweeping raucous epic, *Quin's Shanghai Circus*. By the time he embarked on the Quartet, he was more assured, he was becoming a writer, and he had found a subject that was to engage him for the rest of his life: Jerusalem and the world of Christians, Arabs and Jews; faith and belief; mysticism and religious (and political) fanaticism; nineteenth century; European imperialism, twentieth century wars and terrorism. But above all Jerusalem, the City on the Hill, the Holy City. The novels would still be full of outrageous characters, the humor was still often grotesque and macabre, and there was violence aplenty. But there was also a new understanding of the mysteries of life.

The new novel, finally published in 1979, was *Jerusalem Poker*, the second volume of the Quartet. It involves a twelve-year poker game begun in the last days of December 1921 when three men sit down to play. The stakes were nothing less than the Holy City itself. Where else could a game for the control of Jerusalem be played but in the antiquities shop of Haj Harun? Actually, Ted did not come to live permanently (that is "permanently" according to his ways) in Jerusalem until he was well into writing the Quartet. His knowledge of Jerusalem was based initially on books, but later on he wandered endlessly through the crowded, teeming streets and Quarters of the Old City. Merchants of every kind, butchers, tanners, glass blowers, jewelers, silversmiths,and even iron mongers spoke nearly every known language and dressed in the vibrant and exotic costumes of the Middle East. I once remarked to Ted while we were making our way along a narrow passage in the Arab Quarter, that I fully expected we would run into Sinbad the Sailor coming the other way.

The next time I visited Jerusalem, Ted had settled down with Helen, an American painter, in a spacious apartment in a large, nineteenth-century stone building in the Ethiopian Church compound. The apartment overlooked a courtyard full of flowers and lemon trees. Over one wall there loomed a Cistercian convent, and around the corner there was a synagogue full of Orthodox rabbinical students praying twenty-four hours a-day, or so it seemed to me. And standing or quietly reading in the courtyard were the Ethiopian monks. One morning I woke at six in my sunlit room and heard the Cistercian nuns singing a cappella. They sounded like birds and I thought for a moment I was in heaven.

After a midday nap we usually headed for the Old City, invariably ending up in the same cafe, a pretentious name for what was little more than an outdoor tea garden where hot tea and sticky buns were served. The proprietor sat at one table interminably fingering worry beads and talking to friends, an ever-changing group of local merchants, money changers, students, and some unsavory hard-looking types. They all seemed to have a nodding acquaintance with Ted, who knew as much, if not more, about the Old City as its inhabitants.

*

By 1981, Whittemore was living much of the year in the apartment in the Ethiopian compound, but in the years ahead he also rented a series of rooms in New York, a walk-up on Lexington Avenue, a studio apartment on Third. And he was writing steadily. I had left Holt earlier that spring for another publishing house and Judy Karasik took over the editorial work on Whittemore's new novel, *Nile Shadows*. She has written the epilogue to this book, a eulogy which she should have but didn't give at Whittemore's funeral twelve years after *Nile Shadows* appeared.

Nile Shadows is set in Egypt, it is 1942 and Rommel's powerful Afrika Corps is threatening to overrun Egypt and seize control of the entire Middle East. A group of characters, some old, some new, hold the fate of the world in their hands. At the very beginning of the novel, Stern, an idealistic visionary in *Sinai Tapestry* turned gun-runner a half century later, is killed by a grenade thrown into the doorway of a backstreet bar. Violence as well as mysticism dominates Whittemore's novels. Elsewhere he had described with horrible abandon the "rape" of Nanking and the sack of Smyrna in 1922 when the Turks butchered ten of thousands of Greek men, women, and children. A *Publishers Weekly* reviewer said: "One of the most complex and ambitious espionage stories ever written." And a critic in *The Nation* said: "Whittemore is a deceptively lucid stylist. Were his syntax as cluttered as Pynchon's or as conspicuously grand as Nabokov's or Fuentes', his virtually ignored novels might have received the attention they deserved."

But sales still hadn't caught up with the critics. By the spring of 1985, Ted was finishing the novel that was to be called *Jericho Mosaic*, the fourth of the Jerusalem Quartet. I was in Israel for the biennial Jerusalem International Book Fair. Afterwards, Ted suggested we drive down to Jericho, that oasis to the southeast of Jerusalem from which most of the caravans of Biblical times set out for the Levant, Asia Minor, and Africa. On the way we visited several Greek Orthodox monasteries in the Judean wilderness. Since they were built into solid rock at the bottom of isolated ravines reachable only on narrow paths, we had to leave the car up on the road and scramble down hillsides more suitable for mountain goats than a novelist and a New York editor. However, once we made it safely to the bottom, the monks proved to be extremely hospitable. Whittemore was a frequent visitor and the monks seemed to enjoy his company.

After being shown around the rocky quarters, not much more than elaborate caves, and consuming some dreadful retsina (the monks didn't drink it themselves) we continued to Jericho and a typical lunch of dried figs, a bread-like pastry and melon and hot fragrant tea. Then we made our way to the Negev. Over the years Ted had befriended some of the local Bedouins and we were greeted like old friends at several encampments. We spent one night at an Israeli meteorological center/desert inn near a Nabatean ruin. There seemed to be antennae and electric sensors everywhere, and as we used to say in those days, gray men in London, Washington,

Moscow, and Beijing could probably hear every sparrow-fart in the desert. In retrospect, I sometimes wonder if Ted had ever really retired? Was he still, in this case, visiting his "controller," and using me as his "cover?"

Several months later, when Ted sent me a post card urging me to save a spot on an upcoming list for his next novel, the design on the card was a Byzantine mosaic of "the Tree of Life" Ted and I had seen on the stone floor of a ruin in Jericho. I took it to the art director at Norton where I was then a senior editor. He agreed with me that it would make an excellent design for a book jacket. All we needed was a manuscript.

*

Jericho Mosaic arrived before the end of the year, a fitting culmination to Whittemore's marvelous Quartet. In my opinion, *Jericho Mosaic* is the most breathtakingly original espionage story ever written. The novel is based on events that actually took place before the Six Day War and Whittemore demonstrates his total knowledge of the craft of intelligence and its practitioners, his passion for the Middle East, his devotion to the Holy City, and his commitment to peace and understanding among, Arabs, Jews, and Christians. The novel and the novelist maintain we can overcome religious, philosophical, and political differences if we are ready to commit ourselves to true understanding for all people and all ideas.

This humanistic message is imbedded in a true story involving Eli Cohen, a Syrian Jew who sacrificed his life (he managed to turn over to Mossad the Syrian plans and maps for the defense of the Golan Heights) in order that Israel might survive. In the novel Whittemore tells the story of Halim (who is clearly based on Eli Cohen) a Syrian businessman who returns to his homeland from Buenos Aires to help forward the Arab revolution. Halim becomes an outspoken advocate for Palestinian rights, he is the conscience of the Arab cause, "the incorruptible one." But Halim is a Jew, an agent for the Mossad; his codename is "the Runner," his assignment to penetrate the heart of the Syrian military establishment. At the same time the novel is a profound meditation on the nature of faith in which an Arab holy man, a Christian mystic, and a former British intelligence officer sit in a garden in Jericho exploring religion and humanity's relation to its various faces.

There were fewer reviews of *Jericho Mosaic* and even fewer sales than before. Arabs and Jews were involved in a bloody confrontation on the West Bank, there were lurid photographs in the newspapers and magazines and on television every day, and even more horrific stories. The times were not propitious for novelists defending the eternal verities, no matter how well they wrote. One critic did, however, proclaim Whittemore's Quartet "the best metaphor for the intelligence business in recent American fiction."

Shortly after *Jericho Mosaic* was published Whittemore left Jerusalem, the Ethiopian compound, and the American painter. He was back in New York living during the winter with Ann, a woman he had met years before when she and her then husband befriended Ted and his first wife. In the summers he would take over the sprawling, white, Victorian family home in Dorset, Vermont. The windows had green shutters, an an acre of lawn in front of the house was bounded by immense stately evergreen trees. Twenty or so rooms were distributed around the house in some arbitrary New England Victorian design, and the furniture dated back to his grandparents, if not great-grandparents. Ted's brothers and sisters by now had their own houses and so Ted was pretty much its sole occupant. It was not winterized and could only be inhabited from May through October. But for Ted it was a haven to which he could retreat and write.

*

In the spring of 1987 I became a literary agent and Ted joined me as a client. American book publishing was gradually being taken over by international conglomerates with corporate offices in Germany and Great Britain. They were proving to be more enamored of commerce than literature and it seemed to me I could do more for writers by representing them to any of a dozen publishers rather than just working for one.

I regularly visited Ted in the fall in Dorset. "The foliage season," late September, early October, is a very special time of year in New England: crisp clear days, wonderfully cool moonlit nights. We walked the woods and fields of southern Vermont by day, sat in front of the house after dinner on solid green Adirondack chairs, drink in hand and smoking. Actually I was the one drinking (usually brandy) because Ted had stopped years ago (his "habit" had become so serious that he had joined Alcoholics Anonymous); while we talked I would smoke a cigar or two, Ted would merely smoke one evil-looking cheroot. Comfortably ensconced on the lawn near the United Church, where his great-grandfather had been a minister, within sight of the Village Green and the Dorset Inn, our talk would turn to books and writing, family and friends. To his family, Ted must have been the "black sheep," the Yalie who had gone off to the CIA, had, so to speak, burned out, had come home via Crete, Jerusalem, and New York as a peripatetic novelist whose books received glowing reviews that resulted in less than glowing sales. But they, and "his women," supported him and continued to believe in him.

It was during these early fall visits that I discovered that his Prentiss great-grandfather had been a Presbyterian minister who had made his way up the Hudson River by boat from New York to Troy and then over to Vermont by train and wagon in the 1860s. In the library of the white, rambling Victorian house in Dorset there were shelves of fading leather-bound volumes of popular romances written by his great-grandmother for shop girls, informing them how to improve themselves, dress, and find suitable husbands. I gathered she was the Danielle Steele of her day, and the family's modest wealth was due to her literary efforts and not the generosity of the church's congregation.

We talked about the new novel. It was to be called *Sister Sally and Billy the Kid* and it was to be Ted's first American novel. It was about an Italian in his twenties from the Chicago of the roaring Twenties. His older brother, a gangster, had helped him buy a flower shop. But there was a shoot-out, the older brother was dead, and Billy has to flee to the West Coast where he meets a faith healer not unlike Aimee Semple McPherson. The real-life McPherson disappeared for a month in 1926, and when she returned claimed she had been kidnapped. The stone house in which Billy and his faith healer spend their month of love (from the beginning it is clear that the idyll must be limited to one month) has a walled garden behind it full of lemon trees and singing birds. Although that house is in southern California, the garden bears a close resemblance to another garden in the Ethiopian compound in Jerusalem with a synagogue on one side and a Cistercian convent on the other.

Then one day in early spring 1995, Ted called me. Could he come by the office that morning? I assumed it was to deliver the long-awaited manuscript. There had been two false starts after *Jericho Mosaic*. Instead Ted told me he was dying. Would I be his literary executor? A year or so earlier Ted had been diagnosed as having prostate cancer. It was too far along for an operation. His doctor had prescribed hormones and other medication and the cancer had gone into remission. But now it had spread. Less than six months later he was dead. They were terrible months for him. However, during those last weeks and days while he slipped in and out of consciousness, he was looked after by "his women," one of whom, Carol, had returned to his life after a nearly two-decade separation.

There was a hushed memorial service in the United Church in Dorset that August. Afterwards, a reception was held on the large lawn in front of the family house. It was there that the disparate parts of Ted's world came together, perhaps for the first time; there was his family, his two sisters and two brothers and their spouses, nieces, and nephews with their own families (but not Ted's wives or the two daughters who had flown to New York to say "good-bye" to the father they hardly knew); there were neighbors, Yale friends, and a couple of colleagues from the Lindsay years. Were there any "spooks" in attendance? One really can't say, but there were eight "spooks" of a different sort from Yale, members of the 1955 Scroll and Key delegation. Ann and Carol, who had become allies while watching over Ted during those last, bitter days, were, of course, there.

Jerusalem and Dorset. The beautiful Holy City on the rocky cliffs overlooking the parched gray-brown desert. A city marked by thousands of years of history, turbulent struggles between great empires and three of the most enduring, vital religions given by God to mankind. And the summer-green valley in Vermont (covered by snow in the winter and by mud in the spring) where Dorset nestled between the ridges of the softly rolling Green Mountains. Once one of the cradles of the American Revolution and American democracy, and later a thriving farming and small manufacturing community, it was a place where time stood still since the beginning of the twentieth century. One was the subject of Whittemore's dreams and books; the other the peaceful retreat in which he dreamt and wrote the last twenty summers of his life.

Ted had finally come home to New England. It had been a long journey: Portland, New Haven, Japan, Italy, New York, Jerusalem, Greece, Crete, Jerusalem, New York, and now Dorset. Along the way he had many friends and companions, he was not a particularly good husband or father and disappointed many. But gradually he had found his voice, written his novels, and fallen in love with Jerusalem. I would like to think that Ted died dreaming of his Holy City. In a sense he was at one with that stone-cutter turned medieval knight, turned antiquities dealer, Haj Harun. For Whittemore was the eternal knight-errant who "made it" at Yale in the 1950s, "lost it" in the CIA in the 1960s, and then made himself into a wonderful novelist with the voice of a mystic. The voice of a mystic who had absorbed the best of Judaism, Christianity, and Islam. His great-grandfather the minister and his great-grandmother the writer would have been equally proud of him. His spirit rests peacefully in Dorset, Vermont.

Tom Wallace
New York City, 2002

INTRODUCTION

Jerusalem in the late seventies. Caught eternally, it seemed, between war and peace. That's when a small group of us — writers, journalists, historians, commentators gathering every Friday in a downtown café — discovered Edward Whittemore.

None of us had met him, except through his fiction, but we needed him. We needed him badly. Bogged down in the particularities of daily events, in the hourly newscasts and mind numbing series of military and political skirmishes, we needed someone who could soar above it all. Someone who could take the absurd reality in which we lived and weave it into a rich tapestry of realist absurdity.

More precisely, Whittemore didn't soar so much as tunnel. He tunneled under the surface of Jerusalem, following the three-thousand-year-old antiquities dealer Haj Harun in his tattered yellow cape and dented Crusader helmet down through the physical layers of the place — one era's stones laid on top of the previous one's to create a vertical history — and into the existential city, the one we really inhabited if we could only escape daily reality long enough to see it.

Funny, scabrous, magical, cynical, romantic, clear-eyed — Whittemore was all these and more. Reading him, we felt as though finally someone had come along who could grasp the madness in which we lived. Who could take it and run with it, celebrating its delirious complexity, its fantastic twists and turns, its ramifications though the centuries and across the globe.

Later, when he moved to Jerusalem and lived right by the domed Ethiopian church, a hidden compound where black-robed monks swayed and chanted as they had for centuries, it seemed as though Whittemore were the Pied Piper of the city, playing the hidden tune that would make it dance. He wrote out of an immense affection for the place, its inhabitants and their foibles. Out of pity for the bloodshed yet with calm, Zen-like insight into the passions that led to it. His Jerusalem quartet, now nearly complete, had become a symphony of time and history, innocence and experience.

By then, he could himself have been a character from the Quartet: the ex-CIA agent secluded in the peaceful oasis of the Ethiopian compound, speaking Geez with the monks, juggling the story of Jerusalem at his desk by the arched stone window. There was always something pixie-like about him, but now it seemed he had become a master conjuror who could take your mind and stretch it through time and space, then bring it back again in an arcing circularity, wiser and sadder and yet at the same time happier.

And then he disappeared. And later resurfaced in New York. And in terribly short order, died. Perhaps he knew of the cancer when he walked away from Jerusalem literally in the middle of the night, leaving behind this lovely, wild, time- and mind-bending series of novels.

***

I was the first in that Friday group to discover Whittemore, quite by the kind of chance he loved. On a break from a year's wandering round the Sinai in research for a book, I strayed into Jerusalem's main bookstore and found, in the remainder bin, a paperback titled *Sinai Tapestry*. The cover was luridly sci-fi — the publisher had served him ill — but nevertheless I read the first few pages and knew I had to read them all.

Determined to make the book last, I allowed myself no more than twenty pages an evening. And each day, I'd tell friends what I'd read the night before.

They accused me of making it up.

I wish I'd been able to.

I went back to the store, bought every copy, and handed them out. We became a kind of Whittemore cult, tracing shades of

Vonnegut and Borges, Pynchon and Lawrence Durrell in the man who'd been called "America's best least-known writer."

And then a year or so later, passing by the same store, I saw *Jerusalem Poker* in the window. In hardback — a major investment at the time for a struggling wordsmith. But I had no choice: I walked right in and bought it. And knew instantly that this would be my favorite of the planned Quartet.

If you had to describe the novel in one line, you could say it's about a twelve-year poker game for control of the holy city. But that, of course, is only the top layer, as you realize if you take just the three main players in the Great Jerusalem Poker Game: Moslem, Christian, and Jew.

First, Cairo Martyr, the Nubian dragoman with pale blue eyes who has made a fortune selling mummy dust cut with quinine as an aphrodisiac. Then Joe O'Sullivan Beare, an Irish patriot who now smuggles arms for the Haganah inside giant hollow scarabs, and trades in sacred phallic amulets. And then Munk Szondi, the scion of a powerful Budapest-based banking house run by a matriarchal directorate known as The Sarahs, who trades in futures — any and all futures.

> "Mummy dust. Trading in futures. Religious symbols. With that kind of backing, the three men seemed unbeatable. Year after year, they stripped visitors to Jerusalem of all they owned, bewildered emirs and European smugglers and feuding sheikhs, devout priests and assorted commercial agents and pious fanatics, every manner of pilgrim in that vast dreaming army from many lands that had always been scaling the heights of the Holy City in search of spiritual gold, Martyr and Szondi and O'Sullivan Beare implacably dealing and shuffling and dealing again, relentlessly plunging Jerusalem into its greatest turmoil since the First Crusade."

Familiar and half-familiar characters swirl in and out of the narrative as it arcs from Jericho to Smyrna, Venice to Cairo, the pendulum swinging inexorably back and forth through Jerusalem. There's the seven-foot-tall Plantagenet Strongbow, an English lord who purchased the whole of the Ottoman Empire and wrote a 33-volume study of Levantine sex. Avraham Stern of the eponymous Stern Gang. A Japanese nobleman who becomes a revered rabbi in seclusion beneath Mount Sinai. King Zog of Albania. Warlords and pederasts, eunuchs and bishops, lovers and thieves and soldiers and spies all dancing to Whittemore's tune of time infinite and ineffable.

This is a Jerusalem where time expands and contracts. where it may suddenly, unpredictably, speed up or slow down. "Eternal city and so forth," says O'Sullivan Beare. Daft time spinning out of control for sure on top of the holy mountain." But always in the world of Whittemore, time's swoops and spirals come full circle — as they have now for *Jerusalem Poker*, back in print after the mere eye blink of twenty-odd years.

—Lesley Hazleton
Seattle, 2002

Lesley Hazleton's books include the award-winning *Jerusalem, Jerusalem* and *Where Mountains Roar*. She lived thirteen years in Jerusalem, reporting on the Middle East for *Time, The New York Times, Esquire, The Nation* and many other publications. In a Whittemoreish move, she now lives and writes on a houseboat in Seattle.

Prologue

*I*n the first light of an early summer day a naked Junker baron and his naked wife, both elderly, both heavily overweight and sweating, stood on top of the Great Pyramid waiting for the sunrise.

The air was warm and the desert still, the year was 1914 and the noble couple from Behind Pomerania had just fulfilled a lifelong dream of making love on the summit of the Great Pyramid at dawn, to the point of a final and exhaustive satisfaction.

A few blocks down from the summit sat the man who had performed these various acts upon them, an experienced black dragoman and former slave named Cairo Martyr. For the baron and his wife it was the rarest moment in their long lives, but for Martyr it was just another routine sunrise that had earned him twenty pounds sterling for services rendered.

He yawned and lit a cigarette.

The sun slipped above the horizon and the baron and baroness spread their arms wide to receive it, their skin and hair so fair they were all but invisible in the desert dawn.

Glistening sweat and decaying fat. Sunrise. Cairo Martyr puffed lazily and turned his gaze north when he heard the distant drone of an airplane.

It was a small triplane carrying the morning mail from Alexandria up the Nile to the capital. Martyr watched it grow larger and realized it was heading straight toward the pyramid. In another moment he could make out the dashing figure in the open cockpit, a grinning English pilot in a leather helmet and flying goggles, his white scarf flowing on the wind.

Down, he yelled. Down.

But the delirious baron and baroness heard neither him nor the airplane. The great red ball on the horizon had hypnotized them with the heat it sent rushing through their aging bodies. Gaily the plane dipped its wings in salute to the most impressive monument ever reared by man, then gracefully rolled away and sped on south.

Cairo Martyr got to his feet, not believing what he saw. The nearly invisible man and woman still stood on the summit with their arms outstretched, but now they were headless, cleanly decapitated by the slashing lowest wing of the triplane. The hulking bodies lingered a few seconds longer, then slowly toppled over and disappeared down the far side of the pyramid.

Cairo Martyr stared at the new sun. The cigarette burned his fingers and he dropped it.

The morning mail in 1914.

A gay salute to antiquity.

And an astonishing new flying machine smartly cutting a swath through the leisurely old order of the nineteenth century, a world that could no longer survive in a speeding mechanical age suddenly wagging its wings and rolling in raffish chance.

In the dizzying shock of recognition that came that morning on top of the Great Pyramid, Martyr realized that his days of Victorian servitude were gone forever. Never again would he perform for vacationing Europeans in bazaar back rooms or in rowboats listlessly adrift on the Nile. The era of colonialists sunning themselves on the pyramids was over. The Victorian age had lost its head.

For the Junker baron and baroness, and for Martyr as well, the nineteenth century had abruptly come to an end in that early summer dawn in 1914, although elsewhere in the world a few more weeks were to pass before the radical new state of affairs was generally recognized.

1

Jerusalem
1933

*The end had come. Jerusalem lay
on the table. At last it was a
case of winner take all in the
eternal city.*

he Great Jerusalem Poker Game for secret control of the city, the
ruin of so many adventurers in the period between the two
world wars, continued for twelve years before it finally spent itself.

During that time thousands of gamblers from around the world lost
fortunes trying to win the Holy City, but in the end there were only
three men at the table, the same three who had been there in the
beginning.

Twelve years of ferocious poker for the highest of stakes after an
initial hand was dealt by chance one cold December day in 1921—
seemingly by chance, to pass the time that gray afternoon in Jerusalem
when the sky was heavily overcast and wind whipped through the
alleys, snow definitely in the air.

A cheap Arab coffee shop in the Old City where young O'Sullivan
Beare sat crouched in a corner over a glass of wretched Arab cognac, a

disillusioned Irish patriot who had fought in the Easter Rebellion at the age of sixteen and gone on to be revered as *the biggest of the little people* when he was terrorizing the Black and Tans in the hills of southern Ireland, a fugitive who had escaped to Palestine disguised as a Poor Clare nun on a pilgrimage.

A lonely hero still only twenty-one years old, wearing as an unlikely disguise that day the uniform of an officer of light cavalry in Her Majesty's expeditionary force to the Crimea, 1854, the medals on his chest showing he had survived a famous suicidal charge and been awarded the Victoria Cross because of it, far from home now huddled over a glass of Arab cognac that helped not at all, finding life bleak and meaningless on that cold December afternoon, simply that.

Dice clattered around the smoky room.

Bloody Arab excuse for a pub, he muttered. Just bloody awful, that's what. Not an honest pint in the house and no one to drink it with anyway.

A sudden gust of air struck him. The door had opened.

A tall black man in a stately Arab cloak and Arab headgear, so black he was almost blue, stood rubbing his hands after escaping the wind. On his shoulder crouched a small ball of white fluff, some kind of little animal. The man's eyes roamed the shop looking for empty tables but there were none, only densely packed Arabs sweating over games of backgammon. Then he caught sight of the corner where O'Sullivan Beare slouched alone in the dimness. He made for the table, smiling as he sat down.

Coffee, he said to the waiter.

Dice clattered. O'Sullivan Beare's head jerked back. The smiling black man had light blue eyes.

Hey what's this, thought O'Sullivan Beare. Things just aren't supposed to be like that. Someone's up to tricks again in the Holy City. And what's that little white animal curled up on his shoulder? White as white and as furry as can be, head and tail tucked away ever so nicely out of sight.

He nodded at the black Arab.

Cold out, wouldn't you say?

I would.

Yes, you're right. And who might this little friendly creature be you're carrying around to see the sights? A traveling companion, I suppose. Seems to be sleeping soundly enough despite the wind out there. Has a wicked bite, that wind.

He's a monkey, said the black man.

Oh I see.

An albino monkey.

O'Sullivan Beare nodded again, his face serious.

Sure why not, he thought. A black Arab with a white monkey on his back? Sure, makes as much sense as anything else. Why not, I say.

A few minutes later another man entered the shop escaping the wind and the cold, this time a European, his nationality difficult to place. In his hand he carried a longbow of exquisite workmanship.

Now what's this twist? thought O'Sullivan Beare. What's going on around here? More confusion and things seem to be spinning out of control already. That item's not English for sure, not French or German or anything natural. And armed with a bow no less, just in case a spot of archery practice turns up while he's out for a stroll on a dreadful winter afternoon. Some bloody devious article up to no good in the Holy Land, that's certain. By God, it's pranks for sure and somebody's bent on something.

The man took in the tables at a glance and headed directly toward the corner where O'Sullivan Beare sat with the black Arab. Slung over his shoulder on a cord was a long cylindrical case made of red lacquer. He clicked his heels with a slight nod and sat down. An unmistakable cloud of garlic fumes engulfed the table.

Excuse me for interrupting your meditations, gents, but it seems this is the only table in the room free from backgammon. On the other hand it is a dreary afternoon. Do either of you play poker?

He looked at O'Sullivan Beare, who nodded without interest.

Yes, I daresay you must have picked it up in the army. And you, my friend?

The black Arab smiled pleasantly and spoke with a cultivated English accent.

I used to play before the war, but I'm not sure I recall the rules.

No? Well perhaps we could refresh our memories.

The European brought out a pack of cards, shuffled and dealt five to the black Arab and five to himself. He turned over his cards and set aside what he had, a pair of kings. Then he turned over the black Arab's cards and set aside what he had, a pair of aces.

5

You win, it's as simple as that. Care to try a deal yourself?

The black Arab clumsily put the pack back together, shuffled slowly and dealt. This time when the cards were turned over he had the same two aces as before, plus an additional one. The European had his same two kings and a third to go with them.

The black Arab smiled.

It seems I win again.

Indeed you do, murmured the European thoughtfully. A case of excellent recall. Munk Szondi's my name. From Budapest.

And that's the truth, thought O'Sullivan Beare. Devious pranks sneaking out of the mists of central Europe and lurking on every side. Right you are and I could see that mischief coming.

Cairo Martyr, said the black Arab. From Egypt, a pleasure. Tell me, what in the world is that case you're carrying?

A quiver.

For arrows?

Yes. The Japanese samurai used them in the Middle Ages. And that little creature asleep on your shoulder?

A monkey. An albino monkey.

The two men studied each other for a moment. Then the Hungarian turned back to O'Sullivan Beare who was slumped despondently over his glass, fidgeting with his Victoria Cross. With the eye of a professional military man he took in the rows of medals on the Irishman's chest.

The Crimean War, if memory holds.

It's holding all right. That was the one.

My sympathy, a truly appalling disaster. Pure folly, that charge at Balaklava. But you did survive it after all. And since that was the middle of the last century, perhaps the time has come to put aside the memory of your fallen comrades. Sadness can't bring them back, now can it.

No it can't, that's true. But all things considered I'm still feeling glum today. Gloomy and glum and that's a fact.

How so, my friend?

Don't know, do I. Just guessing though, I'd say it has something to do with having been through too much for my age. Excessive experience, I mean. It's worn me down until now I'm worn out. Here I am only twenty-one years old and I'm already a veteran of a war that was fought nearly seventy years ago. And that's a weight for a man to carry. Do you follow me?

I think so, said Munk Szondi. Are you Irish by any chance?

Not at all, not a bit of it, by no chance whatsoever. By strict calculations at the top, one of those incomprehensible decisions made by Himself and passed on to my long-suffering mother and father, he being a poor fisherman who ate mostly potatoes and had thirty-three sons, me being the youngest and the last. The name's Joe when said in short, but when proclaimed over a proper pint of stout it runs to Joseph Enda Columbkille Kieran Kevin Brendan O'Sullivan Beare, those being saints who came from my island, which isn't much of anyplace you'd ever want to be. The barren Aran Islands, they're called, because they're so rainy and windswept and so poor God didn't bother to put any soil on them, instead leaving it up to His believers to make the soil if they wanted it, figuring somebody in His universe should believe that much. Mere slips of rock in the Atlantic, that's all, outposts against the terrible tides and gales of the Western seas. And now that you know all that, you can see it's not just because of the weather that I'm sagging today. Although young I've had a stormy soilless life, if you catch my meaning.

How bad is it?

Very. Just so bloody awful I can't revive. To be honest, I think it's all over for me.

At only twenty-one?

That's apparent age. The spirit inside is dreadfully elderly and creaking, a regular tottering veteran of the wars at least eighty-five years old. The Charge of the Light Brigade in the Crimea, remember? I'd have to be more or less that old.

The black Arab interrupted their conversation, turning to O'Sullivan Beare.

Those moments of despair come of course, but they can be overcome. Have you ever heard of an English explorer named Strongbow?

I have. I've heard some fanciful reports on more than one occasion and some whimsical allegations too. But the truth is, he never existed. Couldn't have, impossible on any account. No Englishman was ever that daft. A myth in the neighborhood pubs of the Holy Land, no more. Mad tales conjured up by the local Arabs when they're high on their flying carpets, which is most of the time. Opium, it's called. No offense meant to present company.

The black Arab smiled.

And none taken.

Good, we're right then. Now why this reference to the mythical Strongbow who never existed?

The black Arab was about to answer when the Hungarian interrupted him. He also turned to O'Sullivan Beare.

Poker, my friend. That was the subject at hand, not Levantine fables from the last century. And speaking of the last century, why not put your painful Crimean experiences behind you and try your luck today with a spot of cards in Jerusalem? Who knows, it might well be a way of getting things started again. Well what do you think? Will you join us?

Started? said Joe. I was by way of thinking I already had started here, and what it amounts to is heavy lifting that's bloody hard on the back.

He looked down at his hands, rough from handling the giant stone scarab he used on his smuggling trips. A few days ago he had arrived back in Jerusalem with the huge scarab, its hollow bowels stuffed with a secret shipment of arms for the Haganah. And soon there would be another clandestine trip, another load of dismantled Czech rifles, more English pounds for services rendered.

Anyway, he had nothing to do that afternoon.

But there was something else that intrigued him, another possibility. The black Arab was undoubtedly a Moslem and the Hungarian must be a Jew, the Star of David in his lapel showed that.

So just what did they think they were up to in Jerusalem? Working out a little private deal between themselves, was that it? Imagining they could do in a poor Christian just because the weather was cold and gray and bloody awful, not at all what it was cracked up to be in the land of milk and honey? Just doing a quiet little turn by themselves in the Holy City? Pranks and tricks and thinking they could leave him out of the game with their albino monkeys and their samurai bows and arrows?

Hold on, said Joe, I'm in from the beginning. But shouldn't we be giving ourselves a time limit then? Just to keep the winner honest?

Cairo Martyr seemed not to care one way or the other. But Munk Szondi was evidently pondering the matter as he picked up Joe's glass, sniffed it, made a face and poured it out on the floor. He ordered three empty glasses and filled them with cognac from a flask he was carrying in his overcoat.

I just happen to have some of the real thing with me.

Of course you do, said Joe. Now what was that you were saying about a time limit? I don't think I caught it. My ears have a way of ringing sometimes, crowding out all else. It's been that way since the war.

Why? asked Munk Szondi.

That terrible tumble I took when my horse was shot out from under me during the Charge of the Light Brigade. Landed right on my head, I did, and it's never been the same since, this overworked head of mine. It seems to be under a continual siege of unknown nature, by unknown forces, and it just goes right on whistling and shouting and howling and doing all kinds of things I have no control over. But then too, that's how I survived, because my horse went down and I couldn't keep up on foot. Somewhere way back then, you see, the charge went elsewhere and I got left behind. So bless those noises in my head I say, without them I wouldn't be here. Now what manner of time limit did you mention?

The Hungarian brought out a tiny gold pocket watch and placed it in the middle of the table. He pressed the button that opened the lid and they all leaned forward.

They were looking at a blank enamel face, a full moon unmarred by hands or numbers or quarters. Munk Szondi pressed the button again and the blank face clicked back to reveal another watch, the face normal in appearance but with the minute hand moving at the speed of a second hand, the second hand a whirling blur.

I see, said Munk Szondi.

He pressed the button once more to reveal a third face, also normal in appearance but with both hands seemingly stationary. Actually the second hand was moving but with exaggerated slowness. The three men gazed at it for several minutes and in that time it had moved only a second or two.

Cairo Martyr leaned back and roared with laughter. Even O'Sullivan Beare managed to smile. With the same solemnity as before, Munk Szondi clicked all three levels closed and returned the tiny gold watch to his vest pocket. He picked up the cards and began to shuffle.

The way I see it, gents, what we have ahead of us here is a long gray afternoon. Just why we all happen to be in Jerusalem I wouldn't know, other than the obvious fact that it's everybody's Holy City. But in any case here we are on the last day of December, a cold afternoon with snow definitely in the air, a new year upon us tomorrow. So as far as I'm concerned, it doesn't much matter whether time passes slowly or quickly or not at all. How do the two of you feel about it?

Cairo Martyr laughed and cut the pack once. O'Sullivan Beare smiled despite himself and cut the pack a second time. Munk Szondi put aside his bow and arrows and the first cards of their twelve-year game went down on the boards in the Old City, in a smoky Arab coffee shop, where it all began.

Early in the game it became apparent the playing styles of the three founders couldn't have been more different.

Cairo Martyr's was the most unorthodox, since he never looked at his cards until all the betting was over, relying instead on some private law of averages to bring him his winnings. Of course he had to be always bluffing, but outsiders found it next to impossible to outguess a man who could honestly say he didn't know what he was holding.

Munk Szondi used his unique knowledge of Levantine commodities to make money. According to the rules of the game, anything of value could be used in the betting. Thus when a pile of Maria Theresa crowns and chits representing Egyptian dried fish futures were on the table, Szondi would overplay his hand simply to get the fish.

For Szondi invariably knew that Persian dinars were due to weaken in the next few days in relation to dried fish, and that a handsome profit would be his if he discounted the Maria Theresa crowns in Damascus, doubled the value of his fish futures by buying dinars on the margin in Beirut, sold a quarter and a third of each in Baghdad as a hedge against customs interference on the Persian border, and then saw to it that his courier with the fish futures arrived in Isfahan on Friday, a market day, when the fish futures would be most in demand.

Only O'Sullivan Beare played according to mathematical percentages, or said he did, claiming he had adapted to poker the ballistic tables once memorized when he was on the run in the hills of southern Ireland, needing distance then because he was fighting the Black and Tans alone and couldn't afford to approach the enemy directly, instead firing his old musketoon high in the air from far away, in the manner of a howitzer, so that the bullets of his just cause traversed a steep arc and came plunging down on the target as if from heaven.

Inscrutable bluffing in Cairo Martyr's case.

An awesome knowledge of Levantine trade when it was Munk Szondi's turn.

The scientific trajectory of heavenly bullets when the betting passed to O'Sullivan Beare.

Highly individual methods of play, further complicated by unorthodox thrusts at chance, all of it equally baffling to outsiders. Nor did there seem to be any limit to the financial resources the three founders brought to the table.

Cairo Martyr was said to have been looting the tombs of the pharaohs for years and had an immense store of mummies at his disposal. As was well known, pharaonic mummy dust when snorted, or when smoked in its mastic form, was an infallible Levantine aphrodisiac.

If used in sufficient quantities daily it could also provide previously barren women with large families, assure a man of long life and wisdom, and in general serve as a powerful substitute for anything.

And even if the supplies of genuine pharaonic mummy dust were exhaustible, there was still the large number of royal cats the Egyptians had also mummified. And lastly, no one doubted that Cairo Martyr would be more than ready to manufacture powder from old rags, now that he had established himself as the supreme purveyor of mummy dust in the Middle East.

As for Munk Szondi, a Khasarian Jew, it was inconceivable that anyone could ever unravel his arcane knowledge of the values relating Yemeni rugs and Damascus figs with the upcoming spring production of Levantine lambs, the worth of these and a thousand other items bound together in inextricable laws that only he could fathom.

And finally there was O'Sullivan Beare's much more recent wealth, the stupendous business he was doing in religious artifacts, symbolic wooden fish being just one of his profitable lines. The fish were smoothly carved in a cylindrical shape with a nob of greater girth at one end. They came in various sizes but on the average were about the length of an open hand. The Irishman claimed these abstract wooden fish were an exact replica of ones used by the early Christians to secretly identify themselves to their coreligionists in those dangerous times.

But if a mere primitive symbol, why had they suddenly become so popular in modern Jerusalem, spreading from there throughout the Middle East? And if Christian, why were they in equal demand among Jews and Arabs and nonbelievers?

It was true women carried them secretly more often than not, hiding them in their handbags and even appearing embarrassed if a shopkeeper chanced to spy one when they were digging for coins. But men displayed them openly enough in the bazaars, where their uses seemed far from abstract. On the contrary, when greeting one another, men seemed to take pleasure in boldly waving these wooden objects in the air. And when they adjourned to a coffee shop they rapped them loudly on the tables to attract the attention of waiters.

In fact after coffee and tobacco, the Irishman's symbolic wooden fish were the largest-selling staple in the Middle East. They could be found everywhere, in the tents and palaces of all known races, even among bedouin who had never seen a fish.

Mummy dust. Trading in futures. Religious symbols.

With that kind of backing the three men seemed unbeatable. Year after year they stripped visitors to Jerusalem of all they owned, bewildered emirs and European smugglers and feuding sheiks, devout priests and assorted commercial agents and pious fanatics, every manner of pilgrim in that vast dreaming army from many lands that had always been scaling the heights of the Holy City in search of spiritual gold, Martyr and Szondi and O'Sullivan Beare implacably dealing and shuffling and dealing again, relentlessly plunging Jerusalem into its greatest turmoil since the First Crusade with their interminable poker game in the vaulted chamber where they had moved that very first night, after the coffee shop closed.

We shouldn't quit just because it's midnight, Munk Szondi had said.

No reason to stop just because a new year is upon us, Cairo Martyr had agreed.

Well if both you gents see it that way, Joe had said, I know just the place to set up a more permanent table here in the Old City. It's a former antiquities shop that belongs to a good friend of mine, the place largely empty now because this friend is no longer in the business except in his head, an odd proposition as you'll see.

And thus the Great Jerusalem Poker Game came to be played in the back room of an empty shop owned by an obscure dealer in time known as Haj Harun.

On that final day after twelve years of play, O'Sullivan Beare had the deal. His call was for straight poker, three-card draw, and both Cairo Martyr and Munk Szondi nodded with approval when he announced it. A hard and basic hand with nothing wild and nothing stray, the appropriate way to end the game.

And knowing the moment had finally come, they approached it in a leisurely manner. O'Sullivan Beare opened a bottle of poteen and took his time sipping it down. Cairo Martyr filled his hookah with a potent dose of mummy mastic and puffed contentedly. Munk Szondi placed a large bowl of garlic bulbs in front of him and methodically crunched his way to the bottom.

The Druse warriors who guarded the game were paid off and dismissed. In the middle of the table sat a new deck of cards ordered from Venice for the event. Each man tapped the pack once before the cellophane wrapping was carefully removed.

The shuffling began, each man spending fifteen or twenty minutes over the pack to get the feel of it, and after that they spent another fifteen or twenty minutes cutting it in turn. With twelve years behind them no one was in a hurry. Gone were the cunning maneuvers of the past. More than skill was needed now.

The empty hookah, the empty bottle of poteen and the empty bowl of garlic bulbs were set aside. Cairo Martyr gazed at the ceiling and announced his ante.

The goats in the Moslem Quarter, he said.

The other two men looked at him.

Those used for sodomy, he added solemnly.

O'Sullivan Beare's eyes narrowed.

The goats in the Christian Quarter, he countered. Meat.

The goats in the Jewish Quarter, said Munk Szondi. Milk.

The three men watched each other. Over the years it had become customary for them to open a hand in this way, as a reminder to outsiders that only real goods and services had any ultimate value in the Holy City. Because sooner or later the conquering army presently in the city would have to retreat as its empire shrank and collapsed, as all empires had done since the beginning of time, thereby rendering its currency foreign and useless in Jerusalem.

But as the gentle Haj Harun had airily noted once, even a Holy City needs the service trades. In fact it needs them more than most places.

O'Sullivan Beare dealt the cards. He and Munk Szondi raised theirs slowly and held them close to the chest, revealing them one at a time. After a few minutes of study they both chose three for discard. Cairo Martyr, as always, had left his cards lying face down on the table, untouched. With some deliberation he now separated the first and the third and the fifth for discard.

Three new cards were dealt to each man. Munk Szondi's face was grave as he rapidly weighed the comparative values that day of every known Levantine commodity. O'Sullivan Beare seemed a trifle feverish as he calculated patriotic ballistic arcs. Only Cairo Martyr, with his immense self-assurance, seemed completely at ease with what lay before him.

And since he was sitting on the dealer's left, he had the right to open the betting. Again, as usual, he didn't look at his new cards.

No openers, said Cairo Martyr, not this time. I have no intention of wasting time tonight trying to inch the stakes up. I'll start at the top and the two of you can play or not, as you choose. Now I think you'll both agree that through my various illicit enterprises, I control the Moslem Quarter in this city.

The mummy dust king is about to strike, muttered O'Sullivan Beare. But at the same time he knew the claim was true, just as was his own secret control over the Christian Quarter and Munk Szondi's over the

Jewish Quarter, religious symbols and trading in futures being just as essential to Jerusalem as mummy dust.

Well do I or don't I? said Cairo Martyr.

You do. Agreed.

Correct. Now then, that's my bet. Control of the Moslem Quarter. I'm putting the Moslem Quarter on the table. If either of you wins, which you won't, it belongs to you. But first you have to match my bet. No openers. The real thing.

O'Sullivan Beare whistled softly.

That's arrogance and then some, he muttered. You mean the *whole* Moslem Quarter?

That's right. Down to the last sun-baked brick.

People? asked Munk Szondi.

Down to the last unborn babe asleep in its mum's belly, not knowing what it's in for when it has to wake up.

Fair enough, said Munk Szondi, gesturing extravagantly. If that's the way it is I'm betting the Jewish Quarter.

Jaysus all right, shouted O'Sullivan Beare, all right I say. If that's what you're up to I'll put down the Christian Quarter.

He said the last two words in Gaelic but they both understood him. By now they all knew enough of each other's languages to recognize a bet in any one of them.

So there it was. The three men leaned back to savor the moment, a chance that came once in a lifetime, if ever. They had each bet what they controlled and it went without saying that the fourth section of the Old City, the Armenian Quarter, would automatically go to the player who held the best cards.

The end had come. Jerusalem lay on the table. At last it was a case of winner take all in the eternal city.

But twelve years of unscrupulous poker had to pass before that final showdown could take place in the former antiquities shop of Haj Harun, an ancient defender of Jerusalem who even then was wandering around the room in distraction, just a few years short of his three thousandth birthday.

2

Cairo Martyr

Going far? asked Cairo.
All the way, whispered the mummy
with a resigned expression.

*F*rom his earliest years Cairo Martyr had picked cotton as a slave in the Nile delta alongside his maternal great-grandmother, a proud indomitable woman whose passions in life dated from 1813.

In that year, as a young woman in a village on the fringe of the Nubian desert, she had taken into her hut a charming wanderer by the name of Sheik Ibrahim ibn Harun. The sprightly young sheik, who said he was an expert in Islamic law, also claimed his blue eyes were the result of Circassian blood.

But as Cairo Martyr was one day to learn, his wandering great-grandfather had actually been a European in disguise, a highly gifted Swiss linguist with a passion for details whose other descendants, known and unknown, were also to play a crucial part in the Great Jerusalem Poker Game over a century later.

Young Sheik Ibrahim, as always, soon grew restless in the village on the fringe of the Nubian desert. With tears he parted from his new wife to resume his wanderings, promising to return in three months. But when he did come back at the end of that time he found the village had been savagely destroyed and its inhabitants carried off by a Mameluke raiding party.

These dwindling remnants of medieval warfare, originally Mongolian and Turkish slaves who later became the rulers of Egypt, had been driven south into the desert by Napoleon some fifteen years earlier. Although the conditions prevailing on the Russian steppes were fully nine centuries behind them, the memories of frosty gales remained deeply embedded in their sluggish brains and they still wore thick woolen underwear in the ferocious Nubian heat. Dressed in gorgeous robes and enormous jeweled turbans, their swords inlaid with precious stones and their saddlebags stuffed with gold, they rode ponderously through the haze into battle carrying all their riches, their catamites running on foot beside them waving the green banners of the Prophet.

Since the Mamelukes were pederasts, they couldn't reproduce. When they were the rulers of Egypt they had purchased boys in southern Russia and fattened them to be their successors, but with that source no longer open to them they were dying out as a Moslem warrior caste.

Those who survived were aging bloated men, elderly asthmatics tormented by malignant rectal tumors and virulent skin diseases, which flourished particularly in their groins and armpits. In this rampant state of decay, so advanced it could warn local tribesmen of approaching danger when the wind was right, the Mamelukes supported themselves in barbaric luxury by laying waste to the countryside and selling the Africans they captured to Arab slave-traders. After briefly arousing themselves for a sortie they would return to their barges on the Nile and relapse into a deathlike stupor, stretched out under awnings their retainers doused with water day and night in a useless effort to cool their wheezing mountainous bodies.

Since they never took off their underwear, scratching couldn't help. Even flicking a fly away seemed useless. Instead they lay with their glazed eyes fixed on the wilderness, dully wondering how their once lavish life on the Mediterranean, so rich in soothing breezes and perfumes and other extravagant splendors, had been reduced to the parched oblivion of this lizard's existence hundreds of miles from nowhere.

On one of these barges in 1813, Martyr's great-grandmother gave birth to a daughter as black as she but with the light blue eyes of her beloved Sheik Ibrahim. The Mamelukes had no use for a girl, so mother and daughter were sold to an Arab slave-trader who included them in a shipment to the Nile delta, where they were bought to pick cotton. In due time the daughter gave birth to a daughter and that daughter to a son, also deep black with light blue eyes. Both those mothers died of dysentery soon after they bore their children and the boy was therefore raised by his great-grandmother, who finally succumbed to dysentery herself in 1892, after nearly eight decades of servitude.

Upon her death, little Cairo Martyr was freed by his master as an act of Islamic mercy.

Thus thrown alone into the world at the age of twelve, illiterate and without any skills, the boy did what any other black child in Egypt would have done in the latter half of the nineteenth century. He wrapped his kerfiya around his head and walked through the dust to the capital to seek the advice of a former slave named Menelik Ziwar.

Among Egyptian blacks, Menelik Ziwar's position was unusual in several ways.

Since slaves were brought up in the religion of their masters, the vast majority were Moslem. But Menelik's branch of the Ziwars happened to be Copts, and Menelik had taken the trouble to teach himself to speak Coptic, the extinct form of Egyptian that had been used in the country during early Christian times.

He shared this distinction with only one other man, the head of the Coptic Church or Patriarch of Alexandria, whose duty it was to appoint the head of the Church in Ethiopia, the only country where this Christian sect was the state religion, and also the only country in Africa not ruled by Europeans.

Since no one else understood the tongue except Menelik and the Patriarch, they took the opportunity to confer in it whenever they met. Of course no one knew what they were saying, but it was widely assumed among Egyptian blacks that Menelik's influence in independent black Africa, by way of his relationship with the Coptic Patriarch, surpassed that of any other black in the world.

Even his name tended to confirm this special status, the historical Menelik having been the first emperor of Ethiopia.

Nor was it just his political influence that enhanced his standing in the black community. Menelik Ziwar was also the greatest Egyptologist of the nineteenth century.

Menelik's master long ago, a wealthy cotton broker named Ziwar, had sent his own son at an early age to be educated in England. The Ziwar son had returned to Alexandria with a sound knowledge of archeology, but having been away so long he knew nothing of everyday Egyptian corruption. In order to do fieldwork he needed a competent dragoman, or guide and interpreter, who could oversee his thieving workmen and hand out baksheesh up and down the Nile. The Patriarch of Alexandria immediately pointed out that he had to look no farther than his own household and the sagacious slave Menelik.

The Ziwar son and Menelik joined forces in digs throughout the delta. Menelik quickly learned to read hieroglyphs and was soon offering suggestions about where they should dig. Natural intelligence exerted itself and before long the apparent slave was the teacher, the apparent master the pupil.

Yet Menelik remained the perfect dragoman in every respect, even after he was freed. He stayed modestly in the background, so much so that although his discoveries eventually made his master's name famous in all the academic centers of Europe, no one outside the black community in Egypt, and no one at all in Europe, had ever heard of the Ziwar who was important—Menelik, secret scholar and revered African folk hero.

When little Cáiro went to seek his advice the black Egyptologist was already an old man. After years of stooping in cramped tombs he had developed severe arthritis and now he never went on digs himself. Instead he instructed others where to look and interpreted the findings they brought to him, dictating the monographs they subsequently published under their own names, anonymity having long since become a habit with him.

Between times there was an endless stream of respectful young petitioners arriving from all over Africa, black boys and girls starting out in life who wanted to know what to do and how to do it.

Due to his arthritis Menelik was most comfortable when stretched out flat on his back. And since so much of his life had been spent in tombs, not surprisingly he found a sarcophagus most to his liking as a bedchamber.

The one he had chosen for himself was a particularly massive block of stone originally occupied by the mummy of Cheops' mother. Upon his retirement in 1880, Menelik Ziwar had the sarcophagus lowered into a sepulcher he had discovered in Cairo under a public garden beside the Nile. And this was where he had held court ever since, on his back in a bed at the bottom of the sarcophagus. Petitioners were ushered into the sepulcher one at a time for consultations that might last a few minutes or most of a day, depending on how often the old scholar dozed off in his soundproof and nearly airless subterranean vault.

Little Cairo stood in line in the public garden for several weeks, waiting for his turn to come. At last it did and an attendant pointed down the steep stairs that led to the vault. He was told to close the door behind him at once, the master's eyes being no longer accustomed to daylight. He tiptoed down the stairs, took a deep breath and slipped inside the door.

He found himself standing in a small gloomy chamber with the dim outline of a gigantic sarcophagus looming up in front of him, a single taper at its head. He took another deep breath and tiptoed across the floor to peek inside.

He gasped. Far down in the hollow depths of that massive block of stone, amidst piles of books and mysterious inscriptions five thousand years old, lay a withered mummy with a huge magnifying glass on its chest. Little Cairo was terrified. Abruptly the mummy's withered hand floated up in the air and clasped the magnifying glass, then raised it. Behind the lens the enormous unblinking eye from antiquity was fully two inches wide.

Caught you, cackled the mummy.

Little Cairo began to shake. His teeth chattered and sweat ran down his face. A dry crinkled smile spread across the mummy's mouth.

There there, son, stop carrying on like that. I'm only the man you came to see. What's your name?

Little Cairo whispered his name.

Is that a fact? said the mummy. Well you certainly didn't get that from your master, so where did you get it?

From my great-grandmother, sir.

Her last name was Martyr?

No sir. She didn't have a last name, sir. But that's the one she gave me, sir.

Odd. Why?

I don't know, sir.

Never gave you a hint?

No sir.

She raised you?

Yes sir.

Everyone else died before their time?

Yes sir.

Dysentery?

Yes sir.

Hm, that's the paradox isn't it. The Nile gives us the land but takes its toll in return. Good water is also bad water. Now admit it, son. A moment ago I caught you frightened by the past and that's not the way to get ahead when you're black the way we are. And speaking of the past, what do you know about yours?

I know where my great-grandmother came from, sir.

Nubia, I'd say, by the looks of it. Except for those eyes of yours. Where did you get them?

From my great-grandfather, sir. A wandering Circassian, sir.

Is that what he told her? What else do you know about him?

He was an expert in Islamic law, sir.

He told her that too, did he?

Yes sir.

I see. Did he happen to have a name?

Yes sir. His name was Sheik Ibrahim ibn Harun, sir.

The mummy's dry smile crinkled across his face again.

Ah, yes, I do see. That young man *was* a wanderer, there's no doubt about that. In any case he picked himself up and went on his way and your great-grandmother was subsequently captured and sold into slavery?

Yes sir.

The Mamelukes?

Yes sir.

Oafs, all of them. Dazed pederasts running to fat. She wasn't very fond of them, was she?

No sir.

I daresay. But all this happened at the beginning of the century and that's hardly the past. For all practical purposes the past ends with the destruction of the New Kingdom. Know when that was?

No sir.

The XXX Dynasty. An unfortunate period. Yes, I can see it now.

The mummy closed his eyes. After about ten minutes of silence he stirred and scratched his nose. He raised the huge magnifying glass once more and the eye two inches wide reappeared behind the lens.

Did you say you were looking for work, son?

Yes sir.

Any English?

No sir.

No matter, you'll pick it up. You're Moslem, I take it.

Yes sir.

Of course. Your great-grandmother had a long memory and she wanted to see some scores settled. An extremely proud woman?

Yes sir.

It fits, but that's for the future. Right now you need a trade and I think you should start as a dragoman, as I did. There aren't many trades open to us and that's a good way to begin. You need contacts.

Yes sir.

Right. You'll begin as an apprentice and work your way up. Now listen carefully, here are the rules. Be dignified, never cringe or whine or roll your eyes. Be correct but solicitous with the ladies, correct but slightly less stiff with the gents. When you don't understand something always say, Yes sir, and nod vigorously, pretending you do. Upon receiving a tip bow deeply and murmur how happy you are to have performed this service, ending with an air of undefined suggestion, a momentary hesitation will do it, that even more complex services are available, should you be called upon for them. Above all, smile. Smile and smile and look as if you thoroughly enjoy what you're doing no matter how tedious and silly it is. At the same time be absolutely discreet, going only so far as to hint that European travelers often find the desert air invigorating. And be gentle. Never harm anyone in any way. Did your great-grandmother tell you that?

Yes sir.

I thought so. When it comes to settling scores she had bigger things in mind. Well on your way then. The attendant outside will give you an address. Tell them I sent you and return in a week to give me a progress report. In fact return every week until futher notice.

Yes sir.

And you ought to know I wasn't asleep when you came in, nor a few minutes ago either. People think I'm sleeping when actually I'm just taking a trip. You can't understand a particular dynasty without spending time in it. Do you see?

Yes sir.

Nod vigorously when you say that.

Yes sir.

Good. Come around next week.

Yes sir, whispered little Cairo, tiptoeing away from the massive block of stone.

He became an apprentice dragoman and to his surprise he found the profession had little to do with guiding tourists or haggling for them in the bazaars. Instead his duties were largely sexual.

Most Europeans who wintered in Egypt, it seemed, seldom left the spacious verandas of their hotels, where they moved graciously in circles, favorably remarking on the weather and unfavorably deploring the slack manner and slovenly appearance of the natives. The minority who hired dragomen to venture into back streets were those seeking the sexual license associated with the East, an anonymous debauchery far from home, exactly what a dragoman could provide.

In this stolid atmosphere of overt Victorian gentility and covert imperial vice, young Cairo learned his trade without particular ambition. Each day at noon he went to the office of the Clerk of the

Acts, the senior dragoman in the city and the head of their benevolent association, whose job it was to advise apprentices and distribute assignments. The appointments were spaced well apart, in keeping with the leisurely pace of life pursued by the English in Egypt. And in any case a dragoman's clients spent a considerable amount of time sleeping, both because they found the heat enervating and because of the opium they took.

So there were many quiet hours in which young Cairo could dream of the future during those first lonely months in the city, while listening to a man or a woman snore, and inevitably his dreams turned to the astonishing event so often recalled by Menelik, the forty-year conversation the old man had once held with his dearest friend, an English lord and legendary explorer, Plantagenet Strongbow.

Menelik had first met Strongbow in the summer of 1838, a few weeks after the explorer returned from one of his mysterious early excursions, this time to outer Persia.

With his seven-foot, seven-inch frame topped by a massive greasy black turban, and his lean torso wrapped in a shaggy short black coat made from unwashed and uncombed goats' hair, both said to be gifts from a remote hill tribe in Persia, the haughty young English duke was a preposterous figure striding through the dusty native quarters of Cairo. His face was already deeply scarred from his travels and his body, in addition, was severely wasted from a recent encounter with cholera which had nearly been fatal.

But perhaps it was the portable sundial strapped to Strongbow's hip that most amazed Menelik, a monstrously heavy bronze piece inscribed with Arab aphorisms and a legend noting that it had been cast in Baghdad during the fifth Abbasid caliphate.

Menelik had never seen a European dressed in such a manner, let alone an English duke, and never anyone wearing such an outrageous costume in the stifling heat of an Egyptian summer. Immediately he was intrigued.

The young English duke was known to disdain his countrymen but was said to enjoy the company of genuine Levantines, particularly the poor and the devious who made their living as conjurers and gossips and refuse carters. On the basis of this rumor Menelik approached Strongbow in the bazaar one sultry day and introduced himself. Strongbow was on guard as always, carrying under his arm a short heavy club, a kind of polished twisted root which he raised menacingly whenever someone said something irrelevant to his needs.

At the time Menelik was twenty, a year older than Strongbow. He was still a slave and a common dragoman, but he did speak Coptic and clearly possessed the keen powers of observation that would one day decipher the secrets of so many tombs. In fact there were probably very few Cairenes who could have described the lowlife of their city with as much accuracy and gusto as Menelik.

He stepped forward smiling. As Strongbow automatically raised his club, Menelik shouted out an earthy Coptic greeting unheard in over a thousand years, an intricately vulgar expression once used by Nile boatmen who were on the most intimate terms with one another. Strongbow couldn't understand the words of course, but he sensed their trend and liked it. He lowered his club and smiled, whereupon Menelik switched to a raffish Arab dialect and launched into a scandalous diatribe against certain Englishmen involved with criminal elements along the riverfront, which Strongbow enjoyed even more.

The oppressive heat in the bazaar was becoming intolerable. The two young men decided they needed something to drink and entered the first place they came to beside the Nile, as it happened a refuge for off-duty dragomen, a filthy open-air restaurant with trellises of leafy vines and flowers overhead, a pool where drowsy ducks paddled and a cage housing squawking peacocks listlessly twitching their tails. The cheap wine was strong, the spiced lamb tasty, the shrunken Arab waiters somnambulant as they puffed opium and drifted ever more helplessly with the hours.

There in the soothing hum of the shade Strongbow and Menelik spent a long summer Sunday afternoon, eating and drinking and feeding the placid ducks, watching the nervous peacocks mate and enthusiastically discussing whatever stray topic came to mind, the two of them so drunk by the end of the afternoon they threw themselves over the railing into the muddy river before staggering off to late naps.

A firm friendship was established that afternoon by the Nile. Thereafter, when he was in Lower Egypt, Strongbow always sent a runner to notify Menelik and the two of them would meet again on a Sunday in the same filthy open-air restaurant under the trellises of leafy vines and flowers, always at the same table where they had sprawled the first time, picking up their swirling raucous conversation as if they had never left it, heckling the peacocks and feeding the ducks as they gorged themselves on spiced lamb and endless carafes of wine, which they had to replenish themselves, the waiters having become too weak to carry anything as the years went by, Menelik making his way in a career of increasingly brilliant scholarship, Strongbow forever broadening the track of his daring explorations that reached from Timbuktu to the Hindu Kush.

On his weekly visits to the sepulcher beneath the public garden, little Cairo listened in awe to the stories recounted by Menelik Ziwar, these seemingly unimaginable adventures and bewildering changes of fortune that were far beyond anything a lonely boy, only twelve years old and a stranger in a great city, could ever hope to know.

Or so little Cairo felt. Old Menelik thought differently.

Not so, said the wrinkled mummy at the bottom of the sarcophagus, smiling and encouraging the little boy. It may look that way now, son, but we can never be sure what fate may breathe into life. Achievements? Startling transformations? Just consider the Numa Stone for a moment.

Little Cairo was standing with his chin resting on the edge of the sarcophagus. Enchanting names, exotic memories, it was always like this in Menelik Ziwar's quiet vault. A faraway look came into the little boy's eyes.

The *Pneuma* Stone? he whispered.

Deep down in the sarcophagus amidst the stacks of books and the strange inscriptions five thousand years old, the mummy raised his magnifying glass to produce the gigantic eye of antiquity. He cackled dryly.

Are you saying *Numa* or *Pneuma*? Breath is involved all right and a breath of fresh air at that, but the Greeks are in the game only for purposes of scholarship, or by association, you might say. Anyway, it should be *Numa* and Strongbow told me about it on a Sunday afternoon four or five decades ago. He was coming back from the kitchen with another carafe of wine and another plate of spiced lamb, happily swinging his portable sundial on his hip as he threaded his way between the paralyzed waiters, when all at once a devilish grin came across his face. We were getting on toward the end of the afternoon by then and I was so dizzy I almost didn't see it. But when he collapsed in his chair and planted his enormous head in front of me, holding it in those enormous hands, there was no way to miss it. The grin was simply wicked. Roguery itself.

Here, I said, what's this bit of mischief?

Menelik you notorious Nilotic ghoul, he shouted, grabbing my arm and knocking the plate of lamb to the floor as he drew me into the conspiracy, Menelik you astounding black Copt, promise me that if you're ever asked about the Numa Stone, you won't say a word.

Why? I asked, mystified, having never heard of such a stone.

All the while Strongbow was grinning ever more wildly. So wildly that anyone who didn't know him as well as I did would have thought he was in the grip of some terminal fever. The grin was that demented. Then he suddenly made an extravagant gesture that swept across the table, his sundial going with it and sending everything flying. The carafe smashed into the duck pond and stained the water, the glasses crashed against the peacocks' cage and ended their nervous copulations in a shower of splintering shards. He brought his fist down on the table with a roar of laughter that shook everything in the place, even the waiters, it seemed. Of course it might have been only the wine playing tricks with my vision, but I swear I actually thought I saw them quiver at that moment, the first time they'd shown any life in years.

Why? thundered Strongbow. For the sake of Europe. We're going to save Europe from its own unspeakable hypocrisy.

Little Cairo listened, wide-eyed.

Yes, hissed the mummy, the Numa Stone. That vastly controversial slab so named after its discoverer, Numa Numantius, the German erotic scholar and defender of homosexuality. His critics were in the habit of referring to him contemptuously as Aunt Magnesia. But it was also true that no one in Europe at the time was more outspoken on sexual matters than Numantius, a fact that was certain to engage Strongbow's sympathy.

For weeks, continued Menelik, this Numa Numantius or Aunt Magnesia had been up the Nile searching through the ruins at Karnak, trying to find some small inscription in the temple that would suggest the ancient Egyptians had disavowed the persecution of homosexuals. But without success. The hieroglyphs on the columns listed innumerable public works undertaken by various pharaohs, and the innumerable virtues of those pharaohs, without mentioning sex even once.

Numantius was thoroughly discouraged the evening Strongbow happened to come upon him, sitting alone in the ruins of the temple and sighing over and over. Strongbow was traveling in disguise as a poor bedouin navvy from the area of the first cataract, and he began asking Numantius questions as was his habit with anyone he met. He learned what the German was seeking and decided to interrupt his journey in order to help.

The next morning Numantius moved his operations to some ruins on the other side of the river. Strongbow, meanwhile, broke into several nearby tombs to find a basalt slab suitable for his purposes. After inscribing the slab to his satisfaction he treated it with certain chemicals, then buried it in front of the temple entrance, one corner just above the drifting sand so that its appearance would seem to be the chance work of the wind.

A few days later, heaving with sighs and more discouraged than ever, Numantius returned to Karnak for a last reverie in the temple by moonlight. The inscribed corner of the basalt slab caught his eye and he quickly dug it up, Strongbow watching all the while from his hiding place behind a pillar.

Numantius clapped his hands. There on the unearthed basalt slab were three long neat rows of language carved one beside the other, in hieroglyphs and ancient demotic Egyptian and Greek, simultaneous translations of a legal statute from the XXXI Dynasty. In impressive detail the statute guaranteed the right of consenting adults to practice homosexuality to the best of their abilities, when said acts were performed in view of the Nile and were witnessed by a baboon or a dung beetle or some other sacred creature, said best abilities in no way to contravene the pharaoh's divine right to wage interminable wars of aggression in order to acquire more slaves to build more public works to honor the pharaoh.

The statute had been formally promulgated by the priests of Ptolemy V to revive a traditional law of the land that had fallen into disrepute over recent millennia, when recurring conquests from the barbaric north had introduced uncivilized sexual attitudes into the eternal kingdom of the sun.

Specifically *un-Egyptian* attitudes, emphasized the carved inscriptions, the word heavily underscored with chisel marks in the Greek and demotic texts and deeply circled in the hieroglyphs.

Numantius was triumphant. He sailed down the Nile with his precious slab and at once returned victoriously to Europe, where his unique find shocked scholars everywhere. The debate raged and raged, and although the authenticity of the Numa Stone was eventually disproved, Numantius by then had firmly established his reputation in the fields of antique homosexual jurisprudence and homosexual Egyptology.

Yes indeed, mused Menelik Ziwar happily at the bottom of his sarcophagus, smiling up at little Cairo through his magnifying glass, his unblinking eye two inches wide.

Yes, son. A fateful stone from antiquity discovered in a temple beside the Nile. Fate breathing variety into life.

Cairo was twenty before Menelik Ziwar chose to discuss the books he kept stacked in his sarcophagus, which in fact were none other than the thirty-three volumes of Strongbow's monumental study of Levantine sex, published in Basle about the time Cairo was born, and banned throughout the British Empire in perpetuity for being despicably un-English.

There were tears in the old man's eyes when he told Martyr how he had spent months smuggling a complete edition of the work into Egypt, using a giant hollow stone scarab Strongbow had lent him for that purpose. And how, on the very day he had at last assembled the entire set and safely stored it away in his sarcophagus, a special courier had arrived from Constantinople bearing a note from Strongbow along with the explorer's huge magnifying glass, a memento from his old friend who explained he wanted Menelik to have the glass now that he had decided to disappear into the desert forever, to live the life of an Arab holy man.

Included in the note was a request that the giant stone scarab be returned to a certain party in Jerusalem from whom Strongbow had borrowed it, which Ziwar had done.

But *never* to see him again? croaked the mummy, tears running down his cheeks. Never to listen to him roaring with laughter and pounding the table over some recent discovery? Eating and drinking away those glorious Sunday afternoons beside the Nile when we were young and had our hopes before us? Instead just this magnifying glass, even though it had traveled so far and seen so much?

As the old man wept Cairo realized the deep sadness that gripped the scholar even now, two decades later, when he recalled the loss of his friend. But he also knew Menelik Ziwar would always have the memories of his forty-year conversation with Strongbow, those long Sunday afternoons of wine and scurrilous evidence so richly woven under the trellises of leafy vines and flowers, among placid ducks and statuesque waiters and squawking peacocks, in a filthy open-air restaurant on the banks of the Nile, always ending with drunken plunges into the cooling water.

Yes, Menelik had those memories, thought Martyr, and he also had Strongbow's magnificent study. And a magnifying glass powerful enough to read it.

At the bottom of the sarcophagus the mummy wiped the tears from his eyes. It was New Year's Day, 1900. The mummy sighed and opened one of Strongbow's volumes. Briefly he gazed at Martyr through the magnifying glass, then lowered it to the page.

A new century today, he said. I thought I might read to you a few excerpts from the last one.

I'd like that, Menelik.

Good. Here we are then, Volume One.

The author's preface wherein he lays forth his reasons for discussing in three hundred million words an historical topic of general interest heretofore ignored and denied, sex in the Levant or what might more accurately be called Levantine sex, some two-thirds of the entire endeavor being devoted to the author's personal experiences with a gentle Persian girl, once his beloved common-law wife, many years distant but never forgotten.

Magnifying glass in hand, Ziwar read on.

And so it went for the next fourteen years when Martyr made his weekly visits to the sepulcher beneath the public garden beside the river, the old Egyptologist lying at the bottom of his sarcophagus reading aloud passages from Strongbow's study, laughing when he came across incidents he recognized from things Strongbow had said on Sunday afternoons in the course of their forty-year conversation, Martyr totally absorbed as he leaned dreamily against the massive block of stone, listening and listening to the improbable events of an heroic past.

Thus Strongbow's tales were the abiding dreams of Cairo Martyr's early years, yet somehow he was never able to direct his own destiny as Strongbow had done. Decades passed and he was still a common dragoman.

As for Menelik Ziwar, he had taken a special interest in Martyr from the beginning because of a long-ago love affair at the age of sixteen, his first experience with a woman.

She had been much older than he was. Indeed, her blue-eyed daughter was older than he was. Like Menelik, she had been a slave in the delta, although originally she came from a village on the fringe of the Nubian desert. And he would always lovingly remember the gentle way she had initiated him into manhood.

The woman had also told him about her lost husband, and how soon after meeting him she had been carried away by a Mameluke raiding party, and after the birth of her blue-eyed daughter, sold into slavery.

She would never forget that, she said. One day she intended to repay the Mamelukes for their savagery.

Years later when he was able to do so, Ziwar had looked into the background of her dead husband, in his day well known as an expert in

Islamic law in Egypt, and discovered that the wanderer known as Sheik Ibrahim ibn Harun had actually been a Swiss linguist traveling in disguise.

So when a frightened Nubian boy came to him some six decades later seeking advice, an ex-slave with blue eyes called Cairo Martyr, Ziwar immediately understood the significance of the peculiar name bestowed on him by his great-grandmother. Here, in the form of her great-grandson, was the means of revenge against the Mamelukes chosen by that proud and gentle older woman who had introduced Ziwar to sex at the age of sixteen.

Ziwar was determined to honor her memory by helping Martyr when the time came. Yet he remained patient with Martyr, knowing that the tasks his great-grandmother had secretly willed upon him could only be undertaken by a mature man with much experience behind him.

In fact not until 1914 did he decide to act, and even then he did so in a roundabout manner.

It was during one of Martyr's weekly visits and Ziwar had just finished reading aloud a footnote on the gentle Persian girl whom Strongbow had loved in his youth for a few weeks, no more, before she was carried away in a cholera epidemic. Ziwar sighed and laid aside his magnifying glass. He licked his lips thoughtfully. After the silence had gone on for several minutes, Martyr shook himself and emerged from his trance.

What is it, Menelik?

That recurring phrase in Strongbow's study, *a few weeks, no more.* Isn't it extraordinary how such a brief period of time could have come to mean so much to him? Think of the tens of thousands of experiences he had in the course of a haj spread over a lifetime, yet always he comes back to those few weeks. Don't you find it odd in a way?

Yes, said Martyr.

So do I, in a way. But then, time itself is odd. I learned that when I was younger than you, working in tombs. Did you know mummies can grow hairs?

No.

They can. All at once you'll find a fresh hair growing right in the middle of a bald head that's three or four thousand years old. Now that's odd too. By the way, Cairo, how old were you when your great-grandmother died and you first came here?

Twelve.

Yes that's right, and now you're already in your middle thirties. A dragoman then, a dragoman still. What should we make of that? Not stuck in time, are you?

I don't know. I seem to be but I just don't know what else to do.

You're not looking forward to becoming the Clerk of the Acts, are you? To be the senior dragoman in the city in your old age? Is that your ambition?

Certainly not.

I wouldn't think so. I would think you'd want something more meaningful in life than that, and if you do it's about time you got started. When I was your age my name was already famous throughout Europe. Although of course nobody knew it belonged to me.

But you're Menelik Ziwar.

True. And it's also true that notoriety, known or unknown, is worthless. Perhaps no one will ever hear of you when you decide what it is you want to do. Perhaps that's why you'll be so successful at it.

At what, Menelik? What can I do? What should I do?

Hm, let's give it some thought. But in the meantime could you do me a small favor?

Of course.

It concerns a theory of mine. Recently I've begun to wonder whether there isn't a secret cache of royal mummies somewhere. We made a great deal of progress in the last century but it still seems to me the number of pharaohs discovered to date is just too small. Can you get up to Thebes now and then in the course of your work? Luxor, I mean?

Yes.

Well there's a tomb on the west bank that's being excavated. If you can, take your clients there and poke around near the entrance. At night naturally. Unwitnessed. We don't want to alert anyone.

Naturally.

Yes. Just see if you can find anything that looks like it might be covering up a secret passageway. Frankly I'm sure this theory of mine is correct.

In the next few months Cairo Martyr took all his clients to Luxor, to the excavation on the west bank where he said the entranceway to a tomb was especially romantic in the moonlight. There, while squatting and standing and crouching in the entranceway servicing his clients, he dug behind their backs and over their heads but discovered nothing.

Until one night a heavy Italian woman turned her face to the mud brick wall and whispered that she wanted him to mount her from behind, which he did. The woman then redirected him higher according to her pleasure and pushed against the wall with her powerful arms for added thrust, the first outward heaves of her huge thumping buttocks so ferocious Martyr had to grab the wall himself to keep from being thrown backward onto the ground.

He grabbed and his fist went straight through a brick into a hole, around something stiff and straight and thick.

He had his balance now, there was no need for a handhold. As the woman bucked and groaned he removed the object from the hole and gazed at the silver rings and wrappings in the moonlight, at the bracelets of gold and cornelian inlaid with lapis lazuli and light green malachite.

A mummy's arm. Perhaps that of a queen?

Cairo Martyr removed his shirt and carefully wrapped the arm in it. Meanwhile the Italian woman went through four or five howling spasms, shrieked her praise for the mother of God and collapsed on the ground, beginning to snore immediately. Cairo Martyr fixed another brick in the hole he had uncovered and filled the chinks around it.

Had he actually discovered a secret cache of buried pharaohs?

Indeed you have, said Menelik Ziwar, so excited he sat up in his sarcophagus to examine the arm more closely through his magnifying glass, the first time Martyr had seen him rise from his pillows since the old scholar had begun reading Strongbow's study aloud to him fourteen years earlier.

To be exact, continued Ziwar, this belongs to a third-ranked concubine of a pharaoh by the name of Djer. Know him? No? Just as well, rather a drunken dolt. Anyway the history of the tomb is this. It became a shrine to Osiris during the XVIII Dynasty, and since then innumerable people have passed by that brick wall where you found the arm and never suspected it was there. Who was your client by the way?

An Italian woman.

Large and heavy?

Very.

Enormous buttocks?

Yes.

Wanting it in the Mediterranean manner?

Yes.

And with that massive hindside suddenly bucking against you, you had to reach out for support? Your fist smashed through a brick into the hole in the wall? That's how you found the concubine's arm?

Yes.

Menelik Ziwar nodded. He laughed.

What a fine headline that would make in an academic journal. Picture it in impressive type.

> **In hindside, Mediterranean manner leads to most important archeological discovery of twentieth century.**

Well I congratulate that heavy Italian woman. She's proved my theory.

She has?

Yes. You see the mummies of Djer and his women have never been found. Now that shrine to Osiris is of no interest to us. What is of interest is that around 1300 B.C. grave-robbing was becoming such a problem that the high priests had to take steps, because without his mummy a pharaoh's not a god, he's nothing. So they gathered up all the mummies they could and carried them off for reinterment to a secret chamber they'd dug across from Thebes, the present home of our missing mummies. That was my theory and now it's been proved correct.

But what was the concubine's arm doing out there all by itself?

Waiting for a heavy Italian woman's thrusts and groans in the moonlight to make history. Despite the precautions taken by the high priests in 1300 B.C., chanting sacred texts while they slaughtered the workmen and so forth, some clever grave-robber must have found out about the new secret chamber. He was making away with a load of loot when the priests surprised him. He stuffed the concubine's arm into a hole and covered it with a brick, intending to return for it later, but instead he was killed on the spot. So the secret was kept and that was that for three millennia, until your heavy Italian woman squarely faced the wall and revealed the truth to us.

Exhausted with excitement, Ziwar sank back on his pillows and crossed the concubine's arm and the magnifying glass on his chest.

Now listen to this. If my calculations are correct there'll be no less than thirty-three pharaohs in that chamber, not to mention their women and servants and cats. In short, the greatest mummy cache of all time.

He closed his eyes.

What a discovery. What a way to culminate my career. Now listen carefully, Cairo. I want you to go back there at once, alone, and dig behind the hole where the arm was. There has to be a shaft leading to the secret chamber. But just imagine it, thirty-three pharaohs. I'm going to have a lot of traveling to do, a great many eras to visit. This heavy Italian woman simply has no idea what her anal appetites will eventually contribute to our knowledge of ancient history.

She certainly doesn't, murmured Cairo. Quite the opposite.

What makes you say that?

The present she gave me. A little monkey.

Menelik Ziwar opened his eyes. He looked disappointed.

A monkey? You let an Italian woman give you, an African, a monkey as a token of her esteem for your performance? Don't you have any more self-respect than that?

An albino monkey, added Cairo mischievously. Pure white except for his genitals, which are bright aquamarine. He has an extraordinary trick of curling up on your shoulder into a little ball of white fluff, pretending to be asleep, his head and tail tucked away out of sight so that no one can see what kind of animal he is. But when you whisper his name he jumps to his feet on your shoulder and instantly whips into action.

Doing what?

Vigorously masturbating. And with both hands no less. It can be quite a surprise.

Menelik Ziwar smiled dryly.

What name does the little fellow go by?

Bongo.

The old scholar snorted at the bottom of the sarcophagus.

Well Bongo may be bright, Cairo, but all the same we have to find you another profession. I'm more convinced of it than ever. You're just not taking life seriously enough.

Menelik Ziwar nodded with authority and closed his eyes. As the heavy Italian woman had done in the moonlight, he immediately began to snore.

On a dark night, having searched the desert around the tomb to be certain he was alone, Cairo Martyr removed the outer layer of bricks from the wall and started digging. He had only gone a few feet when his shovel broke through into space.

He widened the opening and held a candle inside. Ahead lay a shaft about three feet high and just wide enough for a man's shoulders. He climbed in on his stomach.

The passage was packed with mummies on each side and the only way he could pass through them was by putting his face next to theirs, nose to nose and mouth to mouth. It might have been difficult to move at all if the shaft hadn't sloped downward, allowing the weight of his body to push him through the mass.

He slid and gathered momentum, plummeting down and down for two or three hundred yards in a shower of bones and legs and arms, heads rolling after him, cats flattened under his chin. Abruptly the shaft opened into a chamber and he went crashing down to the bottom, smashing through rags and wooden cases and coming to rest in a suffocating cloud of debris.

When the dust had settled he lit a candle and lay in the stench, staring at the blackened walls and the mummies crowded everywhere in confusion, lying and standing and some on their heads grinning, others slouched against the walls holding on to the stones with shriveled hands. There were gold armchairs and gold sedan chairs, gold drinking cups and gold plates, jewels and necklaces and occasionally, sitting on top of a dusty head, the gold cobra headpiece that was the mark of a pharaoh.

Martyr raised his candle and saw a black square opening at the end of the long narrow chamber. He elbowed his way over to it and pushed through the opening, finding himself in another compartment exactly the same size and shape as the first, also crowded with mummies.

Martyr wiped the dust out of his eyes. What was that at the far end of this chamber? Another door?

Numbly he struggled on through a third compartment, a fourth and a fifth and a sixth, a seventh. Or had he lost count? The chambers were all identical. He started back, barely able to breathe in the stench.

In one of the doorways he paused to lean against a stone and think. Had there been a door at the other end of the original chamber? Did the compartments stretch in both directions? Could he find the way out again or would he have to stumble back and forth forever through the packed compartments of this subterranean train?

The light from his candle seemed suddenly weaker. Perhaps the lack of air was going to make him faint. Maybe he was already trapped on this immobile express train beside the Nile.

He giggled. Where was the express going?

To eternity of course. Here under the desert a party of pharaohs and their entourages were on a trip to eternity, and if only briefly he was joining them.

A mummy next to him stirred. Its shoulders were pinned between four or five other passengers and it looked exhausted.

Going far? asked Cairo.

All the way, whispered the mummy with a resigned expression.

Cairo giggled and nodded and pushed on through the compartment. A cat got in his way and he gave it a kick. The cat dissolved. He came to a royal gold-encased armchair that was blocking the aisle.

Excuse me, madame, he said, trying to elbow his way around the queen who sat stiffly on her throne with a haughty suggestion of a smile. She wore a large emerald on what once must have been an ample chest, now withered.

Cairo had an urge to touch one of her breasts. He did so and his fingers punched through the gold-encrusted rags into an empty cavity. He held his nose as the gases escaped and the queen's smile faded. Her mouth fell open revealing bad teeth and only a stump of a tongue. Martyr laughed and pushed on down the train.

Guv'nor?

He stopped and turned. A mummy pressed into a corner was watching him, a small stooped man with a sorrowful face.

For some reason Cairo wasn't surprised at the working-class English accent. The mummy certainly appeared to be no more than a common laborer, and in any case, if he'd spoken in ancient Egyptian there would have been no way to understand a word he said.

The mummy's narrow concave chest suggested weak lungs, perhaps even tuberculosis. Definitely working class, thought Cairo, and treated no better then than now. The mummy abjectly touched his fingers to his forehead. He seemed to be trying to show respect.

Don't mean to bother you, guv'nor, but could you spare a navvy a light? We don't get many visitors down here.

Cairo lowered the candle in front of the mummy's sickly face and saw him take a deep puff of something, slowly exhaling with a sigh. In your condition, thought Cairo, that's not going to do you any good.

Ah that's better, said the mummy. Thanks, guv. You can't imagine how dull it gets down here. We used to keep each other company all right, but after a few centuries of carrying on no one had much to say anymore. Know what I mean? Down here the party ran out of conversation about three thousand years ago.

Cairo nodded.

And of course I didn't buy this trip in the first place, they put me on it. I mean I can understand why a pharaoh would want to make the trip, being a god, but what's in it for me? You can see how we're packed in down here, the air already stifling and getting worse as time goes on, and you realize what kind of time we're talking about.

The mummy looked down the chamber in disgust.

Like I said, guv, what's in it for me? If you're not a god what's the sense of living forever? But they don't care about that, they don't care how you feel. One morning you happen to be sweeping up an antechamber, a room in the flat belonging to one of the king's third-class concubines, strictly on temporary assignment and minding your business you are, when word comes down that the king has croaked and all of a sudden you're a member of the royal funereal household and being hustled off in official mourning to be mummified. So here I am to no end, an endless no end, and all because I was doing my job one morning. It's not fair and you can't help feeling resentful.

Cairo nodded. The mummy made a face.

What's more, guv, the high priests had it all wrong up there. The pharaoh dies and being a god they're going to send him on his eternal trip. Right. But why do they assume he'd naturally like to have his queen and his playmates and servants on the trip with him? For company? Well they're crazy. We're packed in down here and there's nothing natural about the situation at all. Did they really think we were going to tiptoe around serving him while the concubines flopped on their backs and the queen smiled and the cats did appreciative somersaults? Wrong. Dead wrong. Things don't work that way. He may be a god and used to living forever but the rest of us are just tired to death of this trip of his. Tell the truth. Have you ever seen so many bored faces as you see down here?

Cairo shook his head.

Of course you haven't. They all resent this trip as much as I do. There's not a concubine here who's even looked in his direction in three thousand years. Not a cat who's done a tumble one way or the other, not a servant who's lifted a finger. Why should we? He can play with himself for all the concubines care. As for the queen, you saw what happened when you gave her a poke. Nothing but foul gases inside and her teeth are going bad and she's lost her tongue. Her smile was a fake, as you saw. In fact can you guess what it was that made her teeth go bad and withered her tongue down to a stump? That's right, that's the kind of king our Djer was and drinking all the time too. Her smile was always a fake. But now that Djer's on his trip he can't get even a little cup of drink to help him face the truth. He's dry, as dry as I am, and you can't imagine how dry that is. Well that's some joke on him, but you're not staying down here are you, guv? You'd be a fool to do that. You may think you'd like to live forever, but I can tell you this is no kind of a party to be in.

I'm lost, said Cairo. Where's the exit?

Two cars forward. Look for a large sedan chair on the left, it's right beneath the shaft. Put there a long time ago to serve as a stepladder. He must have caught his though, we never saw him again. Got away with my mistress's right arm but not much else.

Thanks, said Cairo, I'll be going. By the way, how many pharaohs are there down here?

Counting that lout I used to work for, thirty-three in all. And Egypt is well rid of their kind. They did nothing but watch us build monuments to them. Strictly thinking of themselves, and now on this trip that's all they can do forever, and you wonder how satisfying that really is. Well good luck, guv.

The candle flickered. The mummy's face drooped sorrowfully. Cairo waved from the end of the compartment and pushed his way to the sedan chair two cars forward. He lifted himself into the shaft and made the long climb back up through the arms and legs and detached heads, the clouds of dust, to the desert night.

The next morning he boarded a steamer down the Nile. But when the boat finally docked in Cairo on that clear spring day in 1914, when he rushed to the sepulcher beneath the public garden beside the river to deliver his spectacular news, he found an unfamiliar lid on the massive sarcophagus he had visited so often, a painted carving of Cheops' mother in place of the dry crinkled smile he knew so well.

Menelik Ziwar, former slave and unique scholar and absentee discoverer of thirty-three pharaohs, had quietly died in his sleep leaving Cairo Martyr sole owner of the largest divine cache in history, a pantheon of ancient gods with which to avenge the injustices done to his people.

The last day of December 1921.

Snow flurries came and went outside the smudged windows of the Arab coffee shop where Cairo Martyr and Munk Szondi and O'Sullivan

Beare were playing poker. They played into the evening and were still playing the following morning, having moved on at midnight to a curious apartment in the Moslem Quarter which the Irishman said belonged to a friend of his.

The apartment had two lofty vaulted rooms. The front room was empty save for an enormous bronze sundial set into the wall near the door, a set of chimes attached to it. In the back room where they played there was a tall narrow antique Turkish safe in one corner, a giant stone scarab with a sly smile on its face in another corner, and nothing else.

They recessed for a few hours on New Year's Day and were back before twilight, sitting on the floor in their overcoats between the safe and the scarab, Martyr and Szondi wearing gloves, O'Sullivan Beare in mittens. It was almost as cold in the room as it was outside but no one seemed to notice it. Cairo Martyr had the deal. He turned to O'Sullivan Beare.

Who exactly is the friend of yours who owns this place?

Goes by the name of Haj Harun, said Joe. Formerly an antiquities dealer, now on permanent duty patrolling the Old City.

For what?

Possible invasion attempts. These days the Babylonians are worrying him but you can never be sure, tomorrow it could be the Romans or the Crusaders. Keeps a sharp eye out for them. Has to, he says. Knows what kind of havoc they can wreak in a Holy City.

How long has he been on patrol?

Almost three thousand years, answered Joe, studying his poker hand. Cairo smiled and examined the backs of his untouched, downfaced cards. He singled out one for discard.

Now it may be, said Joe, that you're disinclined to believe me, about such an enormous period of time and all, a tour of duty lasting that long I mean. Many are those who have been disinclined over the millennia. In fact he says I'm the first person to believe in him in the last two thousand years, and how's that for a streak of bad luck? I think I'll be taking two don't you know.

Cairo smiled more broadly and dealt the extra cards, three to Szondi and two to Joe and one to himself. He leaned down and patted the giant stone scarab on the nose.

Genuine?

Nothing but. Straight from the XVI Dynasty, according to the old article.

What old article?

Haj Harun, the great skin heretofore mentioned.

Is that a fact. Well why does the scarab have such a sly smile on its face?

Don't know, do I. But my guess is the scarab must be in on a secret we're not. Cunning piece of goods, no doubt about it. Jacks or better you said? Well I think I'll just open with this tidy pile of authentic pounds sterling.

All at once the chimes attached to the sundial in the front room creaked noisily and began to strike. Cairo and Munk raised their heads, counting.

Twelve? asked Cairo. At six-thirty in the evening?

Pay no mind, said Joe. That sundial has a habit of sounding off when it pleases, disregarding the rest of us. It loses track of the hours you see, due to darkness and cloudy days and so forth, and then it makes up for them later. Either that or the other way around, makes up for time beforehand so it can take a nap later on. Confusing, isn't it. Those extra hours we just heard could be already past or yet to come, who's to say.

Cairo nodded.

Was it a portable sundial once?

Strange you should be asking such a question because that's exactly what it was. And a hugely heavy piece it must have been to the soul who was lugging it around. Why such crazed activity I couldn't imagine.

Where did it come from originally?

Baghdad, I'm told. Some era called the fifth Abbasid caliphate, according to the old skin. That is to say, it must have played some role in the *Thousand and One Nights,* which just happens to be Haj Harun's favorite collection of fancies. It was a present to him in the last century from a man who once rented this very room to write a study in.

O'Sullivan Beare smiled.

Haj Harun tried to tell me at first that the man only rented the room for an afternoon. But that didn't seem likely, and then when I heard how big the study was I knew the old man was mixing up time again. More like a dozen years, it must have been.

Why? How big was the study?

Enough to fill a camel caravan that stretched halfway from here to Jaffa. When the gent finished his study, it seems, he packed it up in this camel caravan and sent it down to Jaffa, whence both caravan and manuscript were shipped to Venice to be on their way to publication somewhere in Europe. But here we are on New Year's Day in Jerusalem and aren't either of you two joining me in this interesting game of chance at hand?

Cairo Martyr laughed.

Strongbow's portable sundial? Strongbow writing his thirty-three-volume study, *Levantine Sex,* in this very room? The hollow stone scarab Strongbow had later borrowed from someone in Jerusalem so Menelik Ziwar could use it to smuggle a set of the banned volumes into Egypt?

An uncommon setting, it struck him, for a poker game in the Holy City.

Without looking at his cards, Cairo Martyr raised the bet.

3

Cheops' Pyramid

*Petty dealers were frequently picked up
and jailed for mummy-mastic possession.*

*F*or some weeks after Menelik Ziwar's death in 1914, while continuing to perform his Victorian dragomanning duties in a perfunctory manner, Cairo Martyr pondered the question of what to do with his spectacular cache of pharaonic mummies.

Before Ziwar died he had told Martyr the amazing fact that in his youth he and Martyr's great-grandmother had briefly been lovers. She had vowed then one day to avenge her humiliating life as a slave, and thus Ziwar had understood from the beginning the significance of Martyr's name when he came to him as a frightened boy only twelve years old, alone in the world, seeking the great black scholar's advice.

A proud woman with a long memory, Ziwar had said. She wanted to see some scores settled with those oafish Mamelukes who sold her down the Nile. But time passed and both her daughter and her granddaughter died in slavery, and she knew she would die in slavery, so the best she could do was to give you the name she did, in the hope you might redress the wrongs done to her. So don't deny her, Cairo. Hers was a stubborn, lifelong courage. Honor her wishes if you can.

Martyr wanted to, but how? He was still a common dragoman, although now he had the mummy cache. But what role did mummies have in his life?

And then all at once that stunning incident occurred in the first light of an early summer day in 1914, on top of the Great Pyramid.

An English triplane carrying the morning mail to the capital. An anonymous pilot grinning in flying goggles and leather helmet, white scarf fluttering on the wind. The triplane skimming the top of the pyramid and gaily wagging its wings, gaily saluting the most impressive monument ever reared by man and cleanly decapitating an aging overweight German baron and his aging overweight wife, as if to signal the end of the leisurely old order of the nineteenth century. In the dizzying shock of recognition that came with dawn that morning, Martyr realized that his Victorian servitude had ended forever. And he also understood why Ziwar had sent him to Luxor when he had. Undoubtedly the old scholar had long known the secret pharaonic chamber was there, yet he had waited until he was about to die before he asked Martyr to go find it, so that Martyr would be the sole owner of the mummy cache. Thus had Ziwar placed in Martyr's hands a priceless instrument for retribution, and all for the sake of a woman the old scholar had loved briefly long ago.

Patience.

Extraordinary patience.

His great-grandmother waiting through the nineteenth century for justice to come. After she died, Menelik Ziwar waiting until 1914 before he told Martyr about the love affair of his youth and sent him up the Nile to take charge of the secret pantheon waiting there.

The patience of slaves and former slaves. And now he was determined to be equally patient in devising a master plan for the use of his instruments of power.

Cairo Martyr smiled. He was standing on the summit of the Great Pyramid, the headless naked bodies of the fat German aristocrats having come to rest some yards below him. The sun was on the horizon and he was on top of the Great Pyramid. A new age had arrived.

The mummies, instruments of power. What better place to ponder their future use than the unique hideaway bequeathed to him by old Menelik, sage of sages?

By the second week in August his caravan was ready, the camels laden with a huge supply of tinned meat, exclusively meat, Martyr having early gotten into the habit of eating only protein in order to survive the rigors of dragomandom.

The camels were unloaded at the base of the Great Pyramid and a band of porters labored over a weekend carrying the supplies up to the summit. When the entire top of the pyramid was heaped with tinned meat, Martyr paid off the foreman.

Why up here? asked the dazed man, breathing heavily.

Martyr smiled.

An airplane is picking me up here tomorrow morning. I'm taking this meat to my village in the Sudan. There's a severe drought down there this summer.

The foreman laughed slyly, expecting no better answer from a black man.

And what's that animal asleep on your shoulder? asked the foreman. It looks like a little ball of white fluff.

Martyr smiled more broadly.

He looks like he's asleep but he's not. He's my guardian spirit and he watches over me and warns me if danger is near. Bongo, shake hands with this thieving fellaheen.

Upon hearing his name the little albino monkey instantly leapt to his feet on Martyr's shoulder, masturbating vigorously with his bright aquamarine genitals thrust forward, both tiny fists flailing away.

The foreman screamed and fled with his porters. But all the same Martyr watched them through his binoculars until they were out of sight, porters carrying goods to tombs and returning later to pillage them having always been a curse in Egypt.

After dark he tripped the combination of latches hidden in the crevices around one of the massive blocks of stone near the summit.

Powerful springs creaked. The block pivoted on an unseen iron post and gently swung open. He stepped into the foyer, struck a match and lit the lamp.

At the bottom of a short formal staircase lay the sunken parlor of Menelik Ziwar's spacious nineteenth-century flat.

Martyr gazed at the rich dark wood of the furniture that crowded the parlor, heavy solid pieces arm to arm and back to back, everywhere tassels and laces and doilies, legs that ended in claws crushing the heads of rodents in the thick carpets, lamps thickly shaded and standing only a few feet apart between the innumerable hunting prints on the walls, between the dozens of lacquered Chinese screens that were dividing spaces for no reason, the furniture in this room alone surpassing that to be found in the entire native quarter of any African city.

In style and layout the flat was massively Victorian. Martyr went on to inspect the large library and the formal dining room on the second level down, the well-equipped workshop for archeological restoration on the third level down, the master bedroom and the two guest bedrooms on the fourth level, the kitchen and pantries on the fifth, the servants' quarters on the sixth and the storerooms on the seventh.

Beneath that was a cellar where firewood was stored. Altogether a roomy seven-story apartment, inverted and impressively solid, in the top of Cheops' pyramid.

Martyr spent the rest of the night transferring tinned meat into his new quarters.

In bequeathing the flat to Martyr only a month before his death, Menelik Ziwar had reconstructed its history as effortlessly as if he had been a witness to those events three and a half thousand years ago.

Evidence speaks for itself, the old Egyptologist had said. Remove yourself to the XVI Dynasty if you will, a lawless era. The mysterious Hyksos have conquered the kingdom, the shepherd kings as they're sometimes called, and although we don't know where they came from the epithet does seem apt. That is to say they don't seem to have been too bright, as we'll see. Well as usual when foreigners arrive and take over in Egypt, a lot of them are on the lookout for loot. Tomb-robbers lurk in the countryside waiting for opportune targets, and then as now none loom as large as Cheops' pyramid. Numerous tunnels have already been dug into the pyramid in search of its treasure chambers, but always laterally or uphill. I mention this not because it was hard work, but because direction is essential to our story.

All right, Cairo. One night we find ourselves in a Memphis tavern where a gang of sturdy but not very bright Hyksos adventurers are conspiring over beer. The tavern owner, a native Egyptian, overhears them talking about lost treasure. Now since he is a native Egyptian, and not just another Hyksos who has come out of history from nowhere and will inevitably go back there again, these rootless shepherds turned adventurers naturally respect the tavern owner. They look up to him and that's going to cause trouble, because he happens to have idealistic religious views. You wouldn't know it today but once there were actually Egyptians who had ideals.

Well, whispers the tavern owner as he serves another round of beer to the gang of conspirators, if it's treasure that's on your mind, what about the treasure in the Great Pyramid?

The Hyksos adventurers shake their heads gloomily. Everyone has already tried to look for that, they say, and no one has ever been able to find it.

True, says the tavern owner, but the reason they've all failed is because they always dug their tunnels uphill. Whereas a pharaoh, being a god, wouldn't have allowed his mummy to be dragged uphill to reach his burial chamber. Naturally he would have descended into it with his hands crossed on his chest, a much more dignified position. If you're a god you don't crawl uphill, you descend from the heavens.

In other words, said the tavern owner, the mummy would have been lowered from the top down, and that's how we should dig.

Menelik Ziwar had cackled lightly.

The poor man's deluded idealism at work, you see. And although it seems witless today, that Hyksos gang with their dense shepherd heads believed him. They had another round of beer and that very night followed the tavern owner out to the Great Pyramid with all their tools.

The first thing he had them do was hollow out a base camp, or in this case a top camp, where they could live in secret while sinking their shafts. Then they dug tunnels down toward the bottom, all the way down to the bedrock beneath the pyramid. But they missed the burial chambers and instead broke through into a subterranean stream.

Bad luck for the Hyksos gang, good luck for us. The Nile was flooding and if it hadn't been, who knows? They might have gone on digging vertical tunnels until the pyramid had become structurally unsound and collapsed.

Menelik Ziwar had smiled.

The Great Pyramid suddenly collapsing in on itself? Simply deflating like a balloon? Do you realize there are six and a half million tons of rock in there? Can you imagine the noise it would make?

He sighed.

Pollution saved us. Once again that paradox of the Nile. The Nile was flooding and sewerage from Memphis had infected the subterranean stream. Crazed by thirst after their long dusty dig down from the summit, the Hyksos gang and the tavern owner threw themselves into the sluggish stream to drink their fill and then some.

Ziwar had nodded thoughtfully.

A matter of minutes, I'd imagine. The dysentery endemic to subsurface Nilotic tributaries is particularly virulent. They had enough strength to crawl back up to their top camp, but not enough to budge the block of stone over the entrance when they got there. And that's where I found their skeletons, the bones of the Hyksos telling us nothing as usual, the tavern owner having spent his last moments, by now no longer an idealist, tracing the hieroglyph for *beer* in the dust.

Menelik Ziwar then briefly concluded his tale.

The top camp and vertical tunnels had remained lost until he deduced their existence in 1844 by studying the irregular air currents in the known shafts and chambers of the pyramid. Finding them was a simple matter once he knew they existed. He examined the large top camp and decided it would make an appropriate country retreat and eventual retirement home for the world's leading unknown Egyptologist. Accordingly, he made plans to furnish it, sparing no expense.

The work had taken sixteen years. During that time Strongbow had often stayed in the unfinished flat when passing through Lower Egypt and had always greatly enjoyed it, as he wrote in a letter from Aden around the middle of the century.

My Dear Menelik,

The air at your future country retreat is simply incomparable. And among its many other attributes I would also have to mention the superior quality of the view, the serenity of the sunrises and sunsets as seen from the doorstep, and in general that pervasive sense of solitude men of our nature find so invigorating. Lastly there is the aura of tranquillity that one cannot help but feel when going to bed in the summit of the greatest monument on earth.

Congratulations, my friend. An altogether admirable project. Many thanks for a lovely weekend in this superb perch you have found for your old age.

Yours etc,

Plantagenet

P.S.   I enclose a rare Solomon's-seal as a token of my appreciation. I came across it last month in the Hindu Kush and have never seen a lily-of-the-valley quite like it.

P.P.S.   Are we still on for next Sunday?

Indeed, Menelik Ziwar was convinced he had found the perfect country home for himself. So much so he waited until every detail was completed before he went up to spend his first night in the flat.

He chose his forty-third birthday for the occasion, Christmas, 1860. He would have liked to have asked Strongbow to join him for the celebration, but the explorer was off somewhere in disguise and couldn't be reached.

Ziwar spent the day happily roaming through his new apartment. At the end of the afternoon he prepared a feast of roast beef and Yorkshire pudding accompanied by three wines and two vegetables, a baked potato and a savory, ending with a magnum of champagne and a large serving of his favorite greens, a weed common to the poorer sections of Alexandria where it grew wild in vacant lots, a nostalgic reminder of his youth when there had often been little else to eat.

After dinner Ziwar set up a canvas chair on the summit of the pyramid to watch the sunset while smoking a cigar.

A thoroughly successful day, or so it seemed. Drowsy from his meal and the wine, he retired early to the master bedroom and quickly fell asleep, only to find himself awake in terror a few minutes later, overcome by a sensation of falling, this sudden irrational fear of heights evidently brought on by a lifetime spent in confined subterranean spaces.

In any case, Ziwar knew he could never spend another night in his lofty flat. Sleeping that high in the air was out of the question. When the time came for him to retire, he decided, he would resort to the snug security of an underground sarcophagus, preferably that of Cheops' mother, rather than Cheops' chamber in the sky.

Here Martyr moved with his albino monkey and his tins of meat on August 14, sleeping and reading and exploring the interior of the pyramid by day, sitting on top of the pyramid devising his plans by night, oblivious to the monstrous new war in Europe where massed armies were savagely destroying each other in muddy trenches.

And there in the clear dry air of that ancient pinnacle above the Nile, methodically and relentlessly, Cairo Martyr pondered the injustices suffered by Africans over the centuries, historical crimes he intended to repay in full measure.

Considering where he was living, it wasn't surprising he decided to deal with the pyramids first. Slave labor had built them for pharaohs who thought they were gods, but a pharaonic god was nothing without his mummy and Martyr owned the largest cache of pharaonic mummies in the world.

About the time of the first battle of the Marne, he moved all his mummies in sealed cases to the top of the pyramid. There, in Ziwar's workshop for archeological restoration, he proceeded to grind them down into a fine powder.

So much for the eternal gods of ancient Egypt. He had reduced them to dust but that wasn't enough. After prolonged meditation, coincidental with the second battle of Ypres, he decided to desecrate the once holy remains of the pharaohs as well.

During the Somme offensive he converted Ziwar's workshop into a pharmacy and carefully mixed half of his mummy powder with mastic gum, producing a balm he intended to sell as an aphrodisiac with general magical properties. Thus the tyrannical builders of the pyramids would end ignominiously with a pinch of their dust lodged in the nostrils of wheezing old men greedy for longer life, another pinch served up as mastic to be smeared on the unwashed pudenda of barren women, a third encrusting the slack sexual organs of nervous merchants unable to obtain an erection.

The formerly glorious pharaohs sordidly sold as mummy dust and mummy mastic in back alleys. Available to any corrupt illiterate who could pay for them, just as African slaves had once been.

Martyr now moved forward from ancient to modern Egyptian tyrants. The Mamelukes, as pederasts, had simply disappeared from history. But the Arabs had been their coreligionists in the slave trade and it was therefore through Islam that he would strike. Since he was nominally a Moslem he had access to all the holy places.

A desecration here too then? Some intolerable act that would outrage the entire religion?

Cairo Martyr smiled. He lit a cigarette. The second battle of the Marne had just ended and the Great War would soon be over. And so too the night. Dawn was coming and he was sitting on top of the pyramid, contemplating the last minutes of darkness, when the revelation came to him. Significantly, he was facing east.

Mecca, of course. The navel of Islam inside the Kaaba. The Holy of Holies, a *black* meteorite.

He inhaled deeply.

Black. Islam deprived of its most sacred object. The stone that pilgrims came from all over the world to kiss. To steal the black meteorite from the Kaaba and render the Holy of Holies utterly empty.

Utterly.

Cairo Martyr laughed. And the black stone itself?

To Africa, of course. He would carry it to Africa where the Arabs had grown rich for centuries on black gold, his people. A black meteorite now to pay for black gold then.

Justice.

It had taken him four years to work out his master plan but it had been worth it, no one could hope for more. He intended to steal the black meteorite from heaven and bury it in rich black African soil, where it belonged.

At the end of the First World War a brooding Cairo Martyr, sleek from four years of solid meat, emerged from seclusion at the top of the Great Pyramid and descended into the raucous crowds and swirling flies of the bazaars of the Middle East, there to hire the wholesale dealers who would receive his smuggled mummy dust and mummy mastic in bulk, cut the first with quinine and the second with glue or glucose and distribute both to retailers who would sell them on the open market in tiny oilskin bags, five pounds sterling per bag.

The dose was small and an impotent man or a barren woman needed more than a bag a day for treatment. Three or four bags a day was a common dosage, but habits running to eight or nine bags were far from rare.

Prices varied with the season. In general spring with its illusions of hope was the most profitable sellers' market, winter with its lethargy the worst. But an outbreak of local tribal warfare could drive sales up at any time. Highly spiced foods tended to do the same in the summer, as did aggressive athletic contests in the autumn.

Usage also varied by region and ethnic background. Desert bedouin, the fierce Kurds and religious Jews seemed immune to the benefits of mummy dust and were almost total abstainers. But the sedentary Arabs of the cities, wealthy Persians and lazy Turks of all classes were heavy consumers.

Sales increased substantially near large rivers, near mosques, on Saturday evenings and during full moons, declining dramatically in the weeks before lambs were slaughtered in the spring. Mummy dust was generally preferred by men and women under thirty, mummy mastic by those over that age. But a confirmed user was more than happy to get his mummy any way he could.

The European authorities in the Middle East moved to suppress the clandestine trade as soon as they became aware of it. Both mummy dust and mummy mastic were declared dangerous drugs and treated accordingly in the courts, but the profits involved in handling them were so huge Martyr had no difficulty establishing a marketing network that reached into every corner of the Levant.

Petty dealers were frequently picked up and jailed for mummy-mastic possession, but due to the precautions Martyr had taken it was nearly impossible for his major wholesalers to be prosecuted.

And on the rare occasions when one was, the English or French magistrate in charge of the case immediately received a large anonymous bribe along with detailed dossiers on a dozen underworld figures in his city, previously unknown criminals who could easily be convicted of any crime because they were guilty of every crime.

The wholesaler was then released for lack of evidence and quickly went abroad to the French Riviera for a vacation arranged by Martyr, after which he would turn up with a different name in another Arab capital, where his expertise could be put to work in some other aspect of the overall operation.

In only three years Cairo Martyr's secret balm network was smoothly functioning throughout the Levant, assuring him a large income for life. The time then came for him to launch the second phase of his master plan, the series of deadly steps that would ultimately lead to the theft of the black meteorite from the Kaaba in Mecca.

With typical patience Martyr intended to approach his goal by degrees. First he would gain clandestine control of Jerusalem, the third holy city of Islam. When that was accomplished he would move on to Islam's second city, Medina. And only then, with all flanks secure, would he take his campaign to Mecca for his final triumph.

But when Martyr arrived in Jerusalem in the autumn of 1921, he found he wasn't alone in seeking secret control of the city. Other clandestine operators were at work in the confusion that had followed the war, in particular a Khasarian Jew from Budapest, Munk Szondi by name, who seemed to have immense resources of his own.

If he had been faced with just this one competitor, Martyr was confident he could have made a deal with the man for an equable division of spoils. In fact he had worked out most of the details for a compromise proposal when he accidentally met Szondi for the first time in a Jerusalem coffee shop where they had both chanced to seek shelter on a cold December afternoon when snow was definitely in the air.

But he couldn't make an offer to Szondi then because a third man happened to be sitting with them in the crowded shop, a young Irishman who also agreed to the game of poker Szondi had suggested as a diversion against the gloomy weather.

A game of poker. A diversion. The wind outside whipping through the alleys. Snow definitely in the air.

And somehow a strange design descending upon the three of them that night after they moved the game to the curiously empty shop of Haj Harun, where Martyr soon made another discovery. For some reason as yet unknown, the Irishman was also seeking secret control of Jerusalem.

Chance had apparently brought them together on the last day of 1921, but now none of them seemed able to leave the game, to escape the mysterious spell that had suddenly locked them in around a poker table.

Why? What was the spell? Did it have something to do with Haj Harun?

Cairo Martyr shrugged. He smiled.

There were complications he didn't yet understand but he was as patient as ever, as patient as his great-grandmother and Menelik Ziwar had been. So patient he never looked at his cards before he bet on them, because he knew in the end he wouldn't win out of luck.

In the end he would win because he had to.

Because his cause was just. Because no one could have a cause more just than his.

Even if it meant facing a siege in the Holy City more arduous than any since the First Crusade.

By the closing days of January 1922, with a month of steady play behind them, the three gamblers had begun to realize they were involved in more than ordinary chronic poker. And it had also become apparent they would have to bring outsiders into the game if they were to make any money, the three of them being too evenly matched to win from each other.

It was Munk Szondi who made the suggestion one night when he had the deal.

What about it, Joe?

Suits me.

Cairo?

An excellent idea.

As Munk shuffled the cards he gazed at the tall antique Turkish safe in the corner.

I've been wondering about that, he said.

Have you now, murmured Joe. Well I recall doing some wondering about it myself when I walked in here the first time and saw it standing there so tall and thin. That doesn't look to be a safe, I said to myself. It looks more like an impregnable sentry box on local guard duty.

Joe nodded to himself. He smiled, recalling that afternoon nearly two years ago when he had rapped on the safe and heard the echoes from deep in the ground. Haj Harun had then told him the truth.

The safe was bottomless. Inside it was a ladder that led down to the caverns of the past, the ruins of a dozen Old Cities, two dozen Old Cities. Because Jerusalem was on a mountaintop, as Haj Harun explained it, and since it had been endlessly destroyed and rebuilt over the millennia, no one had ever bothered to dig away what was left from before. Instead they had built over the ruins, raising the holy mountain ever higher. And only Haj Harun knew the caverns existed, because he alone had lived in all those former Jerusalems.

But he had shared the secret with Joe because Joe had not only befriended him but even believed the things he said, the first person to have done so in two thousand years, which had mystified Haj Harun in the beginning.

Why do you believe what I say, he had asked, instead of beating me when I say it? That's what everyone else does. They call me an old fool and beat me.

No reason not to believe you, Joe had answered. I haven't been long in our Holy City, everybody's Holy City, but I've learned enough to know you have to accept twists here the way you might not elsewhere. Different kind of place, that's all. Eternal city and so forth, daft time spinning out of control for sure on top of the holy mountain. Now you say you've lived here three thousand years and who am I to say you haven't? No one, that's who. A man has to be in charge of his own memories all right, otherwise nothing would work. So if you say it I'll believe it and that's the shape of things.

There had been tears in Haj Harun's eyes then, and ever since he had been eager to reveal all he knew to his new young friend. The only problem was that Haj Harun was so old the years seemed to slip and slide together for him, and he could seldom remember what he knew.

Munk Szondi was still gazing at the tall antique Turkish safe in the corner.

What does the old man keep in it? he asked.

Now there's an item for you, said Joe, and would you believe me if I told you? The past. Yes that's right. He keeps the past, no less, in that tall and narrow safe.

Munk smiled.

Is that so?

It is indeed. What he's got in there is three thousand years of history, the Holy City's history, and what do you think of that? You see he's by way of considering himself the custodian of Jerusalem, the one and only legitimate article. And me myself, I'm by way of thinking he's right.

Munk shuffled the cards.

Who appointed him to this exalted position?

Self-appointed he was. Had to be. No one else had been around long enough to do the honors. Not that he wasn't voted into the job too, he was. By general acclamation of the citizenry, accompanied by great applause.

When was that? asked Munk.

Well let's see, it must have been a little before 700 B.C. Seems about that time the accursed Assyrians were ready to make their move in their monstrous chariots, accosting the lands to the north on their way down to a-conquer Jerusalem and everyone in the city was a-scared and agog at the danger. Commerce and the assorted religions were coming to a standstill, don't you see, so maybe soon there would be no Holy City at all here, nothing but gnashing of teeth and lamentations. Do you follow me, Munk?

Yes.

Now first you have to remember Haj Harun wasn't then at all what you see today. He was a greatly respected figure here, a veritable local hero and especially renowned for his oratory. Are you remembering, Munk?

Yes.

All right. He squares his shoulders and strides down into the

58

marketplace to assay the Assyrian situation and assail all doubts and provide assurances or assumptions as the case may be, assuming his role in other words, assiduous defender that he be, just going right out there to arrest the Assyrian confusion with his powerful voice and presence.

Citizens, he shouts, take heart with me.

He stands there smiling and nodding with confidence, shouting this over and over, but his fellow Jerusalemites aren't assimilating any of it. They're just plain scared so there are more teary dirges and dreary threnodies.

The Assyrians are a-coming, scream the citizens. But we can save ourselves, shouts Haj Harun.

How? scream the citizens. By hiding the city's sacred objects, shouts Haj Harun.

Well of course, the sacred objects, no one had thought of that. If they could hide the city's precious sacred objects for a while, say a century or two or three, then the Assyrian danger would surely pass as all dangers do and the Assyrians would have to lug their monstrously heavy chariots back up north where they came from. Then the citizens could bring out their sacred objects once more and be as prosperous as ever, a proper Holy City with its proper holy goods in place.

So it's right you are, *the sacred objects,* and a powerful sigh of relief passes around the marketplace.

Good, scream the citizens, let's hide them for two or three centuries. But where?

Consternation then. Doubt all around. Everyone knows the Assyrians have a dreadful reputation for breaking things up and down to get their hands on sacred objects, especially those of a Holy City, for the Assyrians are nothing if not unholy. So the mob screams again.

Hide them by all means. But where?

Here, shouts Haj Harun in triumph, whipping up his cloak to reveal a gigantic money belt strapped around his waist and a huge shepherd's sack on his back, both previously unsuspected although the citizenry was thinking their hero had looked a trifle overweight and hunchbacked that morning when he got up to address them.

A ruse, they scream. Will it work?

Haj Harun smiles. It will, he shouts. I used the same belt and the same sack in a similar situation some time ago when the Egyptians were coming.

The Egyptians, scream the citizens in dismay, you must have been younger and stronger then. Younger, shouts Haj Harun, but I'm still strong.

A queasy lot, the citizens of Jerusalem, then as now. So many prophets are always passing through here saying this or that is the absolute truth of the matter, and always contradicting each other, that the citizens naturally tend to be suspicious.

Is the money belt big enough? they scream. Is the shepherd's sack? And are you going to sign receipts?

Well Haj Harun shouts he is and all is well and in another minute they're bringing their sacred objects from every corner of the city, jewels and gold in all shapes and sizes and even some wood, and Haj Harun stuffs it all away in his money belt and his shepherd's sack and signs the receipts they wanted. Then he tries to get to his feet.

Groans from the crowd, groans all around.

Can't you even stand up? they scream. If you have to sit there for the next century or two you're certainly not much of a hiding place.

Well it's hard, God knows. It's the hardest thing your man's ever done but he does it, he manages, he gets to his feet. After all he has to, the future of the eternal city depends on it. So he lets fall his cloak and takes one staggering step and then another, looking fat and terribly deformed, not unlike a Jerusalem merchant trying to waddle away from the marketplace under the weight of his profits.

And just in time, because up there on the ramparts the ram's horns are beginning to sound announcing the imminent arrival of the advance Assyrian assault force, which is to say their ferocious and justly a-feared cavalry.

The mob scatters for cover. The marketplace is empty. Only Haj Harun is left behind because he can't move fast enough. Stumbling crookedly with his burden of public safety, he slips into a side alley. Do you see it, Munk?

Yes.

Good. Well the gates bang open and the dreaded Assyrian cavalry comes thundering down the street shaking the cobblestones, and now your man knows why their accursed cavalry is so justly a-feared. I mean, my God, can you believe it? The Assyrians don't ride horses, that's why. They ride winged lions just like you've seen in the pictures.

Great roaring bounding lions with manes a-flowing and wings a-spreading. So it's here come the bloody Assyrians all right. Are you still there, Munk?

Yes.

I thought so. Now here's the difficulty. Your man only thought he was slipping into that side alley. Actually he wasn't. Actually that side alley was far too narrow to accommodate both him and the gigantic stuffed money belt and the huge stuffed shepherd's sack. Actually he's still out there in the open, Jerusalem's portable altar bearing all the goods, right there in the middle of the street with the cavalry bounding toward him, those wicked winged lions breathing fire and looking for a fresh piece of meat to guzzle. Guzzle meat? Of course they could with that fiery breath of theirs, easily and more. What next, you say?

What happened next, Joe?

A miracle of faith, that's what. He wasn't about to drop the goods and run the way you or I would. No, he stayed right there in the open and thought fast. Listen, he said, reassuring himself, if Belteshazzar could do it so can I. He had faith and so do I. I've always served the Holy City and I'm not stopping now, winged lions or no. Jerusalem forever, that's the job. His very words. Are you still with me, Munk?

I am, but who's this new character on the scene?

You mean this fellow Belteshazzar? Apparently he was some gent who was thrown to the lions by an unjust king but who survived because he was innocent and knew it, just as Haj Harun did. Faith, you see. Anyway Haj Harun stands his ground in the middle of the street as the onslaught approaches at a frightful pace. The cavalry comes thundering down on him and the lead lion, near starved for real Jerusalem meat, opens his jaws wide and takes a terrifying snap at Haj Harun.

Well saints preserve us, you could just hear those jaws crack. The lion had aimed at Haj Harun's middle, you see, and planted his vicious bite on the money belt, and with all those precious sacred objects packed so tightly together in there, the thing was harder than stone. So *crack* went the lead lion's teeth, *snap* went its jaw, and the beast rolled over on the cobblestones at Haj Harun's feet, whining pathetically.

Well that slowed the advance. The next lion took a more tentative snap at what looked like a huge succulent deformity growing out of

Haj Harun's back, hitting the stuffed shepherd's sack where it hurt and down he went with his front teeth broken off, howling between the roars, letting the other lions know this article in the middle of the street wasn't worth the biting.

Well to make a long story short, a couple of more lions gave it a try and lost their teeth, so that was that. The cavalry charge was broken, toothless lions were whimpering all over the place, and Haj Harun was able to make his slow escape to a remote corner of the Old City. Then some decades or centuries later the Assyrians were no longer the arrogant power they had been, and sure enough they went slinking away to the north with their chariots, as predicted. Haj Harun brought out the city's sacred objects and redistributed them to the best of his memory, commerce and the assorted religions got underway again and all was well once more in the Holy City. The citizens gave Haj Harun a standing ovation and acclaimed him the unofficial savior of Jerusalem, official status only being temporary and only assigned to prophets before they're discredited and killed.

And that's what I meant, Munk, by the job not being just self-appointed. He did appoint himself all right but later the appointment was approved by all concerned, as you've just heard. For a time, at least. A while after that, during the Persian occupation, things took a turn for the worse for Haj Harun. In fact he went into a straight decline from which he's never recovered.

Why the decline?

Don't know, do I. Time's tricky, tricky times, all manner of possibilities. But I think the money belt was the culprit. You see it weighed on his kidneys something terrible when he was serving as Jerusalem's portable altar during the Assyrian afflictions, so badly he had to urinate every minute or two. And you do that over some decades or centuries and it could well cause your ruin. I mean who could accomplish much of a positive nature if they had to leave every minute or two to go to the bog? In such dire circumstances I think anybody would go into a decline. Well then, Munk. In sum, what do you think of this striking Assyrian adventure?

I think Haj Harun showed extraordinary courage.

He did, assuredly.

But there's one small fact that's out of place.

Do you tell me that? What could the small item be?

When the lions came charging down the street, Haj Harun was reminded of how someone called Belteshazzar had been saved by his faith.

True.

And it was that recollection that allowed him to stand his ground.

Very true. And so?

That was the man's Babylonian name. In the West he's better known by his Hebrew name, Daniel. He was taken to Babylonia at the beginning of the Captivity.

Joe looked confused.

I know the story of Daniel in the lions' den, Munk, I just didn't connect it with this other name Haj Harun used. But why's that matter?

Because it happens that Daniel lived in the sixth century B.C. Did you know that?

I didn't and I'm always glad to have new information, but I still don't see why that matters. Why does it, Munk?

Because the Assyrians conquered Palestine in the eighth century B.C. Now how could Haj Harun have recalled Daniel's exploits two centuries before they happened?

Joe smiled and tapped his nose.

Oh is that all, is that all you had on your mind. Well shouldn't I cut this deck so you can get on with the deal?

Munk put the pack on the table and Joe cut it. The cards began dropping around the table.

Joe?

Hm?

Well what's the solution to that?

To what? Haj Harun recalling something that hadn't happened yet? Something that was still a couple of hundred years in the future?

Yes.

But that's the whole point, Munk. There's no solution necessary for Haj Harun. I mean the past is what's passed and it's all part of Jerusalem to him, and him defending it although always on the losing side, as you always are when defending the Holy City. A Babylonian king throwing someone to the lions? The Assyrians sooner or later charging up these streets with their lions? All just pieces of the same job, defending Jerusalem, a task he says is both immense and perpetual, which is why he fails. Jacks to open, did you say?

No.

Fair enough, I'll open anyway. Hey there, what's the cause of this laughter, Munk?

The idea of Haj Harun keeping the past in a safe.

No laughing matter, as you can see now. And you can also see why he keeps that safe locked. If everyone were to go rifling around through the past the way he does, recalling events before they happen and sorting out confusion to his liking, Jerusalem would be nothing but bloody chaos I say, not able to stand up and do a straightforward job as a Holy City. So it's no bloody wonder the old man keeps that sentry box on duty, on guard and locked so things will be clear for the rest of us. Now just look at these cards. I've no business holding royalty like this, but since I am I'll just add a little sweetness to the pot before we see what you're up to, Cairo lad.

4

Solomon's Quarries

*Ah yes, cognac brought to the Holy Land
by the Crusaders to ease the pains of
pilgrims. Well how's it taste then?
Gone off a bit in eight hundred years?*

On a hot July day in 1922, O'Sullivan Beare lay slumped against the wall in the back room of Haj Harun's shop. The poker table was bare, the game having been recessed because of the severe heat. Listlessly he inspected the empty glass of poteen in his hand and decided it wasn't worth the effort to cross the room to refill it.

Haj Harun wandered in, barefoot as usual. An area of crumbling plaster in the wall caught his eye and he stopped to gaze at himself in a nonexistent mirror. He adjusted his rusty Crusader's helmet, muttering all the while, and retied the two green ribbons under his chin. He also did what he could to straighten his faded yellow cloak, mostly in tatters and hanging unevenly.

A black day, he muttered. Black. A black day for me. Black. A black day for Jerusalem. Black.

Is it now? said Joe from the corner. My sentiments exactly and no wonder in this heat. Just merciless, that's what.

Haj Harun jumped and looked down in surprise.

I didn't know you were here.

Well I think I am, although it's too hot to admit to more.

What are you doing on the floor?

Gravity pulled me down, I'm feeling grave today. Then too the stones down here are cooler than a chair. Then too heat rises, so the lower you are the better, which is also in keeping with my lowly mood. Why don't you try it? It's not half bad.

I can't, said Haj Harun. I can't sit still today. I'm much too restless. It's a black day. Black.

I see.

Haj Harun nodded at himself in a nonexistent mirror on the wall and his helmet went awry again, releasing a shower of rust into his eyes. The tears began to flow and he went on muttering to himself as he drifted out the door.

Black, thought Joe, wiping his face with his sleeve. Black and that was half of it for sure.

It had been only a little over two years ago that he'd been fighting the Black and Tans in the hills of southern Ireland, and all because of something his father had said, his father who'd been the seventh son of a seventh son and therefore had the gift of prophecy.

It was too hot to move, too hot to be in Jerusalem.

Joe closed his eyes and went back to the windswept Aran Islands, to a cool June night in 1914.

It had been a party night, one of the few each year. As usual all the poor fishermen had gathered at Joe's house for singing and dancing and drinking, Joe's father being the undisputed king of the little island, both because he had the gift and because he had thirty-three sons, Joe at fourteen being the youngest and last and the only one still at home. What should have been a wondrous evening of prophecies together with tales of pookas and banshees and the *little people*.

But not so that June night in 1914. On that cool evening his father had stared into his mug without a word, gloomily stared at the floor without a word, until finally toward midnight he began to relate.

All right, said his father, all right now. If you want to know the shape of things I'll tell you what I see. I see a great war coming in two months time. And seventeen of my sons are going to fight in that war and die in that war, one in every army that makes up that bloody war. But that's not what eats at this old heart. They're men now and can decide for themselves. What eats at this old heart is that not one of them is going to die fighting for Ireland. And that's our people for you, everyone's cause but our own.

Terrible, whispered the neighbors.

Terrible it is, said his father. But wait now, there's more. I also see a rising of the Irish nation in two years time, and then at last I'm going to have one son fighting for his country, a mere lad it's true but he'll be there all the same, that small dark boy you see standing perfectly straight in the corner behind you, his destiny now foretold.

And then, added his father, the lad having done his duty here, he's going to go on and become the King of Jerusalem for some reason.

Don't blaspheme, warned the shocked neighbors.

And none intended, said his father at once in embarrassment. I have no idea why I said that.

Nor did Joe. But in 1916 the Easter Uprising came as predicted and Joe was there helping to hold the Dublin post office before it fell, escaping then to the south and fighting alone in the hills of Cork for four long years before the Black and Tans tracked him down and he had to flee the country in the only way he could, disguised as a Poor Clare nun among a dozen Poor Clares sailing on a pilgrimage to the Holy Land.

To Jerusalem. Where he lay in a gutter outside the Franciscan enclave in the Old City, penniless and knowing no one, whispering into the dirt in Gaelic the name of the Irish revolutionary party, *We ourselves,* praying one of the priests who passed would be Irish and take pity on him.

As one did. The former MacMael n mBo, a whimsical man far advanced in years who in the folly of his youth had served as an officer of light cavalry in a British brigade in the Crimea. Who had survived a famous suicidal charge there when his mount fell, and as a result been awarded the first Victoria Cross ever given. Who now for the last six decades had been the priest in charge of the Franciscan bakery in Jerusalem.

Who are you really, lad? the elderly priest had asked Joe as he lay in that Jerusalem gutter, starving and exhausted. And to identify himself with the little breath he had left, Joe had whispered the legend of the O'Sullivan Beare clan.

Love, the forgiving hand to victory.

The baking priest had rescued Joe from that Jerusalem gutter and given him his old army uniform and his army papers so that Joe could move into the Home for Crimean War Heroes, a charity in the Old City. The baking priest, eighty-five years old at least and dancing and singing in front of his oven as he baked his loaves of bread in four shapes, the four concerns of his life, the Cross for God and Ireland for home, the Crimea where he had given up war and Jerusalem where he had found peace.

Singing and dancing in front of his oven and telling Joe not to worry about the date of birth on his army papers. Not to worry about apparent age here because nothing was as it seemed in the Holy City, everybody's Holy City.

Bread for brains? Joe had wondered. Simply gone the other way after six decades of sweating and dancing and singing in front of an oven in Jerusalem?

But he discovered the baking priest had been right about Jerusalem when he made his second friend there, a wizened old man who wore a faded yellow cloak and a rusty Crusader's helmet tied under his chin with two green ribbons, who appeared half-starved and tottered on spindly legs that seemed too weak to support him, a gentle knight named Haj Harun who roamed through the ages recalling the adventures of Sinbad the Sailor and other heroes of old, who remembered the building of Solomon's temple in his youth, and who for the last three thousand years had been hopelessly defending his Holy City against all enemies, always on the losing side.

On that day when they'd met in front of Haj Harun's shop, the old man had taken one look at Joe's Victoria Cross and decided that he was Prester John, the legendary priest-king of an ancient lost Christian kingdom somewhere in Asia.

Come right in, Haj Harun had said happily. I've been expecting you, Prester John. I knew you'd turn up in Jerusalem sooner or later in search of your lost kingdom. Everyone does.

Then Maud. An American and the first woman he had ever really known. Maud and love in the spring.

They met in Jerusalem in the spring and went down into the desert to be alone together. To a tiny oasis on the shores of the Sinai, and to Joe that month on the Gulf of Aqaba was the happiest he had ever known in life. But Maud was different after they returned to Jerusalem. And she refused to marry him, even though she was going to have his child.

When the weather on the heights turned cool in the autumn he found a house for them in the warm Jordan valley, a little house with flowers and lemon trees near Jericho, another oasis it seemed to Joe, where their child would be born toward the end of winter.

But no, he hadn't found another oasis as it turned out. In Jericho he couldn't seem to do anything right, anything that pleased her. No matter what he did Maud seemed angry, often even refusing to speak to him.

Joe couldn't understand any of it. It was true he was away much of the time smuggling arms, had to be away, as a fugitive it was the only way he could find to make a living for them. And his absences especially seemed to infuriate Maud. That and his dream of finding the Sinai Bible, the original Bible with its treasure maps of the riches buried beneath the Old City, which he'd heard about soon after coming to Jerusalem.

The *original* Bible? Discovered in the Sinai in the nineteenth century? Just knowing it existed had been a curse and a hope for Joe, a dream as it had been for so many others before him.

So it became worse and worse in Jericho. Joe totally bewildered, only twenty years old, and Maud more distant than ever, afraid of something perhaps but unable to talk to him about it, ignoring him as he sat up alone late at night in the garden behind the little house, drinking until he fell asleep. Drinking until it was time to leave once more to smuggle arms into Palestine.

And then toward the end of winter Maud left him. Abandoned the little house in Jericho without even leaving a note behind, not even that. Taking with her the son he had never seen. Born while Joe was away running guns to make money.

Money. That's what he needed, he knew that then. Money had kept him away from Jericho. If only there'd been money it wouldn't have turned out the way it had, or so he thought. And he wouldn't have lost the only woman he'd ever loved, or so he thought.

Money. The treasure maps of the Sinai Bible, the original Bible that was now buried somewhere in the Old City. To find it he needed secret control of Jerusalem, and since Maud had left him, the clues to the past that it contained had become his sole interest in life, or so he thought.

Years ago his father had prophesied that he would become the King of Jerusalem. His father had said it unintentionally, not knowing why he said it. But his father's prophecies were never wrong, so Joe knew he could become the secret king. He *knew* he could win the Great Jerusalem Poker Game and go on to recover the Sinai Bible. He only had to want it enough.

And he did want it enough, he wanted nothing else. Money and power and the Sinai Bible, they were everything to him.

Or so he thought.

A black day, thundered Haj Harun, suddenly bursting into the room and angrily stamping his bare feet on the floor.

Black and blacker and blackest, he shouted. As black as the bowels of the devil. Black. *Black.*

Joe stirred and looked up in surprise. He'd never known the gentle old knight to speak so vehemently.

Listen man, why do you keep saying that in all this heat?

Gloomily Haj Harun stared at a wall and retied the two green ribbons under his chin.

Because I can't forget it, he said. I'll never forget it and it happened on a July day just like this one.

When was that?

Haj Harun frowned.

About eight hundred years ago? Is that right?

It could be. Which event are we referring to?

Haj Harun groaned. Joe could see he didn't want to say it, even the words seemed detestable to him. And when the old man finally did say it, cringing as he did so, he spat out the words as if they were the most abominable curse in the world.

The Crusaders taking Jerusalem.

Joe paused, feeling sorry for the old man. He nodded grimly.

Ah, that occasion. And to think a moment ago I was imagining I had troubles. Just nothing compared to the unholy carnage you're talking about.

Haj Harun scowled at the wall.

I wonder if they still have the arrogance to celebrate their conquest.

Where?

In the caverns.

Joe raised his head. He smiled.

The caverns, of course. Why didn't I think of that before? It'd have to be a lot cooler down there. They used to celebrate, you say?

They did. Just shamelessly gloating over their brutal victory.

Well well, cooler at least. Why don't we make a descent to that level and see what's doing?

At the bottom of the ladder that led down from inside the antique Turkish safe, Haj Harun's wizened smile suddenly flared in the solid blackness. He had lit the torch. Joe jumped.

My God man, don't scare a poor soul like that in the underworld. Who's to know whether you're real or not? You could be a caveman's painting or a ghost on the loose or just about anything.

No task, murmured Haj Harun, affords more happiness than being a servant of light. This way now to the Crusades. Just please don't make any noise, Prester John. We don't want them to hear us.

We do not, whispered Joe. And quiet I am in the tunnels of the past, reverent as well. Just please don't get too far ahead of me with that torch. You know where we're going but I don't. And as hot as it is up there above, I don't want to find myself left behind down here in some corner of history.

They walked down tunnels and made innumerable turns. Joe was becoming nervous.

Are you sure you remember the way?

Yes. We're close now.

How can you tell?

The smell.

There was a strange smell in the air, Joe had noticed it. Something very sour and growing stronger every moment. Haj Harun's faded yellow cloak floated around a corner and all at once they were in darkness. Joe bumped into a wall.

Jaysus it's all over now, he muttered. Blind in the underworld with a ghost for my guide.

He groped his way around the corner and was struck by a blast of cool air.

Jaysus again.

Where's Prester John?

Here for God's sake. Where's the bloody torch?

The wind blew it out. Just a minute.

Joe heard a rustling sound. Somewhere nearby Haj Harun cleared his throat. Suddenly an enormous mournful wail shook the blackness. Joe could feel it vibrating against his skin.

Jaysus Joseph and Mary, what's that?

The lighted torch reappeared. A few yards away stood Haj Harun smiling triumphantly, holding a ram's horn.

Did you like it? he asked.

Like it, you say. *Like it?* No I did not. It almost scared me to death.

That's what it's for. I keep it here to frighten the knights away just in case. They don't seem to know about this cellar anymore but it's best to be safe.

Safe, said Joe and choked, overwhelmed by the stench he had forgotten in the excitement. Haj Harun was tying a handkerchief over his face and Joe did the same. They were standing in a large vaulted room lined with shelves cut into the rock, the shelves piled high with

72

rows of dusty bottles. Haj Harun took down a bottle and showed Joe the label, a peculiar white cross on a black background, the arms of the cross in the shape of arrowheads, their points not quite touching at the center. Beneath the cross was a date in Latin, A.D. 1122.

Recognize it?

No. But I'd say it must have belonged to a medieval tippler with a Christian bias.

Indeed it did, they all did. The Knights of St John, no less. Also known as the Knights of Jerusalem and the Knights of Rhodes and finally as the Knights of Malta, since that's where they ended up, but their proper name was the Knights Hospitalers. They became the most powerful of all the warring orders, but originally they were founded here to run a charitable hospital for pilgrims.

What's in the bottles?

Cognac.

True?

Yes, they brought it from France eight hundred years ago. They said it was for medicinal purposes. To ease the pains of pilgrims.

Joe whistled softly.

Ah yes, cognac brought to the Holy Land by the Crusaders to ease the pains of pilgrims. Well how's it taste then? Gone off a bit in eight hundred years?

I'm afraid it has, said Haj Harun. I know cognac is supposed to improve with age but that doesn't seem to have happened here. But it was delicious once, as I well know.

Had a nip or two, did you, over the eras?

Well not regularly. I haven't been able to do much real drinking since my liver gave out during Hellenistic times.

What did it then?

Bad shellfish. A Greek grocer said the mussels were fresh from Cyprus, which they might have been, they certainly made a delicious soup. But they were also polluted.

Oh I see, polluted muscles. Well I guess we all have to expect some toxins creeping in over time. As for me, if my liver had given out twenty-two hundred years ago, I think I'd be an unrecognizable wreck by now.

But there was a period, mused Haj Harun, when this cognac saved my life. It was when I had tuberculosis.

Dastardly, that. When was it?

In the sixteenth century when the Turks arrived. Their breath was so appalling it weakened my lungs.

Bad breath can do that?

When it's as bad as theirs was, yes. I can't imagine the state of their stomachs in the sixteenth century. Excited, I suppose, over all their victories. Anyway, I was employed by the Turks as a distributor of hashish and goats, and as a result of my customers breathing in my face I developed a severe case of tuberculosis.

Dreadful.

So I consulted my local physician and he prescribed plenty of rest and liquids and no heavy lifting.

Sound advice.

So I came down here and spent a year resting and drinking cognac and smoking cigars, catching up on my reading and lifting nothing heavier than a book and a bottle, and by the end of the year I was totally cured.

Does it every time.

And I haven't had a relapse since then. Not one.

It's true, you haven't. You know, there must be thousands of bottles in this Crusader wine cellar.

There are.

Yes, thought Joe, and the baking priest knows his Latin so what's to keep me from getting him to forge a letter from someone to someone, dated in A.D. 1122, proving the stuff is authentic Crusader cognac worth a fortune? There's money in that for sure, and we're talking about treasure even though I haven't found the map to it yet.

Who ran the Knights Hospitalers?

They had a grand master.

A letter from the grand master, thought Joe, that's the job. A formal yet tasty document to the king of France offering warm thanks for his Christmas contribution to the good works being done by the boys in Jerusalem, in keeping with the spirit of charity ten thousand pleasing bottles of much appreciated rare cognac for thirsty pilgrims in the Holy City.

Haj Harun slammed a bottle against the wall and broke off its neck.

Care for a sip?

The fumes rushed up at Joe. He gagged and doubled over, coughing at what might have been vinegar five or six centuries ago but was now a noxious gas unique in the world. He pulled Haj Harun out of the room and the old man followed, still clasping his ram's horn. After walking for another two or three minutes, Haj Harun stopped and whispered that it was just around the corner.

What is? asked Joe.

The great assembly hall of the Crusaders. And we have to be careful now, they carry all sorts of lances and swords and spiked maces. Just terrible to see, more frightening than the Babylonians.

Joe looked down at his shabby patched uniform. He fingered his Victoria Cross uneasily.

The VC was a cross all right and no mistaking it, which might help to establish his Christian piety. But the uniform? How could they know it belonged to an officer of light cavalry in the Crimean War? A hero who'd survived a famous suicidal charge launched on behalf of Christian righteousness? They wouldn't even have heard of that charge.

Are you ready? whispered Haj Harun.

Unarmed, muttered Joe. But as ready as I'll ever be against the combined might of the First Crusade.

Haj Harun got down on his hands and knees and gestured for Joe to do the same. The torch was extinguished. Joe peered down the tunnel and saw a faint light at the end.

The ceiling of the tunnel sloped down to meet them as they crawled quietly forward and squeezed through a hole, emerging on a smooth ledge flat on their stomachs. Joe noticed the rocks around them had been cut away in neat rectangular blocks. They peeked over the edge of the ledge.

Joe's eyes narrowed. They were facing a high square chamber, not a cave but man-made, carved out of the rock. Torches lined the walls and there no more than ten feet below them was an impressive crowd of several hundred men wearing brightly colored robes and a bewildering array of hats, most of them tall and peaked.

Flags and pennants were everywhere. At one end of the subterranean hall an elevated wooden platform had been erected. On it sat a half-dozen potentates in particularly ornate robes, listening attentively as one of their number addressed the assembly.

The new and enlarged College of Cardinals, thought Joe. Rome lost out after all. They've brought their business back here and that must be the new pope who's just been elected. Jerusalem wins in the end.

Haj Harun touched his arm.

The one who's speaking is Godfrey of Bouillon, he whispered.

Has the voice of an English drill sergeant, thought Joe.

And the man to his right, whispered Haj Harun, is his brother, Baldwin I, the first Latin king of Jerusalem. The others on the dais are Raymond of Toulouse, Robert of Normandy, Robert II of Flanders, Bohemond and Tancred. In front of them are the two men who started it all, Peter the Hermit and Walter the Penniless.

A scruffy lot, muttered Joe, trying to read the slogans on the flags and pennants.

From what he could make out between the cryptic symbols, the assembly was a gathering of a group called the Order of the Mystic Shrine, a society of Freemasons made up of men with high Masonic degrees. The speaker was saying that Masons from many lodges in many countries had made the long journey to Jerusalem to take part in this international conclave of the Order, the first ever held in the rock chambers beneath the western ramparts of the Old City that had long been popularly known as Solomon's Quarries, the spot where stonemasons in antiquity are said to have cut and dressed the stone blocks used by Solomon to build his temple.

And since we trace the origins of Freemasonry back to those very stonemasons, continued the speaker on the platform, it is truly a momentous event in history, albeit a secret one the world will never know about, for us to gather here and perform the mystical rites of our fraternal Order in the lofty chamber where Solomon's temple was hewed from the earth, a chamber which can honestly be said to be Solomon's temple in eternity, this spacious area where we now stand, once carved out and emptied by our brothers, being nothing less than the material form of the spiritual shrine we carry within us and treasure in common.

Flags fluttered and pennants waved. There were cries of *here here, yes yes, more more, true true.* The speaker smiled beneficently and raised his hand for silence.

76

By God that's cute, thought Joe, the complicated cant of stones. Cant as can and emptied quarries for heads. Mystical all right, at least to me. What's it all mean?

Haj Harun was urgently tugging him by the sleeve, so distraught Joe couldn't understand his frantic whispering.

What did you say?

I said we have to stop them now before it's too late, before they have a chance to return to their armies. There may never be another opportunity like this, all of them in one room together, to be dealt with in a single blow. Come on. We have to go down there.

We'd be surrounded, whispered Joe. Black and Tans all over us.

When you're defending Jerusalem you're always surrounded.

But the odds are disastrous. Only two of us against two hundred of them.

When you're defending Jerusalem the odds are always like that, whispered Haj Harun hurriedly. They never get better and sometimes they get worse. Come on.

No, I still think we ought to wait for developments. Maybe they'll set fire to themselves or something. Those peaked hats will be a definite fire hazard when the torches burn down a bit.

Haj Harun groaned softly.

But they killed a hundred thousand of us the last time. We simply can't let that happen again. The thought of it is making me hear noises in my head.

Steady man, whispered Joe, easy does it. No unwanted noises in the head at this critical juncture in history.

Noises, repeated Haj Harun desperately, I can hear them coming. Clanging their swords on the cobblestones and slaughtering the innocent until the streets are running with blood, oh it was horrible. The streets were knee-deep with bodies.

Haj Harun shuddered. Then his expression changed and he raised his head defiantly.

They were the ones who first made me wear my yellow cloak. I remember it now.

Why?

To set me apart. To try to humiliate me as a Jew.

Joe looked puzzled.

Are you telling me you're a Jew on top of everything else?

77

Haj Harun waved his hand vaguely.

When you've been around Jerusalem as long as I have, before people were divided into names like that, you're whatever the enemy wants to call you. But I absolutely refused to be humiliated. Instead I wore my yellow cloak with dignity. I've always worn it with dignity. But all the same, Prester John, the noises in my head are getting worse.

No, hold on. Close your eyes and they'll go away.

Noises, whispered Haj Harun and leapt to his feet. He sounded a tremendous blast on his ram's horn. The faces in the hall turned up toward the ledge in astonishment. Haj Harun waved his ram's horn in the air and shouted across the chamber.

Walter the Penniless. I see you skulking down there, you and all the other scheming Franks planning a new conquest of Jerusalem. But it's not going to happen so give it up, I say, don't persist in your wickedness. This city is eternal and can never be conquered by you or anyone else, when will you ever learn that? So take your armed hordes away and never besiege us and starve us and kill us again. We won't be conquered. We simply refuse to be conquered.

Haj Harun sounded a second powerful blast on his ram's horn.

Hear me down there. If you absolutely refuse to withdraw I hereby challenge the bravest among you to individual combat. Step forward, he who dares. Tancred? Bohemond? Peter the Hermit? Raise your sword, any one of you. I'm ready.

Haj Harun sounded a third and final blast on the ram's horn. Joe reached out and tried to stop him, but before he could Haj Harun's spindly legs went churning out into space. His faded yellow cloak flared as he sailed out over the edge of the ledge and plummeted down toward the crowd of stunned faces below.

There was a heavy thud and a terrible cracking of bones.

Joe looked down, horrified. Haj Harun lay crumpled on the stone floor, feebly holding his ram's horn in the air. There was a shiny new dent in the top of his rusty helmet.

The Masons began to yell at each other in confusion. Flags and pennants and peaked hats surged forward as they pressed around the extraordinary apparition on the floor. One of them nudged Haj Harun with his foot and the old man twitched, letting out a low moan. He seemed to be trying to get the ram's horn to his lips for another blast, but he obviously didn't have the strength to move.

Alive, thought Joe. There's that at least.

All at once he realized they were both still wearing the handkerchief masks they had put on in the cognac cellar.

Oh help, thought Joe, two bloody bandits in the underworld, that's what they'll be thinking we are. Hired subterranean thugs and vicious cutthroats come to disrupt their silly revels and spy on their foolish games. We're for it now and what would the baking priest be likely to advise at a time like this? Anything, that's the job. Anything, as long as it's fast.

Joe jumped to his feet and raised a clenched fist.

Hold it right there, he shouted, just hold it, you Freemasonry rabble. This is the Irish Republican Army you're looking at and this uniform is IRA combat issue for special underground warfare in Jerusalem. We've had this quarry mined with heavy explosives for months waiting for you to turn up and reveal your fiendish anti-Jesuit plots, and now that we've heard them all we're taking our information aboveground and going straight to the pope, and dead is the fanatic who tries to stop us. Stand fast or I'll tell the old man down there to sound a fourth blast on his ram's horn, which is the signal for the apocalypse as sure as St John ever wrote the Word. One more blast from his horn and the bombs will blow and you'll all be on your way back to Solomon all right, the world well rid of your black anti-Catholic hearts. *Freeze for your lives.*

Joe leapt lightly to the floor and whirled in a circle, glaring at the stupefied Masons. Then he knelt and gathered up the miserable Haj Harun who had been crawling helplessly in circles, his helmet jammed down on his nose, so that he couldn't see, tears streaming down his face from the rain of rust in his eyes.

We won, whispered Joe in his ear.

We did?

Yes. Not one of them dared accept your challenge. Not Bohemond, not Tancred, not even that scheming scoundrel Walter the Penniless. Paralyzed with fear they were and they're going home without raising a sword. You did it. Jerusalem's saved.

Thank God, murmured Haj Harun as Joe lifted the old man's frail body gently up on his back and staggered away through the masses of pennants and flags and peaked hats, the flickering torches, to limp out the entrance under the northwestern wall of the Old City where the hot July sun was just sinking below the rooftops of the new.

79

Part Two

5

Munk Szondi

You eat pure garlic?
Yes.
How much?
A large bulb before each meal and
two more afterward.

Some slovenly Mediterranean habit
you've picked up, I suppose?

*T*he man with the tri-level watch and the samurai bow hadn't originally acquired his vast knowledge of Levantine commodities through travel, but rather from the unique library of letters that made up the archives of the House of Szondi.

The ancestor who had written those letters, Johann Luigi Szondi, had been born in Basle in 1784, the son of a German-Swiss perfectionist who manufactured very small watches. The smaller the watch the more it pleased his father, and in fact his father's watches were often so small their faces couldn't be read. For that reason few were sold and most ended up strung along the walls of their house like so many tiny beads, ticking inaudibly and keeping precise time uselessly.

But fortunately Johann Luigi's mother was an Italian-Swiss cook who had an unsurpassed talent for baking bread. No better bread could he found in Basle, so while Johann Luigi's father busied himself reducing time to next to nothing, his mother walked around town selling huge loaves of hot bread so the family could live.

Both parents died at the end of the century and it was immediately apparent that Johann Luigi was no ordinary Swiss. To support himself he chopped firewood while beginning his studies in chemistry and medicine and languages. He studied Arabic at Cambridge for a year and decided to make a walking tour of the Levant, a precocious and sprightly young man with light blue eyes, still only eighteen years old.

With his great natural charm, Johann Luigi had no difficulty begging lodgings along the way. In Albania he chanced to knock at the gate of the castle belonging to the head of the powerful Wallenstein clan, where he was duly invited to spend the night. The master of the castle, who bore the Christian name Skanderbeg and was the most recent in a long line of Skanderbegs, was away fighting in some war, as it seemed his predecessors had been doing for the last hundred and fifty years.

Johann Luigi was therefore entertained by the absent master's pleasant young wife. After dinner a wild storm broke over the castle and the young woman invited him to view the lightning from her bedroom. Torrential rains lashed the castle the rest of the night.

By morning the storm had blown itself out. With bright smiles for the young wife, Johann Luigi shouldered his pack to continue his journey, unaware he had planted in his hostess the seed of a pious future hermit, a man whose stupendous forgery of the original Bible four decades later would be universally accepted as authentic, the renegade Trappist and linguistic genius who would be the last of the Skanderbeg Wallensteins.

Johann Luigi traveled briefly in the Levant and liked what he saw. By the beginning of the following year he had walked back as far as Budapest, where he decided to enter medical school, again chopping firewood to support himself. He received his medical degree and set himself up in private practice, specializing in cases of hysteria. Before long he converted to Judaism in order to marry one of his former patients, a young Jewish woman of Khasarian extraction whose family had been engaged in petty local trade in Budapest since the ninth century.

A son was born to the couple and named Munk, a curious tradition his wife's forebears had brought with them from Transcaucasia before they were converted to Judaism in the eighth century, a custom requiring the first male in every generation to be given the same name. In Sarah's family the traditional name was Munk, although no one could remember its significance. As for Johann Luigi, he was more than pleased with the name since it appealed to his own rather monkish tendencies.

About the same time Johann Luigi began planning another brief trip to the Levant. He would travel overland to Aleppo, he told his wife, and spend a few weeks there improving his Arabic. Then he would journey down the Tigris to the Persian Gulf, find a ship bound for Egypt and so back to Europe. In all he would be gone three months, he said, and he promised to write every day, not explaining how his letters could possibly arrive in Budapest before he did, nor how the distances proposed could be covered so quickly.

But little was known of Middle Eastern geography in those days, and perhaps nothing at all in a Budapest family engaged in petty local trade.

Nevertheless, Sarah and her family must have suspected more was involved when they saw how the young doctor went about preparing himself for his trip. Instead of writing to shipping agents, Johann Luigi disappeared into the Hungarian countryside for a full year, walking barefoot in all kinds of weather and sleeping in the open without a blanket, feeding himself exclusively on grasses and returning to Budapest only once, to be with his wife when their daughter Sarah was born midway through the year.

Yet no one mentioned this odd behavior. The women in Sarah's family had always loved their men well and Sarah wanted Johann Luigi to do whatever would make him happy, even if it meant he would be away from home for a while.

On a brisk autumn day in 1809, then, Johann Luigi lovingly embraced his wife and two children and left on a brief journey to the Levant, to be traced by daily letters sent home to Sarah.

That much was true. Johann Luigi did write letters home every day, often five or six times a day.

And given his passion for details, it wasn't surprising his letters also contained long reports on everything he observed, down to the smallest items. Thus mixed in with the lyrical passages describing his love for Sarah, there was interminable information on crops and trade, lists of cottage industries and analyses of local customs, all strung together in what was in effect an exhaustive diary of his travels.

For two years the heavy packets of letters arrived regularly from Aleppo. By then the inquisitive young Swiss had grown a long beard and learned the one hundred and fifty Arabic words for wine, having become to all appearances an erudite Arab merchant, well dressed in the Turkish manner, who went by the name of Sheik Ibrahim ibn Harun and explained his merry blue eyes by saying he had Circassian blood.

So skillful was his grasp of the Arab imagination that before he left his headquarters in Syria, to amuse himself, he transposed an episode from *Gargantua* into Arabic and inserted it in a privately published edition of the *Thousand and One Nights,* the tale so cleverly done it was immediately acclaimed as a lost Baghdad original.

During the next two years Johann Luigi's letters arrived erratically in Budapest. Nothing would be heard from him for months, then hundreds of letters would descend on Sarah in a single day. Now he was in Egypt, having arrived there by way of Petra, probably the first European to have seen that deserted stone city since the Middle Ages.

Pink, my love, he wrote of Petra to Sarah. *And half as old as time.*

In Cairo he established a reputation as an expert in Islamic law. He was urged to take a high position in the Islamic courts but gently refused, saying he had urgent business up the Nile. He was next heard from in Nubia eating dates, marching ten hours a day, covering nine hundred miles in a month.

But in 1813, in Nubia, there were also a few quiet weeks for the restless Johann Luigi. There, in a village on the fringe of the desert, he fell in love and lived briefly with the proud young woman who would one day become the great-grandmother of the Egyptian slave, Cairo Martyr.

Next he pushed south from Shendi down to the Red Sea and across to Jidda, where he disappeared.

Only for Sarah to find a procession of carts drawing up in front of her house a year later, heaped with thousands of envelopes and packets. In his guise as Sheik Ibrahim ibn Harun, it turned out, Johann Luigi had penetrated both Medina and Mecca during the missing year and actually kissed the black meteorite in the Kaaba.

He was the first explorer to see Abu Simbel, then mostly buried by sand, and wrote that Rameses' ear was three feet, four inches long, his shoulders twenty-one feet across, estimating correctly that the pharaoh must have been between sixty-five and seventy feet tall despite his notoriously self-indulgent life.

Once more Johann Luigi went to Cairo intending to lecture on Islamic law, but the plague struck the city and he went to St Catherine's monastery in the Sinai to escape it. There in 1817, two years before the great English explorer Strongbow was born in southern England, Johann Luigi Szondi abruptly succumbed to dysentery and was buried without ceremony in an unmarked Moslem grave at the foot of Mt Sinai, within sight of the cave where the Albanian son unknown to him, the last of the Skanderbeg Wallensteins, would eventually produce his spectacular forgery of the original Bible.

Johann Luigi was only thirty-three when he died and he had visited Mecca fully half a century before Strongbow, who would be the next European to do so. It was true Strongbow's vast explorations would surpass those of the remarkable Johann Luigi. But it was also true the Englishman's haj would stretch over forty years, not a mere eight.

Long after Johann Luigi's death, letters in his familiar handwriting continued to arrive in Budapest from all parts of Africa and the Middle East. Tender letters filled with love, always promising that he would be home within the prescribed three months. Year after year they came—the last, four decades after his death.

But Sarah didn't know he was dead, and who could say that letter was the last?

There was always the chance another letter might find its way to Budapest from some obscure corner of the Levant, where Johann Luigi had entrusted it to a sleepy caravan merchant moving slowly through time on the back of a camel.

So when Sarah looked back on her life she couldn't help but consider her marriage perfect. As she passed into her eighth decade, well after most of her sisters and cousins had been widowed by husbands who had never left home, her husband was still sending her love letters. And even though he had wandered a bit, he had never failed to write home.

So Sarah died embracing his memory, listening to one of her granddaughters read aloud what was in fact Johann Luigi's last letter, delivered on the morning of the day she died, an exquisite description of a sunset at Mt Sinai that ended with the customary promise that soon, very soon now, he and his beloved Sarah would be together again.

And so they were. Smiling gently, she closed her eyes. Those sweet words from her husband the last she heard in life.

For years an exact count couldn't be made of Johann Luigi's love letters. But not long after he left Budapest, two facts had become apparent to Sarah.

First, the love letters were beginning to fill the floor-to-ceiling bookcases she had built in her kitchen so his letters would be near her while she was cooking.

And second, the love letters were likely to become the most complete source of information on the Middle East to be found anywhere in Europe.

By nature Sarah was an imaginative and energetic woman who found housework tedious. Therefore as soon as her children were no longer infants she began to cast about for a project that could engage her talents.

One Friday afternoon while reading a letter from her husband on Damascus cutlery, an idea struck her. As was obvious, the amount of detail on purely commercial matters in her husband's love letters was no less than astonishing. Why not use this information for a trading venture?

Secretly she went to a moneylender and mortgaged her house to raise funds. The sale of imported Damascus cutlery was a success and with the profits she turned to a second scheme, rugs from Persia, as described in another love letter. The rugs paid off her mortgage and after that came cotton from Egypt and jewels from Baghdad.

With business growing, Sarah began employing her sisters and aunts and female cousins as bookkeepers. Momentum gathered as more love letters arrived from the wandering Johann Luigi, detailing possibilities of new markets. Paying interest on bank loans seemed a waste of resources, so Sarah decided to found her own merchant bank.

Banking soon intrigued her as much as trade, so she opened a commercial bank as well. Its operations multiplied and she bought several other banks. By the age of forty her banking assets were the largest in Budapest, and by the age of fifty her branches in Vienna and Prague and elsewhere accounted for the bulk of financial business in those cities. Assets swelled, as did trade with the Levant, based on her husband's love letters.

Until by the time of her death the House of Szondi, as it had come to be called, was the single most powerful financial institution in central Europe.

The executive pattern of the House of Szondi remained the same after her death. From the beginning the boards of the banks had been staffed exclusively by her female relatives, first sisters and aunts, later nieces and grandnieces.

The senior managing board for all the banks, known collectively when in session as *the Sarahs*, in honor of the founder, met upon her death and naturally chose not Sarah's son but her daughter to be the new head of the House.

Sarah the Second assumed her position as managing directress, but being less single-minded than her mother she also took into consideration the men of the family. Now that the House of Szondi had become so rich it seemed ridiculous, to her, for the husbands and sons and fathers of the directors to be still working as petty local traders, the only life they had known since the ninth century.

Even her own older brother Munk was still running a discount dry goods store on the lower east side of Budapest, where he labored long hours stacking imperfect sheets and pillowcases.

Sarah the Second knew that her brother had always secretly loved the violin, which he played at home in a tiny windowless room no bigger than a closet, music being widely viewed as a frivolous pastime in his trade, where men were supposed to have strictly practical interests.

So Sarah the Second made her brother an offer. If Munk would come out of the closet and devote himself full-time to his real passion, music, she would support him for the rest of his life. Naturally Munk was enthusiastic and readily agreed.

At the next meeting of *the Sarahs* she announced what she had done, thereby in effect setting the course for a new family pattern. The directors were quick to follow her example and other secret musicians soon emerged from among the males in the family. Munk himself was immediately joined by three cousins, equally talented men who had also been running discount stores on the lower east side of Budapest. Together they formed a competent string quartet, which was soon in demand on the concert circuit.

The next generation of male Szondis was surrounded by music from childhood. Brothers and nephews and granduncles took to practicing together, under the baton and guidance of the reigning Munk, and over the following decades the all-male Szondi Symphonic Philharmonic, not to mention the numerous Szondi baroque ensembles, became as famous in the musical circles of central Europe as the all-female House of Szondi had become in the world of banking.

Thus while the women of the family made money, led by the reigning Sarah, the men of the family made music, led by the reigning Munk. But in keeping with the new matriarchal traditions of the family the first-born male in each generation, the new Munk, was never the son of a Munk but always the son of a Sarah, and therefore the eldest nephew of the last Munk, a confusing line of descent not easily understood by anyone but the Szondis.

The Szondi women naturally spent long hours doing research in the family archives in connection with their business training, but the Szondi men also had a special obligation in that regard.

Each spring they put aside their music and returned to the roomy old kitchen of Sarah the First, there to spend the months of annual awakening immersed in the bookshelves that contained the sources of the family's material and artistic success, amidst the twitterings of the birds outside in the garden and the heady fragrances of new flowers wafting into the kitchen on gentle breezes, perusing at their leisure those thousands and thousands of tender love letters a wandering Szondi husband had once sent to his loyal Szondi wife.

The future Munk of Jerusalem poker, born in 1890, chose the cello as his musical instrument and naturally he mastered it. But he was also an exception among male Szondis, because music didn't seem enough to him in life. Vaguely he yearned for something quite different, although what it might be he didn't know.

In fact as a boy, young Munk tried every conceivable occupation for a week or a month, avidly pursuing his new role. For a while he was a postman, then a fireman, then a railroad conductor. In the spring of his ninth year he was a surgeon operating in his bedroom, only to turn that summer to hunting lions and elephants in public gardens. By the following autumn he had already tried horticulture and painting and carpentry, and served as a distinguished judge.

When he was eleven he fell under the spell of the letters of his great-grandfather, the tireless Johann Luigi Szondi, and proceeded to relive those prodigious travels up and down the Nile and across the Middle East. He too marveled at the deserted stone city of Petra and marched through Nubia eating dates, covering nine hundred miles in a month, then paused to measure Rameses' ear as three feet, four inches long before pushing south from Shendi to the Red Sea.

But eventually none of these lives satisfied him, not even the splendid journeys of his great-grandfather, perhaps because those journeys weren't originally his. He did come to learn, however, that he wanted to get away from his family and their traditions, which he was beginning to find oppressive. Yet the Szondis never sensed this because young Munk lived so much within himself as a boy. Had they known him better, they might have realized he strikingly combined the qualities of the first Sarah and her wandering husband, energy and imagination and a passion for details.

What are you going to do, young Munk? his relatives asked him again and again in exasperation.

But Munk only smiled and shrugged and said he didn't know, then returned to the family archives to try to discover the secret he knew must be there, the secret of an unusual life, made unique because lived according to its own nature and nothing else.

What was the secret that had driven his great-grandfather to do all the incredible things he had done? Simple curiosity? A fascination with strange customs? To see what others hadn't seen?

In the comfortable kitchen of Sarah the First, surrounded by the enormous bookshelves with their thousands and thousands of love letters, young Munk sat gazing out the window not really seeing what lay beyond it. Certainly his great-grandfather must have had all those feelings, he was aware of that. But what else had there been for Johann Luigi? What *had* driven him? What *was* the secret?

At the age of eighteen, with his family insisting he choose a profession, he finally made a decision. And when he announced his choice they received it in utter amazement.

But why that, Munk? If you're not interested in being a musician, then trade at least would be understandable. We certainly did that for a long time. Or scholarship or one of the professions. Your great-grandfather was both a scholar and a medical doctor, after all. Or chemistry or languages, he did that too. But a Szondi in the army? In the Austro-Hungarian Imperial Army? A Szondi pursuing a military career? It's unheard of.

Yes, said Munk quietly, smiling. I thought so myself.

But after being trained and serving for a short time with a regiment of dragoons near Vienna, young Munk realized everyday soldiering wasn't for him either.

He applied for duty overseas, and as luck would have it an aide to the Austro-Hungarian military attaché in Constantinople died that very week as a result of having eaten bad Turkish meat. Thus in the summer of 1908, Munk found himself seconded to the capital of the Ottoman Empire.

He had been there little more than a month when the Austrian annexation of Bosnia brought on yet another Balkan crisis, causing the

Turks to undertake secret military preparations. Lieutenant Szondi's reports from the field proved so valuable he was promoted to captain early in December.

Then on Christmas the attaché and his entire staff, except for Munk, were violently stricken by food poisoning while consuming a holiday feast of contaminated wild Turkish boar. Munk escaped the poisoning because he had been eating large amounts of garlic since entering Turkey, having learned of this simple yet effective antidote to bad meat from the letters of his great-grandfather, who had used the remedy successfully throughout his travels.

A few of his fellow officers lingered into the new year, but all were dead by Epiphany. Since there was no one else in Constantinople who could fill the position, the ambassador named Munk acting military attaché, an astonishing responsibility for one so young.

But Munk's rapid rise had only begun. The former attaché had not had time to submit his annual summary of the situation in the Ottoman Empire, and Munk took the opportunity to completely revise it.

Of course his superiors had no way of knowing he was able to draw on the vast accumulation of information he had learned as a boy while studying the secret Szondi archives in Budapest. What they did know was that another incident involving foul Turkish meat, a hazard faced by all Europeans in Constantinople, had suddenly brought to their attention a brilliant young officer with an unsurpassed knowledge of the Ottoman Empire.

Munk received a letter of commendation. He was promoted to major and made the permanent acting attaché.

Now Munk had found something that did interest him. For the next four years, eating handfuls of garlic and happily indulging his passion for details, he traveled extensively in the Balkans analyzing the impossible confusion there as Ottoman power disintegrated. None of the other European military attachés could keep up with him, crippled as they were by bad Turkish meat. In recognition of his achievements he was duly promoted to lieutenant colonel.

Then in the autumn of 1912 the Turks announced maneuvers near Adrianople and all the Balkan states mobilized. The first Balkan war broke out with the Bulgarians and the Serbs and the Montenegrins, the Albanians and the Macedonians all rising up against the Turks.

Meanwhile Russia and Austria-Hungary prepared for war against each other to support their various interests.

In this vast maze of intrigue and threats and sudden attacks, young Munk moved recklessly from front to front gathering information, all the while pursuing clandestine meetings in Constantinople and elsewhere with equal abandon.

Tireless and daring, young Lieutenant Colonel Szondi acquired a notoriety that would soon become intolerable to the chief enemy of the Austro-Hungarian Empire.

One of his frequent companions during those last hectic weeks of 1912 was the Japanese military attaché in Constantinople, one Major Kikuchi, a diminutive aristocrat who had become a hero of the Russo-Japanese War by ordering his men to pile up the dead horses of the Cossacks on a barren Manchurian plain, as a barrier against their incessant attacks, a desperate move that had allowed his company alone to survive the massacre of a Japanese regiment, safe behind the eight-foot-high walls of rotting meat that Kikuchi had erected.

Either because he was a Buddhist, or because of the indelible memory of that stench on a Manchurian plain, Major Kikuchi never ate meat, which allowed him to be as mobile as Munk in Turkey.

So they often traveled together, comparing their notes and talking late into the night in the clumsy wagons and lurching trains they shared while moving from front to front, developing a brief but lasting friendship that would one day lead Munk to find what he had always sought in the strange music of a desert monastery.

Late in November, Munk acquired the documents that brought an end to the first Balkan war, certain secret communications from Moscow that proved Russia would not go to war for the sake of the Balkan Slavs. Despite Russian mobilization, the territorial claims of the Serbs were to be abandoned.

These disclosures humiliated and outraged the Russians, and as a price for taking part in peace negotiations they insisted upon a cruel and unusual revenge. The notorious Austro-Hungarian military attaché who had operated so successfully in the Balkans had to be expelled from the army. Furthermore, in order to make certain he was no longer playing a part in Balkan military affairs, he had to be sent into exile in the Ottoman Empire where Russian agents could keep an eye on him.

Munk's orders arrived early in the new year and he sadly boarded the Orient Express for Vienna, where he would experience his last day of military service.

A full color guard greeted him at the station. He was driven to the headquarters of the chief of staff, with a cavalry escort, and ceremoniously promoted to colonel, at the age of twenty-two by far the youngest in the Imperial Army. He was also awarded the Order of the Golden Fleece.

After a formal luncheon with the officers of his old regiment, the dragoons mounted a dress parade in his honor. Finally at sunset he returned to the headquarters of the chief of staff, again with a cavalry escort, to hear read aloud the order of his expulsion from the army, along with an edict from the emperor expressing condolences and decreeing his exile within the week in the cause of peace.

When Munk arrived in Budapest that evening to say good-bye to his family he found only the men at home, some event of great importance having caused the directors of the House of Szondi to gather in emergency session.

Instructions awaited him. Ex-Colonel Szondi responded at once and galloped off to the rambling old house above the Danube that had once been the home of Sarah the First.

The Sarahs were meeting in their boardroom, the kitchen, where the windows between the floor-to-ceiling family archives gave broad views of commercial traffic on the river.

Munk did a sharp military half-turn in the middle of the kitchen and came to attention facing his grandmother, the reigning chairwoman, Sarah the Second. To the old woman's right sat the heiress apparent, his mother Sarah the Third. Ranged elsewhere around the spacious room were Munk's aunts and grandaunts and female cousins, the entire governing board of the House of Szondi.

Good evening, Grandmother, he said, clicking his heels and saluting smartly. It's a pleasure to see you looking so well.

The old woman grimaced.

So well? Stop that nonsense, I look awful and I know it. I can't do a thing with my hair in this damp weather. And what is that perfectly dreadful smell coming out of your mouth?

Garlic.

You eat pure garlic?

Yes.

How much?

A large bulb before each meal and two more afterward.

Some slovenly Mediterranean habit you've picked up, I suppose?

Not at all. It's strictly therapeutic.

Bad Ottoman meat?

Yes.

Oh I remember now, it's in the archives. Well direct the fumes toward the floor as much as you can and say hello to everyone.

Good evening, Mother, said Munk. Good evening, he repeated, nodding politely around the kitchen to the collected assembly of *the Sarahs*, all of whom had knitting in their laps. Those who weren't working their needles in quick agitated strokes were patting their hair nervously or tugging at their bodices. The dozens of women were all dressed in black, without makeup, their hair drawn back into tight buns fixed by a single stickpin with a triangular diamond head. Each also wore a black hat, black gloves, and a modest diamond brooch of triangular shape above the left breast, the customary dress for a formal board meeting of *the Sarahs*.

Outrageous folly, exclaimed his grandmother, opening the meeting. For years now we've asked nothing more from the men of the family than to practice their music and stay out of the way, to behave themselves, and to give a performance or two at family gatherings. Little enough, one would think. But what do we find you doing down in this disreputable place called the Balkans? Making a spectacle of yourself. Attracting international attention. We're bankers, young Munk, and bankers don't like notoriety of any kind.

96

The knitting needles clicked furiously around the room. The crescendo was becoming deafening when his grandmother cleared her throat. Abruptly the clicking stopped. The old woman leaned forwad and everybody watched her. She winked.

We heard you were awarded the Order of the Golden Fleece today. Congratulations.

Thank you, Grandmother.

How was the dress parade your old regiment gave you?

Very impressive.

And the luncheon? How many courses?

Twelve.

You didn't hold back, did you?

No.

Well you're looking a little pale all the same. You should be eating more. Is it true you had a cavalry escort coming and going?

Yes.

And the chief of staff himself read the order of exile? His Imperial Highness sending personal condolences?

Yes.

The old woman leaned back and rolled her eyes. She smacked her lips. Around the room the knitting needles softly assumed a rhythmic clicking.

A grandson of mine, she murmured, just think of it. The youngest colonel in the Imperial Army. Aren't you proud?

Yes. Very.

As well you should be. The Russians are barbarians and not to be trusted. You treated them exactly as they deserved. Now then, down to business.

The old woman stroked her chin thoughtfully. Around the room his female relatives somberly studied their knitting. When his grandmother spoke again the needles clicked quietly.

To be frank, young Munk, your military career has ended at a most opportune time for us. The House of Szondi finds itself facing an extremely grave situation, and a woman just can't do the things in Arab and Turkish lands that she can do in Europe. Even though you've spent time down there I hadn't thought of you before because you're so young, but when we learned of your exile it seemed more than coincidental. One of our musicians would be useless on a mission like this, but with your military experience you might be able to accomplish something even though you are young. Anyway, I've decided it's going to be you.

Munk saluted.

At your service, madame.

His grandmother suddenly frowned and his mother's face was all at once troubled. Others in the room looked variously perplexed or fearful. Again all clicking stopped. The kitchen was hushed as his grandmother spoke.

We haven't told any of the men in the family about this, not wanting to worry you, but we've been aware of the situation for some time. Our information began coming in about twenty years ago. The first clues we had were fragmentary and haphazard, yet even then we filed them away. You can't be too careful in this business. You're not versed in the intricacies of banking and you wouldn't understand such financial subtleties anyway, so I won't bother to go into detail. I'll just say there are definite ways of knowing when a consortium or some other group is buying into an enterprise. Especially if the acquisition is a major one, so large it can only be acquired piece by piece. Can you follow that?

Yes, Grandmother.

All right, that's what happened in this case. During the last twenty-odd years when we've been aware of it, and obviously before that when we weren't, the enterprise in question has been cleverly bought piece by piece. Bought right out from under our noses. And since our very foundations were long ago established there, the effect on the House of Szondi could be catastrophic.

What enterprise was bought from under your noses?

The old woman glared through her spectacles. Her face darkened.

The Ottoman Empire, she hissed.

The *what?*

That's right, you heard me correctly. The evidence is there and there can no longer be any doubt about it. A little over thirty years ago, as unreal as it seems, someone secretly began to buy up the Ottoman Empire.

You mean the Russians have been intriguing with the French or the English again? They've formed a secret alliance with the Germans?

No that isn't what I mean. Politics aren't involved. This is a straight business proposition and only one man is involved. One man has bought the Ottoman Empire.

But that's impossible, Grandmother.

Of course it is. We've been telling ourselves nothing else for years. Haven't we, girls.

She looked sternly around the room and his mother and aunts and grandaunts and female cousins all nodded vigorously. Then they all began talking at once to each other, loudly and rapidly, not listening to what anyone else was saying.

That's enough, girls, shouted his grandmother. Instantly the room was silent.

So you see, young man, the situation before us is more than staggering. It's critical and perhaps even fatal. The House of Szondi was founded on the basis of Levantine trade and now we find one man has bought the entire Levant. Who is he and what does he want? Why did he buy it? What does he intend to do with it?

You're sure it's a man? asked Munk.

His grandmother snorted contemptuously.

Of course it's a man, no woman would ever act so crudely. Perhaps some substantial and influential role behind the scenes, but not a whole empire in one ruthless grab. That's the work of a man.

Munk clicked his heels.

Yes, Grandmother.

Please don't interrupt again.

No, Grandmother.

Now to continue. We've gone back to the beginning to try to reconstruct events and the best we can do, the earliest scenes we can conjecture, are vague reports of an Egyptian emir and a Baghdad banker and a Persian potentate holding shadowy interviews in Constantinople in 1880, sitting down. Remember that, sitting down. The man seems to have been unnaturally tall, but it's impossible for our informants to say how tall because he was always seated. I say *man*, rather than *men*, because it's obvious to us that this emir and banker and potentate, forget the apparent nationalities and the way he paired them up with status for alliterative affect, were one and the same man, a dissembler able to disguise himself cleverly. And how did he disguise himself? Always as a Levantine, which to us means he was obviously a European being clever again. So the available facts are these. A European of untold personal wealth, a man so unusually tall he feared his height would betray his real identity, remained carefully seated while buying all the wells in Mecca and all the wells on all the haj routes to Mecca, while becoming the secret paymaster of the Turkish army and navy, while buying up all Turkish government bonds and issuing new ones, while consulting with pashas and ministers and laying aside trust funds for their grandsons, while firing and rehiring every religious leader in the Middle East so they would have to answer to him, while consummating a hundred other such deals with the goal of making himself the sole owner of the Ottoman Empire. Now only one European in the last century fits that description. Do you know who he is?

No, Grandmother.

Strongbow. First name, Plantagenet. An Englishman who was the twenty-ninth Duke of Dorset. Seven feet, seven inches tall. He took a triple first at Cambridge in botany and was considered the greatest swordsman and botanist of the Victorian era, but he abandoned plants to become an explorer. In 1840 he disappeared from Cairo after attending a diplomatic reception held in honor of Queen Victoria's twenty-first birthday. And in order to outrage English decorum and sense of fair play, which he so dearly loved to do, Strongbow appeared at that diplomatic reception stark naked, save for a portable sundial strapped to his hip that hid nothing. About forty years later a publication of his appeared in Basle, which is the next time we hear of him, just prior to his appearance in Constantinople in various disguises. But the odd thing is, that publication had nothing to do with business or banking. If it had it might have warned us about what was going to happen in Constantinople.

What did the publication have to do with?

His grandmother smiled faintly. She raised her chin.

Sex. It's a study of Levantine sex in thirty-three volumes.

The old woman paused. Around the room dozens of knitting needles erupted into a cacophony of clicks. Munk stood at attention staring at his grandmother, who finally lowered her eyes and removed a lace handkerchief from her sleeve. With slow, delicate motions she dabbed at the beads of perspiration that had appeared around her mouth.

Tut tut, young Munk. *Tut and ho.* This has nothing whatsoever to do with the matter at hand but you seem to want an explanation, and considering what you're going to do for us, I'll give you one. Well then. Strongbow's study was published in Basle and quite naturally the House of Szondi acquired one. I mean of course we did. Everything having to do with the Levant must be our special concern. We can't afford to ignore even the smallest item of scholarship, and Strongbow's study is hardly that. But since it's been banned, and also because it's rather an explicit work, we felt it best to keep it under lock and key and not advertise the fact that we own a copy.

Munk stared at his grandmother in awe.

You mean none of the men in the family has ever known about this?

That's right, and you aren't to tell them. Such matters could only be disruptive to a musician's work. A musician must have discipline and concentration. He needs order in his life to be creative. And let me tell you the information in Strongbow's study is about as disorderly as anything you can imagine. It utterly defies concentration and leads to a complete breakdown of discipline.

I don't doubt that, said Munk. But do you mean to tell me that all of you here have been reading these volumes in private for years?

Strictly for professional reasons, young Munk. Strictly because we handle the business in this family and there would be no music for our men if we didn't pursue business in a conscientious manner. If the House of Szondi is to continue to prosper, we *must* all be current with every aspect of the Levant. That is *the Sarahs* must be. It's our inevitable responsibility. And then too I might add that at the end of a day of hard banking, we find it necessary to take our minds off work. Strongbow's study serves that purpose.

I see. In other words, you mean selections are read aloud here after board meetings?

His grandmother tucked away her lace handkerchief. She straightened in her chair.

That's enough now, young Munk. The agendas of our board meetings are no concern of yours, and all of this has nothing to do with our emergency session tonight. Our subject isn't Strongbow's study but

Strongbow himself, Strongbow in Constantinople thirty-three years ago. What sinister game was he playing out there then? Just who does he think he is going around and snatching up the Ottoman Empire?

The old woman was shaking in anger, her voice low and menacing.

Yes. Sinister. More than any man in this family could ever know. We've always protected all of you and shielded you from the harsher facts of life. We've spared you the brutal experiences that go with dealing in money. But life isn't just music, my boy, not just beautiful concerts played by baroque ensembles on summer afternoons. It has its sinister side as well and we see it here in the case of this Englishman, this former duke and explorer and sexologist who always pretended business was beneath him. *Beneath* him? Why these clever disguises in Constantinople thirty-three years ago when he set in motion the financial instruments to buy the Ottoman Empire? And what he did after *that*? That's even more sinister.

What did he do after that?

He disappeared again, simply disappeared. I told you a banker shuns notoriety. The less that's known about her the better, the more easily she can function and make deals. But to disappear completely as Strongbow did? Now that's truly sinister, truly the act of an arch-banker utterly without scruples. It's a diabolical game he's playing. What fiendish plans does he have? Why does he buy an empire, hiding his hand all the while, and then disappear as if he had no interest in that empire? Well we don't know but we must, and you must find out for us. Young Munk?

Munk clicked his heels and saluted.

Madame?

My yacht is waiting down at the landing for your immediate departure. Like the husband of your great-grandmother, you are embarking on a voyage to the Levant, and I want your reports to be as thorough as his were. Off you go now. Eat plenty of garlic and good luck.

All the women in the room rose. Munk stepped forward and kissed his grandmother respectfully on the cheek. He kissed his mother and went around the kitchen kissing in turn his aunts and grandaunts and female cousins.

They were already beginning to inspect the ovens where a late supper was cooking, by the smell of it nearly ready, when he marched out of the kitchen and made his way down the path to the Danube, smiling as he went over a clear memory from his childhood, his mother calling to say she wouldn't be home for dinner and they shouldn't wait up, the press of business being so great it was keeping *the Sarahs* working late at the office.

One rainy afternoon in February 1924, more than two years after outsiders had first been admitted to the poker game and subsequently spread its reputation throughout the Middle East, Haj Harun came wandering into his back room where the game was in progress, carrying a ladder.

He placed the ladder against the tall antique Turkish safe, climbed up to the top and sat down. He straightened his rusty Crusader's helmet and retied the two green ribbons under his chin, smoothed out his tattered yellow cloak and gazed thoughtfully straight ahead at nothing.

Cairo and Munk smiled up at him. Joe gave him a wave. But the action at the table abruptly stopped as the other players turned to stare at the wizened figure on top of the safe, his spindly crossed legs swinging in the air.

Is he real? whispered a bewildered Iraqi prince.

That he is, said Joe, studying his cards.

But who is he?

Joe looked up.

Well I guess he could be fate, couldn't he? I mean that would be consistent with a game of chance. Fate keeping watch and all.

Is that what he's doing up there? Keeping watch?

Who's to say? Maybe he's surveying the centuries for some forgotten event that ought to be remembered. Now whose bet is it, gents? Let's get on with the bets.

But what does he see up there? Ask him what he sees.

And why not. Haj Harun? Hello up there, what do you see?

How's that, Prester John?

I was just wondering what might be up there on the rainy horizon today. How's the view?

Haj Harun turned to peer into the crumbling plaster of the corner, two feet from his face. He nodded.

I don't like to say it, but the Medes may be coming.

Are you sure? That rabble again?

They may be.

Bad in the rain, very bad, how are the city walls holding up? Safe and strong as they should be? No gates left open? Better check around so we can breathe easy.

I will, Prester John.

Haj Harun looked back at the wall in the corner. He squinted and his helmet went awry, releasing a shower of rust in his eyes. The tears began to flow.

Why does he keep calling you Prester John? asked a Syrian jewel thief.

Because the first time I walked in here I was wearing a Victoria Cross around my neck, being then in retirement and living in the Home for Crimean War Heroes, and because of that he mistook me for the legendary lost Christian monarch of a vast kingdom somewhere in Asia.

Where in Asia?

I don't know and he doesn't know either. I suppose you could ask the scarab, the scarab's likely to know but I doubt that he's talking today. Generally he sleeps away the winter. Anyway, since I was lost he naturally assumed I'd come to Jerusalem to find myself again. Now whose bet is it, I say?

The Syrian jewel thief giggled.

You're both mad. He's just staring at the wall up there.

Not a bit of it, said Joe. That's not a wall he's looking into, it's a mirror. The mirror of the mind, it's called. Believe me it's true.

The Syrian went on giggling.

Well who does he think that is? he asked, pointing across the table at Munk.

He doesn't think, said Joe, he knows. Just watch. Hello up there, Haj Harun, or Aaron as the Jews and Christians call you. Who's this article down here who's being pointed at?

The wizened old man wiped the tears from his eyes and peered down at the table.

That's Bar Cocheba, he said.

Hey Munk, seems he spotted you right off, whispered Joe. Seems he nailed you right down in the course of history. Was he right now? What moment in history would it be for this gent called Bar Cocheba?

First half of the second century, answered Munk, studying his cards.

Role? asked Joe.

Defender of the Jewish faith, said Munk.

Future?

Death in combat. Dying in revolt against the invincible Roman legions.

Is that so? Joe called up. Are the Roman legions really invincible? What do you see up there?

Haj Harun turned back to the wall. He smiled.

Only for a time, Prester John. After a time they lose.

There. You see, Munk, you see how it is? The Romans turn out to be vincible after all. Time it takes, naturally. Time as it was or will be. Time is all.

Time is, murmured Haj Harun dreamily from his perch on top of the safe.

See anything more? Joe called out.

For Bar Cocheba, yes. I predict this game of chance will be very profitable for him. After all, there are nineteen years in a lunar cycle.

Joe looked confused.

According to the Jewish calendar, whispered Munk.

And thus, continued Haj Harun, since you began this game in the Jewish year of 5682, Bar Cocheba should do very well indeed.

Joe looked even more confused.

And why might that be?

Because that year was the first year of the three-hundredth lunar cycle, answered Haj Harun. And that certainly sounds auspicious to me, given the fact there were three of you who founded the game.

Joe whistled softly.

Facts, gents, they're just dropping all over the place. And is that a proper lunar evaluation from the top of the safe or not? Fate on target again as usual, there's nothing like it. But hold on now. I think I can hear a less distant moment in time preparing to announce itself.

The chimes attached to the sundial in the front room creaked and began to strike at four o'clock on that rainy afternoon. In all they chimed twelve times.

Midnight, said Joe. I think we better be adjourning in about an hour. Is the time limit agreed?

That's a good idea, said Munk. I'm rather tired tonight.

So am I, added Cairo, suppressing a yawn.

The other players, who had been heavy losers in the three hours since the session began, were on their feet protesting. A wealthy French merchant from Beirut was particularly angry.

Fraud, he shrieked, shaking his fists. How do you know it's midnight? It could just as well be twelve o'clock noon.

Could be but it isn't, said Joe, smiling. The chimes struck off noon an hour before you arrived. What time did you think you got here?

I know when I got here, shrieked the Frenchman. It was at one o'clock.

Well there you are. The chimes have to be striking midnight, couldn't be anything else. Bets now anyone? We've still got a good hour of fast playing ahead before closing time. Munk, isn't the bet to you?

I believe it is. And since Haj Harun has found lunar evidence for my success in this game, I'm going to take advantage of it by tripling this wager our princely guest from Baghdad has just ventured. Gentlemen, the stakes rise in the cause of lunacy.

Fine, said Joe, very fine. We're off again. No reason to hold back just because there are only three hours between noon and midnight on a rainy day in February. That happens all the time in bad weather. But spring will be coming soon and then we can make up for it.

6

St Catherine's Monastery

Choice is the arrow.

E arly in 1913, Munk arrived back in the Middle East and traveled
widely on his mission for *the Sarahs*. Before the end of the year he
was able to report to them that although there was evidence someone
might have owned the Ottoman Empire once, it was equally obvious
no one owned it now, least of all the Ottomans.

The old jade is tottering to her grave, he wrote in a letter to
Budapest. Once stately, now exhausted, she laments in the twilight,
abused and humiliated on every side. Soon night must take her.

Munk sensed he was also describing the approaching collapse of the
Austro-Hungarian Empire, although he couldn't possibly have guessed
how quickly that would happen. Yet in the next few years not only did
the Empire of *the Sarahs* disappear but with it the once powerful House
of Szondi, both swept away in the First World War.

Young Munk watched it all from afar, no longer interested in
soldiering yet still searching as always for a role in life and pondering

the question that had been with him since childhood, the mysterious force that had driven his great-grandfather, Johann Luigi, a century ago.

Munk traveled alone during the war years, trading throughout the Middle East and sharing his confidences with only one man, an unlikely friend yet also his closest during that period, a wealthy old Greek satyr who lived in Smyrna.

Unlikely on the surface of it, for Sivi was then a man already in his sixties, nearly forty years older than Munk. But he seemed to have known everyone in his time, having long been intimate with every manner of Levantine intrigue, and despite his notorious sexual excesses he was a wise and gentle friend, who adopted Munk as easily as if that had been his purpose in life.

So Munk found himself returning again and again to Sivi's beautiful seaside villa in Smyrna, an exile now from a European era that would soon cease to exist.

It's almost over, he said to Sivi one afternoon in the spring of 1918. My family has lived in Budapest since the ninth century, but with this war a whole way of life will disappear.

They were sitting in Sivi's garden and Sivi was pouring tea, elegant as always in one of the long red dressing gowns that he habitually wore until after sunset, when he dressed for the theater or the opera. He paused to admire the large ruby rings on his fingers. As usual a smile hovered around his eyes and there was a touch of mischief in his voice.

How's this, young Munk? You're not surrendering to melancholy, are you? If I were you I'd look at the matter quite differently. Ten centuries locked in the rain and mist of central Europe? Time to make an escape, I should think, and what better season for it than this one? Ah yes, spring and the sea and a distant shore. Exactly what's needed to stir unexpected juices. But you always said you wanted to get away, and now you have. For good, certainly. Still, a touch of nostalgia perhaps?

Munk shrugged.

I guess so.

Of course, and there's nothing wrong with that. But if I may say so, this twinge of nostalgia you feel has nothing to do with a place really, with a sudden longing for Budapest. It has to do with time, I suspect, with having been a child there, innocent and protected. That rare condition can cause nostalgia in all of us. Am I right?

I suppose. It's true I feel I'm getting old.

Sivi laughed wickedly.

As indeed you are, young Munk. Late twenties? An absolutely ancient age. I had a friend once who felt the same way as he drew near thirty. His youth was behind him and suicide seemed the only answer. He asked me to find him the necessary pills and I said I would, but it might take a few hours. In the meantime I suggested he go out and buy himself a new dress and hat, I mean a quite extravagant dress, and position himself in one of the better cafés on the harbor and wait for me there. I told him if he was going to die he ought to look his best when he went.

So he bought the dress?

He did. But by the time I arrived at the café he was no longer there. It seems a handsome young Greek sailor had come strolling by and winked at him, and they had an aperitif together and one thing led to another, and I couldn't find him anywhere for three days. When I did I told him I had the pills. What pills? he said, I'm in love. And that was that, although of course this occurred around 1880 when gowns were much more lavish than today, and had bustles as well that could give a man an immediate lift.

Munk laughed.

Was this friend a tall man?

He was.

Large and bulky?

More or less.

With an impressive moustache he twirled on occasion?

Indeed, it was probably just such an action that caught the eye of the handsome young Greek sailor as he went strolling by.

How long did the love affair last?

Until the young sailor's ship sailed, a week or so. And my friend was heartbroken when it was over.

Did you consider pills again?

Certainly not. I'd learned what to do. I went out and bought another extravagant gown and positioned myself once more in one of the better cafés. Within the hour events had taken a turn as they will, and a whole new adventure had begun to unfold. You see there's a moral to this tale, although of course it doesn't apply to everyone. I contemplated suicide because I felt my youth was behind me, but the solution was much simpler. All I had to do was put another youth behind me.

Munk laughed again as Sivi happily wagged his head.

That's terrible, Sivi. You're unspeakable.

True. But I've continued to follow this wisdom and it's kept me going quite well.

Sivi delicately raised his teacup and sipped.

And what news do you have from *the Sarahs*, Munk? Have they been making any plans for after the war?

Yes. They've decided to emigrate.

What? All of them?

Yes, all of them.

Extraordinary. Where to?

A few to Canada and Australia and the United States. Most of them to South America.

Sivi sighed.

A new Diaspora, they seem never to end. Yes, well, I guess it isn't all that extraordinary. The banks are finished, I take it? The war has been that hard on them?

Yes.

Sivi nodded gently.

It happens, of course. The Old World becomes too old for some. I have cousins in Argentina whom I've never met. And what of the men in the family? Will there now be all-male Szondi baroque ensembles in various corners of the New World, mostly South America?

Not for a while, I would think. They'll have to give up music and go back to running discount dry goods stores to support *the Sarahs*. Petty local trade again, only this time in São Paulo and Sydney and New York.

But surely only for a time, Munk. *The Sarahs* are too clever not to get something going again before long.

I imagine.

Oh yes, they'll fare well, we know that. It's you I'm concerned about. Dare I be frank?

Munk smiled.

You old sinner. Have you ever been anything else?

Sivi wagged his head appreciatively and examined the flow of his dressing gown, straightening a fold here and there.

Well not for the last four or five decades, in any case. Not since I decided at an early age to recognize the creature I saw leering at me every morning in the mirror. But then too, I had the advantage of growing up in beautiful Smyrna where the light is so pure and the sea so sparkling, well, all things seem natural, even me. So it wasn't that difficult to admit that the lascivious beast I saw in the mirror wasn't a beast at all, just me, basically harmless and in love with love, merely insatiable when it comes to the pleasures to be found on a secluded stretch of beach when the sun is high and the white sand softly burns your skin, and the brilliant blue sea whispers *now and later, now and always,* love and life and the all-healing sea.

Munk smiled. He held his left hand out to the side and strummed with his right in front of him, reciting a verse.

> *Gaily the troubadour touched his guitar,*
> *as he was wandering home from the wars.*
> *Singing from Palestine, hither I come.*
> *Lady love, lady love, welcome me home.*

Sivi laughed.

Quite, he said. The aging troubadour forever wanders, forever singing that sins aren't sins when seen naked in the sun, singing that only darkness and despair can twist an act of love into regret. But we were talking about you, young Munk, and I was going to be frank. Well it's simply this. It's obvious you want something and don't know what it is. I mean something more than an occupation, a home and a family and friends or whatever. That's so, isn't it.

Of course.

Yes, blood tells. Mine is that of the ancient Greeks who reveled in their lucid sunlight, yours is that of your remarkable great-grandfather, Johann Luigi Szondi, his very name suggesting contradictory anteced-ents, a mysterious explorer whose tireless journeys you've never been quite able to comprehend. All that in only eight short years? Penetrating Medina and Mecca and measuring Rameses' ear? Eating dates in Nubia while covering nine hundred miles a month? Gazing upon the stones of a deserted rose-red city half as old as time? Yes, astonishing exploits.

I don't want to leave, announced Munk abruptly, the words said with such force they startled Sivi.

Leave? Indeed, nor do I. But what are we referring to? Life? Smyrna? This garden with its spring flowers in bloom?

This part of the world, added Munk.

Sivi relaxed in his chair.

Ah, of course, the Eastern Mediterranean. No one in his right mind *would* want to leave it. But who ever suggested such a preposterous notion?

You did.

Me? said Sivi, even more startled than before. Me? Impossible. Out of the question.

Yes you did. You were talking earlier about spring and the sea and a distant shore, but I have no intention of going to America or anyplace like that.

Sivi tipped his head and laughed happily.

Oh, is that all. It seems you missed my meaning completely, young Munk. Come along and I'll point it out to you. As it happens it's only a few yards away.

Munk followed Sivi across the garden and into his villa. They walked to the second floor where Sivi threw open the doors to the balcony. The sun was slipping toward the harbor, which was still busy with boats. Strolling crowds thronged the quays in the evening promenade.

There, young Munk, that's the sea I had in mind. The Aegean. And you're already on its distant shore, cold damp Europe is far away to the north. So you see you've already set sail, here and now in sun and light, that's all I was suggesting. It's true, isn't it?

Sivi smiled. Munk smiled too.

Yes it's true.

Good. Now I'm told you're very successful at a special kind of trading, commodity futures are they called? Well then, if you're already trading in futures, why not trade in your own?

Trading doesn't mean anything to me, said Munk. You have your dream of a greater Greece. But as you've said, I don't know what I want.

Sivi laughed. He spread his arms as if to embrace the sea.

What you want? Of course you know what you want. You want a dream like anyone else. But a dream, is that all? Just look out there at what lies at your feet, look and be reassured. For was there ever a man who stood on these shores and *didn't* dream? This is the Eastern Mediterranean, young Munk, the birthplace of dreams. The men who gave our Western world its gods and civilizations came from here, and with good reason.

What is the reason?

I thought you'd never ask. Odd how the young disregard the widsom of age in order to discover things for themselves. It's almost as if matters of the spirit could never be transmitted, only experienced. The reason, Munk? *Light.* The purity of the light here. In this light a man senses there are no limits for him in the world. He can see forever, and that vision intoxicates him. It fires his heart and makes him want to go and do, never to stop but to go farther, to go deeper, *more*. Thus the curiosity of the Greeks of old and their fearless explorations of the soul. Never has man surpassed the dramas enacted on these shores twenty-five hundred years ago, three thousand years ago. That was laughter, that was tragedy, and it is what we know of life. Even today we know no more. And strangely, modestly, they attributed their laughter and their tragedy to the intervention of the gods. But it just wasn't so. The miracle of it all was theirs. It was them. They stood on these shores and wept and laughed and lived those lives.

The old man smiled and stroked his moustache.

Well now, what do you think of that?

You're shamelessly romantic, Sivi, that's what I think.

It may be so. Yet all the same the light here *is* different. It's a palpable thing and its effect is inescapable, which is why Greece has always been more of an idea than a place. When the modern nation was founded in the last century, Alexandria and Constantinople were the great Greek cities in this world, and Athens was but a lonely plain where a few shepherds grazed their flocks at the foot of the Acropolis. But no matter. An idea doesn't die. It only slumbers and it can always be resurrected. Tell me, would anyone have ever heard of the Dorians if they'd stayed up there in the north puttering around the Danube? Just one more minor central European tribe three thousand years ago, passing the time with their crops and domestic animals and setting out for an occasional foray a few miles downstream? Exactly, and enough to put anyone to sleep. But the Dorians didn't stay up there. They had the luck or good sense to come trotting down here where they could learn to dream, and dream they did, and the result was ancient Greece in all its splendor. Ah yes, Munk, the Dorians should be a lesson to you. By the way, when you were on your mission for *the Sarahs,* how far were you able to trace Strongbow?

South of the Holy Land, that's all. Nothing more specific than that.

No? Well it was the Yemen where he ended up, and died.

Strongbow's dead?

Yes, four years ago, just before the war broke out. Appropriate, wasn't it. One of the towering figures of the nineteenth century, and the successor to the explorations of Johann Luigi Szondi in this part of the world, dies on the eve of the Great War that will bring an end to his century.

How did you find that out?

How? murmured Sivi. Don't I have a reputation for knowing everyone's secrets? Well so I do, but in this case it was simpler than that. Strongbow's son told me.

His son? I didn't even know he had a son.

He did, but the son's identity is a confidence I can't reveal. He's always gone by a different name.

Munk laughed.

Is there anyone at all in this part of the world who hasn't come to you with their confidences at one time or another?

They had returned to the garden. Sivi uncorked the bottle of ouzo standing on the table and sniffed it. He nodded approvingly and filled two glasses.

Tea won't help us now. Ouzo is definitely wanted, a substantial measure over ice to cloud the clear liquid, the better to clear our minds as evening falls. As for people confiding in me, there must be some who haven't yet, but then I wouldn't be surprised if they were getting ready to do so this very evening, after dark of course. You see the truth is, a juxtaposition of facts in my case tends to reassure people. On the one hand it's known that my father was a leader of the Greek war for independence and a great friend of Byron. Masculine heroics, in other words, the sound of the bugle and the charge against the oppressor, flowing capes and drawn swords and fierce eyebrows, the poet-warrior in a headlong gallop and all that. Yet on the other hand, it's equally well known that when I attend the opera and take off my evening cape, the gown and jewels I will be wearing will be so elegant no woman could possibly hope to match them. I am, in short, an embodiment of life's bizarre contradictions. Therefore trustworthy.

Munk laughed.

What brought Strongbow to mind, Sivi?

Dreams, of course. The dreams we have when we're young.

Ah yes, mused Sivi. My dream at your age was to become a great scholar, and all because of Strongbow's study.

What? You're not going to tell me you own a set too?

Certainly. Thirty-three volumes on Levantine sex and I shouldn't own them? Is such a thing conceivable? But why me too?

It turned out *the Sarahs* had a set. None of the men in our family ever knew it.

Sivi chuckled happily.

Is that so? Well apparently life wasn't as bleak up there as I'd thought. It seems there were certain diversions on rainy evenings by the Danube when *the Sarahs* had to stay late at the office. But they were probably just being sentimental. The study isn't exactly what people think. Two-thirds of it, in fact, is devoted to describing a love affair Strongbow had with a gentle Persian girl when he was nineteen, the most complete love story ever told and a pastoral idyll that could make any woman swoon. Anyway, what I wanted to do was compose a companion study on Byzantine sex. Levantine is one thing, but Byzantine? It could have been truly arresting.

What happened?

I did a two-page outline and began to have doubts. Strongbow rightly notes that there are nine sexes, and being only several of them, how could I attempt to be accurate overall? No, I realized I couldn't be so I abandoned the project. Such grand designs seem to be no longer possible. Now Alexander the Great would have been much better prepared for such an undertaking. We know he loved several women and a number of boys, his horse, a male companion or two and at least one eunuch. And if we know all that, just imagine what we don't know. Indeed, a person could be more comprehensive in those days.

Sivi laughed. He raised his nearly empty glass of ouzo and tipped it, gazing at the milky liquid left in the bottom. Munk shook his head.

You're not just a shameless romantic, Sivi. You're a shameless *aging* romantic and that's the very worst sort. To be young and romantic is understandable. But at your age? After all the grief and torment you've seen in the world?

Sivi nodded. He stroked the end of his white moustache.

It's true. I used to try to fight it, to get up each morning prepared to curse and be gloomy. An ache here and a pain there? Neither mind nor body functioning as well as the day before? Evidence, you would think, that the world is indeed a dreadful place to live. Yes, I had my good intentions of a dark nature, but as it happened they never survived the bedroom where I found myself that morning, no matter how sordid the place might appear at first glance. I'd wake up and look around me and think, Oh my God, what have you done now? What have you gotten yourself into this time? How could you possibly have behaved that way last night? Yesterday at this hour you were a total wreck, but to have sunk even lower? It's unimaginable. This is the very end.

And so on. Darkness at dawn, in other words. Terminal despair at dawn. The worst thoughts to be found in the land of the living. But then what did I spy as I lay there beyond hope in that ghastly place? What else, a window. Even the most wretched bedrooms in Smyrna have windows. So over to the window I'd go and raise the shade and stick my head out, what little was left of it, and what do you suppose was waiting for me out there? The Aegean, and the light of the Aegean. And at that moment I knew any attempt at despair that day could only fail. There was too much to see out there, and to feel and hear and smell and taste. So in time I stopped fighting it. I had no choice but to accept my love of life, and of love, as incurable.

Then too I was lazy, which was the real reason I never got on with a massive scholarly study. It would have meant giving up too many things, added Sivi, wagging his head and staring lasciviously at the thin milky dregs in his glass of ouzo.

Munk laughed.

In your hands everything becomes obscene.

Not so, said Sivi. Merely observed in its true light, which is essentially sensual.

I'm afraid the sun with its true light has already set, you old rogue. Put down your suggestive glass.

Almost three years passed before Munk found his dream as Sivi had predicted he would, not by the sea but in the desert. And he did so, curiously, through the unexpected intercession of his old friend from the hectic weeks of the first Balkan war, the diminutive officer who had been the Japanese military attaché in Constantinople.

Then Major, now Colonel, Kikuchi had returned to Japan before the First World War. Toward the end of the winter of 1921 he wrote an urgent letter to Munk from Tokyo saying he had just learned that his older twin brother, the former Baron Kikuchi, an esthete and collector of French Impressionist paintings, had converted to Judaism while visiting Jerusalem on his way home from Europe. He was now residing in the town of Safad in Palestine.

The colonel explained that his brother's health had always been delicate and he was concerned about living conditions in postwar Palestine. Furthermore, in the last months his brother's letters had taken on a new feverish quality that disturbed the colonel, remembering as he did the virulent diseases that had stricken foreigners exposed to Turkish meat during the days of the Ottoman Empire.

Is the situation still as dangerous as before the war? wrote the colonel in his precise hand. Or have the Allies cleaned up the meat in the Middle East? When my brother was a Buddhist he never ate meat, of course, but now that he's a Jew I don't know what he might be eating. Please, dear Munk, could you possibly go to this town of Safad, which looks pitifully small on the maps, and see if my twin brother is well?

Munk cabled that he was on his way and left for Safad immediately. With his affectionate memories of Colonel Kikuchi he would have gone in any case, but the circumstances particularly intrigued him.

In Safad he learned that the former Baron Kikuchi had pursued rabbinical studies there, specializing in medieval Jewish mysticism. He was now known as Rabbi Lotmann, a highly respected but eccentric figure in occult circles. It seemed he had left Safad a few weeks earlier, although no one could quite remember the day. Nor could anyone say when he might return, or where he had gone. As Munk questioned the scholars it became obvious they were being evasive.

Why? What were they afraid he might discover?

You know I'm Jewish, said Munk, and of course they did, the Szondi name having been made famous by *the Sarahs*. Yet still the scholars would tell him nothing. Finally Munk went to the chief rabbi of Safad to try to find an explanation for the way he had been received.

In the case of Rabbi Lotmann, answered the old man solemnly, the fact that you're Jewish isn't enough.

It's not?

No.

Why?

Because there's more these days. But *I'll* say nothing more.

Bewildered, Munk went on to Jerusalem hoping to find another man he had met during the first Balkan war, an Arabic Jew named Stern who ran guns against the British and French in the Middle East, an agent who knew a great deal about clandestine affairs in Palestine and elsewhere.

Fortunately Stern was in Jerusalem. As usual he asked Munk for money and Munk gave it to him. Munk then explained whom he was seeking and what he had been told in Safad.

Stern nodded. Slowly he smiled.

The Japanese rabbi? Yes, I've heard of him. He's an underground Zionist. Newly involved but very active.

Munk was astounded. Stern's smile broadened.

I agree, Munk. Stranger things may have happened lately but none that I'm aware of. There was a possibility the British had begun to watch him so it was decided he should go into hiding for a while.

Where? Turkey? Europe?

Stern shook his head.

Not that man. Hiding, yes. Running away, no. He's still here, he's in the Sinai. St Catherine's monastery. And I'd advise you to approach him in a circumspect manner. They say he's an expert archer. He can hit a shilling at a hundred yards.

What?

Stern laughed.

Zen and archery, Munk, the way of the Japanese warrior. It seems the former Baron Kikuchi had an old-fashioned upbringing. And take a coat with you if you're going down to the Sinai. The nights are still very cold down there.

It was Munk's first visit to St Catherine's. He learned that Rabbi Lotmann was using his Japanese name at the monastery, to avoid the possibility of informers identifying him with the Lotmann occultist in Safad whose clandestine Zionist role was under suspicion. Accordingly, he had presented himself to the Greek monks of the place as a Nestorian Christian from China on a pilgrimage to the Holy Land, his wish to stay at St Catherine's motivated by a special interest in praying on Moses' mountain.

Being unfamiliar with Oriental names in that remote setting, and oblivious to transitory historical matters, the monks had readily accepted the presence of a pious Chinese Christian called Baron Kikuchi, unaware the name couldn't be Chinese, unaware as well that the Nestorian community in China had ceased to exist centuries ago.

During the hours of daylight, Munk was told, the Chinese pilgrim removed himself to the far side of the mountain to pray in solitude at a collapsible altar he carried over there in two parts, setting up collapsible altars on holy mountains evidently being a Nestorian custom.

Upon returning at sundown the Chinese pilgrim ate his evening meal and then sat up late in his cell praising God by playing music on an unusual stringed instrument that lay flat on the floor, evidently another Nestorian custom. This peculiar form of nightly Oriental worship, said the Greek monks, went on for at least three or four hours every evening.

From its description Munk recognized the stringed instrument as a koto, the ancient Japanese harp he had heard Colonel Kikuchi play in Constantinople during their rare moments of leisure. As for the collapsible altar in two parts, Munk understood what that was when he saw Rabbi Lotmann returning to the monastery that first evening with a cylindrical red lacquer case slung over his shoulder and a light thin canvas case over six feet long swinging in his hand.

A samurai bow and quiver.

Evidently the former Baron Kikuchi was taking advantage of his stay at the monastery by practicing his archery.

After the evening meal Munk joined the Greek monks in the dark corridor outside of Kikuchi's cell, where they regularly gathered each night to sit on the floor and listen to Kikuchi's exotic music. The selections that evening ranged from sacred Japanese court music to Noh drama. Sitting very erect in a formal kimono with his feet tucked beneath him, Kikuchi announced each piece beforehand to the assembly of totally baffled Greek monks.

The closing selection was especially beautiful to Munk's ears, a thirteenth-century kagura used for the most solemn Japanese religious rites. Maintaining his disguise, Kikuchi had referred to it as a weird Chinese composition. In any case the Greek monks found it incomprehensible.

At the conclusion of the concert the Greek monks crossed themselves and drifted away. Only then did Munk step forward from the shadows into the doorway of Kikuchi's cell, which was lit by a single candle. He had decided to speak in German so they wouldn't be understood by any monk who might still be lingering in the corridor.

Baron Kikuchi, that was lovely.

Thank you, sir.

And I suspect it may be the strangest music ever heard at St Catherine's.

I suspect you may be right.

Especially that last piece you played. Your *weird* Chinese composition, as you called it.

Weird, murmured Kikuchi. That's what it is all right.

Because of its semitones?

What?

Yes. In fact there were semitones all evening.

Now *I* think that's definitely weird, said Kikuchi. But why do you think so?

Because I've been told Chinese scales don't have semitones. Japanese scales do.

Is that so? You mean that although I'm a Chinese pilgrim, my music is Japanese? This is certainly getting weirder all the time. Do you think there could be some sort of divine influence radiating from the holy mountain above us and splitting my tones? Just halving them on the spot, so to speak?

Kikuchi laughed gaily.

Well it's weird all right. Weird. I picked the right word. By the way, where did you learn about Oriental music?

From a friend. A hero of the Russo-Japanese War who saved his company on a barren Manchurian plain by piling up the dead horses of the Cossacks as a barricade against their incessant attacks. Later, I might add, when we were both serving as military attachés in Constantinople, the meat served by the Turks was just as bad as any rotting Cossack horse.

The little Japanese aristocrat jumped to his feet.

Are you Munk, then? My brother often spoke of you.

Kikuchi, delighted, shook hands. Their conversation lasted most of the night and the next morning they went out to walk across the hills together, talking all the while, Kikuchi occasionally pausing to take aim at some distant patch of sand and fire off an arrow.

Gentle in manner and tiny in stature, the present Rabbi Lotmann had been born the hereditary leader of a powerful landowning clan in northern Japan, but both his title and his numerous estates had passed to his younger twin when he embraced a foreign religion. To anyone this would have been a striking testament of faith, but what most impressed Munk was that Kikuchi had then gone on to become a passionate Zionist.

Munk himself, although recognizing the appeal of Zionism to the oppressed Jews of eastern Europe, had never taken any particular interest in it himself. Somehow it had seemed irrelevant in the Empire of the Habsburgs before the war.

Yet here was an aristocrat from an utterly alien land halfway around the world, a rich esthete from a unique ancient culture who had

121

devoted the first thirty-five years of his life to archery and painting, now pacing the foothills of Mt Sinai eagerly quoting *Der Judenstaat* from memory to prove the absolute necessity of a Jewish homeland.

Munk was astonished. The tiny man's fervor was undeniable, his arguments were entirely persuasive. Munk found himself being drawn in more and more deeply.

On his third day at the monastery an incident occurred that he would never forget. It was late in the afternoon and the two of them were walking along a lower slope of the mountain, a broad descending sweep of sand. A sharp wind had risen and was buffeting them from the east.

By now Munk was more than a little dazed by their hours and hours of conversation. The wind distracted him and he found himself listening to it. Kikuchi, noticing this, had been silent for some time.

All at once Kikuchi stopped in the middle of the expanse of sand and began tracing Japanese characters with the tip of his bow. He worked quickly, scrambling up and down the slope slashing away at the sand, leaving behind him long columns of intricate curves and crossed lines and softened angles that flowed effortlessly from one complex to the next. When he was finished he came sliding down the slope and stood beside Munk once more, leaning on his bow and smiling up at his handiwork.

It's a cursive script, he said. Not much used anymore, I'm afraid. Difficult even for us to understand.

What does it say? asked Munk dreamily.

Kikuchi laughed.

Several things. At the beginning up there to the right is a haiku, written by a poor poet upon the death of his youngest daughter. He had twelve children and they all died before him, but that little girl was his favorite. It translates, *The world of dew is a world of dew, and yet. And yet.* Beneath it is the name of a famous Shinto shrine in northern Japan where our ancestral lands are. Up at the top again are some technical terms used in esthetics. Below that the name of the seventh Taoist sage, below that my mother's name, she taught me to play the koto. The next column is breakfast.

Breakfast? said Munk.

Yes, the breakfast my brother and I always ate as boys. Rice and

122

pickles and a certain kind of white fish, grilled, served cold. Lastly, lower down and off to the left, are two signatures. Baron Kikuchi and Rabbi Lotmann. The hillside is me, in short. Watch.

He fitted an arrow to his bow and took aim. The arrow sped up the slope and buried itself deeply in the middle of the swirling characters. Munk stared at the arrow standing there in the sand. After a moment Kikuchi touched him on the sleeve.

Well?

I'm sorry, I must have been lost somewhere. What did you say?

The hillside, Munk. What do you see?

Munk gazed up at it. The wind was blowing away the characters, filling the lines with sand. Already they were mostly obliterated. Only a few dissolving strokes remained here and there. Kikuchi was laughing loudly, tugging at his sleeve.

So quickly and nothing but my arrow is left? What happened to my delicate script? All those beautiful suggestive characters with the myriad meanings and memories they hold for me. Where have they fled?

By the time the former Baron Kikuchi had retrieved his arrow the sandy slope was bare again, swept smooth by the wind. The present Rabbi Lotmann snorted and laughed as they turned back toward the monastery.

When you told me about your great-grandfather, Munk, the one who was an explorer, you implied that some mysterious force had driven him to do so much in only eight years. But I don't think it was mysterious at all. I think he decided he wanted to drive an arrow into the hillside and he did so. Your family remembers that arrow as the love letters he sent to his wife. But as marvelous as they were, and as important as they became to your family, I don't imagine it was exactly that way for him. For him, the pride he took in those eight years was his arrow.

Kikuchi snorted, he laughed.

Yes. Despite the ultimate mystery of the universe there's still one small truth we can live by. Choice. Never merely to take what we are given or inherit, but to choose. It may not seem like much but it's the difference between meanings and memories that disappear in the sand, and something that doesn't. Choice is the arrow. For then, at least, we play a part in making ourselves.

The next morning Munk said he was going away for a few days to be with himself. In answer Kikuchi merely nodded, his face expressionless.

The nightly koto concert was already underway the evening Munk arrived back at St Catherine's. Quietly he walked down the corridor to Kikuchi's cell, with a chair and large case, and sat down in the doorway. The Greek monks looked at him in surprise but Kikuchi seemed not to take any notice.

The first notes from Munk's cello blended uneasily with the koto, but after a few minutes the two men found their way together and the music from their instruments mixed richly in accord.

Kikuchi smiled happily up at him.

A wise decision, Munk, an arrow in the hillside. There is never any better cause than a homeland for people who lack it. And tonight, I think, we are definitely hearing the strangest music ever played at St Catherine's.

After he had begun his Zionist activities in Jerusalem, Munk returned to St Catherine's to visit Rabbi Lotmann. He could see the Japanese wasn't well and Lotmann finally admitted he was suffering from some severe unknown ailment that caused him to pass excessive water. Medical treatment in Palestine was inadequate and his condition had worsened in recent weeks. Munk urged his teacher to return to Japan to receive proper care. Reluctantly Lotmann agreed it was the best course.

On the last day of May the two men stood on a pier in Haifa. There were tears in Munk's eyes but Lotmann's face was impassive.

I'll be back soon, he whispered.

Of course.

No later than the beginning of the year.

Good.

124

Tiny Rabbi Lotmann reached into the cart that held his luggage and removed the quiver made of red lacquer and the familiar long thin canvas case.

I've never been without these, said Kikuchi. I'm not sure exactly how old they are, they've been in my family a very long time. But now that my true home is here, I'd like them to stay here. You'll keep them until I return?

Certainly.

Lotmann smiled and took a tiny gold pocket watch out of his vest. He placed it in Munk's hand.

I found this some years ago in an antique shop in Basle. What appealed to me was the extraordinary miniaturization. Can you imagine how small the parts must be to fit inside this case? But look, they're even smaller than you think. There's more going on inside this watch than anyone could ever suspect. Like the universe?

Kikuchi laughed and pressed the button that opened the lid. Munk found himself staring at a blank enamel face. Lotmann pressed the button again and the blank face clicked back to reveal another watch, the face normal in appearance but with the minute hand moving at the speed of a second hand, the second hand a blur. Kikuchi pressed the button once more to reveal a third face, also normal in appearance but with both hands seemingly stationary.

They're moving, said Lotmann, but very slowly. Depending on the temperature and tides and your mood, it takes the second hand two or three hours to make a full traversal.

He snorted and laughed.

You'll also keep this for me, Munk? I've always been fond of it and it would make me happy to know it's here waiting for me. For my return.

The ship's whistle blew. Kikuchi went on board and stood by the railing. As the ropes fell and the ship drew away from the pier, Munk thrust the samurai bow in the air in salute. For a long time he stood there watching the ship become smaller, the tiny gold watch clicking all but inaudibly next to his ear, rendering time slow and fast and nonexistent.

An antique shop in Basle.

One of the masterpieces of miniature clockwork constructed long ago by the father of Johann Luigi Szondi?

That summer Lotmann wrote that he had been diagnosed as a diabetic and confined to his home in Kamakura. There he lived for the next quarter of a century, translating the Talmud into Japanese and eagerly awaiting Munk's monthly reports on Zionist progress in Palestine.

But the gentle Kikuchi twins seemed destined for violent ends. In 1938 Munk learned that General Kikuchi had been grotesquely murdered on the night his army occupied Nanking. And then late in 1945 the general's widow wrote that Rabbi Lotmann had died in an American fire-bomb raid toward the end of the war, a mysterious passing that consumed him and all his translations in a sudden ball of fire while leaving his house and the garden where he was working untouched.

To Munk, Lotmann's death was inevitably reminiscent of the chariot of fire that had carried the rabbi's favorite prophet, Elijah, to heaven in a whirlwind.

The wind was whistling through the alleys of the Old City early one March morning in 1925 when the Patriarch of the Syrian Greek Church in Aleppo rose from the poker table. The other three visitors to the game, a wealthy Sumatran slaver and two Belgian embezzlers of food relief funds from Flanders, had dropped out shortly before dawn. The session had begun at noon the previous day and everyone was exhausted. Both Cairo and Munk were slumped in their chairs with their eyes half closed.

Most curious, murmured the Patriarch, a large man with a massive gray beard and watery eyes. Joe had risen respectfully with the Patriarch and now stood with his head cocked, sipping from his glass and listening attentively.

How's that, Father?

The symmetry of it. Those three men who left all lost a great deal of money, but by amounts differing as much as several thousand pounds. Yet the three of you here have come out winning almost exactly equal amounts, while I've ended exactly even. How strange it was. I admit it seemed to be heading that way some time ago, but I just couldn't believe it.

Game of chance, Father. No way of foreseeing how the cards are going to account for themselves.

Divine intervention in my case, mused the Patriarch. The neutrality of providence. It was uncanny.

It may be so, Father. Me, I wouldn't be knowing about such higher designs and all.

A veritable heavenly design, mused the Patriarch. God's very hand at work, showing me the futility of this way of life. Telling me to put this affliction behind me.

Affliction, Father?

Gambling. Throwing away the Church's money on cards. At a wicked table like this, using the contributions meant for the poor to pursue my own evil gratification. For years I've sinned in this manner but I never will again.

Oh I don't know, Father. As far as I can see cards just come and go like that wind outside. Pure chance in the alleys of Jerusalem is all I see.

The Patriarch smiled dreamily through his watery eyes.

Perhaps it's that way for you, my son, but no longer for me. This night, through His mercy, I have been freed from my vice forever. Divine intervention was at work here. The Almighty's hand was upon me.

Too lofty for me, Father. But this is certainly a blustery March morning on the heights of the Holy City. Sign of a new season, I suppose.

A new season for the soul, mused the Patriarch. *My soul.*

Cairo scratched himself. He seemed to have been growing increasingly restless during the conversation. Curled up on his shoulder, as so often, was a furry white little creature apparently asleep, its head and tail tucked away out of sight. A loud fart suddenly cracked against Cairo's chair when the Patriarch said *my soul.* Cairo looked up and grinned.

You know what I think, Father? I think some people's souls must resemble monkeys. Yours, for example. Ridiculous.

The startled Patriarch, in his new state of grace, recovered from the insult almost immediately. He smiled benignly in answer and made the sign of the cross over Cairo's head.

No thanks, Father. And speaking of monkeys, I own one. He helps remind me what people are up to when they're sounding high-minded. Bongo, say hello to this pious crooked freak who calls himself a patriarch.

Upon hearing its name the ball of white fluff on Cairo's shoulder erupted. Instantly the little albino monkey leapt to its feet, its bright aquamarine genitals thrust forward, and began masturbating itself vigorously with one fist and then the other, alternating hands every few seconds to maintain speed, not missing a single furious stroke.

The Patriarch reared back in horror. Munk laughed. Joe took the Patriarch by the arm and quickly steered him toward the door.

May God have mercy on that man, murmured the Patriarch.

Never mind, Father, said Joe, you can never tell what sort of horrid elements are going to turn up at a poker game. You're best out of it and that's for sure. There are people who've missed the path, that's all, I mean hopeless cases. A crazed Arab with a white monkey on his back? Obviously he's got his troubles, both of them have, or they wouldn't be carrying on like that. Forget about it, I say, you can't save them all. Some have to drop by the wayside and that's the truth. Lost cases, hopeless. There are a lot of wrecks like that around here, especially here, Jerusalem seems to attract wrecks. They're looking for the cure of course, deathly ill in their heads and in need of a fast miracle in the Holy City. Depraved, that's all, better to forget it. Back in Aleppo things will be different, better, looking up. Sure.

Joe eased the Patriarch out into the alley and came back and collapsed in a chair. The little albino monkey had curled up again on Cairo's shoulder.

A disgraceful deception, said Munk, smiling. *His* merciful hand? As I recall I saw the Almighty's hand hoisting a glass of illegal Irish spirits only a minute ago.

By God and not a bit of it, where's your heart for grace this morning? Are you of the same opinion, Cairo?

It took three hours longer than it should have, muttered Cairo. He should have been out of here before dawn with those other scoundrels.

Well of course, said Joe, I know that and I'm sorry. But that large sneaky article with his watery eyes just refused to see the light before dawn. Staying on here like he did, still hoping his luck was going to go up or down while your local bogman was dumping contrary evidence all over the table. Well he came around in the end, but Christ it's hard maintaining that kind of balancing act.

How much was the difference? asked Munk, rubbing his eyes and yawning.

His money you mean? Twenty hours from arrival to departure and he left two shillings ahead. But that's what he paid for mineral water, so your man came out exactly on the line. Not a ha'penny above or below.

Marvelous, Joe.

But was it worth those three extra hours? asked Cairo, also yawning.

My God it seems to me it was. Seems to me that any bloody Church situated in a thieves' den like Aleppo, and finding itself both Syrian and Greek in the bargain, needs all the honest help it can get, and especially at the top which is where we started. Seems to me the devious machinations going on in such an enterprise must be staggering. Syrian tricks *and* Greek tricks and God as a front for the two of them? Frightening, I say. Perversity itself and just crying out for reform at the top.

Cairo smiled. Munk laughed. As they slouched in their chairs, too weary to rouse themselves to leave, an eerie baying sound, soft and distant, suddenly swelled and filled the room.

What was that? asked Munk.

Of course it was the wind outside, said Joe quickly, sitting up and whistling. Hear it? Just the wind outside but with the twists and turns of the alleys throwing it off-center.

It didn't seem to come from outside, said Munk. I swear it sounded as if it were in here.

From the corner, added Cairo.

Yes I thought so too, said Munk. The corner where the safe is.

The safe? asked Cairo.

I swear it.

Inside the safe, Munk?

It sounded that way to me.

Here here, said Joe. I do believe we're all so exhausted we're hearing noises in our heads. Next thing that giant stone scarab is going to start talking to us from the other corner. Could it be so? Let's tip an ear in that direction.

Joe cupped his hand over his mouth and a rasping voice rose from the corner where the huge squat scarab watched them with a sly smile carved on its face.

Ah ha, doomed mortals. Did you really believe you could learn the scarab's secret? Never, I say. It's locked here in my black heart for all time, still as stone in the smiling scarab of eternity.

The voice trailed off in cackling laughter. Munk and Cairo groaned. Joe nodded thoughtfully.

Well what do you make of that? Quite plainly we're all in need of some rest after a long tiring night at the gaming table. Now I was the one who kept you here so it's only right I do the cleaning up while you both go home to the comfy rest you're deserving. No that's fine, no objections, I know my duty when I see it. Here we go, my Munk. Give us a hand there, Cairo lad. My God but the two of you are dreadfully heavy when not in motion.

Joe got them both to their feet and pushed them out into the alley. He stood there smiling and waving as they walked away, but the moment they turned the corner he slipped back inside and closed the door. He dropped into a chair and put his feet up on the table, muttering to himself.

By Christ, that was too close by far. Another minute and the great skin would have surfaced and we'd have been for it, the secret of the caverns done and finished and no return.

He sat up. The handle on the tall antique Turkish safe was turning. Hinges creaked. The door opened and Haj Harun stepped out into the room carrying a pile of neatly folded laundry, his ram's horn under his arm.

Oh hello, Prester John. I thought you'd be home in bed by now.

Thought so too but I got carried away last night, divinely intervening with a merciful hand and so forth.

Is something the matter? You look upset.

Just with meself I am. We nearly had a disaster here.

What happened?

There were early morning rumors that the Crusaders were coming back.

What? Again? And we're just sitting here? Quick, we must sound the alarm and go to our posts.

Hold on there, it was a rumor merely and it turned out not to be so. Isn't that lovely?

Haj Harun sighed and his helmet went awry, releasing a shower of rust into his eyes.

It certainly is. What a relief.

Precisely my feelings.

Well tell me about it.

About what?

The rumor.

Oh yes. Well it seems the sightings were real enough. The Crusaders had set out all right, over their heads in clanking armor and monstrous horses and lumbering siege machines, swords banging and clubs swinging and studded maces and heavy lances all clanging together, the full regalia it was.

Tears had come to Haj Harun's eyes.

Please, he whispered. I know what they look like.

Hey I'm sorry, of course you do. Well what happened was that these noble Christian knights got as far as Constantinople and decided to take a break there and maybe give that good Christian city a good Christian sack, and the sack turned out to be so much fun and the killing and burning so satisfactory, dividing all that Christian loot so enjoyable, such a good game all around up there, that they just called it a day and never left to push on down to Jerusalem.

That was the Fourth Crusade, said Haj Harun, wiping the tears out of his eyes, smiling now and fully recovered.

Exactly. It was.

And the Fifth through the Ninth Crusades will amount to very little.

I'm glad to hear that. It means you and I will have some time to ease up around here and get some rest. Well I see you're carrying your reliable ram's horn. Some blast that was, the number you gave us a few minutes back.

I was at the end of the tunnel approaching the ladder.

I see. Were you just treating yourself to a toot or was there deadly intent behind the signal?

I thought I saw someone lurking behind a rock.

Ah.

But it was only my imagination.

Only that, you say?

Yes, it was a shadow cast by my torch.

They do that, I know it. And how was it down there? Anything special to report?

No. I was just doing my laundry down on the Persian level.

Why that era precisely?

Their mountain water is very fresh and sparkling.

I see.

And then I was waiting for it to dry. I like to hang my laundry out overnight.

Do you now. And why might that be?

It gets much whiter.

So it does. But why?

The moon.

Of course, I forgot.

Laundry gets much whiter in moonlight, you see.

I do now although I didn't before. Fresh facts have a way of just popping up.

Look here, Prester John. Have you ever seen dishcloths as white as these?

Surely never. Remarkably white they are.

Thank you. Would you like to go for a walk?

Fine, very fine. I do sense the need for fresh air, to clear the mind after a smoky night at the table. A walk, yes, that's the job wanted.

They locked the ram's horn in the safe and left, Haj Harun taking his dishcloths with him and proudly holding them up to show to the people they passed on the street.

That's it, thought Joe, the evidence is continuing to mount in the cause of lunacy. Just no holding it back as time goes on and comes around. Striking, it is. Impressive, it is. More so every day I live.

7

Haj Harun

It wasn't my physical condition that caused me trouble during the Persian occupation. It was the fact that as a result of those sexual experiences, I was incoherent for the next hundred years.

aj Harun and O'Sullivan Beare were strolling through the Moslem Quarter in a generally easterly direction.

Just ahead, said Haj Harun, is a famous Crusader church. Do you know it?

St Ann's, you mean. I do.

And have you visited the grotto?

Birthplace of the mother of our Blessed Virgin. I have.

Haj Harun nodded pensively.

Then perhaps you can tell me why so many important events in the Gospels took place in grottoes. Why was that so? Why did everything happen in caves? Was it more comforting?

Caves, muttered Joe. It started out as an underground religion, like most I suppose. But listen, why is it you talk so little when Cairo and Munk are around? Don't you like them?

Oh yes I do, said Haj Harun shyly. In fact I like them very much.

They're kind and gentle and I admire their determination. They're good men.

And so? Why don't you feel you can talk around them?

Haj Harun turned to Joe and opened his mouth. Most of his teeth were gone, only a few stumps remained.

Rocks, he whispered. For two thousand years people have thrown rocks at me and run after me yelling insults because they said I was a fool. Well maybe I am.

Joe put his arm around the old man's shoulders.

Here now, what's this all of a sudden? You're not a fool, we know that. The city depends on you, it's survived because of you. You're the one who patrols the walls and guards the gates and sounds the alarm when the enemy's coming. If you weren't here who would rebuild the city after it's destroyed? How would the mountain keep growing higher? Who would take care of the caverns?

Haj Harun lowered his head. He was weeping quietly.

Thank you, Prester John. I know I've always failed but it still means a great deal to me to have someone know I've tried.

Not *tried* man, said Joe, you did it. Now get ahold of yourself and let's forget this nonsense.

Haj Harun wiped his eyes. As he did his helmet tipped and released a new shower of rust in his face. The tears began to flow again.

Thank you, he whispered. But you see it's going to take me time to get used to having friends again. To be able to trust people again. After so much ridicule and humiliation, and the slaps and the kicks and the punches that go with it, you can't help but be afraid. When we met and you believed what I said rather than beating me when I said it, that was wonderful, the best thing that had happened to me in two thousand years, ever since I lost my credibility in Jerusalem. But I don't want to rush things with Munk and Cairo, I have to have some confidence in myself again. I'm so afraid they might think I was mad and it's terrible when people think that, it hurts much more than the slaps and the kicks and the punches. You can understand that, can't you? Please? A little?

Of course I can, all of it. Now then, let's both of us stand up straight. It's a March morning and spring is coming and we're walking through the streets of your city. Let's smile too.

Haj Harun tried to smile and a shy little twisted grin flickered across his face. Two well-dressed young men were going by and he tentatively held up one of his newly laundered dishcloths to show them. With a single glance they took in the dishcloth and the old man's faded yellow cloak, his spindly legs and bare feet, his rusty Crusader's helmet with the two green ribbons tied under his chin.

As if on command the two young men noisily coughed up phlegm and spat into the gutter. They both turned their heads away as they went striding by, one holding his nose and the other making an obscene gesture.

Haj Harun dropped the dishcloth to his side and shrank back against the wall, cringing pathetically. An enormous sigh escaped his lips.

You see? he whispered sadly. The younger generation doesn't believe in me at all. They think I'm just a useless old man.

What? said Joe. Those fat werewolves from the merchant class? Who cares about them? They've already taken a turn on their morning hookahs and they're so dazed they couldn't believe in anything. The hell with them, we were talking about Munk and Cairo, two very fine gents. I mean I don't think you have to worry with the likes of a Munk or a Cairo.

Maybe I don't, but I still feel shy around them. Anyway a time will come, Prester John, and I'd rather wait until I feel easy about it. I do like them though. Isn't that enough for now?

It is, certainly, so let's be on our way. Say, did I ever tell you I used to have a regular name before I came to Jerusalem five years ago?

Everyone always has other names before they come here.

I believe it. But how would you like to call me by this other name once in a while?

Haj Harun looked puzzled.

Why?

Just so I won't be confused, just because it was the name I was born with. Sometimes I do get confused when we're together. You know, time and all, it can be a jumble.

Time is, murmured Haj Harun.

By God I know it, but just occasionally. O'Sullivan Beare's the name. Or just O'Sullivan if that seems too long.

That's Irish.

That's what it is all right. Now can you use it now and then so I can keep myself straight?

If you wish.

Yes, that would be nice.

They walked into the garden in front of St Ann's and sat down on a bench. Haj Harun untied the two green ribbons under his chin, removed his rusty helmet and held it out to Joe.

Do you see these parallel dents on each side, O'Rourke? I got them one day five or six hundred years ago when I was on my way out of the grotto in this church.

A fight to the finish, was it? You were emerging from the caverns and the Crusaders had the exits blocked?

Oh no. That is, I was emerging from the caverns but there was no one around at all, unfortunately for me. You remember how low the ceiling is on the stairway up from the grotto? Well my torch had gone out and it was night and I kept banging my head with every step I took. Finally I became so angry I butted the ceiling and got stuck.

Stuck?

My helmet did, O'Banion, in a cleft between two rocks in the ceiling. And then I lost my footing and there I was hanging in mid-air by my helmet. It felt like the top of my head was coming off.

Awful, I know the feeling. I have it some mornings myself. How did you escape?

I didn't. I had to hang there the rest of the night. The next day a group of pilgrims came along at last and freed my by pulling on my legs, which was terrible. Then I really felt as if the top of my head was coming off.

Haj Harun stirred uneasily.

O'Donnell?

Yes?

O'Driscoll?

Still here as best I can be.

You know all at once my mind seems to be a perfect blank.

Why?

I can't imagine. I'll have to think about it.

Good.

But that won't help, will it, if my mind's a perfect blank to begin with? Oh dear, I just seem to be going around in circles today.

Suddenly Haj Harun laughed.

I know why it is. It's because we're here. This is a very special place to me.

The old man chuckled and put his helmet back on his head. He drifted over to the church where a part of the wall attracted his attention. He examined himself carefully in a small nonexistent mirror, then stepped back to examine himself again in a full-length, nonexistent mirror. All the while he was humming and smiling and raising and lowering his eyebrows.

Seems unusually concerned with his appearance, thought Joe.

O'Brien?

Yes?

I've never seen a helmet with more dents in it than mine, and isn't that just like history? Always new blows to the head? Inevitable blows it would seem?

Seems so, yes it does.

But there are other moments in life, O'Connor, truly unforgettable moments. Here in this garden, for example, in my youth.

Your youth? A journey, I'd say. How far back are we going?

To the Persian occupation. Oh those were the days, you can't imagine.

Haj Harun laughed softly.

Such long lazy afternoons, O'Dair. I ate garlic incessantly during the Persian occupation and always wore my leather bracelet, the one with the right testicle of a donkey inside it.

Do you say that. Why these customs?

To increase my sexual powers.

Ah.

Yes. And when it was necessary I induced abortions through the mouth.

By way of, you mean?

No, out of. That could still be done then.

I see.

And I had to do it frequently because I was very active with the ladies. Feverish days, O'Casey, when the Persians were here.

Feverish?

Sex. Just sex and more sex. Rampant sex. I was insatiable.

Groin fever in other words. Couldn't get enough of it?

137

No, never. Not until the princess finally accepted me as her lover. I even remember the year. It was 454 B.C.

True? Garlic and a donkey's right one doing the job in 454 B.C.? That strikes me as uncommonly precise dating for you. Generally an era is as close as we get.

But I'm not in error on this one. My experiences that year were wholly unique. Let me show you where it started.

Joe followed him across the garden. Haj Harun kept stopping to admire flowers, referring to each one as a Solomon's-seal.

How can that be? asked Joe. They're all different. Don't they have different names?

Not here. Here every flower is a Solomon's-seal. Do you see that pool, O'Nolan?

Oh nullify me, I do.

Well that's where I met her, right there. And she was holding a Solomon's-seal in her hand.

Who?

The princess.

Where's the sun gone? said Joe. Why is it looking like rain?

Joe sat beside the pool rolling a cigarette while Haj Harun roamed around the edge of the water, absentmindedly straying into the mud. Every so often he paused and shouted.

Right here, O'Ryan. The pool was also called Bethesda then, did you know that?

O'Ryan am I now, muttered Joe. A constellation prize if that's any help when Jerusalem time is out of control. Daft heavens above and a daft gathering of the clans below in the Holy City, everybody's Holy City.

He leaned back against the bank and closed his eyes.

It smelled like rain but it was a good time for a nap all the same. Late game last night persuading a patriarch from Aleppo to see through his watery eyes. And too much poteen for sure so forty winks, why not.

The cigarette fell out of his hand. His head rested on the grass. From far away a faint wail came to him in his sleep.

I'm sinking, O'Meara. Sinking.

And so he is, thought Joe, and so are we all. Hour by hour and day by day, that's what's happening to us.

O'Boyle, clay feet, wailed the voice, louder now and much closer.

That's it all right, thought Joe. That's what we have and none other. *O'Halloran, please.*

A voice of desperation? Joe opened his eyes and saw Haj Harun stranded in the middle of the pool. The old man had wandered in to see his reflection in the water and gotten stuck in a mudhole. He was in up to his knees and unable to move. Joe scrambled around to find a pole and pulled the old man out.

A close call, whispered Haj Harun.

No it wasn't that bad, said Joe. The water's not very deep.

Not very deep? Two thousand four hundred years ago is not very deep?

Oh that's right, I was forgetting. Now just sit down here beside me where you'll be safe.

Haj Harun smiled and did so.

It's just as well, he whispered. I shouldn't have been over there shouting in the first place. It wouldn't do to have other people overhear. It might excite them too much. I mean sexual exploits like that are unheard of today.

All true.

Well, whispered Haj Harun, where shall I begin?

At the beginning I suppose. Right here by the pool where you met her.

All right, said Haj Harun proudly. And will you keep in mind that I was quite a different person in those days?

I will.

Not at all what you see today? Strong and energetic in my youth? At the peak of my sexual powers?

The very peak, yes.

Well then, I met this Persian princess here and she was so beautiful I immediately fell in love with her. I told her so and she was also taken with me. But first, she said, she wanted to be sure I could truly satisfy her. Of course I already had a great reputation in such matters but still she wanted to be sure, given the fact that she was a princess from Persia while I was just a youth in conquered Jerusalem.

139

Given. And so?

And so she said she would set three tasks for me to accomplish. The first task was to come to her castle on the next full moon and deflower eighty virgins from her court, in one night, without ejaculating.

Saints preserve us. You *were* at a peak in those days.

And that was only the first task of three. Are you still with me, O'MacCarthy?

I am in one guise or another, some as unheard of as the sexual adventures of your youth. Now please to proceed. How went this heroic effort?

As required. Fortified by garlic and wearing my leather bracelet and bursting with love for the princess, I did what was necessary.

The donkey's right one was there on the job, I can see that.

Indeed it was. And then the next morning the princess presented me with my second task. I was to spend one full month standing naked in her court with a full erection, and the ladies of the court were to come and go as they pleased in any state of undress, fondling me as they might as frequently as they might, while I was neither to ejaculate nor go limp in all that time. I was to begin this task, O'Gara, on the next full moon.

I sense a lunar presence in all this too. Next?

The full moon came and I took up my position. It was agony but so great was my love for the princess, I managed it. The month was over at last and the princess was growing more eager, I could see that.

I can too.

Awed even.

And no wonder, I say. The third and last task then?

She was secretive, she wouldn't tell me what it was going to be. Return at the next full moon, she said, for a deed that will take forty days to perform.

Lunar presence confirmed and a surprise performance surfacing. How to prepare for such a chronic sexual task of unknown nature?

Haj Harun smiled.

Garlic.

Ah, I was forgetting.

I ate garlic.

You did, it's true.

Whole bowls of garlic.

Of course you did.

Then I ate more.

I see.

And more.

Yes.

More still.

Good.

Yet more.

Fine.

And more and more and more garlic, just on and on and on.

Oh God that's enough man, my stomach's on fire already, let's go to the event. The night finally came, the full moon was overhead. What state of mind?

No mind, whispered Haj Harun. I was too hot inside. Fires raged within me and flames shot from every orifice, I swear it.

You don't have to, I can see it happening. You were roaring to explode when the princess presented you with your third and final task.

I was, I truly was. Love had overwhelmed me.

Oh Christ man, on with it. Three hundred women? All at once? I can't stand it.

No, whispered Haj Harun. I was ready for something like that but it turned out I was going to be with only one woman.

One? True? Is that all?

Yes, but that was enough, O'Donoghue. In the princess's court, it seemed, was a very large woman who was round and thick in every part, with a measureless treasure and an inexhaustible appetite to have it filled. All day she lay with half-closed eyes thinking of nothing else, and why? Because this large and round and thick woman, sadly, had never had her treasure filled and her appetite slaked. Never once. Can you imagine her physical and emotional state?

No I can't. It was a case of many having tried, yet never had the large round woman's eyes closed more or opened less? Is that the way it was? No satisfaction ever? Oh help.

That's exactly the way it was. And my third and last task was to do this woman's business unrelentingly for forty days and nights and thereby bring off success.

Not a job for a casual interloper.

By no means, O'Sullivan.

Who?

O'Reilly, I meant. Well I approached the sumptuous couch of this enormous female creature, breathing my withering fumes, and what a creation she was. Her breasts were as vast as sand dunes in the desert, her bellies were a mass of heaving mountains and at the base of these lofty ranges was an immense dripping tangle exuding the steam and the gases and the juices of a primeval jungle. Although to be frank, I've never really seen a jungle.

In short?

In short she was as magnificent a creature as God ever made, and there was no question she would test all my powers.

I'm tired already.

Ha. I went to work and at the end of ten days one of the princess's handmaidens tiptoed in to see how matters were progressing. She whispered into the ear of my female continent, whose eyes now seemed slightly more open, slightly more alert.

Has he tired yet? asked the little girl.

Noooooooooooo, came the rumbling gurgle from deep down in the mountain beneath me.

Is that the truth?

It is, O'Shea. And when the little girl returned again at the end of twenty days, she could see without asking that my continent's eyes were round and bulging, glassy and unfocused.

Oh my God. At the end of thirty days what further developments?

That's when it began. First a muffled groan from the hinterland, then one vast prolonged spasm moving down her central ridge. And so it was to continue for the next ten days, O'Flaherty, ten full days without rest or interruption. Eyes clamped shut, screams and gurgles and hiccups shaking the jungles and mountains and deserts for ten full days. So long had she been waiting for that moment that when it arrived, it arrived with force and duration.

Amazing.

Yes, O'Regan. Then on the fortieth day, spent, she rolled over and began to snore at last.

At last I say, at last I repeat, agreed. What an ordeal. And the princess accepted you after that?

142

She did.

Lovely.

It was, O'Leary. In fact it was incomparable.

I can believe it.

Joe stood and lit a cigarette. He walked up the bank.

I think it's going to rain, he said.

Haj Harun turned and gazed at him. He smiled.

What do you mean, O'Geraty? It *is* raining.

Joe shrugged.

You're right. You know maybe it would be better if you called me Prester John after all. Maybe I could keep track of myself better that way.

As you wish.

Yes.

See here, said Haj Harun as he climbed up the bank and looked back at the muddy pool. Do you realize those adventures I had while winning the heart of the princess were the talk of Jerusalem for centuries?

I didn't, no, but I can understand it. Spectacular, that's what they were.

Later on they even wrote them down as stories in books. But do you know they never once mentioned my name? Not once? They always attributed those adventures to others, to people whose names they made up.

Maybe it's that way, said Joe. Maybe we never hear about the real heroes. Maybe that's what being a hero is.

Like the dents in my helmet, you mean?

How's that?

No one knows how they got there except me.

True.

Curious, murmured Haj Harun.

Hold on there, said Joe, I just thought of something. Haven't you always told me that it was during the Persian era when you began to lose your influence in Jerusalem?

That's right.

Well did it have something to do with the princess and your heroic exploits on her behalf? Were you just completely worn out or something like that? Staggering exploits after all.

Haj Harun sighed.

It wasn't my physical condition that caused me trouble during the Persian occupation. It was the fact that as a result of those sexual experiences, I was incoherent for the next hundred years. I was totally preoccupied with visions of sex, which severely limited my vocabulary. When I opened my mouth the only words that came out were things like *cunt* and *lick* and *fuck* and *suck*. They hadn't been bad words when the princess and I were whispering them to each other, but afterward, with the general public, their connotations seemed to change. They no longer seemed acceptable. To be frank, I could only use about a dozen words in all.

Limited, yes. I see.

And after a hundred years of that no one took me seriously anymore. Especially my speeches in the marketplace. Before then it had been my oratory that swayed people and made me influential in Jerusalem, but during that hundred years when I was using only a dozen words, people got in the habit of laughing at me.

I see.

So by the time I could speak normally again my credibility was gone. Not that I blame my fellow citizens, it was my own fault. After all, if you said good morning to a person and they always answered by shouting *cunt*, and then you said good afternoon to them and they always shouted *lick*, and you said good evening to them and they always shouted *fuck*, and you wished them a nice weekend and they always shouted *suck*, how would you view them after a while?

Not too optimistically.

And after it had gone on for a hundred years?

Pessimistically.

Of course, said Haj Harun with a sigh, and that's what happened to me. But if I could go back I'd do it all again, I wouldn't change a thing. I'd love the princess just as I did then, even though I knew it would cause my ruin.

True?

Haj Harun smiled shyly. He nodded.

Oh yes, Prester John, absolutely. We're holy men now, you and I, and our concerns are spiritual ones. But even a single night with the princess is worth a century of incoherency.

Ah, now that's a fine sentiment.

And it's worth the twenty-three centuries of abuse and ridicule and humiliation.

Fine, very fine.

Yes, Prester John. If we were young again, I tell you, the ladies would know it. They'd hear our knock on the door and see the gleam in our eye and know our intent.

We'd be lusty, you say? Not taking no for an answer? Doing a proper passionate job in Jerusalem?

Giving the dear sweet souls God's gift, murmured Haj Harun. Unabashedly giving them love.

Unabashedly, I say. Why not.

But unfortunately we're no longer young, Prester John, and we have our mission before us.

Before us, yes, along with a rainy March day in 1925. Well I do feel like I'm going the other way sometimes, but do you know how old I am according to the calendar?

Younger than I am, certainly.

True. Soon to celebrate my twenty-fifth birthday to be exact.

But of course that's apparent age, which doesn't mean anything here.

I do know it. That information was passed on to me during my first foodless days in the Holy City. By the baking priest who gave me this uniform and awarded me the Victoria Cross and set me up in residence at the Home for Crimean War Heroes. Take the uniform and the medal for bravery, he said, apparent age is no problem in Jerusalem. So said the former MacMael n mBo, baking priest and my first benefactor here.

Haj Harun leaned over and picked up a flat worn stone. He peered into it.

The baking priest, you say?

That's who he is, the very article. And when I ceased to be a Poor Clare nun upon my arrival here and joined the ranks of the Jerusalem unemployed, outcasts on the summit, he was the one who put me on my feet.

I know him, announced Haj Harun, still peering into the flat worn stone.

You do?

He always bakes his loaves of bread in the same four shapes, I believe. That's him all right.

One in the shape of his homeland and one for his God, a third in the shape of the land where he gave up fruitless strife, and a fourth in the shape of Jerusalem where he found peace.

All true, that's him. Ireland, the Cross, the Crimea and Jerusalem.

And that's all he does. He bakes and bakes his four shapes in the Old City and is content.

Very true. But how do you happen to know him?

I've known him a very long time, ever since he arrived. His role is a traditional one here.

Ah. And when did he arrive?

In the first century. Soon after Christ died.

Ah.

Yes. Baking his bread in the Old City, a cheerful man then as now. Given to little dances in front of his oven as he shovels in his dough and shovels out his bread, sandals clapping on the stones as he does his little dances.

That's him.

Bits of wisdom flying between the loaves, and laughter and merriment and rhymes as well, tales to hum to and a gay glint always in his eye.

By God, for sure.

A cheerful man, our baking priest, we've always relied on him. Of course we have. We couldn't possibly get along without him.

Haj Harun looked up from the stone mirror. He smiled.

Yes. Jerusalem must have its merry baking priest with his leaven and his laughter, his leaven and his dances in front of his oven. He gives us something we in the Holy City must have, something simple yet special that we will never be able to do without. And we're thankful for that.

I'm ready, whispered Joe. That something is?

Haj Harun nodded gently.

Bread, Prester John. Even here men can't live by spirit alone.

8

Joker Wild

Change the view, that's the article.
If you're down on the coast, bugger it
up to the mountains. If you're up in
the mountains, bugger it down to the
coast. Do you follow me?

Still the Old City, still everybody's Holy City. In the back room of Haj Harun's shop the high round table was heaped with currencies and jewels and precious metals, the Great Jerusalem Poker Game now in its ninth year and notorious throughout the Middle East as the place where fortunes could be quickly made or quickly undone, the game still run by its three founders and only permanent members, an enigmatic African, a clever Hungarian, a wily Irishman.

From the far side of the table Munk Szondi snapped his fingers, signaling to the Druse warrior on mess duty to refill his bowl of garlic bulbs. The warrior took the bowl to the corner where the garlic bunches hung and lopped off a load with his sword, returning the overflowing bowl to the table.

Munk picked up a handful of bulbs, crunched his way through them and yawned. It had been a long evening of seven-card high-low, and business was slow. In front of him lay a meager supply of chits representing Jericho orange futures, Syrian olive-oil futures and not much else. Munk sighed, rippling his cards with garlic fumes, and gazed dully around the table.

To his left, a lean leathery British brigadier on long leave from the Bombay Lancers.

Next to him a limp cringing Libyan rug merchant who had stopped off to pray at the Dome of the Rock after shamelessly and successfully beating his dying cousin with a stick, somewhere to the east, in order to acquire the cousin's valuable collection of Bukharas.

Continuing clockwise, a French dealer in stolen Byzantine ikons, a shifty-eyed pederast who regularly visited Jerusalem on his trips of desecration up and down the Levantine coast.

An elderly Egyptian landowner, cotton-fat, spastic when excited, said to be impotent if his favorite hunting falcon, hooded, wasn't perched on the mirror that ran the length of his bed.

Two enormous Russians with shaved heads, ostentatiously dressed as kulaks and picking their teeth with knives, pretending to be mining technicians interested in sulphur deposits on the shores of the Dead Sea, obviously Bolshevik agents sent to foment atheism in the Holy Land.

A commonplace group, in short, with the players dropping in and out of the game.

Off somewhere to Munk's right was Cairo Martyr hunched beside his hookah, not doing very well either, in front of him a small stack of Maria Theresa crowns which the African fingered from time to time, listlessly polishing the impressive breasts of the former Austrian empress with his smooth thumb.

And also off somewhere to his left, as usual, O'Sullivan Beare, quiet tonight for a change and apparently more interested in his antique cognac bottle than his cards, the bottle actually containing his fiery home-brewed poteen. The Irishman absentmindedly traced with his finger the distinctive cross that appeared on all his bottles, in front of him an insignificant pile of Turkish dinars, backed up by a totally useless reserve of Polish zlotys.

Munk yawned again and gazed down at the cards he held. The betting had come around to him.

Fold, he said, reaching under the table to scratch himself. Joe also folded, as did Cairo.

The servile Libyan rug merchant and the French ikon thief went on to win. But the British brigadier and the spastic Egyptian landowner had been more than holding their own all evening and the two noisy Bolsheviks seemed on the verge of a breakthrough. Luck was running to the strangers at the table.

Hello there Munk, called Joe from across the table. Would you be having the time on this dreadfully dreary evening?

Munk took out his three-layer pocket watch and began flipping through the faces. Eventually he came to one that satisfied him and glared at it. A heavy garlic belch erupted from deep inside him.

Hello there Munk, called Cairo from his side of the table. How's it read?

Slow, answered the Hungarian.

Right, said the African.

Figures, muttered Joe.

All three men nodded vaguely at each other and went back to their diversions, garlic cloves and poteen and the breasts of the former Austrian empress. While the cards were being shuffled, Joe recited some lines in Gaelic.

Know that one, Munk? Cairo? It's a pome I used to be telling myself back when I was doing my jig around the Black and Tans. Roughly speaking, it says a man should never sit still when he has a dose of the slows. Change the view, that's the article. If you're down on the coast, bugger it up to the mountains. If you're up in the mountains, bugger it down to the coast. Do you follow me? You have to get yourself to where you were or might have been, then there's a chance of something happening. And that, gents, is the meaning of the pome in all its brevity.

Both Munk and Cairo nodded sleepily, although it was only eleven o'clock. Munk yawned and pushed back his chair, gathering up his few remaining chits of orange and olive-oil futures. As he did so the chimes attached to the sundial in the front room began to strike, tolling twelve times in all.

An early midnight and bedtime for me, said Munk. I trust no one cares if a loser leaves the table?

No one did. Munk drifted out the door as the new hand was being dealt. The Libyan went high and won, the Frenchman went low and won. Cairo folded on the next hand and pocketed the only two breasts of Maria Theresa still in his possession.

That it, sport? mumbled the British brigadier. Not your night either?

Cairo shrugged and swayed out the door in his stately robes, trailing the sweetish smoke from his final puff on the hookah. The chimes in the front room creaked and inexplicably tolled midnight for the second time, although it was only eleven-fifteen. The Russians took a hand, then the Egyptian and the brigadier. The French pederast and the limp Libyan shared another pot, the rug thief going low and the ikon thief high.

Joe had only three Polish zlotys left when the Druse warrior on duty in the alley entered the room and stood at attention behind Joe's chair.

I believe your batman wants you, mumbled the British brigadier.

Joe looked up and the Druse warrior handed him a calling card engraved in gold. Joe looked at it and his eyes widened. He sat up very straight, whistling softly.

What is it? someone asked.

Jaysus.

A new player? asked one of the Russians.

Jaysus Joseph and Mary.

Three new players? asked the other Russian.

Rather late, mumbled the brigadier, but of course there's still room if they have money to lose.

Joe whistled very softly and tapped the calling card. He leaned back and licked his lips hungrily.

Now it's just too bad, he murmured, that Munk and Cairo packed it in and left when they did. I'd just like to see their faces now.

Well? asked someone.

Well you can't blame me for being shocked, said Joe. I mean who'd ever have believed that item would dare show up here again after the bundle he dropped in '24? Not me, I couldn't have imagined such a thing was possible. Sat right where you're sitting, Mr Brigadier, and just as coolly as you please gambled away three villas in Budapest and two in Vienna with all their treasures included, paintings and statues you could hardly count, regular palaces they were, and if that wasn't enough he threw in a Czech hunting estate and a piece of Bohemian

150

forest and a whole Croatian lake jammed with fish, all over two aces can you imagine. Two aces? That's right, mad arrogant he is. You'd have thought he was the former owner of the old Austro-Hungarian Empire, which isn't far from the truth as it happens. And another thing he was big on betting that night was musical instruments.

What? mumbled the brigadier.

That's right, violins and cellos and so forth. You could have equipped a dozen string quartets with the instruments he lost here. Now I wouldn't venture a miserable zloty on two aces in a game like this, but there was just no holding him back. He goes off the deep end, you see, when he spies an ace. By God and he must have collapsed between the ears to be coming back here looking for more of the same.

Joe shook his head in disbelief. Everyone at the table was watching him. He opened a tin of imported Irish butter and snapped his fingers. The Druse warrior on mess duty dragged a heavy lumpy sack out of a corner and over to the table. Joe rummaged through the sack of cold boiled potatoes, looking for one to his liking.

Who is this mad rich man? someone asked.

Joe split a potato down the middle, tested the pulp with his finger and smeared it with butter. He took a bite, decided on more butter and chewed thoughtfully. When he leaned forward at last his voice was conspiratorial, little more than a whisper.

Who is he, you say? Well I don't want to alarm anyone, God knows we see all manner of rogues and cutthroats sitting down at this table. But this great skin is simply something else, and if the cards weren't running against me tonight I'd bet everything I own against the fool. Know what I mean? This item sees an ace and just loses control. Always bets on aces and won't bet on anything else. Discards three kings, he does, in hopes of getting an ace in return, it's that kind of madness. Of course it's criminal to throw money away like that, but he's so bloody rich he doesn't care. Just showers money down on the table like next year's olive crop. I tell you, if this were only my night.

No one moved. There was utter silence in the room. Joe noisily blew his nose and examined his handkerchief. He ripped off another hunk of cold potato and chewed.

What a chance, he muttered, his mouth full of potato. A man who'll put money like that on two lonely aces? I told my friend the baking priest about it and he straightaway hustled me off to mass. That's dangerous, he said, your soul's in mortal danger. Anyone who throws money away like that can only be in league with the devil. Tempting poor souls to leap into the abyss by dumping filthy money all over them, that's what he's doing, now off to a special mass with you to clean things up. So said the baking priest, word for word.

Joe nodded vehemently. The eyes of the other six players never left him. He scooped out the rest of the butter in the tin, loaded it on his stump of potato and closed his eyes to chew.

Delicious, he murmured. Beats all.

But who is he? someone whispered.

Sorry?

My God, the man outside, Who *is* he?

Ah, that one. The worst villain ever to come out of central Europe, that's who. Not that he was a central European to begin with, there's too much perversity in his black heart for anything as simple as that. No, his people came from farther east, around the Volga they say. Or perhaps as far out as Transcaucasia who knows.

The two Russians narrowed their eyes imperceptibly.

Anyway, he first surfaces in Budapest before the war, and then on to Vienna, where with stealing his way with lies and more lies he somehow manages to get in with the royal family. How? Faith-healing at first, that kind of thing. Then advising on financial investments. And he uses his powers while he's scheming in the shadows don't you see, hinting here and coaxing there, probably a potion or two secretly administered in what looks like a nice harmless cup of tea to ease things along, until finally the royal dukes and duchesses won't make a move without him. I mean if you've ever heard anything about vampires and werewolves lurking in the mists of central Europe, forget it. This fiendish monster was in a class by himself. So he got his teeth in all right and that's when they say he got in touch with Trotsky. Broadening his horizons so to speak, an eye out for every eventuality. Well that's the general picture.

The two Russians seemed to have stopped breathing. Sweat ran down their shaved heads. Joe rummaged in his potato sack and came up with another potato to his liking.

Plots, he whispered. Laying diabolical plans for the future, he was, and what did the future just happen to bring? The Great War, that's what. Now is it true he arranged that war so the Austro-Hungarian

Empire would do a tumble and he could pick up what he wanted from the pathetic ruins? Is that why he'd been talking to Trotsky? We'll have a war, Leon old chap, and you take what you want over there and I'll do the same over here? And just to get things started right, Leon old fruit, why don't I see that our archduke over here just happens to get shot dead as dead? By a patriot of course, ha ha.

The British brigadier looked appalled.

Well yes, whispered Joe. There are those who swear that's the truth of the matter but I won't argue it one way or another, not being familiar with the intriguing that went on up there before the war. But the fact stands he got his loot out in plenty of time, to Brazil where it would be safe, then just sat back and cruelly calmly watched the dottery old Habsburg Empire go down and fall flat and decompose like so much carrion. And do you think he gave a thought to the dukes and duchesses who'd made him what he was? Not a bit of it. Down you go, he said, with a wicked smile on his face as the old Empire collapsed. Sorry about that, old girl, but you're just carrion now. Do you see what I'm getting at? He had what he'd come for so away he went with his bundle. A regular imperial jackal, that's what. And of course he'd been dealing on all sides, we know that now.

Munitions? whispered the Frenchman in awe.

Cruelly calmly watching the Empire crumble, murmured the Egyptian wistfully, his spastic hand jerkily trying to rearrange the currencies he had won into two separate piles, those that fell within the British Empire and those that didn't.

Play fair at cards, does he? asked the brigadier briskly.

That he does, said Joe, and it's the only time he does play fair. Has a curious habit too of liking to play with the joker wild. Says he likes the idea of having that extra card in the game. Probably because it means he has a chance of getting five aces.

Fair play, said the brigadier, that's the important thing. It's no concern of ours how he happened to make his money.

How important has he become in Brazil since the war? asked one of the Russians.

Important? You couldn't call it that. What it amounts to is he owns half the bloody place outright and runs the rest with an iron fist. But no one knows it because he uses women to front for him, to run all his financial transactions. He calls them *the Sarahs*, just one name for all of them, and pretends they're his aunts and grandaunts and female cousins, although of course no one would ever dare to be related to a fiend like him. And he always wears disguises, that's another thing. Has his enemies naturally. A blond wig is what I remember, that and a gaudy military uniform. You know, as if he were some bloody Prussian aristocrat or something.

Shit my God, said the Frenchman, who cares about a wig or two?

Runs Brazil with an iron fist, mused one of the Russians.

The Habsburgs paid extraordinary prices for good carpets, murmured the Libyan. Especially Bukharas. They loved Bukharas.

The biggest country in South America, whispered the second Russian. Someday it could be as rich as America, and he runs it with an iron fist.

I don't like any of it, said Joe. That monocle and that Junker sneer on his face, looking down his nose at you. Treats ordinary people like peasants, that's what.

Joe grumbled and made a face. He reached into the sack and pulled out a potato without looking at it, devouring it noisily in three huge bites. The other players were watching him dumbly, either daydreaming or hypnotized by his gyrating mouth.

All at once the Frenchman exploded. His fists came crashing down on the table.

Shit my God, what are we doing just sitting here? He may have gotten tired of waiting and left. Quick. Call him in before it's too late.

Everyone nodded eagerly. Joe shrugged.

Suit yourself then. The jackal from central Europe now joins the game, he said, initialing the engraved calling card and handing it back to the Druse warrior on alley duty.

The man who marched haughtily into the room wore a full-dress military uniform, recognizable to the British brigadier as that of a colonel of dragoons in the prewar Austro-Hungarian Imperial Army. Also recognizable to the brigadier was the newcomer's highest decoration, the Order of the Golden Fleece. A ceremonial sword clanked at his side and an ivory and leather riding crop was tucked smartly under his left arm.

He was wearing a blond wig as Joe had mentioned, Germanic in appearance and obviously false, and a closely clipped blond beard, also false. He wore not one monocle but two, both tinted different colors, so his true features were completely hidden. In the middle of the room he snapped to attention and clicked his heels.

My compliments to the Irish peasantry, he said to Joe in thickly accented English. Gentlemen, he added, making a curt bow to the rest of the table.

The Libyan was already on his feet with an oily smile, making a place for the colonel beside himself. The man adjusted his blond wig and accepted the chair with a look of complete disdain for the Libyan. The British brigadier, meanwhile, was studying the numerous decorations on the colonel's chest. He cleared his throat with authority.

A most impressive display of medals, colonel. But you must excuse my ignorance when it comes to obsolete decorations from empires that no longer exist. What is that small black ribbon, for example?

Meritorious behavior in the Balkans, said the colonel. With special reference to Bosnia, the crisis of 1908.

Ah yes. And the purple and black ribbon?

The Balkans again, still Bosnia. For the crisis of 1911.

And the orange and purple and black ribbon?

Once more Bosnia. This time for the crisis of 1912.

Very interesting, colonel. You seem to have had a specialized career.

The colonel's heels clicked under the table.

Minor local affairs, sir. Of no possible interest outside of the Habsburg Empire, now defunct.

Yes, I daresay the Balkans with their tiresome crises did seem a bore to most of us at the time. But then when your archduke was assassinated in Bosnia a few years later, we all had quite a different show on our hands, didn't we? Or at least a good many of us did.

The colonel's heels again clicked under the table.

So it would seem, sir. But I have to say Bosnia was unstable from the beginning. The very concept of a Bosnia is ridiculous and untenable. As I should know, my decorations testify to that. And now to matters more of the present.

The colonel removed a thick packet from his tunic and placed it on the table. He turned to Joe who was sullenly munching another potato.

You will recall from my visit a few years ago, young man, that I do not favor large sums of money on the person. But see here, I'm addressing you. Take that disgusting lump of vegetable matter away from your mouth this instant or I shall leave immediately.

Joe put his potato down on the table as the other players glared at him. Slovenly Irish peasant, muttered the colonel under his breath. Joe rubbed his beard around his mouth, knocking off bits of potato that fell into his lap.

Now to begin again, said the colonel. What I have here are deeds to gold mines on the South American continent, mostly in Brazil. Acceptable as wagers? Yes?

Joe was about to say something when voices erupted around the table.

Shit my God, shouted the Frenchman, of course.

An exquisite pleasure, shrieked the Egyptian.

But shouldn't we play with the joker wild? screamed the Libyan. Just to enliven our little game of high-low?

High-low Brazilian gold mines, thundered the two Russians, jumping up from the table in their excitement and nearly knocking each other down.

Good show, said the brigadier. On with the game while there's still time.

Reluctantly Joe pushed aside his potato. He wiped his hands on his shirt and began to deal. The colonel lost heavily on a single ace, king-high, to the Egyptian and the first Russian. On the next hand he lost just as heavily with another single ace, jack-high, to the Frenchman and the Libyan. The third time it was the British brigadier's turn to share the winnings with the second Russian.

No one was really sure whether the colonel was trying to go high or low with his single aces. But they were all suddenly winning so much, except for Joe, they didn't care. Nor did they care that the colonel had discovered the bowl of garlic bulbs left behind by Munk Szondi and was now sneaking handfuls of them to munch. Nothing mattered with that kind of wealth on the table.

The game was moving quickly now, cards and gold mines flying around the table. Joe had just turned in his last Polish zloty, in exchange for one hundred perfectly worthless Polish groszy, when the Druse warrior on alley duty reappeared with another calling card.

Your batman again, mumbled the British brigadier.

Joe peered at the card and read the name out loud.

Evelyn Baring? Is that a him or a her? Anybody know?

Isn't it all the same where it counts? giggled the Egyptian, spastically prodding Joe in the ribs.

Shit my God, let it in whatever it is, screamed the Frenchman gaily, his fingers stroking a long thick deed in his pocket.

I seem to recall having heard that name somewhere, mumbled the British brigadier.

More, roared the Russians, who had broken out a bottle of vodka and were rapidly emptying it.

We have to have unanimous agreement, said Joe glumly, rules of the game. You only play with those you want to play with. What's the view from Libya?

Rugs, answered the Libyan with a gurgle.

Vote recorded. Colonel?

I couldn't care less.

Well all right then. Evelyn is admitted by popular consent.

Joe put his initials on the calling card and the Druse warrior withdrew. A tall, dignified black man entered the room wearing dark glasses. He was dressed in a long black robe and a formal white wig, not unlike those worn by English judges presiding at the bench. On his shoulder a little animal was curled up asleep, its fur pure white, its head and tail tucked away out of sight.

The black judge placed a large pile of English banknotes on the table and sat down beside the Frenchman, his expression contemptuous and even insolent. But no one took any particular notice of him. They were all too busy reading the deeds to the gold mines they had just won.

Or pretending to read them. By now the Europeans at the table were drunk. The Libyan and the Egyptian had fired up Cairo Martyr's hookah and were lazily passing the tube back and forth, their eyes glassy. The Russian comrades patted each other on the head and hummed the Third Internationale.

Joe lost his hundred groszy and got up from the table. He rubbed his eyes and took a last potato from the sack on the floor. The brigadier was grinning at him crookedly.

That it for you too, sport? Don't tell me the famous high-low

Harrigan of Jerusalem poker has lost for a change?

Afraid he has. Looks like one more poor Irish bogman is down and out in front of the mighty British lion.

Want your hundred groszy back? asked the brigadier. You could always give them to a beggar if he didn't know what they were.

Joe shook his head. He looked exhausted and dejected.

No thanks, I'll just shuffle along home now. Play as long as you like, the man at the door will lock up.

As he left the chimes attached to the sundial in the front room inexplicably struck midnight for the third time that evening.

During the next half-hour the haughty black judge wearing the white wig joined the reckless colonel wearing the blond wig in betting more and more heavily and losing hand after hand. It must have been at least an hour after midnight when the Druse warrior from the alley entered once more to announce a prospective player. The Frenchman, who was stroking the hairs in one of his nostrils with a fingertip, read the card and giggled.

Why are you doing that to your nose, sir? demanded the colonel.

It's very sensual, murmured the Frenchman.

Well stop it this instant, ordered the colonel, or I'll close down all the gold mines you've won.

The Frenchman reluctantly removed his finger from his nose. He giggled again.

This card is a joke. It must be.

What name, sir?

No name. There's a crude drawing, done in crayon, of a bear holding a bottle. That's all there is.

The colonel reached over and took the card. His voice was grave.

Not crayon, you fool, charcoal. And that bottle is the mark he always uses. Now stop giggling like the empty-headed idiot you are.

What do you mean, *he*?

I mean I recognize his mark. Most people in the New World would. But I am surprised to find him so far from home.

Home?

The western half of North America. The ancient domain ruled by Chief Sipping Bear and his ancestors since the dawn of time. No native American was ever more powerful. Among other things, he's heir to the Seven Lost Cities of Cibola.

The lost cities of what? mumbled the British brigadier, pouring himself more whiskey.

Indeed sir, said the colonel, undoubtedly you've heard similar tales in India. The Seven Lost Cities of Cibola are legendary cities of gold located somewhere in the deserts of the southwestern United States. The conquistadores searched for them but were never able to find them because they were outwitted by the Chief Sipping Bears of the time. For my part, as an emigré to the new world, I would welcome such a distinguished player in the game.

And I, said the Egyptian quickly. Lost cities on the Nile have always been a source of treasure throughout history.

Historical treasure, bellowed the Russians, show the oppressed red man in.

The Libyan concurred, suspecting American Indians might well have use for a certain number of rugs if they lived in deserts like the bedouin. The British brigadier admitted he was always curious to see another breed of native. As for the black judge known as Evelyn Baring, he simply rapped the table once, loudly, to show his approval.

By unanimous proclamation, screamed the Frenchman, Chief Sipping Bear from the New World is invited to join the game.

But can he outsip an O'Sullivan Beare? whispered the colonel to Evelyn Baring, who for once relaxed his severe expression and flashed a broad smile, brilliant white teeth in a face so black it was almost blue.

The door banged open and the odd figure who stood facing them was certainly neither as noble nor as savage as everyone had been led to expect by the colonel's comments. In fact he looked rather shabby and harmless.

He was a small dark man, his face and chest haphazardly painted with drab vertical streaks of dye, and he wore a loincloth held up by a rope tied around his waist. His moccasins resembled well-worn cheap

Arab slippers, the threadbare khaki blanket wrapped around his shoulders looked like some shoddy army issue from the last century, and his ill-fitting feathered headband kept slipping down over one eye, giving him the raffish look of an itinerant entertainer and low-level charlatan. Nor were the feathers eagle, rather some common pigeon variety.

Thrust through his rope belt was a crude tomahawk, a stone tied to a shaft of wood that might have been cut from a broom handle. The long bow he carried in his hand was of the finest workmanship, however, thin and powerful and exquisitely wrought, and the quiver made of red lacquer was equally beautiful. So much so that both seemed out of place.

That gave the white man trouble? giggled the Frenchman.

There's no hope anywhere, murmured the Egyptian.

Stunted, mumbled the brigadier. The need for empire was never clearer.

If that's his idea of a blanket I'd hate to see his taste in rugs, said the Libyan.

Oppressed red man, muttered the Russians darkly.

The colonel groaned and shook his head as if in despair. The black judge sighed and gazed up at the ceiling through his dark glasses as if invoking the immediate intervention of some higher power.

Nevertheless, despite his seedy appearance, the Indian seemed determined to act as fierce and menacing as he could. He scowled and began a slow shuffling dance around the table, lifting his knees high and brandishing his bow, reciting a war chant in some barbaric tongue. It was the quiver that caught the brigadier's attention.

I've seen those, he whispered in astonishment.

You have? said the Libyan.

Yes, in the Orient. It's Japanese. The samurai used them.

Valuable? asked the Frenchman.

I should say so. That one could be at least six or seven hundred years old.

The samurai? muttered one of the Russians. Their time will come.

Do the Japanese live in America? asked the dazed Egyptian.

That's right, said the brigadier. What's he doing with that?

Nonsense, interrupted the colonel, suddenly recovering his composure. Everyone knows the American Indians originally came from Asia, and Chief Sipping Bear's forebears have always been proud warriors in the best samurai tradition. The heritage is altogether natural.

Those slippers, wheezed the Libyan, look like the ones my servants wear.

But before there could be any more comments the chief all at once silenced them with a ferocious whoop. His war dance around the table had come to an end. He shook his bow in the air, whooped again and glared down at them.

Me Sipping Bear, great chief of west. *How.*

The colonel rapped his riding crop on the table for order. He rose and clicked his heels.

How indeed. Welcome, chief. We're playing seven-card stud, high-low, joker wild. Let's see the color of your wampum.

The Indian took a leather pouch out of his quiver and removed a gold nugget the size of a pigeon's egg. He took out three more nuggets equally large and placed his tomahawk on the table in the middle of them. The Frenchman, although drunk, couldn't help but notice the savage had accidentally made the sign of the cross on the table with his gold nuggets and tomahawk.

Here Cibola pebbles, grunted the Indian, thumping his chest, which made him cough. All Cibola made out of this, pick up in streets to use as wampum.

Fine, chief, no problems with that. Tell me, how do you happen to be over in this part of the world?

Come to see Holy City East. Tomorrow journey west again home to wigwam in setting sun. But first play joker wild, Holy City East.

Fair enough. Make yourself comfortable.

The chief spied the bottle of poteen Joe had left behind and grabbed it, taking a long swallow.

Ummm, firewater good, Sipping Bear like firewater. Tonight play poker, win fortune. Tomorrow do sun dance at dawn, go home. Now give cards.

He grunted and reached into his quiver again, this time coming out with an ear of corn.

New World food, he said, baring his teeth and gnawing away at the ear of corn as he glanced suspiciously around the table. He picked up his tomahawk.

No cards for great chief? No cards go on warpath. No play with Indian?

Easy there, sport, said the brigadier. No one here minds playing with an Indian.

That's right, added the colonel. This is a friendly game.

Until now, thundered the black judge, speaking for the first time since he had entered the room, his stern voice so authoritative everyone turned to stare at him. And it was also the first time that anyone had really noticed the furry little white creature curled up on his shoulder, its head and tail tucked away out of sight.

My deal, announced the black judge. Yes it's my turn now and I think it's only appropriate that you meet the spirit who watches over me, my guardian spirit who appears to be slumbering by my ear but isn't, because he never sleeps. Bongo, say hello to these greedy crooks.

Upon hearing his name the little albino monkey instantly leapt to his feet with his bright aquamarine genitals thrust forward, wildly flailing away at himself with both fists, alternating them and not missing a stroke.

This jungle beast, said the black judge ominously, likes to eat cucumbers. And although he's small he can eat a surprising number. The ante for the next hand is a cool three hundred pounds sterling, or its equivalent. I'll see the glint of your money now.

The black judge raised his hand and gave the table a solid rap.

Time, gents. The court is in session. Chief Sipping Bear? Try to keep that bottle from dancing around in front of your face. Colonel? I'm not impressed by Bosnia so blow those garlic fumes in another direction. As for the rest of you, I suggest you keep a firm grip on your luck. You'll need it.

Mouths fell open, the black judge laughed. And the little albino monkey pounded vigorously away at his lurid parts as the cards began to spin once more in the swirling haze of alcohol fumes and hashish clouds that had come to envelop the table, causing heads to float and minds to wander in the dark Jerusalem night, the sundial in the front room all at once catching some illusionary ray of light that set its chimes tolling an invisible hour.

162

Just after three in the morning the dazed Libyan rug merchant slipped out of his chair and slid limply down under the table, in passing clutching the trouser leg of his neighbor, the former colonel of Austro-Hungarian dragoons.

Excuse me a moment, said the colonel to no one in particular, bending over to see what was going on. He found the Libyan collapsed in a heap, one arm loosely thrown around the colonel's boot.

Here here, whispered the colonel. This is no way to act.

Ruined, wailed the Libyan. Haven't you seen the chits I've been giving him?

Giving whom?

The black man.

No, I've been concentrating on my own game. How much did you lose?

Everything. First the Bukharas went, my precious Bukharas that I've only owned a week. Then all my rugs back in Tripoli, then the shop the rugs are in. Then my villa in town and my other one by the sea. Then my wives and my children and my servants.

In that order?

Yes.

Your greyhound?

He took that too. Then he took my steamship ticket home so I'd be trapped here at his mercy. Finally there was that last fatal wager.

What was it?

Goats. I indentured myself to serve as a goatherd for the next year. Tomorrow evening I'll be standing on a barren hillside eating yogurt and talking to goats.

The colonel tried to move his foot. The man's slobbering mouth was dulling the polish on his boots.

In other words he wiped you out? Hm, yes. Well that formal white wig and the black robe did seem to indicate he was a judge. Perhaps he held a trial and found you guilty of shameless dishonesty in acquiring those Bukharas from your dying cousin.

He's a judge?

I suspect so. Take another look.

The Libyan crept to his knees and peered over the edge of the table at the black man.

See how severely his lips are pressed together? whispered the colonel. The heavy brooding nose? The stern unwavering eyes?

I can't see his eyes behind those dark glasses he's wearing.

No, but you can certainly imagine them. Cold blue and unrelenting. Merciless even.

Blue eyes? In a face that color?

Yes, blue. I'd bet my life on it. And look at the arrogant way he waves his hand in the air when he deals. More like a pharaoh wafting his divine wand aloft.

Frightened and confused, the Libyan slipped back under the table. The colonel gave him a sharp rap on the head with his riding crop.

What is it? whispered the Libyan.

This is extraordinary. Take a look at what he's just put on his head.

The Libyan crawled up and peeked over the edge of the table again. The black man had placed a gold cobra headpiece on top of his wig, the mark of a pharaoh.

Evelyn Baring, whispered the colonel, of course. I should have recognized the name. He's better remembered today as the Earl of Cromer.

Who's that?

You don't know? A modern pharaoh, the consul general in Egypt. He ran the country for twenty-five years around the turn of the century. No one was more powerful in this part of the world.

English?

Of course.

An *English* lord? I didn't know they had any that color.

Oh yes. His is an old line that far predates the Anglo-Saxons.

The who?

The people you're accustomed to thinking of as English, fair-skinned. His line goes back much further to the time when the Phoenicians were sailing to England to buy tin. Along the way they stopped off in North Africa to replenish their water jars and apparently an ancestor of his joined one of these trading ventures.

Is that why he has a white monkey on his back? Because his ancestors were originally from Africa?

It might be. In any case, once in England that ancestor went into tin and became a titled magnate, and thus we find the origins of the black strain in English aristocracy. And he has many other famous ancestors. Merlin, for one, was also in the line.

Who was Merlin?

A wizard and general handyman at magic. King Arthur couldn't have gotten along without him.

Who was King Arthur?

My dear fellow, you're already sounding like a goatherd. Your knowledge of history is appalling.

The Libyan slipped lower down the colonel's boot.

History? How can I think about history when I've just lost everything, even the future.

Ah, futures, I almost forgot. I'm very fond of futures and there seem to be some interesting ones on the table at this very moment.

The colonel raised himself from under the table, glanced at his cards and tapped his riding crop three times to indicate he was tripling the bet.

An hour later the two Russians staggered out the door in each other's arms, weeping noisily. Having squandered not only their funds meant to foster atheism in Jerusalem but sold all their Bolshevik secrets as well, there was nothing left for them to do but return directly to Moscow, sign confessions that they were undercover Trotskyite agents in the pay of Rockefeller and Krupp and Ukrainian nationalism, and be strangled in an OGPU dungeon which had recently been set aside for criminals guilty of that specific offense.

In the alley outside, the black judge in the cobra headpiece had just finished urinating against the wall. He was straightening his robe when the Russians lurched into the alley, tripped, and went crashing down on the cobblestones at his feet, crying on top of one another.

Time, gents?

Ruined, the two Russians blurted out together.

Indeed, I did notice the colonel seemed implacably opposed to you tonight. But then, the Austro-Hungarian army was always concerned about securing its eastern front.

At four-fifteen the spastic Egyptian landowner grabbed the Indian chief's arm with shaking hands.

Can you understand English?

The Indian stopped gnawing on the ear of corn stuck in his mouth and thumped his chest with it.

English bad but since me great chief, understand words from heart. Firewater good, have drink.

Thank you but I'm too dizzy. That black man with the monkey on his back, why did he play so hard against me? Why does he dislike me? He won my cotton crop for the next ten years. I'm finished, it's all over now. Why?

Cotton. Black man think only cotton. You have cotton, he take.

Over, moaned the Egyptian. Somehow he even knew about my falcon and took that.

You old man now, too old for mirrors and hooded falcons. Better retire and watch setting sun over pyramids. How.

What?

Heart. From heart. Sipping Bear knows.

At five-thirty the British brigadier sank forward onto the table, his head in his arms. The colonel nudged him.

What seems to be the trouble, sir?

It's disastrous, I just can't believe it. Do you realize I actually gambled away my regiments on that last hand? That shabby Indian in the loincloth, swilling firewater and wearing an old army blanket, is now in command of the Bombay Lancers.

The colonel thoughtfully stroked his false blond beard.

Disastrous, yes, I see what you mean. Of course I've always known the chief had a reputation for cunning, but even I wouldn't have imagined he'd go so far as to take over an entire English brigade in India.

But what can I do?

Nothing, unless perhaps you can find an Irishman who'll talk the chief into giving you back your regiments. That seems to be the only hope. You'll have to go begging to an Irishman.

An Irishman?

Yes. For some strange reason the chief has always had a weakness for the Irish.

Why, for heaven's sake?

I can't imagine. Maybe it's because he thinks they like firewater as much as he does. After all, his name is Sipping Bear.

At six-twenty the French ikon thief and pederast leapt from the table and began beating his head against the wall. The black judge pulled him away and led him outside.

Steady, boy.

But shit my God, did you see what that seedy savage has done to me while gnawing on his ears of corn? He's won every ikon I've ever stolen and every one I ever will steal. For the next ten years I have to turn them all over to him and tell him where they came from. Boys too. And in addition to everything else I have to spend time in purgatory.

Where's that?

Someplace here in the Old City. An elderly ecclesiastic known as the baking priest runs it. I'm to come in here tomorrow afternoon and the Irishman who's generally in the game is going to take me there. And every day for as long as the baking priest wants, I'll have to slave in front of a hot oven baking bread in the shape of a cross and saying Hail Marys. This baking priest is going to be my parole officer.

Time in purgatory, mused the black judge, time spent slaving in front of a hot oven. And all because of stolen ikons. It's true the Indian chief seemed to single you out tonight as a special target. Do you think it's possible, despite his primitive brain, that he resented the fact that you traffic in stolen Christian artifacts?

Shit my God, why? He's a savage, I just don't understand it. I wish I'd never come to Jerusalem and gotten mixed up in this poker game.

Yes, said the black judge. There are those who've said that before, and I suspect there'll be others who say it again.

Back in the poker room Chief Sipping Bear was doing a final jig around the table. The black judge came in, picked up the tube to the hookah and sat down beside the colonel of dragoons, who was contentedly crunching garlic cloves. He took a puff on the tube. Only the three of them were still left in the room.

Joker Holy City East, chanted the chief. Day coming night ending, time now make water and rest head, snooze happy dreams in happy hunting ground, happy sleep for Chief Sipping Dancing Chanting Bear, Chief O'Truly O'Sullivan Beare.

With a whoop he went spinning out the door. The black judge removed his cobra headpiece and straightened his white wig.

Going my way, colonel?

The colonel nodded and tucked his riding crop under his arm. Together they strolled down the alley away from Haj Harun's shop. Dawn had come to the city.

A long night, said Munk.

They often are, answered Cairo.

As they turned a corner they came face to face with an English policeman. The man stared in amazement at their wigs and costumes. Munk touched his riding crop to his cap.

As you were, officer, we're quite capable of finding our way. This is the Chief Justice of the Sudan and I'm his aide-de-camp, seconded here by the late Emperor Francis Joseph in accordance with security arrangements for the Holy Land. We're out on an early morning pilgrimage to see some of the sights before the crowds gather.

Sah, barked the policeman, stepping back and saluting. Cairo nodded pleasantly, Munk smiled, they strolled on.

You know, said Cairo, the night was worth it if for no other reason than to ruin that Frenchman.

A detestable wretch, I've never cared for him. But you mean he's UIA as well?

Yes. He was recruited by Nubar's Dead Sea Control about a month ago. I have a dealer who sells down there and keeps me informed.

Munk nodded.

It must cost Nubar a great deal to be always sending players into the game to lose his money. You'd think he'd be tired of it by now. Rather desperate, that little Albanian.

Mad is more like it, said Cairo. But no matter. We won't have to put up with him forever.

What's he got?

Syphilis, acquired through the anus about ten years ago. And they tell me it's moving into the tertiary stage.

Who tells you that, Cairo?

The UIA people who inform on him to my dealers, in exchange for a discount. Still, that's not his most serious problem. The other thing will probably get him first. Apparently little Nubar Wallenstein is a hopeless mercury addict.

Munk smiled.

In certain esoteric areas your knowledge is astonishing. What in the world are the symptoms of mercury addiction?

In his case, said Cairo, severe megalomania compounded by hallucinations. Self-starvation will set in at some point. It's an uncommon way to go these days. In fact there haven't really been any European mercury addicts around since the sixteenth century, when a fairly large number turned up among the alchemists. Before that it occurred among the Arab alchemists in the twelfth century. In other words, not an everyday matter.

Munk smiled again.

I see. Speaking of the twelfth century, have you noticed anything strange about the cognac bottles Joe puts his poteen in?

Only that they're hand-blown and old and have dates on the labels in Latin. As I recall the bottle he had with him tonight said A.D. 1122. Why?

Because there's also that mark on all the labels, a white cross on a black background, the arms of the cross shaped like arrowheads with their points not quite touching at the center. Are you familiar with that cross?

No.

Well, said Munk, it was the insignia of the Knights of St John of Jerusalem, more commonly known as the Knights Hospitalers because they were founded here after the First Crusade to run a hospital for Christian pilgrims. But they soon grew into the most powerful of all the orders and dominated the Mediterranean for centuries. Their loot was enormous.

And so?

And so how does Joe happen to have cognac bottles with their cross on them?

Cairo suddenly smiled, knowing exactly what it meant. After all, he had extensive experience himself with secret caches of history.

You say the Knights once ran a hospital in Jerusalem?

Merely a sideline, answered Munk, an excuse for getting started. Very soon they were marauders and wealthy oppressors.

The pharaohs were also wealthy oppressors, said Cairo. And they weren't just knights pretending to fight for some god. They *were* gods.

So?

So now they're just so much mummy dust available in any bazaar in the Middle East. At a high price to be sure, but still available to anyone who can raise the money for a snort.

You're talking about your own game, said Munk.

No, about Joe's bottles. Wouldn't it be reasonable for a hospital to have medicinal cognac on hand?

Cairo smiled more broadly. Munk stopped and stared at him.

You're saying you think the bottles are genuine?

Yes.

Imported into the Holy Land by the Knights Hospitalers early in the twelfth century?

Strictly for medicinal purposes, answered Cairo, laughing.

Munk took out his watch and clicked open the face that showed no time. For a moment he gazed at it.

Then you're also saying Joe has discovered a hidden wine cellar that once belonged to the Knights?

Yes.

170

But where?

Cairo raised his patent-leather slipper and gently tapped the cobblestones where they were walking.

Down there? Somewhere beneath the city?

Very far beneath it, I would think. Jerusalem has come and gone several times since then and they've always rebuilt the city over the ruins.

Munk stopped and gazed down at the cobblestones.

Caverns of the past? But how could he have found a way into them? If they were known to exist people would have been looking for them for centuries.

Perhaps there was only one man who knew they existed and Joe learned the secret from him. A man no one else has ever believed or even listened to.

Munk put his watch away. They walked on in silence for a time.

Obviously Haj Harun, said Munk.

It seems likely.

But he's mad.

Of course.

He even claims he's lived three thousand years.

Which is why no one listens to him. But tell me, Munk, would you be interested in the caverns if that's what they are?

Not really. Futures are my specialty, as you know.

Yes, a new Jewish homeland. I know.

And what about you? asked Munk.

Not my line either. In my own way I'm looking to the future too.

For what?

Justice, said Cairo with a smile. He removed a small gold container from under his robe and extracted a pinch of dust. He sniffed and the pupils of his clear blue eyes dilated. The muscles around his mouth relaxed in a familiar manner. The two of them had emerged from an alley near Jaffa Gate.

It's quite extraordinary the effect mummy dust has on you, Munk commented dryly.

Cairo smiled into the distance and nodded gently as they separated to go their different ways.

Part Three

9

ℕubar Wallenstein

*Nothing less than a vast criminal
organization operating throughout the
Balkans, its scheming employees chosen
by Nubar solely for their abilities in
intrigue and intimidation, burglary and
embezzlement.*

In the tower room of the Albanian castle where his grandfather had
memorized Bibles early in the nineteenth century, Nubar Wallenstein
sat brooding over a report that suggested the possible existence of yet
another obscure treatise written by the most renowned alchemist in
history, Bombastus von Hohenheim, more often remembered as
Paracelsus.

Nubar's library contained all the works commonly attributed to the
great sixteenth-century Swiss master, and in addition thousands of
smudged pages that were either forged or illegible. Acquired over the
last six years, the collection represented an immense effort by his
network of agents in the Balkans.

Paracelsus Bombastus von Hohenheim.

Hohenheim Paracelsus von Bombastus.

To Nubar, those syllables held mystical implications, sonorous suggestions of secret knowledge that had immediately captivated him when first he came across them, in 1921, at the age of fifteen.

Indulged as always by his grandmother, Sophia, he had begun writing to literary dealers and bibliophiles throughout the Balkans, offering huge sums of money for any works by Paracelsus that they could procure. Fortunes had changed drastically in the Great War. Powerful families had sunk into ruin, estates had been broken up. The tracts and treatises flowed in and before the end of the year, due to Sophia's enormous wealth and influence, Nubar had owned the largest collection of Paracelsus in the world.

But for Nubar the largest collection of Paracelsus wasn't enough. While growing up in the ancestral Wallenstein castle in Albania, Nubar had early fallen victim to those traditional suspicions and rampant fears that had plagued the first Wallenstein master of the castle in the seventeenth century, and thereafter all the Skanderbeg Wallensteins save for the last, Nubar's grandfather, a fanatical renegade Trappist monk who had discovered an ancient manuscript in the Sinai that was in fact the oldest Bible in the world. His horrified grandfather had found that Bible untenable in every respect, denying every religious truth ever held by anyone, and out of piety had proceeded to forge an acceptable original that could provide grounds for faith.

Parabastus Hohencelsus von Bombheim.

Fear in the case of the first Albanian Wallenstein that the enemies of his murdered uncle, the once all-powerful Generalissimo of the Holy Roman Empire, were sending out spies to kill him.

Suspicion in the case of subsequent Skanderbegs, those illiterate warriors who had spent their lives away from the castle fighting in any army that would have them, because they were incapable of combining love with sensual pleasure and were therefore impotent with their wives, able to be aroused sexually only by very young girls of eight or nine.

Suspicion feeding on itself and eventually giving birth to its own reality as successive Skanderbegs, who when young had always sensed that their fathers were strangers, grew up and came to know for a fact that their own sons were fathered by strangers, a terrible burden of isolation causing lifelong instability, the sons fatherless and the fathers sonless generation after generation in the family's dark dank castle perched gloomily on a wild Albanian crag, a windy and insecure

Balkan outpost in the precarious marches separating.Christian Europe from the Moslem realm of the Turks.

Hohenbomb von Celsus Paraheim.

Excessive doubts and traditional fears harrying Nubar as they had harried Wallenstein men for centuries, those unrelated and suspicious warriors who had violently distrusted everyone at home while imagining extravagant plots against them abroad. Vague yet pervasive plots that explained all events on earth. The entire universe, as they saw it, secretly arrayed against these insignificant masters of a remote Albanian castle.

And so too Nubar, even though his grandmother, Sophia, still ran the castle as she had for the last seventy-five years, ever since her common-law husband, Nubar's grandfather, had returned home from his stupendous labors in the Holy Land, broken and insane. Nubar sensed those same plots from the past and he could no more control his fear of them than keep his left eyelid from drooping when he was excited, another affliction of the first Wallenstein master of the castle that had subsequently been visited upon all Wallenstein males.

Inexplicably so. For since none of the Wallenstein males had been related prior to the time of Nubar's grandfather, how could they possibly share such specific characteristics?

The question had never been answered, and with good reason. Because to do so would have been to admit a-causal relationships in the Balkans, influences removed from logic which would have been highly confusing in their disorderly ramifications, and had therefore always been thoughtfully ignored as nonexistent.

Hohenbastus von Heim Parabomb.

Or in short, Paracelsus, the master alchemist of all time.

Briefly professor of medicine at the University of Basle early in the sixteenth century. Forced to leave because of his defiance of tradition, which took the form of explaining things that had never been explained, relating things that had never been related, and conversely, unrelating other things that had always been seen as tightly wedded. In general, then, wreaking havoc throughout the entire shadowy terrain that lay between cause and effect.

Brilliant and eccentric and quarrelsome, renaming himself Paracelsus because he felt the name he had been born with was insufficient for his needs. Prodigiously learned, vitriolic in debate and psychotically self-confident, believer in the four Greek elements of earth and air and fire and water, and the three Arab principles, mercury and salt and sulphur. Discoverer of the philosopher's stone which would allow him to live forever. Successively a profound scholar, a miner, a mixer of metals in dim cellar laboratories, a dreaming wanderer, a political radical, a barefoot Christian mystic.

And finally the magus himself, Faust, first modern scientist of the soul. The genius who first used minerals to treat internal diseases, who scorned remedies such as bloodletting and purging and sweating.

Unswerving advocate of opium and mercury compounds in search of the spirit.

Celsusheim Parahohen von Bomb.

Nubar hadn't been satisfied to have the largest collection of the magus's works, he had to have *all* of them. Because if he didn't it meant that someone, somewhere, would have the power to plot against him, to use an unknown page of the master alchemist's conjectural knowledge to harm him.

Once more Sophia had indulged him, this time providing him with unlimited funds to hire full-time literary agents whose job, as Nubar innocently explained it, would be to track down the lesser known works of Paracelsus and buy them.

Admirable, thought Sophia. For a boy in his sixteenth year, he's already displaying his grandfather's scholarly bent to a remarkable degree.

But in fact Nubar wasn't scholarly at all. His bent was elsewhere and his network of literary agents had soon expanded into a private intelligence service with its own complete hierarchy of control centers and agents and informers, nothing less than a vast criminal organization operating throughout the Balkans, its scheming employees chosen by Nubar solely for their abilities in intrigue and intimidation, burglary and embezzlement.

This had been necessary because the works Nubar now sought were either so rare or so treasured by their owners no amount of money could buy them. They could only be extorted from their owners, or failing that, stolen.

Thus for the last six years, since the closing days of 1921, Nubar had been regularly receiving secret reports in his Albanian headquarters, the tower room of the ancestral Wallenstein castle. These reports he studied suspiciously before issuing the daily directives to his agents that would eventually lead to another illegal acquisition, by blackmail or bludgeoning, from a monastery in Macedonia or a bookdealer in Bulgaria, or perhaps from a private library in Transylvania.

Celsus Heimbomb von Bastus.

When Nubar had founded his criminal organization in 1921, he had decided to name it the Uranist Intelligence Agency, because it pleased him to associate himself with the Greek sky-god Uranus, the personification of heaven and the first ruler of the universe, and the father as well of those deformed creatures of old, the cyclops and the furies.

Hulking mindless shepherds with their single round eyes fixated on the hindquarters of retreating sheep? Frenzied raving women so grotesque they had snakes for hair?

Yes, the images pleased Nubar. Their implications were close to his heart, and thus he had chosen Uranus for the name of his secret network.

And also because he knew that if any planet guided his destiny it would have to be Uranus, remote and mysterious, its true nature unknown, its astrological sign a variation of the male symbol, twisted, punctuated with a black hole.

Paraho von Bomb von Heim. Eternal Bombastus.

Since the agents of the UIA came from the most disreputable elements in the Balkans, it was inevitable they couldn't all be professional criminals. Naturally there were also clever charlatans lurking in the ranks, along with the outright quacks and impostors, unctuous fabricators whose only talents lay in inventing ever more intricate and fantastic schemes for squandering Nubar's money.

Nubar was aware of this. He knew perfectly well that his network had given rise to a whole new industry in the Balkans in the 1920s, the marketing of fake Paracelsus treatises and tracts by unscrupulous entrepreneurs who pretended they were selling him translations of original works that had been lost.

In order to mislead him these forgeries were often concocted in obscure languages such as Basque and Lettish, occasionally in dead local languages such as Old Church Slavonic, and at least once in a tongue so remote and archaic no one who ever spoke it could possibly have heard of Paracelsus, a ludicrous gibberish from central Asia known to scholars as Tokharian B.

Yet Nubar was so obsessed with Paracelsus he always paid in the end to have these outrageous forgeries checked by experts, this profitable sideline for academics being another whole industry he had created in the Balkans in the postwar period. For Nubar invariably preferred to waste money on a worthless sheaf of nonsense, no matter how illegible, rather than take the chance of letting one authentic remnant of the master slip by him.

Bombast Paraheim von Celsusho.

Nubar turned away from his workbench to gaze at the enormous sword that stood in the corner of his tower room, a replica of the one the great doctor had brought back with him from his mysterious travels in the Middle East, before he had gone to work in some Venetian mercury mines on the Dalmatian coast, exact location unspecified, perhaps not that far from the Wallenstein castle.

The great doctor had claimed the sword was given to him by a hangman. In its hollow pommel he had stored a supply of his wonder drug, laudanum, made from a recipe acquired in Constantinople. Laudanum had been Paracelsus' most valued treasure, and as a result he had never parted from his sword, not even in his sleep.

Nubar also kept laudanum in the hollow pommel of his sword and he also never slept without it, cold and hard and comforting as it was with him in bed at night.

Parabast Celsen von Heimbomb.

On his workbench lay several volumes of the master's *Philosophia Sagax,* and others of the *Arch-wisdom.* Nubar owned dozens of copies of both works and all the copies violently disagreed with one another. Paragraphs were misplaced or truncated, changing the meaning entirely. Formulae contradicted each other and proposals cancelled out each other. Whole pages were missing here, entire chapters added there. In short, a maze of discrepancies.

One problem was that the great doctor had never read anything he wrote, preferring to leave that task to others.

Then too, many of the works published under his name were transcripts of his lectures that had been recorded by dazed students, or dictations he had given to inept amanuenses, who hadn't been able to keep up with the master's brilliantly explosive diatribes. So scholars were in complete disagreement over which books should be recognized as genuine.

It was as if this great doctor of the soul, the magus, Faust, after penetrating all the mysteries, had thrown the ingredients of his knowledge into the air to let them reshape themselves in endless variations through the centuries, the indisputable truths he propounded forever as profuse and contradictory as life itself.

In addition, causing yet more confusion, were the code words.

Like all the alchemists of his era, the great Swiss master had disguised his discoveries by using metaphors to describe his successful methods for transforming base metals into gold. Thus *soul* and *chaos* could also mean *gold*. And *chaos* might mean *essence* or *gas*. As *sulphur* might mean *gas*. Or *chaos* used to indicate a certain element he didn't wish to name at the moment. While *mercury* was the first heaven of the metaphysical heavens to come.

Heimbomb Celsushohen von Para.

Discrepancies, clues, cryptology.

Omitted references in the sixteenth century.

Incomprehensible additions and deletions made by dazed scribes suffering from poor candlelight, weak from unbalanced diets, given to sudden attacks of vertigo as they struggled through the night with pen and paper in vaulted medieval laboratories, hopelessly trying to record the great doctor's mutterings, his whispered arcane wisdom that rose with the fumes spiraling up from his vast array of pelicans and alembics, crucibles and athanors.

Dizzy scribes numbly scribbling in the smoke as the great doctor now loomed up in the shadows, now shrank back in the shadows, now disappeared altogether in the darkness behind his workbench, mumbling as he sank out of sight, only to rear up a minute later in the haze in front of his workbench, bellowing out eternal formulae and startling truths that had never been heard anywhere before that moment. While all the time explaining the secrets of Mercury, both the god of knowledge and of the marketplace, and mercury the cure for syphilis and mercury the mother of metals, to be purified before long up through the seven stages to the gold of the seventh heaven. Gas and chaos and soul.

Gas, the magus. Chaos, the soul. Faust in the fumes peering into his pelicans and alembics, igniting ever new secret solutions in the crucibles and athanors of time.

Hohenbastus von Heim von Ho.

The gas erupted inside Nubar with a roar. A powerful fart lifted him off his chair. He belched loudly, painfully, and fell back in his chair to quiver through the diminishing explosions of thumping farts and fiery belches that were racing from his stomach in all directions, unloading his gas into the air.

Mercury poisoning, and merely one of its symptoms, the result of his chronic alchemical experiments with that metal. Certainly an excessive inhalation of mercury fumes over the years could be harmful, perhaps even dangerous. But Nubar accepted that possibility, knowing it was unavoidable when in pursuit of the great doctor's secrets.

Merely one of the symptoms, there were others. Gastrointestinal inflammation. Excessive saliva and excessive gas. Urinary complications. Tremors. Skin ulcers. Mental depression.

The master, chaos. The soul of secret fumes, a fart, gaseous gold, to be purified up to seventh heaven. Magus and mystery, in short.

Ho Parabastus von Heimenbomb.

After six years laboring in his tower room, Nubar sometimes gloomily wondered whether he would ever reach his goal. How could he acquire all the great doctor's works when scholars couldn't decide which were genuine? When forging the master had become an entire industry in the Balkans? When analyzing those forgeries had become another entire industry? Both of those industries aimed at Nubar, exclusively supported by him. Whole armies of quacks and scholars living off his obsession.

Sagax, for example. Which was the correct version? Was there a correct version or were they all equally correct? Equally incorrect?

A case of *Sagax* you are if you think you are? *Sagax* as you like it?

A pelican of tremors and gas and ulcers? An alembic mixing urinary complications with the soul? A crucible of excessive saliva? An athanor of chaos and mental depression? *Arch-wisdom* into infinity?

Nubar shook himself. *No.* He had to be careful, he was drifting again. Slipping into that vague state of confusion that often followed the sour belches and pungent farts produced by a sudden racking attack of mercury poisoning. He had to get back to work, there was still a great deal to be done before lunch. For a young man of twenty-one, the tasks he had set for himself were awesome.

Nubar sat up straight in his chair on that mild December day in 1927. He busied himself rearranging the papers on his workbench. A limp pamphlet bound in pale violet velour, small enough to fit inside a coat pocket and not be seen there by anyone, caught his eye. Not the great doctor, surely? He retrieved it from the pile of documents where it was hiding.

The Wandering Bulgar's Unofficial Guide to Boys' Orphanages in the Balkans, Illustrated, Complete With Diagrams of Fire Escapes and Suggested Cross-Country Itineraries. Anonymous, Mol, 1924.

Nubar smiled and stuffed the pamphlet into a drawer. He couldn't imagine why one of his UIA agents had seen fit to submit that very naughty guidebook as background material for an intelligence report. Nubar had read the report and it had seemed to have nothing to do with the pamphlet written by the wandering Bulgar. Had the agent made a mistake or was he making some sly comment about Nubar? Anyway, there would be time to study the diagrams of the fire escapes that evening while he was doing his mercury experiments. Now there was a more immediate problem.

For the third time that morning Nubar read through a perplexing document that had arrived just after breakfast, an appendix to the monthly summary of activities submitted by his control center in the Bulgarian seaport of Varna, which was responsible for monitoring all activities on the Black Sea.

The appendix was purported to be a verbatim record, taken down in shorthand, of a conversation between one of his Bulgarian agents and an underworld informer on the Adriatic island of Brač. The agent had gone to the island to investigate a rumor provided by a confidential source in Varna.

The rumor claimed that an unemployed Croatian peasant on the

Adriatic island of Krk, after stealing a well-worn manuscript from a tourist, had gone into hiding on Brač. The stolen manuscript was said to be Paracelsus' *Three Chapters on the French Disease*, dated 1529, which had appeared in Nuremberg in 1530.

The underworld informer said the Croatian peasant in Brač was drunk most of the time on slivovitz. Nevertheless, despite his drunken incoherency, he was still stubbornly insisting on a fee of three thousand Bulgarian leva just to let the manuscript be reviewed by an expert.

And the underworld informer, added the agent, although just as drunk as the peasant and also on slivovitz, was being just as stubborn, demanding a fee of three thousand Bulgarian leva for himself before he would reveal the peasant's hiding place in Brač, so the agent could contact the man directly.

The agent concluded by recommending payment of both sums, and his chief in Varna concurred. Routine permission to proceed was requested.

Routine?

Nubar snorted. Was there ever anything routine about a manuscript that just might possibly be a genuine Bombastus? In fact the longer Nubar considered the report the more suspicious he became.

Why hadn't this Adriatic information, for example, come from Belgrade Control? With the whole Black Sea to monitor, what was Varna Control doing conducting an operation all the way over on the other side of the Balkans?

More specifically, how competent was the agent's shorthand? As a Bulgarian, did he speak Croatian that well?

There were other seeming irregularities.

Could there really be any need for an underworld informer on an island as small as Brač? Could there even be any role for an underworld there?

Why was a peasant on Krk stealing well-worn manuscripts from tourists and then fleeing to Brač? How did he happen to be interested in learned sixteenth-century speculations, written in Latin, on the French disease? Would a drunken Croatian peasant know what the French disease was? Or did the peasant have the disease himself, and in that case was it so advanced his mind had already deteriorated to the point of insanity?

Would a tourist be likely to carry such a valuable document with him while taking a holiday on a tiny island like Krk?

Or to approach the problem differently, how did a confidential source in Bulgaria happen to be familiar with rumors on Brač? And how could an unemployed Croatian peasant from Krk, in the first place, afford to stay drunk on imported plum brandy in Brač, in the second place? The third place being reserved for the fact that the plum brandy everyone was drunk on, curiously enough, just happened to be Bulgarian.

And along that same line of reasoning, why was everybody involved in the case asking to be paid in Bulgarian leva when the two islands in question were both Yugoslavian? What was the matter with good Yugoslavian dinars?

Nubar sat very straight in his chair, his pencil poised, well aware of his role in history. The great doctor had cloaked his discoveries to confuse the unworthy, but Nubar intended to be worthy and he wouldn't be so easily fooled. Could anyone in Krk be trusted? Could anyone in Brač? What were his people over there on the Black Sea really up to with their routine requests to proceed in the Adriatic?

Krk-Brač. In short, what was the truth?

Nubar wrote down an extensive list of questions to be answered before any more money was spent on the Krk-Brač operation. Having done so, he felt much better. He left his workbench to go to the window for a breath of air.

In the distance lay the Adriatic. Nubar looked down on the valleys where peasants were farming the Wallenstein land, at the workers several hundred feet below who were clearing the castle moat so that it could be filled with water again, a little more than a century after his grandfather had disappeared in the Holy Land and caused the castle to fall into ruin.

It had been his idea and Sophia was enthusiastic, but he hadn't suggested it out of devotion to his grandfather's memory. Rather, having turned twenty-one and become legally a man, he wanted the added protection of the moat, a hygienic insulation between himself and the outside world.

As he leaned on the windowsill Nubar noticed that one of the stones in the sill had become loose. Abruptly his left eyelid drooped in excitement. He worked the stone free and leaned out the window with it, taking aim at a peasant laboring in the moat.

Down and away, down and down. The stone didn't hit the peasant on the head as he had hoped, it struck him on the shoulder. But from that height it was enough to knock the man down. There was a roar of pain far below, then one of anger. When last seen the man was scrambling out of the moat swinging a pickax, heading toward the workmen on top of the embankment.

Nubar giggled and pulled in his head.

Order. Alignment. Hygiene.

Nubar spent the rest of the morning straightening his bookshelves, nudging the books forward or backward so the bindings made a perfectly flat surface. To facilitate this daily task, tiny metal conductors had been inserted at the base of the bindings in all his books, the conductors resting on metal contacts in the shelves that led in series to a circuit breaker. Ceramic insulators had been installed at both ends of every shelf. Nubar only had to stretch an electric wire taut down the length of a shelf, and throw a switch, to know whether the alignment was perfect or not.

Buzz.

Nubar nudged the offending book into place and moved to the next shelf.

When he was a little boy he had liked to lean forward on the toilet bowl and peek through his legs to see what was happening. A brown round head appeared and slowly lengthened, longer and longer. He held his breath. *Plop.* Another. The little brown logs circled peacefully down there. He pulled the chain and waved as they spiraled away.

Good-bye, little friends.

When he was nine he had become fascinated with butterflies and wanted to learn how to embalm them. Sophia wrote to Venice and soon a slender young Italian lepidopterist arrived at the castle to assume his duties as Nubar's private embalming tutor. The Italian also taught him other things as Nubar, wide-eyed, bent over the trays of butterflies, his lips nestled between their richly colored spread wings.

On Sunday afternoons the Italian tutor took him to band concerts in towns on the Adriatic. Nubar sat sorely but happily on the hard wooden chairs, entranced by the uniforms, especially the conductor's with its cascading loops of gold braid.

Someday, he decided, he too would have a gorgeous uniform.

That winter he found himself attracted to one of the mechanics who maintained the automobiles at the castle, a hairy man who was always covered with grease. By then Nubar knew how to embalm butterflies so the Italian tutor was sent back to Venice. Throughout the chill rainy weather little Nubar's experiences in the grease pit of the garage, his hands pressed against the cold slimy walls for support as the hairy mechanic bucked and grunted behind him, were far more delirious than the languid summer encounters he had known with the slender young Italian over trays of butterflies.

By the end of the Great War, Nubar had grown into a small adolescent with an unusually large head, a narrow sunken chest and a prominent potbelly. His face was small and round and pinched, and his tiny weak eyes were very close together. He wore round glasses, wire-framed in gold, that seemed to push his eyes even closer together. Two of his front teeth were gold.

He had a small nose and a small mouth and lips so thin he couldn't make them whistle. He cultivated a short straight moustache and combed his straight black hair low over his forehead to hide his baldness, his hairline having already begun to recede by the time he was fifteen.

A mild December day in 1927, in the tower room of the ancestral Wallenstein castle.

Nubar finished putting his books in order with a frown on his face, having recalled the dream that was disturbing his sleep lately. In the dream he entered a restaurant carrying a baby and asked the chef to cook it rare. The chef, in a tall white hat, bowed respectfully while three young men sat at a table crunching chicken and grinning up at him with lascivious expressions, their hands and mouths dripping with grease. The unpleasant noise of the chicken bones cracking in their mouths woke him up and he found he had a painful need to urinate.

Mercury poisoning again?

Parabombheim von Ho von Celsus. Immortal Bombastus.

The gong sounded in the courtyard announcing lunch with Sophia. Nubar gathered up his queries on the Krk-Brač operation and started down the long winding stairway.

10

Sophia the Black Hand

She put her tiny right fist in the fragile porcelain cup of crude, wiggled it around and brought it out dripping. With a gesture of authority she flattened her hand in the very center of the map.

When Sophia entered the dining room the opening chords of Bach's Mass in B Minor boomed forth from the organ in the balcony at the far end of the room. That piece of music had been the favorite of her common-law husband, Nubar's grandfather, and Sophia always had it played during meals in the castle. Nubar kissed his grandmother lightly on the lips and went to his chair in the middle of the table. At the far end, nearer the organ and facing Sophia, the usual place had been set for his dead grandfather.

Sophia was then in her eighty-sixth year. She was dressed entirely in black as she had been for half a century, ever since the last of the Skanderbeg Wallensteins had ceased to recognize her upon the birth of their natural son, Catherine, Nubar's insane dead father. She wore a flat black hat and black gloves and a thin black veil, raised only at meals. But the firmness of her unlined face made her look much younger than she was.

Her stature gave the same impression. Sophia was a tiny woman who had shrunk with age, and who kept on shrinking, until now she was not much bigger than a large doll. In fact Nubar sometimes wondered what would happen to her if she lived another ten or fifteen years. At the rate she was disappearing, wouldn't she be the size of a baby by then?

Or was that the point. There was no denying Sophia's whimsical eccentricities. Having been grown up for decades, had she now decided to retrace the stages of her extraordinary life back to its origins?

In order to sit at the table, Sophia used a special high chair with a folding stepladder built into it. Except when eating she chain-smoked black Turkish cheroots through a hole in her veil, an extremely mild cigar made to order for her in Istanbul. Nubar's earliest memories were of a soft white face in black lace hovering over his cradle, a mixture of lavender scent and pungent cigar fumes suddenly engulfing him.

Then she had seemed large to Nubar, but of course he hadn't been aware that she was standing on a chair beside his cradle.

Once long ago when she had been rebuilding the Wallenstein fortune lost by his grandfather, and modestly saying very little as she did so, she had become known in the district as Sophia the Unspoken. The name had lingered into Nubar's youth, but now she was always referred to as Sophia *the Black Hand*.

Various explanations for the name existed. Among the local peasants it was assumed she was called this because she always wore black gloves. Farther afield in the Balkans it was suspected she must have played some decisive part in the Black Hand terrorist organization that had been active in Serbia before the war. While elsewhere in Europe the name was considered a natural epithet for someone whose manipulations in oil were vast and conclusive.

All of these explanations were true as far as they went. Sophia obviously did wear black gloves and she had assisted the Balkan nationalist movements before the war. And her influence in the Middle East had made her the single most powerful oil merchant in the world.

But none of these facts had given birth to her epithet, which had actually come from an unpublicized meeting that took place on a lemon barge in 1919, an event so ruthlessly suppressed only a few men in the world knew about it.

And with reason, they felt, since it proved that an international oil cartel of scandalous proportions did indeed exist in Europe after the First World War.

The steps that led to that highly secret meeting had begun a decade earlier. For three years after the death of her beloved husband in 1906, Sophia had remained in absolute seclusion in the castle caring for Nubar, who had been born prematurely the day after his grandfather died. But then the resilient powers of her forebears had reexerted themselves.

Although no one in the twentieth century suspected the truth, Sophia wasn't an Albanian but an Armenian, the descendent of a woman who had been brought to the castle two hundred years ago by an illiterate Wallenstein warrior serving in the forces of the Ottoman sultan. That Skanderbeg had helped crush an uprising in Armenia, and for his part in the brutal slaughter he was offered the pick of some captured prisoners. As would any of the Skanderbegs save for the last, he naturally chose only very young girls of eight or nine. With a half-dozen of these little girls roped behind his horse he began the journey back to Albania, looking forward to a lusty military holiday.

But that early Skanderbeg fared poorly. Before he reached the Black Sea a raiding party of Armenian patriots managed to free three of the girls. While waiting for a sailing vessel a fourth girl escaped in a rowboat, and the following night a fifth slipped away while he was getting drunk in order to rape her. Thus only Sophia's ancestress reached the castle in Albania, still a virgin because the Wallenstein warrior could only rape when thoroughly drunk, and he had been too afraid of losing the last of his spoils to drink on the latter part of the journey.

By the time he sighted his castle, that Wallenstein was desperate with craving. He locked the girl and himself in a tower room and emptied a flagon of arak in a frenzy.

After weeks of abstinence, the drink had an immediate effect. He was insensible and slobbering, the room a blur, his mind a cave of swirling bats. His left eyelid was drooping heavily and an unmistakable tightness was in his groin. On his hands and knees he groped his way ecstatically across the room toward the little girl cowering by a window.

The girl was frightened but not incapable of thought. She was ready to jump out the window, but first she wanted to see if she could take advantage of his drunkenness as others had done. In particular she noticed how the drooping left eyelid seemed to confuse his movements.

She therefore praised his magnificent virility. She said she had been waiting weeks for this moment and offered him another flagon of arak, hoping, she said, that this would double the time he spent on top of her. The Wallenstein warrior, laughing hysterically at his own prowess, staggered to his feet and drank off the arak.

His left eye snapped shut. He lunged and smashed into the wall, reeled backward blindly and went crashing through the window, landing on his face in the moat several hundred feet below, instantly dead in his sexual frustration.

The little Armenian girl was put to work in the castle stables until she was ten, old enough not to attract the attention of the next Skanderbeg. When she was fifteen she began to sneak down into the villages at night, determined to find an Armenian who could father a child for her and thereby keep alive her Armenian heritage in the barbaric foreign land where fate had brought her. Before long an itinerant Armenian rug dealer chanced to pass through the district and was happy to oblige her. A girl was born and fifteen years later another itinerant Armenian rug dealer spent a pleasurable week with another young Armenian woman in one of the villages.

Thus these mothers and daughters, while cleaning the Wallenstein stables, maintained their pure Armenian blood down to the middle of the nineteenth century, when Sophia broke the tradition by becoming the common-law wife of the last of the Skanderbegs, the forger of the Sinai Bible.

In 1909 Sophia ended her period of formal mourning and emerged from seclusion in the castle. Agriculture no longer interested her so she turned her attention to the problems of energy, opening several low-quality lignite mines on her estate. Then when the British navy switched from coal to oil in 1911, Sophia decided she should go to Constantinople and learn what little was known about oil in the Middle East. She studied diligently there and became convinced that oil could be found along the Tigris.

In 1914 she executed the second most brilliant maneuver of her career by putting together a syndicate, in Constantinople, of English oil companies and German banks to exploit the oil along the Tigris, obtaining a charter from the Ottoman government for that purpose.

As broker of the agreement, Sophia retained for herself a share of seven per cent of all future profits.

Because of the war the syndicate was inactive for the next five years. Then in 1919 Sophia convened the highly secret meeting of its members.

The English responded eagerly and so did the French, new partners in the syndicate, Sophia having cleverly transferred to them the shares formerly owned by the defeated Germans. England and France now administered the Middle East through various mandates. And the oil companies of the two countries, at her insistence, had successfully persuaded their governments that the syndicate's charter should apply not just to the Tigris valley, but to all the lands that had previously been a part of the Ottoman Empire.

The meeting was to be held on a barge in the middle of Lake Shkodër, on the Albanian-Yugoslav border, thereby allowing members to approach the meeting from different countries for added diplomatic security. Sophia herself spent the night before the meeting in the city of Shkodër.

So as not to arouse suspicion by her presence in the city, she had arranged to dine with the archbishop and formally announce her endowment of a chair of moral metaphysics at the Jesuit college there. But she retired from the banquet early, telling the archbishop that her kidney stones were bothering her.

Well before dawn a fishing boat, with rags tied around its oars, was carrying Sophia silently across the dark lake toward the barge.

The barge had formerly been used to transport lemons from the lake down to the Adriatic. Its old worn planks were deeply impregnated with a rich lemon smell, and in fact Sophia had sentimentally chosen the barge for that very reason.

For nearly seventy years she had treasured the smell of lemons above all others, ever since that distant afternoon in her youth when she and her Skanderbeg had wandered hand in hand through the lemon groves beneath his castle, smiling and laughing and finally sinking into the grass to become lovers, both of them knowing another for the first time in the heady perfume of that blossoming Mediterranean spring of long ago.

The exterior of the barge had been disguised with earth and bushes and vines to make it look like a small island, but inside it was nothing less than lavishly decorated. Magnificent Oriental rugs and tapestries abounded, giving the chamber an opulent Levantine atmosphere. Instead of a conference table there was a circle of thick satin pillows where the syndicate representatives could lounge comfortably while sipping cups of strong Turkish coffee. The soft flickering light cast by the tapers along the walls, together with the dishes of delicate incense and the sweet all-pervasive smell of lemon trees in bloom, added to the sense of Oriental ease.

Above the circle of pillows a small yet particularly splendid Oriental rug had been cleverly suspended on thin wires, the wires invisible in that dim light, which gave the impression that the rug was a flying carpet from one of the traditional Arab tales of romance. On this Sophia had positioned herself to meet her guests, standing on the flying carpet which had been raised to a height where she could greet the men eye to eye.

The English and French representatives began to arrive, dressed as gentlemen on a fishing holiday, rowed to the barge by Sophia's servants dressed as local fishermen. They presented their credentials to Sophia, who indicated the circle of pillows. When everyone was comfortably stretched out she sat down on her flying carpet and gave a short welcoming speech, emphasizing that the syndicate now owned all the oil reserves in the former Ottoman Empire. She then asked for presentations from the floor.

It was immediately apparent the other members of the syndicate had no idea what the boundaries of the former Ottoman Empire enclosed. Maps were spread out in the middle of the circle and consulted, but none of the maps agreed with one another. The extent of the former Ottoman Empire was utterly confused by its long history of decay.

An hour passed. The English representatives were still mumbling repetitiously, the French still jabbering passionately, but nothing had been jointly discerned. Throughout this time Sophia had remained absolutely silent, sitting on her flying carpet overhead, chain-smoking cheroots and watching the proceedings. At the end of an hour, however, she apparently said something in Tosk or Gheg to her servants, because the flying carpet suddenly began to move.

Everyone in the room stopped talking. The men lounging on the pillows watched in wonder as the flying carpet slowly descended into the middle of the circle, coming to rest a few inches above the floor,

Sophia sitting rigidly in her flat black hat and her black gloves, her thin black veil with the cheroot sticking through it. They could now see she was holding something in her left hand, what looked like an exquisite porcelain cup.

Sophia raised the cup in front of her and leaned out over the edge of the flying carpet. She studied the large map laid out on the floor and dipped her right forefinger into the cup. She touched the map.

The men gasped. A heavy black viscous substance spread where her finger had been. *Pure crude.*

Sophia nodded to herself and blew a smoke ring in the air. She had touched Constantinople, obliterating it with oil. Now the flying carpet moved gracefully around the circle, still hovering inches above the floor, and the steady black line traced by Sophia's finger began to lengthen.

From Constantinople she was floating with conviction down the coast of the Eastern Mediterranean.

The flying carpet paused. Sophia again dipped her finger in the milky white porcelain cup. The spellbound delegates leaned forward on their pillows, holding their breath, as Sophia arrived at the Red Sea and banked to the left, speeding east around the tip of the Arabian peninsula, heading now across the water toward the Persian Gulf, the line of crude advancing with her.

Their eyes narrowed. The flying carpet drifted over Ābādān and floated inexorably north in the direction of the Black Sea, the space enclosed by Sophia's black line gradually taking on the shape of an ellipse, an enormous area that would contain all the future oil-producing lands of the Middle East except for Persia.

A final dip in the cup of crude and the ellipse was closed. The line had returned to Constantinople, the former capital of the Ottoman Empire.

Sophia triumphantly raised her veil, the only time the men in the room would ever see her face. She was smiling happily and puffing her cheroot, but perhaps what they would all recall later was the dreamy quality of her eyes. It was true she looked no more than half her age, if that, which was astonishing in itself. But it was the softness of her eyes that held them, not at all what they would have expected at a time like this.

It was almost as if she had created the drama of this momentous occasion with the guileless simplicity of a child.

Yes, they were sure of it. *Innocence.* That's what they saw.

Sophia smiled shyly, then all at once her face was serious. Another command in Tosk or Gheg and the flying carpet floated to the middle of the circle above the map. She put her tiny right fist in the fragile porcelain cup of crude, wiggled it around and brought it out dripping. With a gesture of authority she flattened her hand in the very center of the map.

An unmistakable *black* handprint on the heart of the Middle East. Sophia blew a smoke ring. The men on the pillows gasped.

Now the flying carpet gently rose in the air, withdrawing to a position of height just outside the circle. After fixing each man in the room with her eyes, Sophia lowered her veil. She waved her cheroot commandingly and spoke in a quiet voice.

Yes, gentlemen, there you see it. This is the former Ottoman Empire for our purposes, and this is the area covered by our charter. We have the agreement of your governments and I now solemnly declare the syndicate in operation. You will return to your countries and issue the necessary orders. We begin digging, pumping and distributing at once.

Thus the most brilliant moment of her career. Speeding on an exquisite flying carpet, tiny Sophia the Unspoken had silently circled the entire Middle East in minutes and transformed herself into Sophia the Black Hand.

From an opulent Oriental chamber on a lemon-scented barge, a vast international cartel had been launched. And the tiny Armenian woman in black would thereafter be known, among the very few men in the shadowy upper reaches of power who were aware of her true role in the world, as the phenomenal *Madame Seven Per Cent* of the earth's richest oil fields.

Oil and immense wealth.

Yet within the tiny old woman there still lived a haunting innocence, as witnessed by others on the lemon-scented barge where she had once floated on a flying carpet, the innocent simplicity of an eight-year-old peasant girl who had found a broken man lying at the gate of a ruined castle, the last of the Skanderbeg Wallensteins home from his unparalleled ordeal in the Holy Land, and with the perfect faith of her years fallen in love with him forever.

Indeed, there were still mornings when Sophia rose long before dawn with a strange distant smile on her face, silently to descend the stairways of the castle to a small unused room in its foundations, a servants' kitchen where she had been born and lived in poverty with her mother during her first years, the room where the two of them had tenderly nursed the last of the Skanderbegs back to life on their bed of straw, while they slept on the stone floor.

Sophia had kept the room exactly as it had been then, with its bare walls and its little hearth, the one or two pots and the bed of straw, the broom by the door.

On those mornings she took the broom and proudly swept the floor of the little kitchen. Went down on her knees in her plain black dress and her flat black hat and her black gloves to scrub and scrub the worn stones. Chopped a few imaginary vegetables and kindled a meager imaginary fire, setting the pot to cook the morning meal for the lord of her ruined castle.

Later she drifted up to the courtyard to gather imaginary firewood and tend the imaginary garden where imaginary vegetables grew, down on her knees once more washing out imaginary rags and hanging them up to dry, humming Armenian nursery rhymes as she did the chores of her childhood.

It's on her, whispered the servants in awe, peeking out the windows.

Sophia had broken her hip and the bones had mended poorly, causing her to totter when she walked, bent forward from the waist with her hands groping in the air for balance. And on those special days the bent old woman wandering in the courtyard, so tiny and frail, seemed at any moment about to grasp some passing breeze that would lift her above the walls and the lemon groves on the soft sunlight of her memories.

It's on her, whispered the servants in awe, peeking out the windows to see whether their tiny mistress was still with them. Or whether she had already taken flight, and the strange distant smile of a child's dreams had finally found its way to heaven.

In the dining room Bach's Mass in B Minor progressed from a chanted solo to a choral response. Sophia accepted two lamb chops, waiting until the empty place at the far end of the table had been served before she picked up her fork. Nubar was already chewing a slice of brown bread and cutting up boiled vegetables.

I wish you'd have just one of these chops, she said gently, but Nubar ignored the comment. Vegetarianism was one of the important resolutions he had made on his twenty-first birthday.

I've come across a fascinating historical study, he said to change the subject.

Sophia sighed.

What is it this time?

It was written by a Scotsman. It's called, *Proofs of a Conspiracy Against All the Religions and Governments of Europe, carried on in the secret meetings of Freemasons, Illuminati, & Reading Societies.*

Sophia shook her head.

Really, Nubar, spare me. What is that supposed to mean?

Just what it says. It turns out, you see, that the Knights Templars weren't really exterminated in 1364 as everyone has always thought. They survived as a secret society dedicated to abolishing all monarchies and overthrowing the papacy in order to found a world republic under their control. From the beginning they were poisoning kings, slowly, so the kings would appear to be insane, as so many have. Then in the eighteenth century they captured control of the Freemasons. In 1763 they created a secret literary society ostensibly led by Voltaire and Condorcet and Diderot. But it wasn't really the Templars who were doing all this. *They* were behind it.

Plots? asked Sophia. Still more plots? Who were *they?*

The Jews of course.

Oh Nubar, spare me. Not that kind of nonsense.

But it's not nonsense, Bubba, it's fact. And it goes back much further than the Templars. I can prove it to you.

Now Sophia tried to change the subject.

What was in those crates the workmen were carrying up to your tower this morning?

Cinnabar, Bubba.

Cinnabar? *More* cinnabar? I thought there was a shipment just last week.

197

There was, but my experiments use up a great deal of mercury.

Tell me about the experiments. Are they interesting?

Yes, but another time. Have you ever heard of Mani or the Old Man of the Mountain? Or of Osman-Bey?

Sophia looked confused.

I'm not sure. Are they local people?

Not at all. Mani founded Manichaeism in Persia in the third century. The Old Man of the Mountain was supreme ruler of the Assassins, the Moslem sect that was also founded in Persia. Both men were Jews. As for Osman-Bey, he fearlessly exposed the Jewish plot to take over the world.

Oh Nubar. Why don't you try reading the Catholicos Narses IV instead of things like this? It's such gentle poetry. It would soothe your nerves.

And the founder of the Freemasons, continued Nubar excitedly, was also a Jew and so are many of the cardinals in Italy. They're hoping for a majority soon so they can elect a Jewish pope. Didn't you know the French Revolution was a Jewish-Masonic conspiracy?

That's ridiculous. And I thought you just said the Jews captured control of the Freemasons in the eighteenth century. Why would they have to do that if they'd already founded the Freemasons?

It's the same thing. The Jews made a secret pact with the Templars and then took them over, later they did it again with the Freemasons. The grand master of the Freemasons has always been a Jew and every Freemason must assassinate anyone the grand master orders him to, even a member of the inner council. You can't become a Freemason of the thirty-third degree unless you're a Jew. The symbols they use in their lodges are the snake and the phallus.

You ought to find a wife, Nubar.

Have you ever heard of Sir John Retcliffe?

No.

He was an Englishman who wrote an autobiographical novel called *Biarritz*. There's a chapter in it that describes the secret meetings held in a cemetery in Prague by twelve Jews, representing the twelve tribes. The novel has two versions. In the first version Sir John is the chief rabbi at a meeting in the cemetery in 1880, when he delivers a speech calling for world domination by the Jews. He wrote that to try to fool them but it didn't work, so then in the second version he told the truth. ·

What was the truth?

That he was an English diplomat, a Catholic, and that he might well have to pay with his life for revealing, fictionally, the Prague cemetery plot.

What happened to him?

He paid with his life.

Sophia shook her head.

Such lurid fantasies, Nubar. And you've never even known a Jew, have you?

No one who was openly a Jew or admitted to it. But I have my suspicions.

Oh dear, Nubar. I think it's time you took a vacation with the Melchitarists.

Nubar scowled. The Melchitarists were a monastic literary order of Catholic Armenians, formerly in Constantinople and now in Venice, who published works in Armenian. Sophia admired their combination of monastic piety and literature, perhaps because it reminded her of his grandfather's labor in the Holy Land, and whenever she thought Nubar was becoming overexcited she suggested he go off and visit the Melchitarists. They would have been more than happy to welcome him, Sophia being their chief financial benefactor. But he had no desire to vacation with monks in Venice or anywhere else.

I'll tell you one thing, he said. I'm never going to a city that has underground transportation tubes.

Why not?

Because that's the way the Jews plan to blow up cities when the time comes. They'll take over the subway trains and race around setting off bombs behind them.

Is that bread really good for you, Nubar?

Yes, it's a new kind of whole wheat.

Won't you have even a small glass of wine? It helps the digestion.

No thank you, Bubba. Teetotalism and vegetarianism must go together. Cleanliness within and without is of the utmost importance.

Ah, sighed Sophia, I just don't understand you. But then, I'm old and the world is full of riddles.

Nubar nodded enthusiastically. He leaned forward.

Seemingly insoluble riddles?

It would seem so. Digging for oil is so simple compared to understanding human beings.

Let me quote something to you, Bubba. *The whole truth is to be found in this formula, which provides the key to a host of disturbing and seemingly insoluble riddles.* What do you think of that?

I think it's nonsense. The whole truth can be found only in God, and He surpasses human understanding. What does the formula refer to, some Fascist or Marxist ideology?

But Nubar was suddenly evasive.

Not exactly, he said, and went on to ask a question about his grandfather, the spiritual presence at the end of the table whose plate of lamb chops was now being replaced by a bowl of fruit, a subject that was guaranteed to make Sophia forget everything else as she lapsed back over the decades.

Two weeks later on a dark stormy evening, Nubar sat hunched over the workbench in his tower room inhaling toxic mercury fumes, brooding, his mood one of rambling speculation. He had been conducting mercury experiments since the middle of the afternoon and by now his workbench was a complex jumble of pelicans and alembics, crucibles and athanors that seethed and gurgled and hissed and bubbled.

Nubar sniffed. He breathed deeply and coughed.

He was well aware that chronic mercury poisoning could produce a delirium akin to madness, but that in no way deterred him. The dangers inherent in his experiments were unavoidable.

Perhaps it must be repeated thousands of times, Paracelsus had written, in order to achieve the unique set of circumstances that produces the philosopher's stone of eternal life.

The philosopher's stone. Immortality. Had he at last found the way to achieve it? And all because of a bizarre report that had been smuggled out of a communal Polish farm in Palestine?

Nubar had come across the report on New Year's Day, after lunch. Normally he took a nap after lunch, and he always carried a handful of

UIA reports to bed with him to help him fall asleep. But there had been no nap that day. Instead he had found himself sitting up in bed reading and rereading an unusual report with a thoroughly odd title.

The Lost Greek and the Great Jerusalem Poker Game

The Greek in question, now lost, was named Odysseus and had been the chief of the UIA station in Ithaca. The previous autumn he had used his annual leave to go to Jerusalem, claiming he wished to make a pilgrimage to the holy sites. But then he had disappeared, simply dropped out of sight. Nothing had been heard from him or about him until this report, in a plain brown wrapper, had suddenly turned up one December morning in the office of the UIA chief of station in Salonika, apparently thrown over the transom by a person of unknown identity. The report was both a confession and a desperate plea for help.

The lost Greek began his report by admitting he hadn't gone to Jerusalem with any intention of visiting holy sites. He couldn't care less, he said, about holy sites there or elsewhere. His sole reason for the trip was to try to make a fortune in the Great Jerusalem Poker Game.

The *what?* wondered Nubar, never having heard of such a game. Intrigued, he read on.

The lost Greek had entered the game one afternoon with a substantial amount of money. By the end of the afternoon he was well ahead. However, he had made the mistake of drinking while he was playing, which tended to loosen his tongue even though he was normally a wily man with a reputation for shrewd and clever tactics. Overconfident and perhaps a little drunk, he began to brag about his prowess as a burglar and the easy targets to be found in Palestine. In particular he mentioned burglarizing something called a kibbutz on his way to Jerusalem. It had been a small dusty place, very poor. The farmers had been out in the fields and in a matter of minutes he had made away with all their valuables.

If you can call a suitcase of old cracked Polish clocks valuable, he had added with a laugh. That's all they had so I scooped them up.

Most of the players at the table laughed with him but several did not. The one who seemed least amused was a man named Szondi. What followed was a disaster for the lost Greek.

First he lost all the money he had with him to this man Szondi. That took only two hands. Then he lost the reserve he had hidden in his hotel room, in a single hand, with the best cards he had ever held in a poker game, along with the suitcase of worthless old Polish clocks and his shoes and socks. He wanted to leave for Ithaca then, even though it would have meant going barefoot, but he found he couldn't rise from the table.

As soon as the man named Szondi had started betting against him, it seemed, another player at the table had begun pressing a bottle of very old cognac on him. At least this other player, a carefree Irishman, implied it was cognac and the bottle certainly looked very old. The lost Greek had accepted the offer and drunk freely straight from the bottle, emptying it. The drink had seemed smooth enough when it was going down, but obviously the Irishman had tricked him. It turned out the bottle hadn't contained cognac at all but some kind of Irish home brew called poteen. All at once the lost Greek found he was paralyzed below the waist.

It can have such a temporary effect, noted the Irishman merrily, until you become used to it. Then it generally paralyzes from the neck up, rather than the waist down. Do you follow me?

The lost Greek had shaken his head. He knew now he wasn't following anyone anywhere, he was trapped at the table. The deal passed to a black man dressed in an Arab cloak and Arab headgear, a man who smiled broadly, his skin so black it was almost blue. The beaming black man dealt the cards quickly and the lost Greek went on losing to Szondi, who seemed especially adept at gambling commodity futures. The Greek lost the future olive-oil production of his family farm back in Ithaca over the next twenty years. He then lost the olive oil that would be produced by his brothers and uncles and cousins over the same period.

By now the lost Greek was weeping noisily. His family had no future in Greece, the next two decades had disappeared. He begged for mercy, wanting to do so on his knees but unable to move because of his temporary paralysis below the waist.

Finally Szondi made him an offer. They would play one last hand and if the lost Greek won, all his debts would be cancelled. But if he lost, he would have to do manual labor for an unspecified period of time at a place Szondi would designate.

The lost Greek had no choice, he knew that. He had to chance it. So the hand was played and the lost Greek lost.

The designated place for manual labor turned out to be the dusty poor Polish kibbutz where Odysseus had stolen his load of worthless old cracked Polish clocks. He had been laboring there ever since in the fields, in the hot sun, and it might go on forever unless a ransom were paid.

Despite his exhaustion at the end of the day, he had written the report bit by bit by candlelight over the weeks, under a blanket at night, all the while being eaten alive by mosquitoes. Early in December he had managed to persuade someone to smuggle the report out of the country and throw it over the transom of the UIA chief in Salonika.

The report had been written in pencil, and not a very good pencil at that. Nubar noticed there were water stains around the signature, probably tears.

> *Your most loyal employee in the UIA*
> *And your former chief in Ithaca,*
> *Now somewhere in Palestine farming with*
> *Poles in the dust,*
>
> Odysseus
> *The Lost Greek*

Beneath that the chief of station in Salonika had typed a few questions asking for guidance.

> *Ransom acceptable? How high do we go?*

Nubar had snorted and fired off a cable immediately.

ARE YOU MAD? NO RANSOM OF ANY KIND FOR THE LOST GREEK. WHO NEEDS A LOST GREEK? AND WHERE DID THIS FOOL EVER GET A REPUTATION FOR BEING WILY, LET ALONE SHREWD WITH HIS TONGUE OR CLEVER WITH HIS TACTICS? HIS OWN FAULT ENTIRELY, FORGET HIM.

At the time, on New Year's Day, Nubar hadn't been exactly sure why
he had reacted so quickly to the report. But something had been
working at the back of his mind, something having to do with
Jerusalem and the Holy Land.

The answer to his cable had finally arrived that morning, a thick
folder of briefing material, and Nubar found the information in it
shocking.

The game, it seemed, was notorious throughout the Middle East.
Anyone who hadn't been in it at one time or another had at least heard
of it and wanted to be in it. And its reputation had spread far beyond
the Levant, witness the lost Greek's eagerness to go there to try to win
his fortune. The game had already been going for six full years, in fact it
had just entered its seventh year with no end in sight. The money
changing hands was incalculable.

Three men had founded the game and were its only permanent
members, all mentioned in the lost Greek's report.

Szondi, the defender of old Polish clocks that belonged to poor
kibbutz farmers, was a dedicated Zionist. And as a Zionist, quite
naturally, he traded in futures, as noted by the lost Greek, since there
was no Jewish homeland at present. His first name was Munk, perhaps
because he liked to think of himself as the monk of the coming Jewish
revolution.

The Irishman, who merrily offered paralyzing drinks from antique
cognac bottles, was one O'Sullivan Beare. He had made a fortune selling
spurious Christian artifacts that were undeniably phallic in shape. And
he was still selling them, claiming they were blessed by an ecclesiastic,
obviously fictional, known as the baking priest.

The beaming black Arab, actually a Sudanese, had the unlikely name
of Cairo Martyr. He was also making a fortune on the side by selling
pharaonic mummy dust and mummy mastic, renowned in the Levant
as aphrodisiacs and euphoric agents.

As for the grandiloquent name of the game, that came from the fact
that the ultimate prize at stake was nothing less than complete
clandestine control of Jerusalem. That was the goal sought by each of

the three founding members, and of course by anyone who challenged them, whether the challenger realized it or not.

Nubar was stunned.

Complete clandestine control of Jerusalem?

Now he understood why the lost Greek's report had immediately caught his attention. Jerusalem was where his grandfather had buried the original Sinai Bible after producing his forgery of it. The real original was still there and he, Nubar, was its rightful owner.

Jerusalem, the Holy City. The *eternal* city. Could it be, then, that the Sinai Bible was the philosopher's stone he was seeking? Containing all the ancient eternal truths, the one sure way to immortality?

Was it time to put aside the gaseous, chaotic mercury experiments of his youth and boldly take what belonged to him?

Nubar was beginning to think so. He was ready to make a momentous decision. And that's why he felt that today, Epiphany, 1928, might well be the most important day of his life.

The pelicans and alembics on his workbench, the crucibles and athanors, seethed and gurgled and hissed and bubbled as he hunched over them, engulfed in their mercury fumes. Midnight was near. Around his tower the storm raged. The moment had come for the third eye of occultism to see the unseeable in the darkness.

Nubar took the small sphere of polished obsidian from its hiding place in his workbench. Attached to the sphere was a loop of nearly invisible gold thread. He smiled at the black volcanic glass and rubbed it against the side of his nose, the oils of his skin bringing it to a high luster.

He placed the gold thread around the top of his head so that the obsidian sphere hung in the middle of his forehead, his third eye. Now he possessed supernatural powers of perception.

The power to sum it all up. To consider the totality of the universe and make his decision.

Nubar mixed mercury, heated mercury, mechanically repeating the master alchemist's instructions. He lowered his head into the fumes as his mind wandered through the stormy night from plots and stratagems to the possibility of joining Paracelsus in an exclusive society of immortals, to Zog, to the Black Book, to the muscular stable boy with curly hair, to teetotalism, the Protocols, a primitive volcanic eye.

To vegetables and black glass and a dark cemetery in Prague, to the Theban Sacred Band and the original Bible discovered by his grandfather in the Sinai, to the moat around the castle and hygiene in general.

The Uranist Intelligence Agency and whole-wheat bread and Krk-Brač, *the whole truth* and the Great Jerusalem Poker Game, the Assassins and subterranean trains and the Old Man of the Mountain.

Black glass, primitive volcanic eyes. A third eye, bombs.

The Black Book. Said to have been compiled by the German secret service before the war. Said to contain the names of forty-seven thousand English homosexuals in high places, both male and female. Entrusted to the care of Prince William of Wied when he came to Albania in 1914 to serve briefly as king. Who had the Black Book now? Could it be bought or stolen? Did Zog know where it was?

Zog. Born Ahmed Zogu of the Zogolli clan of the Mati district. Dictator of Albania for the last three years and soon to crown himself King Zog I. Sophia had worked for the liberal leader, Bishop Fan Noli, but Nubar had backed the cause of the reactionary Zog. What rewards would be his after Zog's coronation?

The Uranist Intelligence Agency. His own private network of Paracelsus agents and informers, feared throughout the Balkans and perhaps beyond. Criminals of the highest caliber making up the largest private intelligence service in the world.

The Theban Sacred Band. Three hundred heroic young warriors of noble blood in ancient Thebes, bound together by oath in defense of their ideals and their city-state, an elite homosexual brotherhood that had lived and fought in mutual passion until slaughtered by Philip of Macedonia. Could the Band be reborn in Albania? Would that be the reward he requested from Zog?

The stable boy had rolled his eyes as he lit Nubar's cigarette, forbidden to Nubar according to one of the resolutions he had made on his twenty-first birthday. But Nubar had rapidly inhaled the cigarette anyway in the dizziness of the moment, in the shadows at the back of the stables where he had slipped down onto a pile of damp hay, a sudden weight on him and a fiery pain rushing up to cleanse his body.

Mercury fumes, chronic poisoning, delirium.

Using the crucibles on his workbench, Nubar mixed equal amounts of sulphur and lead and iron and arsenic, copper sulphate and mercury and opium. Equal amounts as he poured and mixed, as he drifted above his workbench through the stormy night numbly repeating the experiment again and again in search of the unique set of circumstances, in search of Paracelsus and his secret society of immortals.

While in a dark cemetery in Prague aging men with long thick noses bent over a little boy, holding him tightly and taunting him, their white beards matted and filthy, the Old Man of the Mountain slowly thrusting a dull rusted knife between the little boy's legs.

Nubar shuddered and found himself standing in front of a military formation, three hundred handsome young men at attention. They wore the helmets and swords and tunics of ancient Greece, identical in cut and color. Courageous invincible warriors waiting for him to address them, to lead them again into victorious battle as only he could do, their immortal commander Parastein von Ho von Heim, Celsus of Bombastus, the incomparable von Wallenbomb.

The handsome young warriors cheered him, holding up their clenched fists in salute. Nubar nodded solemnly and waved for silence. With a flourish he slipped his right hand around his right buttock. The lines and ranks watched him breathlessly.

Wild cheering erupted. Nubar grinned and nodded. For a moment he was able to thrust his whole fist in up to the wrist. The massed young warriors were screaming ecstatically. The muscular stable boy knelt beside him, waiting with bowed head. Nubar carefully wiped his fist on the boy's curly hair.

Whole-wheat bread and vegetables, curly hair and bombs.

Fumes. More mercury fumes and a moat, hygiene in general and the Assassins and subterranean passages. Brač. A dull rusted knife. Explosions.

And across the sea a poker game being played by three ruthless criminals for control of Jerusalem. The Sinai Bible discovered by his grandfather, still buried in Jerusalem, now rightfully his.

The original Bible, the philosopher's stone, and a secret society in Jerusalem plotting against him to get it. A secret triad of players trying to steal what was his.

Through his third eye Nubar saw it all clearly, through his obsidian eye of primitive glass. Nothing could escape his black volcanic eye on that dark stormy night of Epiphany.

Nubar fell forward. His head struck the boards of the workbench and rested there, his poisoned delirious brain adrift in visions of immortality and the Sinai Bible.

The next evening when they sat at dinner, the Mass in B Minor booming forth from the organ, Nubar was unusually subdued.

I've had a few things checked into, said Sophia. I thought you might be interested in the facts that turned up.

What facts, Bubba?

For one, the English diplomat and autobiographical novelist known as Sir John Retcliffe. His real name was Hermann Goedsche, a former German postal clerk. He later admitted *Biarritz* was a total fabrication, including of course the chapter set in Prague.

Nubar smiled faintly.

What about Osman-Bey?

An even worse fake. He also used the name Kibridli-Zade, but his real name was Millinger, a crook of Jewish origins from Serbia. He wrote in German and published in Switzerland, peddling his anti-Semitic works door to door from Constantinople to Athens. He was expelled from every country he ever entered for every kind of swindle, always on the move and always being arrested. His career began in 1879 with his expulsion from Venice, and ended with his death in 1898. The Russian secret police sent him to Paris with four hundred rubles to uncover evidence of a Jewish plot to take over the world. He used the money to manufacture *World Conquest by the Jews* and have it published.

Ritual murder of Christian boys by rabbis? murmured Nubar vaguely.

The most recent documentation of that comes from a Roman

Catholic priest of Polish extraction who was defrocked for a variety of offenses, ranging from embezzlement to rape. In 1876 he wrote a book on the subject, then made an offer to some leaders of Russian Jewry to publish a refutation of his own book if they paid him. He also offered to lecture against his book if they paid him a little more. Don't you understand what kind of company you're keeping, Nubar?

The whole truth is to be found in this formula, murmured Nubar, *which provides the key to a host of disturbing and seemingly insoluble riddles.*

I know. The line refers to the Protocols of the Elders of Zion and was written in Paris by one Rachkovsky, head of the Okhrana outside of Russia. He spent his time writing attacks on everyone and then answering his own attacks, all under the names of real people. He also had the habit of fabricating nonexistent organizations, issuing pamphlets under their names and then refuting those same pamphlets, using the names of other nonexistent organizations. And so on endlessly. Can't you really see what this kind of thing leads to?

Nubar murmured that he would reconsider his theories of historical conspiracy, but actually he no longer cared much about them. It was the Great Jerusalem Poker Game that now obsessed him, the secret reasons for the game and especially the three evil criminals who had founded it and were now trying to deny him immortality by keeping him from the philosopher's stone, which lay hidden somewhere in the Old City where his grandfather had buried it.

Sophia placed a thin volume of poetry by the Catholicos Narses IV, a twelfth-century Armenian prelate, at his elbow.

Just read a little, Nubar. It will soothe your nerves.

Nubar nodded.

And promise me you'll at least consider a vacation with the Melchitarists in Venice in the not too distant future. I know you'd find it restful.

I promise, Bubba, he said, already immersed in the details of shifting the operations of the UIA from the Balkans to the Middle East.

11

Gronk

To counteract the chaos of eternity
there, utter order here.

T he task Nubar had set for the UIA was to uncover every particle
of information related in any way to the Great Jerusalem Poker
Game. Once armed with that knowledge, he would then move to
destroy the game and ruin its three criminal founders. And with that
accomplished he would at last be able to seize clandestine control of the
Holy City himself, resurrect the Sinai Bible that had been buried there
by his grandfather and use it as the philosopher's stone that would
guarantee him immortality.

The first step, relocating the UIA in the Middle East, turned out to
be surprisingly easy. In fact Nubar's network functioned far more
effectively in the bazaars of the Levant than it ever had in the
bookstores of Bulgaria and the private libraries of Transylvania. His
agents began collecting information on the poker game in Jerusalem
with an enthusiasm they had never shown when dealing with
Paracelsus and alchemical mysteries.

One of the most disturbing facts they uncovered initially concerned the sundial that hung by the door in the vault where the game was being played. In the nineteenth century, according to information collected by his agents, this monstrously heavy bronze piece had been a portable sundial, the property of a fabled English explorer named Strongbow who was said to have been the secret owner of the Ottoman Empire at the end of the century.

That immediately struck Nubar as important. So too the fact that this sundial had chimes attached to it that sounded erratically, belying any orderly concept of time and thoroughly disorienting visitors to the game. But not, apparently, confusing the three founders of the game. On the contrary, they obviously thrived in the chaotic atmosphere caused by this unnatural timepiece.

What was the connection then? Was it possible his three enemies were using this strange sundial to try to negate time in order to recreate Strongbow's nineteenth-century empire? Secretly playing with time in the eternal city not just for control of Jerusalem, but with the aim of controlling the entire Middle East?

Oil. Not only were they trying to deny him immortality, they wanted all the money he was going to inherit as well. The cunning of those three men was appalling.

Nubar's eyes narrowed.

The poker game was even more dangerous than he had suspected. Never would he have imagined the conspiracy against him in the Holy City could be so vast.

The massive reports Nubar's agents sent to Albania proved to be stunning mixtures of hearsay and hints and shadowy allegations, each more improbable than the last. And even when hard factual evidence was available, it seemed to drift away almost at once and lose itself in the twisting alleys of Jerusalem with the ease of a Haj Harun, that unreal phantom figure who somehow embodied the spirit of the mountaintop, everybody's mythical Holy City.

Numbingly complex reports, and Nubar spent long days brooding over the confusion of the eternal city. In the beginning he toyed with the idea of making a journey there, in disguise, to assess the situation himself. If he did go to Jerusalem he might even enter the game one evening with some of his stronger agents along as bodyguards, cleverly passing himself off as deaf and dumb so as not to reveal anything he knew.

But no, thought Nubar. Not yet. It would be far too dangerous now to enter Jerusalem and confront the three vicious poker players, even in disguise and surrounded by bodyguards. Too much was at stake. The UIA had to complete its work before it would be safe to venture there. For the present it was necessary to remain hidden securely in his castle tower far away from Jerusalem, methodically perfecting his theories and carefully arranging thick sheaves of charts and numbers.

And perhaps not just for the present. Nubar was already beginning to sense that the myth of a Holy City might always remain as allusive as a butterfly in flight, forever defying order in its eternal quest. As a boy he had been fascinated by butterflies, but only when they were dead. Their erratic passages when they were free on the wind, colors suddenly flashing and just as quickly gone, had always disturbed him, and as a result he himself had never caught the butterflies that were to be embalmed for his collection. Servants had done that.

So perhaps even then Nubar suspected that he would never dare to go to Jerusalem and subject himself to the realities of that myth with its worn cobblestones beyond time, its massive walls that had drifted over the ages sheltering hope and safeguarding in their shadows the cherished water of sacred wells, the secret byways of faith and promise, a mountain of many dreams reared above the wastes by many peoples.

No, the implications of the myth were abhorrent to Nubar and the myth itself was intolerable, too mysterious and too intangible, too far beyond the control of any power on earth. So even in the beginning he sensed that he would never be able to deal with the city and its players except from afar, in order for the players to remain faceless and the myth remote, while the UIA served as his net for catching the changing colors of life. Butterflies, but only when embalmed for Nubar. Order and alignment and the safety of abstractions, the security of concepts, and as with butterflies, so too with Jerusalem.

Thus the bulky UIA reports arrived month after month, endlessly piling confusion upon confusion as his three distant enemies across the sea laughed and joked and dealt the cards that spun out their game over the years in the eternal city, as Nubar brooded over hearsay and hints and shadowy allegations in his castle tower in Albania, safe and far away as he wanted to be, as indeed he had to be so great was his fear of the conflicting clues of the Old City that rose above time and the desert, at home in his castle tower safely handling charts and numbers to his satisfaction, safely arranging concepts.

But at the same time finding it increasingly difficult to relax in the evening, unable to escape the contradictions in the reports he read during the day. To be able to do that Nubar decided he needed a practical diversion that would be the exact opposite of the chaotic poker game in the Holy Land, a diversion that would be wholly under his control. To counteract the chaos of eternity there, utter order here.

But what form should it take? Nubar's mind wandered and a number of boyhood memories nudged one another.

The Sunday afternoon band concerts he had gone to with his first lover. The uniforms worn by the band members, the far grander uniform worn by the conductor whom everyone watched and obeyed. Returning home at the end of the afternoon to nestle his lips in orderly trays of embalmed butterflies, his lover on duty behind him.

Band members. Embalmed butterflies in neat rows. Colors and uniforms, the conductor.

Nubar smiled. Of course. A private army.

An elite private corps devoted to pomp and regularity, to discipline, recruited by him and commanded by him and bound by the strictest oaths of obedience, to be ruled with an iron fist by Generalissimo Nubar Parastein von Ho von Heim, Celsus of Bombastus, the incomparable Field Marshal von Wallenbomb, Maximum Leader and Number One, future Supreme Commander of the *Albanian Sacred Band.*

Nubar lounged happily at his workbench far into the night playing with crayons. Nothing could have been more soothing to him than pondering the uniforms of his elite corps and musing over its ceremonies.

A code of conduct?

Naturally similar to that of the Theban Sacred Band, those noble warriors of ancient Greece with their traditions of honor and physical cleanliness, homosexuality and fanatical brotherhood. But couldn't he add to that a final irrevocable act of initiation? Something along the lines of the vicious crimes perfected by the Spartan aristocracy?

In ancient Sparta each young officer had been responsible for planning and committing an atrocity at the end of his military training, sneaking out at night alone to secretly massacre an entire Spartan peasant household as brutally as possible, this crime against his own people seen as proof that he was worthy of being a leader for his country in battle.

Probably out of the question in modern Albania, thought Nubar. But still, the idea of secret crimes binding his men together strongly appealed to him.

Uniforms?

Nubar spent more time designing them, coloring everything in with crayons, than he did on any other aspect of the future Albanian Sacred Band. After all, uniforms were vital. Nothing was more important for the pride and bearing of men, for the sense of honor his elite corps would feel. It took Nubar months but finally he developed a portfolio of crayoned sketches that satisfied him.

The black leather tunic was skin-tight with a high round black leather collar. The black leather pants were skin-tight. The black leather jackboots flared above the knee, and the black leather military cap rose high in front with a massive silver skull mounted over the visor. A black leather trenchcoat was to be worn at all times, indoors and out, as were black leather gloves long enough to reveal no flesh at the wrists.

An animal skin would be thrown over the right shoulder and gathered together by a silver skull on the left hip. The rank and file would wear leopard skins, the officers tiger, he himself, as king of the jungle, lion.

The belt of the trenchcoat would be a heavy silver chain. Hanging from it would be a large spiked mace and a rusty straight razor in a thick cylindrical black leather sheath, a leather blackjack, a black leather fist and a long black leather truncheon.

Loops of heavy silver chain would gird the chest between medals awarded for merit, the medals depicting stags and stallions and bulls, wolves and jackals and hyenas. A large silver skull would hang around the neck on a silver chain.

His own uniform would have gold everywhere instead of silver.

Ceremonies?

They would be held exclusively at night, by torchlight, his men facing him in perfect lines and ranks. The ceremonies would consist of him ranting at the top of his lungs, strutting back and forth, while the men listened. He would deliver interminable speeches detailing all his theories and concepts, talking as long as he liked about whatever he liked, while the massed corps remained rigidly at attention, expressionless, the slightest movement by anyone cause for immediate disgrace and expulsion. Then when it suited him he would distribute awards for obedience and give everyone minute instructions about what they were going to do next.

An elite private army. Spiked maces and skulls and truncheons, fists and black leather by torchlight, iron discipline.

Nubar completed his plan in his tower room late on a Sunday night. For the third time that evening he mixed equal amounts of sulphur and lead and iron and arsenic, copper sulphate and mercury and opium. Tomorrow he would have to return to the unsettling reports from Jerusalem, but now at least he was at peace with himself.

Nubar marched to the window and stood with his hands on his hips staring defiantly out at the darkness, at nothing, profoundly immersed in visions of order and obedience and deeply satisfied with himself, unaware that his old friend Mahmud would be responsible for both the initial success and the sordid destruction of the Albanian Sacred Band.

He had first met Mahmud when he was twelve and Mahmud a year older.

In the spring of that year Sophia had vacationed in Rhodes. One evening at sunset on the walls of the Crusader fortress there, Sophia had chanced to fall into conversation with another tourist, an elderly princess connected to the Afghan royal family. The two old women took an immediate liking to one another and retired to Sophia's hotel to dine. The princess was on her way to the Riviera but promised to stop in Albania on her return in September, bringing with her a young grandson as a playmate for Nubar.

When they arrived at the castle Nubar thought the Afghan prince looked much more than a year his senior. Mahmud was a head taller than he was, his voice had deepened and there was hair growing on his flabby chest. Nubar, still without body hair and speaking in a high squeaky voice, hid in the castle in embarrassment and refused to come out and play.

At the time Nubar was fascinated with bad Albanian poetry as a result of having met a man named Arnauti, a young French national of Albanian descent who had shown him a battered yellow volume of his poems while passing through the country on his way to Alexandria. The poems were grossly sentimental but they had beguiled Nubar and he was now writing poems himself, imitating Arnauti by cramming his verses with the names of rare minerals and semiprecious stones, a device Arnauti had developed to make commonplace colors seem exotic.

After hiding for several days Nubar finally agreed to show Mahmud his poems. Mahmud said he liked them very much. The boys began giggling and before long they were panting together on a couch, whispering lurid accounts of real and imagined experiences with animals and household objects and adult male servants.

Of all Mahmud's tales the one that intrigued Nubar the most was his account of an exclusive medical clinic outside of Kabul. Nubar had never been treated in a hospital and the descriptions of somber men in white coats, coming and going with strange instruments, fascinated him.

When he was eleven, it seemed, Mahmud had begun to manifest signs of a nervous disorder. He laughed hysterically at inappropriate moments and then broke into tears for no apparent reason. Afghan specialists were called in and diagnosed dementia praecox with possible overlays of adolescent catatonia. The psychiatric clinic on the outskirts of Kabul was recommended for intensive observation.

Mahmud spent the next year and a half at the clinic, which was situated in a pastoral setting that included brooks and ponds, sheep and goats and many wild flowers. Every morning the doctors treated him with hypnotism and every afternoon his mother faithfully visited him, to take him for a walk on the grounds of the clinic. But no progress was made. If anything Mahmud wept more violently and laughed more inappropriately.

One fine sunny day Mahmud had been out for the usual afternoon walk with his mother when a doctor had stumbled upon them behind a bush next to a bubbling brook. The doctor had suddenly begun shouting at his mother and angrily waving his arms.

What are you doing, woman? yelled the doctor.

Mahmud was lying on his back in the grass giggling inaudibly, gazing up at the rays of sun slanting through the bush while his kneeling mother performed fellatio on him. His mother, an unsophisticated Tadzhik woman whom his father had married for political reasons, raised her head in confusion and wiped her mouth.

But he began to cry, she said simply. I always do this when he cries. Look, now he's smiling again.

Which Mahmud was, although the vacant leer on his face dangerously resembled the demented grin of a congenital idiot. His mother was immediately hustled out of the clinic and told she could never return. Within a month Mahmud was pronounced cured and sent to the Riviera with relatives for a rest.

The Albanian sojourn of the Afghan princess and her grandson ended in late October. They left the castle to return to Afghanistan and there the elderly princess soon died from a concussion suffered when her horse went out of control on a cliff. Nubar wrote to his friend once or twice but Mahmud was too lazy to answer. So Nubar knew nothing of him until he turned up in Albania unexpectedly in the autumn of 1929, in disgrace, his furtive note to Nubar from a cheap hotel in Tiranë saying that he had just arrived in the country and was badly in need of help.

Nubar went to the shabby hotel in Tiranë and found his old friend stretched out on a filthy bed, dressed in the shapeless costume of a Turkish peasant. After a separation of ten years, they embraced with tears. Mahmud then produced a bottle of cheap mulberry raki from under the bed and went on to give an account of himself.

It seemed the coming world economic crisis had already been anticipated in the palaces of the Afghan royal family. Various speculative ventures were collapsing and Mahmud had been implicated in a plot to poison the minister of finance, his paternal uncle, with whom he had been maintaining a secret sexual relationship in order to gain access to economic information.

Mahmud had just managed to flee the country in disguise, traveling overland by way of Baku and Odessa, distributing heavy bribes along the way, his uncle's jewels and some other valuables he had stolen at the last moment. He still had a small income from a few holdings on the Riviera, but it was absolutely essential that he go into hiding in some obscure place until the scandal was forgotten at home. He felt there surely must be such a spot in a corner of Albania, and he asked his old friend's help in finding it.

Mahmud was equally frank about other things. In the last ten years he had become an alcoholic, he said, and having always had a low opinion of man's bestial nature, he was now slowly starving himself to death. He totally lacked the courage for a more abrupt departure, and besides, he quite enjoyed the routine he had set for himself. In fact he had adopted the Mediterranean habit of taking a siesta in order to have the pleasure of getting fully drunk twice a day.

His regimen was orderly. Upon awakening in the morning he drank several quarts of warm beer, in bed, to soothe his stomach. By the middle of the morning his stomach was sufficiently inactive for him to get out of bed and go to a café for mulberry raki, which he drank by the tumbler until noon while reading literary reviews. His intellectual work for the day thus accomplished, he went to a restaurant and ate one baked chicken wing with his fingers because his hands shook so badly a knife and fork made too much noise clattering around the plate.

After lunch he returned to the café and drank unwatered wine until he went to bed toward the end of the afternoon, reawakening around eight in the evening to repeat his earlier cycle, this time minus the literary reviews of course. His second performance ended in oblivion sometime after midnight, when by prearrangement a waiter carried him home and dumped him in bed.

And there you have it, said Mahmud with a smile, emptying the bottle of mulberry raki and going down under the bed to look for another.

Nubar listened to all this with sympathy and agreed to do whatever he could. Accordingly, the next morning, he donned his white duster and racing goggles and set off through the mountains in his Hispano-Suiza in search of an Albanian hideout for Mahmud.

He found it that very day but not in the mountains. After driving for several hours through one drab village after another, Nubar decided he needed some grilled crabs for lunch to buoy his spirits. He asked for the nearest fishing village and was given directions to a place called Gronk.

The olive groves gave way to orange trees as he dropped down out of the hills and sped along a flat sandy stretch of coast, a beautiful deserted beach that must have been five miles long. And then all at once he came around a headland and stopped the car in amazement.

Exquisite little Gronk. Why had he never heard of it before?

A Venetian wall around the village, a crumbling Venetian fort on the promontory. Minarets from the Turkish era rising beyond the small placid harbor, which was ringed by the stately stone arches of what had once been the high narrow houses of Venetian merchants, their walled courtyards set behind them for protection from the winter seas. Tiny alleys wound around and around back there away from the harbor, the overhanging upper stories nearly obscuring the sky.

A brilliant autumn day, the blue water sparkling, the brightly painted fishing boats rocking gently by the quay where a few old fishermen mended nets or rinsed sea urchins and pounded small octopuses on the rocks. There was only one café-restaurant on the harbor, a large simple place with its tables set out by the water, a huge stove at the back and arches inside that showed it had been a boat-builder's shop under the Venetians. In the stillness of the little harbor Nubar ate and drank, warmed by a sun casting soft russet colors over the worn stones of the old Venetian houses.

After lunch he talked with the couple who ran the café. They said the only people who ever visited Gronk were the peasants from the surrounding farmlands bringing in their produce. Other than that men fished and grew oranges, women cared for children and chickens and it was a forgotten corner of the Mediterranean with Venetian and Turkish memories. Half of the houses on the harbor were empty and could be bought for next to nothing if anyone wanted to buy one, which no one ever did.

Nubar was excited and returned at once to Mahmud to describe the beauties of little Gronk. Mahmud liked what he heard but he also had practical questions.

Of course, Nubar assured him, the café would serve him a single baked chicken wing twice a day. And it was well supplied with beer and mulberry raki and wine, and the large stove inside would be warm and cheery during the winter months of rain, the tables by the water lovely the rest of the year. Here Mahmud could happily spend his waking hours following his usual routine. Nubar had already talked to the café owner and he had agreed, in exchange for the steady patronage of a foreign resident, to carry Mahmud back to his house every night and put him in bed.

Mahmud became enthusiastic. They returned to Gronk together and Mahmud bought one of the Venetian villas on the harbor and set about having it repaired. At the pleasant café beside the water that was now his headquarters, Mahmud was also enthusiastic about the idea of an Albanian Sacred Band, when Nubar explained it to him.

But I have a few suggestions, said Mahmud, flashing a swift toothy grin and pouring more wine as their first afternoon in the Café Crabs swirled drunkenly on toward evening.

For one, Mahmud thought the uniforms of the Supreme Field Marshal Generalissimo and his deputy, Nubar's and his own, would be more impressive if the skull hanging from the neck were discarded in favor of a large ivory mask that would fit over the entire head, making their heads look like skeletons' skulls.

Yes, Nubar? A grinning death's-head in cold carved ivory?

Nubar nodded eagerly.

And for another, said Mahmud, refilling his glass, shouldn't we change the name of our elite corps to the Albanian-Afghan Sacred Band, thereby suggesting an international brotherhood reaching far beyond the confines of Gronk? Indeed, one that goes so far as to embrace the outer limits of the empire created by Alexander the Great?

Nubar nodded dizzily.

As for the secret crimes Nubar wanted committed as final acts of initiation, Mahmud agreed that full-scale Spartan atrocities were simply no longer feasible.

220

No, Nubar, times do change and we can't kill any children, he said, brushing away an imaginary bat that was nibbling at his ear. But what a noble vision you've had, resurrecting ancient Greece like this in all its glory and even improving upon it. The truth is you must be a mad genius. I've always suspected it and now I know it.

Nubar laughed.

I'm not mad, he said.

Mahmud downed another glass and brushed at his ear.

Do you see anything hovering above my shoulder?

No.

Odd. I could swear something's taking little bites at my ear, and yesterday it was the back of my head. Anyway, you're going to order the masks and uniforms right away?

Of course, immediately.

Excellent, Nubar, uniforms ·are crucial. I've never known why exactly, but they are. I've never felt really comfortable except when I'm wearing a uniform or someone else's clothes. Do you know what I mean?

Nubar nodded, Mahmud smiled, and thus as the world sank into the ruinous despair of the Great Depression which would give rise to so many historical extremes, an elite organization devoted to honor and physical cleanliness, homosexuality and fanatical brotherhood, was born in the autumn of 1929 over a daily regimen of beer and mulberry raki, single baked chicken wings and unwatered wine, and the rites and rituals of the Albanian-Afghan Sacred Band, to be known affectionately to its two founders as the *AA*, came into being beside the beautiful little harbor of Gronk.

Over the next three years during long lazy Mediterranean afternoons, from clear evenings listening to the cicadas down through the soft shadows of night to the brilliant still sunlight of morning, a vast succession of peasant boys passed through Mahmud's stately sixteenth-century Venetian villa on the harbor, being initiated into the wonders of the *AA*.

In order for darkness to be perpetual in the villa, shutters had been nailed closed over all the windows. Candlelight played on the pale violet drapes and on the soft low couches where the boys lay while Nubar and Mahmud reclined in their elaborate *AA* regalia, raising themselves languidly to sip mulberry raki and discourse on ancient Greece.

In practice the boys dressed up only once a year, on Easter at sundown, when the villa's locked closets were thrown open and uniforms and chains and leather fists and truncheons were distributed to everyone, the solemn oaths in the cellar then followed by a feast of lambs roasted over pits in the privacy of the walled courtyard, and thereafter by a long fiery night of drunken dancing in the villa, the anonymous black figures spinning from floor to floor and room to room in an unbroken chain.

But it was the summer scenes on the beaches outside of Gronk, the daring watermelon parties held by moonlight, that were perhaps the most delicious of all to the two founders of the *AA*. The parties began with a brief lecture by Nubar on some aspect of Greek philosophy while Mahmud hacked up the first watermelon and passed out the slices. But almost at once the two of them dropped out of sight among the boys and rich slippery sounds spilled over the sands as sticky fingers squeezed off seeds, sweet juicy pulp everywhere as more rinds were ripped open amidst the rhythmic munching of mouths and the rhythmic roll of the sea, eager eyes exploring the insatiable sources of blackness and the lapping waves stirring ever more quietly with the late hour, ever more softly, finally washing a summer night into oblivion.

For Nubar and Mahmud, delirious years on the timeless shores of Gronk. Watermelons and rituals and pleasures without end for the two friends in their lavish, ancient dream.

Until one winter morning a cleaning woman entered the stately Venetian villa on the harbor and found Mahmud's mutilated body in all its *AA* splendor, without a head, disfiguring the orderly lines of his bed.

The terrified woman's hysterical screams shook the little harbor as she came running out onto the street. When the police arrived they found a grinning ivory skull staring out from under the bed, with Mahmud's head inside it. They broke into the locked closets and discovered racks of black uniforms and heaps of *AA* medals. Huge *AA* banners were hung on the walls along with photographs of mass meetings by torchlight, long straight lines of rigid warriors, faceless, seen from the back, being harangued by a small strutting figure in black wearing a death's-head and gold chains and alternately waving truncheons and straight razors and black leather fists in the air, his identity hidden by his ivory mask.

The police went at once to the Café Crabs to learn what they could of Mahmud's last movements, but the moment they entered the café a stolid peasant boy, who was eating breakfast, came forward and confessed to the crime. The boy was led away. An investigation began.

Nubar, asleep in his castle tower room, was awakened by a telephone call as soon as the police left the Café Crabs. Fortunately Sophia was in Istanbul on a business trip so he didn't have to do any explaining. Immediately he cabled the Melchitarist monks in Venice, signing Sophia's name, saying that he was coming there to marry and that they should find him a suitable wife. Just before noon, after making several confidential calls to Tiranë, he boarded a chartered yacht for Venice.

By the time he arrived there the Melchitarists had found him a respectable young woman to marry from the Armenian community in Venice. The wedding ceremony was performed as soon as Nubar disembarked. That night, terrified by the events he had fled in Albania, he was somehow able to arouse himself briefly through fear, the only time he ever had in his life. The marriage was thus consummated and there could be no grounds for divorce later on charges of impotency, Nubar's lifelong affliction.

As it happened, he also impregnated his wife during that momentary encounter.

The investigation in Gronk was quickly concluded. From the beginning the Albanian authorities had been inclined to believe that a foreigner, and especially a prince from a country as barbaric as Afghanistan, was capable of the most unspeakable behavior. They were therefore more than ready to put most of the blame for the murder on the murdered man himself, the headless Mahmud.

The trial opened and the peasant boy explained that he had accidentally strangled Mahmud with one of the chains Mahmud was wearing around his neck. Unknown to the boy, the chain had become entwined around his foot while they were lying together on the bed. The moment he realized what had happened, said the boy, and that he would be blamed for Mahmud's death, an uncontrollable rage had seized him, directed toward that grotesque mask that was grinning up at him from between his legs, its frozen leer an unbearable mockery. In a frenzy he had rushed to the kitchen to find a cleaver to deal with the death's-head as it deserved. After he had done so, the head had apparently rolled off the bed and under the bed and, still grinning, come to the upright sitting position in which the police had found it.

Other citizens from Gronk then took the stand to descibe what they knew of Mahmud's activities and background, although no one could bring himself to utter the dead man's name. Instead, without exception, Mahmud was referred to as *that disgusting Afghan, that despicable Easterner,* or simply as *the filthy foreigner.*

And then all at once there was an immediate sensation in the courtroom when it was learned that *the filthy foreigner* had first arrived in Albania by way of Baku and Odessa, where he might well have acquired secret Bolshevik links, shocking information that somehow managed to emerge in the rambling testimonies of several illiterate Gronk fishermen, all of whom were retired and poor and elderly, but who had also been in the habit of loitering around the Café Crabs from time to time, hoping to receive a bone.

By the end of the afternoon the judge was convinced the extenuating circumstances in the case were many. *The filthy foreigner's* rank perversity had been more than made evident, as had the extreme provocation to violence that he had provided at the time of the crime by his ugly costume and uglier weapons, and especially by his abominable death's-head mask. The peasant boy was therefore sentenced to only twenty years in an agricultural prison where tomatoes were grown, each day of labor to serve as two days off his sentence, so that with good behavior he could be out in only six years.

But meanwhile, and more important for the nation, the entire contents of Mahmud's villa were to be sent under guard to Tiranë for inspection by higher authorities, possibly to include King Zog himself, to see whether the *AA* might indeed have been a cunningly disguised Bolshevik plot to invade the country and assassinate the king, after entry had been achieved by corrupting youths at a key point on the vulnerable Albanian coastline.

As soon as the trial was over Nubar received detailed reports in Venice on the proceedings. Sophia returned from Istanbul and wrote to him in amazement asking what he was suddenly doing in Italy. Nubar replied vaguely that he had felt the need for a vacation. Lately he had been working too hard on his mercury experiments, he said, and had decided to come to Venice for a rest, following Sophia's long-standing advice. The city enchanted him so much, he added, that he had bought a palazzo on the Grand Canal for other vacations in the future. Sophia, delighted that he was at last getting out of his tower room and into the world, immediately sent him a cable. Over the next few days there was a brief exchange.

WONDERFUL NEWS, NUBAR, I'M SO HAPPY FOR YOU. NOW TRY TO GET OUT AND ENJOY THE SIGHTS. DON'T SIT INSIDE YOUR PALAZZO ALL DAY BROODING, AND STAY AWAY FROM MERCURY FOR A WHILE. READ POETRY. IT WILL CLEAR YOUR MIND.

· · ·

MY MIND AND CONSCIENCE ARE PERFECTLY CLEAR, BUBBA. FURTHERMORE, I'M OUTSIDE A GREAT DEAL. I SPEND MANY HOURS IN THE PIAZZA IN FRONT OF SAN MARCO'S.

· · ·

LOVELY. NOTHING COULD BE BETTER FOR YOU. IT'S SO BEAUTIFUL THERE. DRINK PLENTY OF MINERAL WATER FOR YOUR GAS, GET A LOT OF SLEEP AND HAVE A GOOD TIME.

· · ·

THANKS. GAS UNDER CONTROL. HAVING WONDERFUL TIME IN THE MYSTERIOUS WINTER MISTS THAT CLOAK THE CITY. PERFECTLY ENCHANTING.

If only she knew, thought Nubar, setting out again in the cold fog at sundown, heading for San Marco's with his stack of thick journals, the rambling testimonials to himself that he spent all day, every day, writing.

The journals contained passages describing his sadness for the fate of the peasant boy convicted of murder in Gronk, who had originally been his lover, not Mahmud's, although no mention was made of that. But most of the pages were devoted to long incoherent attacks on every conceivable aspect of Mahmud's character and behavior.

In addition the journals contained lengthy spurious histories of the *AA*, which proved beyond any reasonable doubt that the organization had been founded and run solely by Mahmud, while he, Nubar, hadn't really known of its existence. In fact, he had never even suspected that it existed. He simply had no idea there could ever have been such a monstrous group as the *AA* operating secretly in sleepy little Gronk.

Furthermore, the correct name of that foul organization, spelled out in large letters at the top of every page in the journals so no one could mistake it, was the *All-Afghanistan Sacred Band,* proof of the utterly foreign nature of the conspiracy which had always been completely alien to the Albanian way of life and the Albanian national character, not to mention Albanian ideals and the Albanian work ethic, and in its lazy decadence, even contrary to Albanian efficiency. As Nubar made perfectly clear in the journals, the *AA* could only have been the product of *a filthy foreigner's* diseased and totally aberrant mind.

The entire affair, in short, was a frightening case of Afghan mountain madness let loose in a small, quiet, civilized, respectable, law-abiding Albanian fishing community.

And lastly, there were numerous eulogies to the Albanian prison system in the journals, particularly to its agricultural prisons, along with arguments that showed a few years in one of them, growing tomatoes, couldn't help but be a healthy experience for a peasant boy who had previously known only the confines of a small seaside village.

The Boy.

The letters appeared on the covers of each of Nubar's journals. All day long he scribbled illegibly in his journals, sipping mulberry raki to steady his nerves, then gathered up the journals at twilight and went off to San Marco's where he moved from café to café, accosting strangers to read to them passages aloud from the journals, or thrusting the journals into the hands of astonished tourists and trying to run away, so they would be trapped with them and perhaps read a page or two.

Spring passed into summer and summer into autumn. Sometime before the winter fogs descended once more, the Melchitarists informed him that his wife, who had deserted him on their wedding night upon seeing what kind of person he was, had given birth to a son in the Armenian community in Venice where she had returned to live. Nubar told them the boy was to be named Mecklenburg Wallenstein, an effort by Nubar to retain a small measure of self-respect by recalling past family glory, the uncle of the first Albanian Wallenstein having once been created the Duke of Mecklenburg by the Holy Roman Emperor for his extraordinary military services during the Thirty Years War.

But past glories couldn't relieve the restless despair Nubar now felt as he made his nightly rounds of the cafés in the piazza in front of San Marco's, hiding in archways until the waiters were looking the other way and then darting between the crowded tables, quickly squeezing along trying to distribute his journals, trying to make people see the truth, trying to get someone, anyone, to listen to his absolutely accurate account of past events in Gronk.

In *what?* asked a startled tourist.

Nubar thrust his journals forward.

Gronk, he raved. Are you mad? Are you deaf? *Gronk*, I said. *Gronk*.

By now even the most worldly tourists were thoroughly alarmed. Sticky pastries and cups of thick coffee came flying, the weapons at hand used by waiters and café patrons who were outraged by his skulking behavior around their tables, his furtive whispers as he sneaked up behind them and tried to drop one of his journals into their laps before they knew what was happening.

So the sticky pastries rained down on him, the cups of thick scalding coffee shot by his head and Nubar had to turn and run, crashing into walls in the darkness, in the eerie fog-bound emptiness of the huge deserted piazza where a distant footfall sounded as if it were right beside him, fleeing around and around through the night on the slippery cobblestones, lost in the mists and the drizzle of a Venetian winter, stumbling and falling and clutching to his chest the precious journals that were capable of explaining Gronk in its entirety, if only someone would read them, which no one ever would.

Just before dawn he collapsed in a gondola and ordered the gondolier to hurry down the Grand Canal so he could reach his palazzo before daylight came. Gliding over the water then with bits of stale pastry clinging to his face, his evening clothes muddied and his opera cloak ripped and his top hat newly dented, he lay in the bottom of the boat haggard and trembling and dizzy, sinking deeper into a stupor, dangerously weak because he now ate only a single baked chicken wing twice a day, a morbid compulsion toward self-starvation that had come to overwhelm him in the last year. And deliriously drunk as well from the mulberry raki he always carried to the piazza at night in a wooden canteen slung over his shoulder, another compulsion toward self-destruction that had come to overwhelm him in the last year.

But finally home. Nubar lurched for the landing and nearly missed it, lost a shoe and his top hat in the water, lost his opera cape on the landing, muttered incoherently as he staggered across the wet stones pulling off his clothes and disappeared at last, mostly naked, through the door of his elegant palazzo, there to hide until night came once more to cover his movements.

Thus lived Nubar in the closing days of 1933, a crazed phantom figure haunting the winter mists of Venice, never farther from the eternal city of his dreams. Yet soon now, very soon, to achieve his goal of immortality after reading the UIA's last staggering report on the Great Jerusalem Poker Game.

Part Four

12

Maud

*Afraid of Jerusalem, just imagine
it. Afraid of something, unlike
the rest of us.*

$\mathcal{N}$ot surprisingly, Maud's long friendship with Munk began in Smyrna. Many years later when she looked back on her four decades in the Eastern Mediterranean, it was one of the two cities that meant the most to her, Smyrna in her mind somehow embodying the secrets of profane love just as Jerusalem held the secrets of more sacred dreams.

In fact Maud lived only briefly in each of them, about half a year in Smyrna and a little more in Jerusalem. Yet so changeable was the flow of time for her in retrospect, reducing whole years to a few experiences dimly recollected, surging elsewhere to transform an afternoon or an evening into months of memories, that the importance of those two cities in her life far surpassed the actual decades spent in Athens and Istanbul and Cairo.

Jerusalem, because she met Joe there. Smyrna, because of Sivi and Theresa.

Munk she met in the one, but she always associated him with the other.

Smyrna, then, in 1921. Maud in flight from the little flowered house in Jericho that Joe had so lovingly found for her so she could escape the wintry blasts sweeping the heights above. The child she was awaiting had been conceived the previous spring in their first days and nights of love in a tiny oasis on the shores of the Gulf of Aqaba. One month of exquisite solitude in that tiny oasis, one boundless month in a world of fiery desert sunsets and star-filled darkness, of sun-soaked hours on the brilliant sands, lacing the Sinai and the blue cooling water in the fingers of their love.

Winter in another oasis after that, in flowering Jericho awaiting the birth of their child, Joe away most of the time smuggling arms because he could find no other way to make a living for them as a fugitive in Palestine, away because he had to be, yet Maud's old fears of being abandoned returning from her childhood, asking those terrible questions from childhood.

Why did everyone leave? Why did they go away?

As her card-playing father had done when he left the farm in Pennsylvania to go west. As her mother had done when she swallowed Paris green in despair, and when that failed went out to the barn and hanged herself at suppertime. As her Cheyenne grandmother had done behind the counter of the grimy saloon she ran in a Pennsylvania mining town, the old Indian woman hardly saying a word for days on end as little Maud learned arithmetic by adding up what the miners drank, hearing from them that her grandfather was a convicted murderer who had been sent away, never to return.

And then the dream of her youth, to become the best figure skater in the world, which she still might have become when she escaped to Europe at the age of sixteen as the youngest member of the Olympic skating team. But instead, being totally ignorant of men, she had made the disastrous romantic mistake of marrying a man she knew not at all, a man who lived in a seventeenth-century Albanian castle, the depraved Catherine Wallenstein.

Catherine raging insanely between the twin curses placed upon him by his father, the last of the Skanderbeg Wallensteins, who had come to think he was God and that his son was therefore Christ, who had named his son after the monastery in the Sinai where he had discovered the original Bible, twin unbearable burdens for Catherine Wallenstein, hopelessly lost as he staggered ever deeper into the symbols attributed to St Catherine, a sword and a crown and a wheel and a book, using a wheel to torture boys in the Albanian forests and a sword to kill them slowly as he bled from a crown of thorns and covered the book of his short violent life with sacrificial human skin, in savage madness reenacting on others the martyrdom of the historical Catherine and her mystical marriage to Christ.

Fated from the beginning, Catherine Wallenstein. Doomed by an intolerably pious act in the last century, his father's forgery of the original Bible, a stupendous task meant to bring order out of chaos and give grounds for faith where there were none.

Maud saved from him by the intercession of a mysterious old woman who had a strange hold over the castle, Sophia the Unspoken, at the time not known to be Catherine's mother, who helped Maud flee the castle in 1906 when her time was coming to give birth to Catherine's child, which Maud did prematurely in a peasant farmhouse, Catherine in pursuit with forty horsemen finding the farmhouse where she lay and slaughtering all the inhabitants before ordering some of his party to carry his newborn son back to the castle, Catherine himself galloping on ahead intending to murder Sophia, who instead at last brought an end to the curses on her son by striking him dead on the road in front of the castle. With her eyes, as she thought, and by making the sign of the cross.

Maud's Wallenstein son, Nubar, thus lost to her on the day of his birth. And seven years later in Athens an infant daughter dead while her second husband, the Greek patriot Yanni, was away fighting in one of his wars, Yanni himself dead in 1916 on the Macedonian front.

After four long years of sadness a dream in Jerusalem, where she met her magical Irishman just as he was emerging for the first time from Haj Harun's mysterious caverns of the past, Joe all whirling words and visions in the shadowy crypt of the Church of the Holy Sepulchre, Maud in wonder and silence slipping to her knees and performing a first wordless act of Communion there.

To be followed by beautiful Aqaba in the spring, the worn stones of Jerusalem in the summer and flowering Jericho in the autumn when the evenings were turning cold on the heights. And Joe away although he couldn't help it, and the terrible fear tormenting Maud as she gazed into the currents of the Jordan flowing near their little house, the muddy river of miracles by then reaching the end of its brief and steeply falling course from the rich slopes of Galilee down to the utter barrenness of the Dead Sea.

Fear that Joe would leave her. That this love would also go away. At her feet a rushing river and Joe too young to understand the terrified silences that gripped her that winter beside the Jordan, Maud unable to raise her eyes from the water and reach out and touch the man she loved.

So she had run away from the little house where Bernini was born toward the end of winter. She had left before Joe had even seen his son, not leaving a note behind for him because there was no way then that she could explain her dreaded memories of a barn in Pennsylvania and a castle in Albania, a daughter dying when Yanni was away at the front and Yanni's death, all those restless demons that had returned to shatter the dream of peace she thought she had found in the stillness of a crypt in Jerusalem.

Abandoning the little flowered house in desperation and going up to Galilee, where she rested until she could travel with Bernini. And then in April sadly journeying on to the only sanctuary she knew in the world, the lovely villa by the sea in Smyrna that was the home of Yanni's elderly half-brother, the elegant and kindly Sivi.

Sivi was then nearly seventy. He was unusually tall for a Greek, as Yanni had also been, both of them having inherited their large strong frames and deep blue eyes from their father, a famous leader of the Greek war for independence who had come from an isolated corner of Crete where the people were said to be direct descendants of the Dorians. The fierce old man had married twice late in life, fathering Sivi when he was in his fifties and Yanni when he was well over eighty.

So nearly thirty years had separated the half-brothers and much else as well, Yanni a warring patriot who had lived by the Cretan war cry against the Turks, freedom or death, Sivi a sophisticated arbiter of art and society at his famous teas in Smyrna, where everyone seemed to turn up sooner or later.

In the past year Maud had written Sivi only once, soon after returning from Aqaba, a short note saying she had fallen deeply in love in Jerusalem. But later when her fears had begun to paralyze her she hadn't dared to write. So Sivi had no way of knowing who was at the door on that April afternoon when he answered the bell and found her standing in the rain, thin and wasted with a baby in her arms, one battered suitcase at her feet.

Maud had memorized what she was going to say but the words left her the moment she saw Sivi suddenly towering above her. She couldn't speak. She broke into tears.

She didn't remember everything that happened after that. Sivi embraced her and swept her inside, delivered the baby into the care of his housekeeper and helped her upstairs, called Theresa, his French secretary, to draw a bath and provide new clothes, talking happily all the while in a warm excited voice as if the visit had been planned for months, as if the only misfortune on that dark April afternoon was that it had been raining when she arrived.

Later they sat with cognac in front of the fire, Sivi's deeply lined face all smiles as he wagged his massive head and chatted on about Smyrna and his recent adventures, never once mentioning Bernini or alluding to Maud's life during the last year, simply accepting her presence in his home and delving into ever more elaborate anecdotes to distract her.

Constantinople, 1899.

While Sivi was entertaining a young sailor in his hotel room the sailor's regular lover, a hulking customs inspector, had arrived and begun chopping down the door with an ax, shouting that he was going to kill Sivi. The only escape was the window and the door was giving way so fast there was no time to dress. With an open umbrella over his head to serve as a parachute, Sivi went sailing out the window in a long red nightshirt and nothing else, the hotel room having been cold enough to warrant a nightshirt no matter what activities were under way.

The nightshirt billowed up, revealing his nakedness to the pedestrians below. And what was worse, it made it impossible for him to see where he was going.

To not even know, intoned Sivi, gesturing extravagantly, what manner of grave I was going to fall into? A diabolical trick of fate.

As it happened he found himself landing on his bottom in a pool of water, raising a great spray, in the back of a madly careening water wagon driven by an Armenian whose horses had gone out of control, attacked by a yapping dog. As the customs inspector shook his ax from the hotel window the wagon thundered away up the street followed by the noisy dog, Sivi sitting up to his waist in the water and still holding his umbrella high, his nightshirt spread around him like a gigantic red water lily, smiling and nodding pleasantly at the astonished spectators on the sidewalks who had seen him come sailing out the window at precisely the right moment to make good his escape.

Or Salonika, 1879.

Being given to pranks in his youth, Sivi had not appeared in his box at the opera until just before the end of the first intermission, when he presented himself dressed in an enormous red hat spilling with roses, long red silk gloves and a flowing red gown complete with an impressive bustle, a fake ruby brooch of extraordinary size fitted into the cleavage of his chest.

Whispers were rampant through the tiers of the opera house but Sivi kept his eyes fixed on the stage, ignoring everyone, slowly stroking his thick moustache with a forefinger.

The curtain rose. Siegfried marched to the middle of the stage and spread his arms to proclaim a mighty deed, whereupon Sivi swept dramatically to his feet and thundered out the first bars of the solo in a basso profundo that not only shocked Siegfried into silence and stunned the audience but immediately brought the curtain crashing down.

And Alexandria and Rhodes and Rome, Venice and Cyprus and Florence, Sivi recounting tales from over the years to amuse her until Maud was laughing in spite of herself, whispering as he kissed her goodnight that this was expected to be an especially beautiful spring in Smyrna, his way of saying she was welcome to stay as long as she liked in his villa by the sea.

And later that night as she lay sleepless in bed, sobbing quietly in the darkness as the rain beat down on the house, she marveled anew at this gentle courtly man who had somehow come to accept everything in life, and everyone, without asking why it should be so.

At peace. She wondered if such serenity would ever be hers.

She met Munk for the first time in June and found him to be so close to Sivi as to be almost his adopted son, which surprised her initially because she herself had known Sivi so long and never heard him mention Munk. But then she remembered that had always been Sivi's way. So flagrant in his own behavior, he was yet extremely discreet when he came to others and never talked about one friend to another. And in the same manner, Munk was surprised to learn that Sivi had a sister-in-law.

And an American with beautiful green eyes at that, said Munk, taking Sivi's arm. Why didn't you ever tell me, you old sinner?

Sivi wagged his head and smiled wickedly.

Tell you? Why should I have told you? I didn't want to complicate your lives. A handsome young widow from the New World? An itinerant bachelor from Budapest? No, I would never take responsibility for initiating such an enterprise. Who knows what might come of it? But the truth is my closets are seething with relatives and friends neither of you have ever heard of. The condition is a common one as you'll come to understand when you get to be my age and have a long and varied background behind you. It's just extraordinary how events over the decades can multiply the people in your life. And even when you're just out for a stroll and strictly minding your own business. Come now, this way for tea. Young Munk is bursting to tell us something. The signs are unmistakable.

In fact Munk had come to Smyrna to tell Sivi of his recent conversion to Zionism, and he could talk of nothing else as they all sat together in the garden behind the villa that first afternoon, Sivi nodding paternally at Munk's enthusiasm over what would be done in Palestine, Sivi's secretary Theresa appearing indifferent. But by then Maud knew the young Frenchwoman well enough to understand her exaggerated calm.

When did they stop being lovers? she asked Sivi later, when the two of them were alone and he was preparing to go out for the evening. Sivi smiled happily and came back to sit down beside her, more than ready to tarry, as always, when the talk turned to love.

But my dear, he said, patting his closely cropped white hair, they still are lovers.

I don't think so. He may not know it yet, but she does.

You mean his new interest in politics, a homeland for his people and so forth?

Yes.

Sivi waved his hand majestically.

Nonsense. Passion in one sphere induces passion elsewhere. Our friend Munk has been looking for a cause for years, long before that stately old Empire of his began to crumble in the cold damp mists of central Europe. The blood of the great Johann Luigi Szondi flows in his veins, the indefatigable spirit of exploration, and now that Munk has found his cause on the shores of the Eastern Mediterranean, his flame will burn ever more brightly casting light in all corners. Love, in short. A lifetime to come exploring the landscape of love. The Mediterranean has him at last.

Sivi, you do carry on so. You should be back on the stage.

I don't recall ever having left it. Now, a wager of a drachma on the case in hand? I say the passion between the two of them will be greater, if anything. And you say it's already gone?

All right, a drachma.

Sivi suddenly leaned forward, his face serious. He put his hand on hers.

No, Maud, don't do that. Don't you see it's wrong? You must never do that, you can never be happy that way. Not even one drachma. Don't you see you're betting against love?

I suppose I am.

Then the bet is summarily withdrawn?

Yes.

Sivi smiled and squeezed her hand.

Excellent. The least we can do on these beautiful Aegean shores is honor our pagan gods, and there's never been any question they're on the side of love. Heavens, how they did carry on. Swans and bulls were no obstacle whatsoever. In comparison our very best efforts are meager indeed.

Your gods, Sivi. I don't know that they're mine.

Not so, my lady, simply not so. They belong to all who pause in this sunlight, and whether for a day or a lifetime is no matter. We have no control over it, you see. Summoned or not summoned, the gods are there.

Yours?

Heavens no, much too profound for me. The words of a revered counselor of antiquity, the Delphic oracle to be exact. Spoken to the Spartans when they were contemplating war against Athens. Well they made their war and they triumphed, but then the Thebans triumphed over them so where did it get them in the end? Ah yes, in the end. In the end we're all sodomites.

Maud laughed.

Sivi. That's awful.

Indeed it is. An atrocious pose to strike so early in the evening. But you do see my meaning? You see how impossible it is for us to escape love? Even when we turn our backs we're not safe.

Sivi, that's enough.

The old man wagged his head happily and got to his feet.

You're right of course. In the cafés of this city, where every sort of depraved creature dizzily nurtures his obsession, such mild remarks would go unnoticed. But here, it's true, we're standing beside a hearth in the presence of motherhood, while upstairs an innocent babe waits to be nursed. As for him, by the way, you've already decided it.

What?

His future, by naming him Bernini. With that name there's simply no chance the pagan gods will overlook him. Whether he likes it or not the sunshine of the Mediterranean will be his home and he is blessed with it, I predict it. Yes and now you're off to your maternal concerns on the second floor, and Munk and Theresa have left to relish the mysteries of the harbor by moonlight, and it's time for me to venture into the shadowy recesses of Smyrna to discover what spiritual nourishment this soothing June evening has in store for me. Shouldn't you be wishing me success? I'm not as young as I used to be.

Maud laughed. Sivi stroked his moustache in the doorway.

Well? Not even a wisp of a wish for success?

You don't need it, you old goat.

I don't? In the end? Hmmm. A felicitous turn of phrase. It suggests philosophical resignation. But naturally I've always been a stoic on top of everything else, although naturally I'm not always on top. Now if you chance to hear whispers in the early morning hours, don't be disturbed. It may well be some thoughtful young rogue in search of the wisdom of Smyrna's Zeno, who is rightly famed for living consistently with his nature in darkness as well as light. And the consistency of that nature? Undeviating. Without the confusion of mixed sexes. Addio then. Yet again Smyrna beckons, and who am I to resist love's caressing whispers? Addio, my lady Maud.

That summer Sivi planned to go to Crete to visit his father's village. He asked Maud to go with him but she refused, Yanni's birth there signifying to her all the pain of loss in life that she couldn't bring herself to accept.

Yanni himself had never told her the story. It was Sivi who did after his half-brother's death, when he was trying to help Maud understand why Yanni had lived the way he had.

Sivi's mother had died giving birth to him. A wealthy sister who lived in Smyrna offered to take the baby and raise Sivi as her own. Sivi's father, in despair over the loss of his wife, agreed to this and also decided to give up politics and return to the isolated village in Crete where he had been born.

He became a goatherd again, as he had been in his youth, spending six months of the year alone in the mountains with his flock, running his goats from dawn to darkness to find the meager feeding, in lonely solitude sleeping in one of the huts made of broad flat stones that had been up in those mountains for centuries withstanding the ferocious winds of the lunar landscape, never able to take off his boots or his coarse woolen garments in the frigid nights of those mountain summers, in darkness before the sun rose and again after it set, hurriedly eating his meals of goats'-milk yogurt and twice-baked bread, rock-hard until soaked in water, brought with him from his village in the spring.

Occasionally his keen eyes spied movement on a far slope and there would be a chance to call from peak to peak to other roaming goatherds. And since the distances were too great for words to carry, they didn't use words, rather a shouted singsong code that passed their messages through tone and cadence. As for talking to another man face to face, that opportunity seldom came until the snow began to block the passes in late October and it was time to descend to the villages and await the ebb of the melting snows in April.

Over a quarter of a century passed before Sivi's father, then eighty-four, took a second wife, a woman of nineteen from his village. She conceived and complications appeared toward the end of her pregnancy. In her eighth month the two of them set out across the mountains for the north coast, to the nearest town where a doctor could be found.

It was early October and snow flurries were already worrying the passes. It took them two days to reach the last northern ridge and see the Cretan sea opening up beneath them. That night she went into premature labor and by dawn the baby was breeched and suffocating.

They exchanged a few words, the old man who had lived a long full life and the young woman who was only beginning hers. The wrong one was being taken but there was nothing to be done.

He held her. They both made the sign of the cross. Then he placed a rock in each of her hands and a twisted root of wild thyme between her teeth and cut open her belly with his hunting knife and removed the baby as she went into shock and died.

That morning he walked into the town on the north coast with the infant Yanni in his arms and the rigid body of Yanni's mother strapped to his back.

Oh I know, Sivi had said as she sat with her head in her arms.

It's cruel and brutal and it sounds barbaric, but you have to remember the life those people have. When you're up in those mountains you might as well be on the surface of the moon. There's only a little wild thyme clinging to the rocks here and there and a man has to run all day to find it, from five in the morning until ten at night, so his goats can eat. And they do that, those men, they run up mountains. It's almost impossible to believe unless you've seen it. The life is hard and violent and although they live to be very old when left alone, often they're not left alone and death can be quick.

Not long ago a child in one of those villages was playing and as a joke took the bell off one of his father's goats and put it on a neighbor's. A goat stolen? By nightfall the boy's father was dead and the neighbor was dead and three other men were dead, and by the next morning the village was deserted, not a soul there. Because if all the families hadn't left at once, the killing of brothers and cousins by brothers and cousins would have had to go on until all the men in the village were dead. They knew that and they had no choice but to abandon their homes and go away.

So the way life works for them is that everyone has his duty and death can never be feared. Of course Yanni could have come back from the front when your daughter was due to be born, and he could have come back when she was taken ill, but I doubt that he ever even thought of it. To him he was where he belonged as a man, doing what he was supposed to be doing. The mountain people in that corner of Crete were never conquered by the Turks, the only Greeks who never were. For two hundred years the Turks burned down their villages, but they went up into their mountains until they had a new generation of sons to fight, and then they came down and fought, and saw their sons die, and went back up into the mountains again. For two hundred years they did that, and when the resistance was particularly heroic the Turks impaled those they had captured and put mirrors in front of them so they could watch themselves slowly die in the hot sun. The best remembered of all their leaders was a Captain Yanni who died that way when he was a few years younger than your Yanni. So that's where your Yanni came from, and that's what he was.

Maud shuddered. She understood it was a way of life. But she herself never wanted to see those mountains.

When Maud said she hoped to be alone with Bernini that summer, Sivi offered to let her stay in the villa in Smyrna. She quickly accepted, planning now to move back to Athens in the fall and find work as a translator, after Sivi returned in September. As for Theresa, she had already left to spend the summer in the islands, her affair with Munk having abruptly ended in June as Maud had foreseen.

Munk was in Smyrna twice that summer and on his second visit Maud spent a night with him, an evening brought on by wine and loneliness on her part, by wine and uncomplicated need on his. They smiled over it the next day, both aware it wouldn't be repeated, Munk hurrying on with his Zionist concerns and Maud preoccupied as before with beginning a new life in Athens in the fall. But it had been a long, intimate summer night that they both also knew would give rise to friendship.

One of their conversations late that night had turned to Theresa, and they realized all at once that neither of them knew anything about her past. Three years earlier at the age of nineteen, according to Sivi, she had gotten off a boat in Smyrna, alone and friendless and without any money. Another passenger from the boat, whom Sivi knew, had brought Theresa to one of his afternoon teas and Sivi had offered her a job as his secretary, as a way to help. Soon he had become strongly attached to her and now he liked to refer to her, mischievously, as his unnatural daughter.

Another adopted stray, said Munk, like me before the war. And it's been wonderful for him since she moved in. Despite what he says the old sinner has his bouts of gloom and loneliness, and it's made a great difference to him to have her here. She's family to him and he loves her enormously, and I'm sure she loves him in her way. But there's a kind of intensity about Theresa I've never understood. Something hidden. Something that won't allow her to be really close to anyone. I don't know how to describe it.

Is that all Sivi knows about her?

Yes, other than the fact that she was educated in a convent in France, apparently very strictly, although she's not a practicing Catholic now. But about her family or lack of it, or how she happened to turn up in Smyrna, nothing. Of course he never asks people who they are or where they've been. If they want to tell him he's glad to listen, no one could be more sympathetic. But if they don't he just accepts what he sees and plunges ahead without any reserve whatsoever, just assuming you deserve his confidence, his friendship. It's an extraordinary trait, as if he had no guile at all. Of course he must have some or he wouldn't be human. But I've never seen it. And anyway, Maud, surely you already know all this.

She nodded.

Yes. When I came here the first time as Yanni's wife, an American no less with no family, out of nowhere, there wasn't a single question about who or what. And this spring when he found me standing at the

243

door with Bernini, not having heard from me in almost a year and having no idea I'd had a child, well he burst into a smile and threw his arms around me and that was that. *Ah, here you are, how lovely.* That's all he said, only that. And they weren't just words. I swear there was no question in his eyes, either.

Munk rose from the bed to pour more wine. Maud took a sip and gazed out the open window at the lights in the harbor.

When did it start between you and Theresa?

About a year ago. I've been visiting Sivi since before the war and I suppose it was only natural that Theresa and I should fall in with one another. But I was never in Smyrna for more than a few days at a time, and I didn't think it was a particularly serious matter for anyone. Certainly Theresa didn't act as if it was.

That distance you mentioned?

Yes. Not cold exactly, but as if she didn't really care one way or the other. She never asked me if I could stay another day, for example. In fact she never even asked me when I would be back. When I turned up that was fine, and when I left that was fine too. But then when I came here at the beginning of June, she suddenly got all upset and said she didn't want to see me anymore. It was strange though. When she told me that I had the sensation she wasn't there somehow, not with me I mean. She was somewhere else, talking about something else. To be frank I don't think it was me, her interest in me or lack of it, that caused her to become so emotional.

I know, said Maud.

Why? How, I mean.

Well we talked several times too, before she left for the summer. She was terribly guarded but a feeling came through all the same. It's odd, but it almost seemed as if what bothered her were the places you kept talking about. Palestine, I mean. The Holy Land. Particularly Jerusalem. I don't know why I had that impression. Maybe it has to do with the fact that she was religious once and isn't now. Do you think she could be afraid of Jerusalem for some reason?

Maud shook her head. She laughed harshly at herself.

Afraid of Jerusalem, just imagine it. Afraid of something, unlike the rest of us. Aren't you afraid of anything, Munk?

No. What we have to do will take time, but it will happen.

Maud smiled. She put a finger on his nose.

It will? It just has to happen? What's that? The faith of the fathers?

More, my lady, much more. Remember that I became a Zionist because of a former Japanese baron. And the reason I happened to meet my Rabbi Lotmann was because I once discussed cavalry tactics with his twin brother, Baron Kikuchi, who was a hero of the Russo-Japanese War.

And so?

And so Baron Kikuchi and I chanced to meet in Constantinople while we were both covering the first Balkan war. And then years later he writes to me asking me to check on the well-being of his twin brother, who has converted to Judaism and is supposedly studying medieval Jewish mysticism in Safad. But the twin isn't there and eventually I trace him to St Catherine's monastery in the Sinai, where he's gone into hiding because of his Zionist activities and is pretending to be a Christian pilgrim, a Nestorian from China. At St Catherine's I listen to the evening concerts on the koto of this man who is now Rabbi Lotmann, and the music is so haunting and strange in that unusual setting that I find I can't sleep at night. Instead the former Japanese baron and I stay up and talk and talk, and the result is that a Hungarian Jew is converted to Zionism in the Sinai by an aristocratic landowner from northern Japan who was raised as a Buddhist in matters of death, and as a Shintoist in matters of birth.

Maud laughed again.

All true. And so?

And so given these vast implausibilities, geographical and racial and religious and esthetic, it immediately becomes apparent that much more than just the faith of my fathers is involved. Quite obviously, someone with an extraordinary overview has taken a hand in the matter and given me faith in this task.

Maud reached out and tweaked his nose.

It's always useful to have that kind of help, she said. The only thing you haven't explained is why these Japanese twins happen to figure so prominently in God's plan?

But that's easy, said Munk, tapping her nose in turn. The Japanese are a unique people who arrived in their islands more or less as an entity, with a culture of their own, just before and after the time of Christ. But no one has ever been quite sure where they came from. Now it was suggested more than once in the last century, by them of course, when they'd opened up their country and begun to Westernize themselves, that they just might be the survivors of the ten lost tribes of Israel. No one has ever taken that seriously but the time span wouldn't have to be wrong if you consider a leisurely journey across Asia, with time out to plant crops and care for livestock as a wandering people must, and also with time out to develop their unique culture, so they'll definitely be an Asian people when they eventually arrive in their Asian islands. And lastly, I don't think I mentioned that both Baron Kikuchi and his twin, Rabbi Lotmann, are very small men with very short legs. Legs that short, if not in a hurry, would cover distances sparingly and take some centuries to cross the world's largest continent from its western end to its eastern tip. So in conclusion, God's plan for the last two and half millennia has been to have His chosen people stationed at both extremities of Asia to see that nothing untoward occurs in the interior, which as we know has been a notorious birthplace for marauding tyrants throughout history. And those are the facts, in brief. Well what do you think?

Maud smiled and filled both their glasses. She raised hers in a toast.

Chapeau, Munk.

Thank you, madame.

Before she moved to Athens in September, Maud saw the changes in Theresa. She couldn't believe it was really as bad as it appeared but in fact it was worse, as Sivi told her the next time they met, in Athens late in the spring of the following year.

She's coming apart, said the old man sadly. She just doesn't care about anything. Drugs and alcohol and practically any man who speaks to her on the street. She told me there were thirty-five last month and she didn't even know the names of most of them. Then she laughed and said they all had beards though.

Beards?

Yes, it's crazy. I don't know what that was supposed to mean, or whether it meant anything at all. But I didn't like the way she said it and that laugh was more a scream of desperation, just horrible to hear. But she won't let me help her, she says it's not my concern and there's nothing I can do. Well if it's not my concern, whose can it be? She doesn't have anyone else. Oh I tell you, Maud, I feel sick about it. It simply can't go on like this much longer. There has to be an end in sight or it will be all over for her. And she's so young, just a child.

Maud took his hand and agreed with him, not knowing the end was indeed in sight because a gunrunner named Stern, the man in Jerusalem who had told Munk where he could find Rabbi Lotmann, had recently arranged for O'Sullivan Beare to meet Sivi in Smyrna in September.

Sivi providing arms for Stern and Joe smuggling them. Sivi a secret patriot with his dreams of a greater Greece, his clandestine life unknown to Maud then and for many years. And Stern, the sad shabby gunrunner who would save Maud's life more than a decade later when she stood in despair beside the Bosporus in the rain, ready to give it all up at last, the past too much for her, ready to throw herself into the currents when night came.

Sivi, Theresa, Stern, Joe. Only a few months from then to be together in Smyrna when a raging massacre would break loose and change all their lives.

Leaving Stern a tormented man forever. Driving gentle Sivi into madness. Theresa's tortured visions in the fire and smoke of that terrible slaughter to be revealed so painfully to Joe when their time came, on the small lonely rooftop where he kept watch in the Old City.

Smyrna and Jerusalem. The profane and sacred cities one day to be inextricably entwined in Maud's memories.

13

O'Sullivan Beare

*Signal night, he thought, quiet place
for sure. Demanding night up here
beneath the murmurs of heaven.*

*A*nd there were other, quieter moments during the twelve-year
poker game when one of the three friends would disappear for
days or weeks to pursue his dream. Munk Szondi building a future
Jewish homeland, Cairo Martyr on his quest for the black meteorite of
Islam, O'Sullivan Beare pondering the enigmas of the lost Sinai Bible
and his lost love as well, Maud, the woman who had abandoned him in
Jericho in 1921, taking with her their infant son.

When those moods came over him Joe left Jerusalem and traveled
down to Galilee where he kept his tiny seaplane, a Sopwith Camel.

Joe had won the Camel in a poker game during the great blizzard of
'29. That spring he learned to fly the Camel and had a hangar built for
it on the shores of the lake, and his first flight that spring became the
pattern for all the subsequent ones.

Late in the evening he taxied out onto the still water. He pushed the
engine to full power and the Camel broke free to rise above what had

once been Beth Jarah or the Temple of the Moon, sped south above the Jordan down the sinking valley past Naharaim and Bethshean and Jabesh-gilead, past Jabbok and Adam and the Jungle of the Jordan where lions had once roared, above the little flowered house somewhere below that he and Maud had once known near Jericho, whose ancient name also spoke of a lunar god, between the Moabite hills and the Dead Sea along the slopes of Mt Nebo where Moses had seen the promised land that he would never enter, rising to speed above the wastes and reaching Aqaba, tracing the west coast of the gulf until the configuration of a promontory and a mountain told him the Sinai oasis was coming up beneath him.

There Joe landed the Camel and pulled it partway up on the sand. He took ashore a small wicker basket and a bottle marked with the cross of St John, dated A.D. 1122, and sat crosslegged under a palm tree eating fresh figs and drinking raw poteen, waiting for the last hours of night to pass and the sun's first rays to rise above the mountains of Arabia, to warm the sands and glitter upon the waters where he had long ago spent a month with Maud.

Once he had a strange visitor in that remote spot, and the episode was so curious he wondered later if it might not have been a dream, a vision brought on by poteen and the dark loneliness of his mood.

In the very first light he had seen the figure, small and indistinct, coming out of the Sinai and moving in his direction. The minutes passed and the figure became an Arab, still striding directly toward him. He remembered being puzzled that the Arab had known he was there in the darkness, so complete in that last moonless hour before dawn that even the plane would have been invisible to anyone more than a few hundred yards away. Yet from the time he first saw the Arab, the man's line of march had never changed. He came walking straight from the night toward Joe, straight from the vast black hills of the desert to the mound where Joe sat on the beach.

A gray light now lay on the sand. The Arab kept coming until he was no more than ten yards away, then stopped and smiled. The stave he carried was that of a shepherd. His cloak was tattered and he was barefoot, his head tied with an old rag, a poor man of indistinct age. Gesturing, smiling, he made friendly signs that Joe was to follow him.

And there was the dream, for Joe got to his feet. Why? He didn't know, it just seemed there was nothing else to do. There were more reassuring nods from the shepherd and Joe found himself trailing along behind the man, down the shore away from his plane.

After they had walked some distance down the sand the Arab stopped and handed Joe his stave. He smiled and pointed at the water. Joe took off his shoes and shirt and trousers and waded in up to his knees, holding the stave.

A sandbar ran along the coast there and after going fifty yards Joe was still only up to his waist. On the beach the Arab was still smiling and nodding and pointing farther out. Joe smiled and took a few more steps, the water now suddenly up to his chest. He had reached the end of the sandbar and the bottom was dropping sharply away.

An absurd thought came to him. What if the shepherd kept pointing to the east? How far would he have to swim? Across the Gulf of Aqaba to Arabia? Around Arabia to the Indian Ocean? From there to the Pacific?

Why? Where would it end? He might have to go on swimming forever. Swimming for the rest of his life until he finally reached the Aran Islands and died. And what would the bedouin think when they found a Sopwith Camel abandoned on the shores of the Sinai, near it a wicker basket containing fresh figs and a bottle of home-brewed Irish liquor dated A.D. 1122, bearing the cross of St John?

The Arab was suddenly shouting in excitement. Joe heard a frightened whine. He turned, the water now up to his chin.

He hadn't noticed it before. Off to his left beyond the end of the sandbar there was a small clump of rocks. The shepherd was gesturing wildly for him to swim over to the clump of rocks.

He began to swim. A terrified dog was huddled on the rocks. The shepherd was shouting and waving his arms and Joe understood. He pushed the stave toward the rocks and the dog leapt for it. He started back toward shore with the stave stretched out behind him, the dog swimming after it. When they reached land the Arab was beaming. Joe smiled and returned the stave. He picked up his clothes and together they walked back up the beach with the dog happily prancing at his master's heels.

Joe offered the shepherd a drink of poteen but the man sniffed it and politely refused. He pointed at the cross on the bottle and laughed. Solemnly, then, he put his hand on his heart and bowed his head before striding off in the direction from which he had come. On the top of the first ridge the shepherd turned and waved his stave in salute and exactly at that moment the new sun rose above the horizon and fell on the barefoot man.

The shepherd was gone. Joe sat down on the sand and watched the sun come up across the gulf, curiously wondering what manner of being could come striding out of the Sinai and have the wordless power, expressed only through smiles and gestures, to cause him to enter the sea without knowing or caring why he did so, even if it meant he might have to go on swimming forever.

The god of dawn? The god of light?

Strange presences, it seemed, on the shores of the Sinai where he and Maud had once known love.

It was late one afternoon in the autumn of 1933 when Cairo made his way through the still streets of the Armenian Quarter and knocked on the door that was Joe's address in the Old City. An elderly Armenian priest appeared. Cairo looked puzzled.

Were you looking for the Irishman? asked the priest gently.

Yes, said Cairo. I thought he lived here.

He does. You take those outside stairs to the left.

Cairo thanked the priest and the door closed. He started up the winding stone stairs. Apparently the old house had been added to at different times, for the walls jutted out at irregular levels. The stairs twisted steeply around them and led up to a short stone bridge, an arch connecting the main structure with a smaller one behind it. Cairo crossed the bridge above a narrow courtyard, climbed a last flight of stairs and stopped. Now he was even more puzzled.

He had emerged on a roof and save for a small square shed at one end, low and windowless, there was nothing else there. He tried the door to the shed but it was locked. Bewildered, he sat down on the low wall that enclosed the roof and gazed out over the Old City, lost in thought. He didn't know how many minutes had passed when he suddenly heard the soft familiar voice behind him.

Like the view then?

Cairo turned and broke into laughter at the sight. Joe was wearing the baking priest's shabby uniform from the Crimean War, flyer's goggles around his neck and a flyer's leather helmet. The goggles bounced on his Victoria Cross as he bounded up the last few steps and walked across the roof scratching his beard.

Here now, Cairo, what's so funny?

That outfit of yours. I never knew they had fighter pilots in the Crimean War.

Didn't you now. Well I don't think I did either until I was almost thirty. History can be a mystery when you're young. Were you looking for me then?

Not at all. Just roaming the roofs of the Old City in my spare time. You can't see as far up here as you can from the top of Cheops' pyramid, but there's more variety certainly. Where do you live by the way?

Here.

No, I believe an elderly Armenian priest lives here.

Ah, you met Father Zeno downstairs. A fine oul article that one, none better.

I'm sure.

Runs the library in the Armenian compound and also makes pottery. First a baking priest took me in, then a potting priest. Just seems to be how things go for me in Jerusalem. Care for a drink?

Fine. Where did you say you lived?

Joe shrugged. He walked over to the shed and unlocked the door. Cairo followed him and stood outside the door, gazing down at the narrow iron cot, the battered wooden footlocker, the small cracked mirror above a small table that held a basin and a pitcher, a bar of soap, a comb and a toothbrush and a towel neatly folded over a rack. A kerosene lamp hung on one wall beside a shelf of books. There was a crucifix above the head of the cot. The ceiling of the shed was so low Cairo wouldn't have been able to stand up inside, but of course he was much taller than Joe.

A cupboard sat on the floor and there was a little fireplace in one corner. Joe took a bottle and two glasses out of the cupboard and poured poteen. They went back to the wall around the roof and sat down.

Well here we go, Cairo lad, home-brewed and the best poteen in the

Holy City by far. But don't go thinking I'm religious just because you saw that crucifix. It's a habit merely, kind of thing I grew up with. Would you say the view is best to the north? I'm generally of that opinion.

Cairo nodded.

What's the meaning of that anyway?

Of what?

That peasant's hut. That monk's cell.

I don't know what you're talking about. It's where I live, there's no special meaning to it.

There isn't? When one of the richest men in Palestine lives like that?

Oh those schemes of mine, Christ they're nothing really. I was born a peasant you know so there's no reason why I shouldn't live like one.

Joe took off his leather helmet and goggles. He lit a cigarette and sipped from his glass. Cairo clasped one knee with both hands and leaned back, silent for a while, his eyes closed.

Do you cook in there too?

That I do. The very best stews to be found east of Ireland. Hearty and nourishing on a winter night.

What do you do for heat on a winter night?

A nice cozy turf fire, nothing like it.

I can imagine how cozy it is up here when there's a winter gale blowing down from the north.

Anyway, Cairo, aren't you richer than I am?

Probably.

And Munk too?

He might be if he didn't give it all away.

Sure and that's true, Munk's our very own idealist. Knew another man like that once, a man who had that kind of dream, a homeland for his people. But his people were Jews and Arabs and Christians all together, if you can imagine such a hopeless situation. Hated him at the time I did, but I was young then. Anyway, I've nothing but affection for our dear Munk of the revolution and his three-level watch, time as time is at any hour of the day or night, fast or slow or not even there. And he'll make it too I think, Munk will. Hope so certainly. Be good to see someone who believes in more than money make it. But is that why you came dropping in today? To see if I was properly prepared for winter?

We were worried about you, Joe. Munk thought one of us should look in.

Nothing to worry about. I was just off with the Camel taking in the fine autumn sunsets.

Aqaba?

That's right.

For three whole weeks?

Was it that long now. Yes I guess it was. I was having a snort or two you see.

Drunk for three weeks, in other words.

Couldn't have been that long, I'm sure of that.

Yes you're right. It must have taken at least a sober day or two before you were steady enough to fly back.

It's not being unsteady exactly, that's not the problem, it's the danger of falling down that alarms you. Who wants to take a terrible tumble? Not me. So you just daren't get in the plane at a time like that. You just have to sit still as still watching the water and holding on to yourself until things get right inside. Even walking is alarming. Dreadful feeling, the falling-down sickness.

Joe tried to smile but his face was sad and weary. He emptied his glass and lit another cigarette.

There's a pome, he said, that describes my last three weeks and it goes like this.

> When things go wrong and will not come right,
> Though you do the best you can,
> When life looks black as the hour of night—
> A PINT OF PLAIN IS YOUR ONLY MAN.

Like it, Cairo? Has a ring to it I say, a touch of majesty, and it'll live as long as the tongue is spoken. But since we don't have any plain on the premises, I think I'll just help myself to another glass of this most friendly dhrink that looks like water, yet is far friendlier than that. Care to join me?

No thanks. It's a little raw for me.

Guess it would be. Guess you have to be born to the stuff. But it can help all right when you're feeling like last winter's turf fire, all cold gray lumps and ashes. Well I'll just be helping myself now.

Cairo squinted at his hands as Joe went inside to fill his glass. Behind him he heard a beating of wings, a pigeon alighting on a little roof just below them. There were two small wooden shelters on the lower roof. A short ladder led to it.

You keep pigeons, Joe?

For company don't you know. After he eats he'll sleep, so will the others when they arrive. They'll be tired certainly.

Where are they coming from?

Joe shrugged.

Aqaba, I suppose.

You take them down there with you?

It's company, and then when I'm getting ready to leave I give them a wave and tell them they can go anywhere they want. Amazing, isn't it, how they can fly all the way back from the Sinai to find a little roof like this? One tiny roof in Jerusalem when they've got the whole world to choose from? Makes you think about home and wonder where it is.

Joe went down the ladder and put out some grain for the pigeons. Cairo was standing outside the door of the shack, gazing at the crucifix, when Joe came back and sat down.

I just knew you'd be going and thinking I was religious when Christ it's just not the truth. Why are you thinking that anyway?

Cairo nodded. He put his hand on Joe's shoulder.

Say, what's the hand for? Am I in need of support or something? Do I look like the falling-down sickness is on me again?

Joe, why don't you tell me about her?

Who?

The woman you went to Aqaba with once. It was when you first came to Jerusalem, wasn't it?

Yes.

Well?

Well I met her here.

Where?

Here. The Old City.

Where exactly?

In a church.

What church?

A church that's all, what's it matter.

Say it, Joe.

Oh all right, my God, it was the Church of the Holy Sepulchre. I'd been in Jerusalem only a few weeks after spending four years on the run in the mountains of Cork never talking to a soul, and before that nothing but the Dublin post office which we held for a couple of days, and before that just a boy in the Aran Islands. Well that's where we met and she didn't say a word then, she just did this thing in the crypt of the Church of the Holy Sepulchre. I mean I'd never done a thing with a woman before, not one thing. Will you understand?

Yes.

All right, so we met, me just out of four years on the run in the bogs fighting the English, cold and wet all the time and sinking up to my knees with every soggy step, and then this woman and I went off to the desert. Haj Harun suggested that. It was spring and Haj Harun said spring was the time for the desert, the flowers were blooming and they only had a couple of weeks before they all died. Well bless his bones, bless the oul article for telling me that because we did go, we went to Aqaba and down the coast of the gulf and we found a tiny deserted oasis and the two of us were alone there, the Sinai red on one side and the gulf blue on the other and the sand so hot and the water so cooling and arak to drink and fresh figs to eat and other than that just nights and days that had no end or beginning. Do you see, Cairo? A month we were there and I was just twenty years old and I'd never known there could be sun like that and sky like that and nights and days like that. By God, just never knew it, do you see?

Yes.

Well it turned out I didn't know her. After we came back here it wasn't the same and it got worse and worse, me not understanding any of it, and finally she left our little house in Jericho where we'd gone for the winter, taking our baby son with her, I was away and never even saw the lad, had to go to the midwife to find out it was a boy. So that's all there is and that's enough. Twelve and a half years ago she left me and that's how I got into our bloody poker game, by God that's how. Money and power I wanted after that. What else is there?

Yet you keep going back to Aqaba.

I do, surely I do, and I also go back to the crypt in the Church of the Holy Sepulchre. Just go back and back for no reason. Makes me tired, going back. Makes me dreadfully tired, Cairo.

Wasn't there ever another woman after that?

Yes, one only, Theresa's her name. And it's strange because Munk knew her before I did. They were together once.

Who was she? Who is she?

Yes, there's that difference all right. When Munk knew her in Smyrna she was young and carefree, and when I knew her in Smyrna she was still young but she was going mad. And here, well here she's something else.

Joe looked down at his feet. He tipped his glass.

Now she lives downstairs, he said softly. She lives with Father Zeno. He takes care of her and protects her and keeps anyone from seeing her because of what she has. Good man that he is, he protects her because of that, so the world won't flock and gape at her and make her miserable.

Because of what?

The stigmata. She has the stigmata. I've seen it, and besides him I'm the only person in the world who has.

The sky was brilliant with stars that autumn night above the roof in the Armenian Quarter where Joe sat with Cairo turning over the years amidst the domes and spires and minarets of the Old City, the shadows of the Judean wastes dropping away into blackness.

Theresa?

There was the one who'd been Munk's lover in Smyrna after the First World War, and there was the other Theresa whom Joe had seen during the massacres at Smyrna in 1922, shrieking and beating her head on the floor in the frenzy of her torment.

Smyrna?

Joe had gone there for a man named Stern. He was running guns for Stern then and there was a man Stern had wanted him to meet in Smyrna, an elderly Greek who provided Stern with guns, so that Joe could deal with him directly. The Greek's name was Sivi, Theresa was his secretary. That was in 1922, September. Joe had taken Haj Harun with him.

But there had never been time to discuss their business in Smyrna, Stern's cause and Sivi's cause and Joe running guns from one to the other. The massacre had begun on a Sunday in September and there was nothing but slaughter and fire as the Turks butchered Armenians and Greeks. Joe and Haj Harun had gone to the address they'd been given, Sivi's villa on the harbor, and there they found Stern and Theresa trying to drag Sivi to safety, the old man bleeding from a head wound and raving incoherently, having been beaten by the Turkish soldiers who were inside his house, looting and setting fires.

Stern and Joe managed to carry the old man away. Theresa was still calm but later she too collapsed and began raving. And the slaughter went on as the city went up in flames, and Joe shot a Turkish soldier who attacked them, and Haj Harun killed a blinded old Armenian who was burning to death, and Stern slit the throat of a little Armenian girl who was dying in unbearable pain. Screams and smoke in the alleys of Smyrna, screams and death everywhere in that nightmare on the waterfront.

They all managed to escape. Joe was finished with Stern after that and told him so. Never another rifle smuggled for anyone, not for any cause, no cause was worth the slaughter.

Sivi?

He'd gone mad during the massacres.

Theresa?

Joe didn't know what had happened to her after Smyrna. Having broken with Stern, he lost touch with all of them except for Haj Harun. But Munk also knew Stern, as it turned out, and later Joe learned from him that Stern was still running guns and Sivi had never recovered his sanity. Of Theresa, however, Munk knew nothing. She'd simply disappeared.

For a year. Until she came to visit Joe on his roof a little over a year after Smyrna, on a clear evening early in November. November 5, to be exact. In Theresa's tortured mind there was a reason for the date, as Joe eventually discovered.

He didn't know why she'd sought him out, nor did he ask her. She'd brought a bottle of cognac with her and they sat here where he and Cairo were sitting now, having a drink and talking and neither one of them mentioning Smyrna. It was as if they'd met once pleasantly somewhere, chance acquaintances together again, who knew? A clear night with cognac and stars and stray sounds drifting up from the alleys.

To Joe it seemed better for them not to have a past that night. Not their past. Not the horrible hours they had known together in Smyrna. Better to have another drink and listen to the murmurs of the Old City, which never quite slept.

Time passed, they made love. It had been Theresa's doing but afterward she sat up in bed crying hysterically. Joe thought she was drunk. He tried to quiet her but she was screaming so wildly he had to slap her and slap her a second time, a third time before she stopped. She began talking feverishly then and her voice was terrible to hear.

She was evil, she said. For a year before Joe had met her she'd been sleeping with every man she could find in Smyrna who had a beard. Because she was obsessed with Christ, she said, laughing hysterically. Because she was obsessed with finding Christ and all she could remember from the paintings in the convent school of her youth was that Christ had a beard. A beard. *I've lost His face,* shrieked Theresa, laughing hysterically.

Well none of those men in Smyrna had been Christ, she said. Until in the flames and the smoke of the massacres she'd seen a vision, and that's when she'd collapsed. She'd seen Joe standing over her with his beard and his burning eyes, the fires of Smyrna burning in his eyes, and she thought she'd found a face for Christ at last and that's why she'd come to him tonight. To make love with him, to use him to fulfill her twisted vision.

And how do you like that? she screamed. *How do you like that?*

Joe moaned.

Let it go, he whispered sadly. Let it go.

But she wouldn't. She kept on screaming and taunting him until finally he could stand it no longer and in another moment he was screaming too, calling her wicked, saying she was evil, shouting that she was damned forever. *Damned forever.*

Theresa heard those words and suddenly she was sober, her face grave. She looked up at him.

I *am* damned forever, she said simply. And then all at once she was a small naked woman huddled on his narrow iron cot, cowering and terrified and whispering naked words, terrible naked words.

Normandy. The château where Theresa and her brother had been born. Their father, a count, was a fanatically religious man, their mother a plain and quiet woman. Theresa would one day look like her.

A whore, shouted their father. That's what you were when I saved you.

Little Theresa and her brother crouching in a corner hearing the same dreadful words shouted over and over, their mother with a bowed head never saying anything. Then their mother began to stay in bed all day, and in the kitchen they heard the servants whispering of opium.

Their father dismissed the servants from the château. He told his children his shame before God was too great to allow anyone to see their mother in such a condition. They would live alone in the château and pray for her redemption, which would come if they prayed hard enough.

But it didn't come. Instead the children were out playing one afternoon when they heard pounding in a tool shed. They peeked inside. A cross made out of old lumber was leaning against the wall. Their father was nailing their mother to it.

They threw themselves at him and he knocked them down. They attacked him again and he drove them off with a hammer. They ran across the fields to the nearest neighbor, a curate, who ran back with them. Their father was sitting at the foot of the cross, weeping. Their mother's head had fallen. She had already suffocated.

The curate went to his bishop and it was decided the scandal had to be suppressed because of its religious nature. The bishop made arrangements with a magistrate and it was agreed the count shouldn't be sent away for fear he might talk about what he had done. He would remain in the château and the curate would move in to live there. The children were made to place their hands on a crucifix and swear under threat of eternal damnation never to say anything about what they had seen. A certificate of death by natural causes was issued for their mother.

The curate moved into the château. Theresa and her brother almost never saw their father, who went to church seven times a day with the curate, observing the canonical hours. Other than that, obeying the curate's orders, he stayed in his rooms.

Their father did penance but no one knew he had carried his fasting to the point of giving up food almost entirely. For sustenance he had turned to raw Calvados, and over the years the small amounts of wood alcohol in the Calvados slowly ate away his brain.

The sudden outburst of submerged decay occurred five years later in the family chapel on the anniversary of the murder, at the special mass performed each year by the bishop for their mother. During the final benediction the emaciated old count shrieked and suddenly rushed forward. Before anyone could stop him he had climbed up on the altar. His arms were open to the crucifix on the wall and the words he screamed were those of the leper on the shores of Galilee.

Lord, if thou will thou can make me clean.

He leapt to embrace the crucifix and missed it, crashing through a window at the side and shattering the richly stained colors that had depicted a garden below Jerusalem, and the meeting there of two kinswomen who would one day know sorrow, Mary and Elizabeth.

The window was gone, the old count's throat was severed, the chapel was rendered into the silence of its candles.

Theresa and her brother returned to the château and went on living as they always had, alone with each other in a private world, secluded in their love. And gradually under those gray skies of Normandy, far from the black twisted roots of the past, there was born within them the dream of another and timeless land by the Nile where the blue heavens were unbroken and the distant horizons limitless, an ancient dream of an eternal pharaoh wed to his eternal sister.

One day Theresa threw herself down the stairs. Her brother carried her to her room and that night he went out into the drenched forest to dig deeply the grave of their hopeless love in the loose stinking earth, there to bury the tiny bundle of unborn flesh wrapped by Theresa in her own Confirmation dress, once spotlessly white and flowing and now bloodied to the ends of its delicate lace, soon to rot in the undergrowth of fallen vines and blind nibbling creatures.

That winter the howling winds of trapped memory had come to haunt her brother. In the tool shed where their mother had been crucified he soaked himself with kerosene and struck a match.

And so at the age of nineteen Theresa had left everything behind and fled south to the Mediterranean, by chance to beautiful Smyrna where kindly Sivi had taken her in and where she had known a few peaceful years because of him, only to find the horrors of the past were inescapable, abandoning herself then to her sins and spiraling downward in a life of degradation.

Until a terrible massacre descended on Smyrna and Sivi was raving in pain, and a wizened ageless man abruptly appeared to defend them, an apparition in a rusty helmet and a faded yellow cloak, trailing a long sword.

Who is that? she had screamed, and a soft Irish voice had whispered near her that it was all right, the old man thought he was the archangel Gabriel now, come to smote God's enemies.

She had turned. She had looked up and seen a small dark man standing over her, a man with the beard and the burning eyes from the paintings on the convent walls of her childhood.

Christ in the gloom and smoke with a pistol in his belt. Christ in the fires of Smyrna.

Dawn had come to the roof in the Old City by the time Theresa had finished speaking. Joe stroked her head and wrapped another blanket around her naked body. She had refused to dress until she had told him everything. He rose and went to the door, leaving her sitting on the narrow iron cot. He opened the door and stood there gazing north in the gray light.

Joe?

Yes.

I've never told anyone before. Never. Do you mind my having told you?

No, he said sadly. No. It's better to tell someone.

Joe? That stained-glass window in Normandy? The garden beneath Jerusalem where Mary went to meet Elizabeth?

His shoulders suddenly sagged in the doorway. He leaned against the wood and sighed.

Yes I know it, Ein Karem. I've been to the village. And yesterday was St Elizabeth's feast day. You chose that day to come here, to come to me. Why?

Because that's where I've been living, Joe. Since Smyrna, for the whole last year, that's where I've been. There's a leper colony there and

262

I've been working in it. Joe? Please? These hands that held you last night wash lepers. *Wash lepers.* They're not good enough for anything else. Joe? Could you forgive me for what I've done in life? I know God never will, but could you? I've been wretched for so long, and I know I don't even have the right to walk in these streets where He came to suffer and die for us. Yesterday evening when I entered the gate I thought I'd be struck dead. But I had to come and tell someone here and you're the only person I dared to speak to, because you've never really known me. I've been terrified of Jerusalem for so long, Joe, you can't imagine, no one can. And I'm weak and I've done one awful thing after another in life, and I've suffered for it, but that was why I went to Ein Karem. To be near Jerusalem, to be able to look up at it, the Holy City that will never be mine. Oh Joe, please? I know what I did to you last night was horrible, but if you say you'll forgive me I'll go away and you'll never see me again, I swear it. I'll go away and never bother you again, Joe. Only here, now, just once let me be forgiven here. Just once. *Please?*

He stood in the doorway. The new sun was touching the domes and the spires and the minarets with gold. The tears were running down his face and his voice was choked.

Yes, little Theresa, poor tormented little one. Of course I forgive you.

With His words, Joe? Could you please? I'll go and you'll never see me again. In His city? Please?

Joe nodded. They weren't his words to give but he repeated them anyway because there was no one else to speak them, no one else to utter the healing words. So he looked at the floor and whispered what Christ had said to the woman in the house of the Pharisee.

Thy sins are forgiven, thy faith hath saved thee. Go in peace.

A scream, an almost silent scream that cut through him with all the pain of Smyrna. Joe looked up, he looked at the bed. Theresa was sitting with her hands up in front of her, staring at them and screaming silently.

Joe stared too. Punctures had appeared in her palms. Christ's wounds. She was beginning to bleed.

Joe got up from the wall and paced back and forth.

I don't know how long I stood there, Cairo, right there in that doorway. It seemed forever. And she didn't move either. She sat there naked on the bed with the blankets falling open, her hands in front of her, staring, watching the wounds form, watching the blood come out, both of us watching it happen, not believing it and watching it happen. I don't even remember whether either of us spoke after that or how I got her down to Father Zeno or why, but I did.

She was in some kind of shock and I wasn't much better. He bandaged her and put her to bed and prayed beside her all day and all night. He asked me not to say anything about it and of course I wouldn't have anyway, we were both pretending it might have been anything.

But it wasn't, Cairo. It wasn't just anything. The wounds went away in a few days but they came back the next month and the month after that, and they have ever since. Ever since that night we made love in there ten years ago.

What does Father Zeno say?

Only that he hears her confession and I'm to tell no one what she said that night. She never goes out anymore, she prefers it that way. She has a room down there somewhere, I don't know where, and she keeps to it most of the time, and after the wounds come she doesn't see anyone, not even Father Zeno. I respect him. What he's doing is best for her.

Do you see her?

Never.

Would you like to?

I don't know. I did the first three or four months she was there. She seemed to want it, to need it. We wouldn't do much, hardly even talk, just sit together in the courtyard in the evening. But then one evening Father Zeno met me and said she couldn't see me then and it would be better if I didn't come anymore.

Did he say why?

No.

Did you ask him?

No.

Cairo nodded. Joe sat down again. The moon was gone now and the domes and spires and minarets of the Old City were waning in the soft starry glow of midnight.

You know, said Joe, I don't think I'm going to be in the game much longer.

How's that?

I'm not sure, but it's been almost twelve years now, hasn't it. Twelve years in December.

The last day of December, said Cairo. You were sitting in that coffee shop feeling bitter because you were a few months away from your twenty-second birthday and already eighty-five years old, and I came in with Bongo to get out of the wind, and then Munk turned up with his samurai bow and his three-level watch, and that's when it all began. A cold winter day with snow definitely in the air.

Yes. You know I was doing some thinking when I was down in Aqaba this time. Thinking it might be time to move on. Thinking that what I've been telling myself I wanted for the last dozen years, well maybe it's not what I want at all.

Joe waved his arm toward the city.

The things that happen here, what can you say about them? They happen, that's all. Have you ever heard of something called the Sinai Bible?

What is it?

Well it's supposed to be the original Bible. Supposedly it was written three thousand years ago, more or less.

Cairo smiled.

And how's that possible?

Who knows? Who knows what's possible around here? Not me, I don't, I'm just a poor fisherman's son from the Aran Islands, a windswept place and barren and nowhere, so poor that God didn't even put any soil on them. We had to make it out of seaweed and manure. Well the point is the Sinai Bible is buried near here.

How did you learn about this Sinai Bible?

Oh I've been hearing about it since I arrived in Jerusalem. It's the kind of thing that will fascinate me every time. And you can pick up clues when you're looking for them.

Joe laughed.

Ah and I was innocent when I first got here. I actually believed then that this Bible was something Haj Harun had written. I heard about it and got it wrong, and Haj Harun confused me more, and off I was just spinning like a top around the idea of a Sinai Bible. You know what Haj Harun likes to call it when he's mixing up the ages? *The story of my life.* But of course it could be, depending on your point of view. It could be that as well as anything else. After all that's about how long he's lived, three thousand years or so. So why shouldn't he think the original Bible is the story of his life?

It's a nice way to look at it, said Cairo.

Yes. Anyway, after a time I learned that such a Bible actually had been found in the last century, in the Sinai I guess, that's why it has that name. A Trappist monk found it, but that's all I know about him, and he was so appalled by its chaos he decided to forge a new original and let it be found, then buried the real original here in Jerusalem, the Holy City don't you see. Well he did that and the fake original was acquired by the czar in the last century, and just this year the Bolsheviks sold it to the British Museum for a hundred thousand pounds. So how's that for a saga and a half? But the real one, the real one's still here.

Where?

Right here, somewhere in the Armenian Quarter. Buried in a basement hole.

And that's why you wanted to live here? You moved in to be close to it because you wanted to find it?

I did, I mightily did, but now I'm not so sure. I'm not so sure I really want to see what's in it. Something along those lines, I just don't know anymore. Maybe it'd be better to leave it alone. Better to think of it as the story of Haj Harun's life, and remind myself that I've been fortunate enough to have been able to keep the old man company these dozen and one years, better just to let it go at that. There are more than enough mysteries in *his* life to think about, certainly more than enough for me, so why go on looking?

Why? asked Cairo.

Joe smiled.

Well there you are. I don't think I will. I think it's time for me to give up the seeking and the search for lost treasure and go take my ease in the west, Holy City West, wherever that might be. It's time to become Chief Sipping Bear at home in the setting sun.

Are we to be treated to a Zuni sun dance now?

Go on with you, Cairo. We're hours away from sunup and any dance of that nature could only be a failure at this hour. No, there are other matters before us. Now that it's midnight and a little more we have to hear from a very important spokesman who goes by the name of Finn MacCool.

Joe cupped his hands around his mouth and pretended to shout out over the rooftops.

Hey *Finnnnn,* he whispered, we're right here in Jerusalem. Lend us a hand if you will.

Do you think he heard me? whispered Joe. I was aiming in a generally western direction but I don't know how well my voice is carrying tonight. What do you think?

Cairo laughed.

He heard you, definitely. And I take it he's some tribal god native to the bogs of Ireland?

Now why would you be guessing as wildly as that? Well as a matter of fact that's just what he is, a great strong giant of a man whose favorite pastime on nights like these is telling stories. In fact he's got so many stories to tell, most of them about himself, that he never runs out of them. He's been doing it for ages already and it looks like he just might go on doing it to the end of time. Now back home when you want Finn to tell you a story you say, *Please relate.* Will you do so?

What?

What you're doing, Cairo. I've noticed you might be getting tired of the game yourself. The signs are there and of course with my keen eye, I wouldn't be missing them would I. Why the poker game for you originally? Why did you want control of Jerusalem? Please relate.

It is true that I will not.

Joe laughed.

Ah Cairo, there you go using my very homespun English, bad as it is

267

and getting no better. But with that accent of yours you'll never be taken for an Irishman, not even in Africa. Your tone is too aristocratic by half. Well then, will you relate?

I'll compromise with you, Joe. I'll go so far as to tell the tale the way your Finn MacCool might.

Which is to say?

Stretched and distorted and made outrageous.

Fine, very fine. That's tale-telling for sure and nothing could be more accurate anyway. So please to begin. And as you do I think I'll just be taking a shade more of this drink that looks like water but definitely isn't, is definitely not.

That won't help at this hour of night.

You're right, Cairo, it won't, it surely will not. Makes a good man old before his time and a bad man young before he's ready, a curse on the race and that's a fact. But if it's any help to you I have some of that other stuff here for a smoke, and maybe you'll be wanting a puff or two before the night's out. Well maybe you will so I'll just lay the pipe and the mixings beside you in case you feel the urge sneaking up in the darkness, a late evening in the Holy City being no time to exert yourself unduly. Now, you're the African Finn MacCool you say?

I wasn't aware of saying that.

Ah come on, Cairo. After all these years of us playing poker together, how could you possibly mislay your name? I've always known you weren't in the game for money, something else has been up. What's the deed?

It was going to be Jerusalem first, then Mecca.

Has a ring to it all right. What in Mecca?

The Holy of Holies.

Ah.

The black meteorite.

Ah.

You may not know it, but that black meteorite is the most sacred object in Islam. It's in the Kaaba. I was going to steal it and take it to Africa and bury it in good rich African soil. Black soil. Where no one would ever find it.

Why?

Cairo grew somber then. He described Jidda, for centuries the great depot of the slave trade, and how many of the African children who arrived there had already walked more than twelve hundred miles to reach the Arab ferries on the other side of the Red Sea.

He described the small wells he had seen across the Sahara, surrounded for miles with dry bleached bones, the skeletons of slaves who hadn't survived the forced marches of their Arab owners. And although the footprints of the slaves had fled where the earth was hard, straight deep troughs still ran from horizon to horizon to show where the countless slave caravans had passed century after century in the desert, grooves once cut by lumbering camels laden with Arab slavers and their tents and their food and their water, for them, not for those who stumbled starving in the dust behind them.

Joe listened to it all in silence. And not for the first time he felt the enormous sadness that was in Cairo, a sadness that would have seemed unbearable to Joe had it not been for Cairo's great strength. Cairo with his brilliant smile, Cairo who laughed so warmly, his huge hands so gentle when he reached out and laid them upon you, when he embraced you in greeting and simply lifted you up off the ground in his exuberance, tenderly, gently, with the natural ease of a man picking up his child. Indomitable in the end. There was no other way to see him.

So Joe listened in silence, and after a time Cairo broke through his somber mood.

Anger now, Cairo?

There was.

Vengeance too?

There was.

Well by God, I can see how you've been able to bet all these years without looking at your cards. It's there in the very name you bear.

Given to me by my great-grandmother, a slave from the Sudan. I was going to do it for her and all my people, to repay the Arabs for the black gold they've carried out of Africa over the centuries.

But now you're not so sure that's what you want to be doing?

No. Somehow my passion has been spent along the way. Building something would be better. Perhaps it's because of the game. Perhaps I learned that there.

From our Munk?

From Munk, yes.

I know what you mean. But here now, what's this? Do I see you filling that pipe and preparing a smoke?

You do.

Curious. Never understood the stuff myself. Why would anyone want to bother with that when there's genuine poteen on the premises? A mystery to me, one more among the many. But since we find ourselves taking our ease in our different ways, shouldn't we be talking about our futures? You know how Munk does nothing but deal in futures. Well what about us? Isn't it time we did a little dealing in that line ourselves?

Cairo smiled. *Time,* he said.

Right. How's that stuff taste by the way?

Good.

Now that's odd, it is. That's exactly how this tastes and poteen is nothing like that at all.

It was dawn before Cairo and Joe embraced on the roof and Cairo made his way across the little stone bridge and down the twisting stone stairs to the street, quiet at that early hour but not deserted, the beggars and madmen and pious fanatics of the Old City already out pursuing their vocations as they had been for millennia.

Cairo walked slowly through the alleys toward the bazaar, thinking he might have something to eat. Soon he would be going back to Africa, he knew that now. He and Joe had talked away the night making their plans, deciding that December 31 would be the appropriate time to play their last hand with Munk, the twelfth anniversary of the game. They had also agreed to make it a surprise to Munk, what they were going to do on that last hand.

But would Munk be surprised? wondered Cairo.

Probably not. They all knew each other too well by now.

Dawn after a long autumn night. Ten years, thought Cairo, after Joe and Theresa had spent their hours of darkness and light together on a rooftop in Jerusalem, and conceived a child.

Did Joe know?

Cairo nodded. Of course Joe knew. No one had told him but he knew. He had admitted as much when describing how Father Zeno had told him that it would be better if he didn't come to see Theresa anymore.

Did he say why? Cairo had asked.

No, answered Joe.

Did you ask him?

No, answered Joe.

And so Joe had known it all these years, a secret borne for the sake of others and never to be spoken, until last night when he had finally shared it with a friend, finally, in his weariness after returning yet again from Aqaba.

And where, wondered Cairo, would Father Zeno have placed the child? With a family? In a foundling home?

In any case, not a religious home. That much was certain. From what Joe had said about Father Zeno, Cairo knew that the gentle old priest would never have presumed to choose a faith for the child. Thus no one but he would ever know who the child really was. Cairo was sure of that. Father Zeno would have made the arrangements very carefully and the secret would die with him. And somewhere in Jerusalem, or in an encampment near it, a child would grow up not knowing he or she had been born to Christ and Mary Magdalene.

Cairo paused in front of a blind beggar and dropped a copper coin in his cup. Ever since that spring when he had come down the Nile to find the lid on top of Menelik Ziwar's massive sarcophagus, the crinkled smiling face gone, he had never once passed a beggar without giving him something, his way of recalling the kindness an old man had once shown to a frightened twelve-year-old boy, illiterate and without any skills, who had suddenly found himself alone in the world.

The elderly blind man whispered his thanks and Cairo moved on.

Only to stop a few yards away and look back. For a long moment he gazed at the beggar where he sat on the worn stones in the dust, then he retraced his steps and placed three gold coins, one after the other, in the beggar's scarred hand. The beggar heard the coins ring and his blind eyes turned upward. He murmured in disbelief.

Gold?

Yes. I would like you to say a prayer for a child, if you will.

With all my heart. Tell me the name of the child and I will pray.

I don't know the name and I've never seen the child. Or perhaps I have seen the child and don't know it. In this I am as blind as you.

And so are we all, murmured the beggar. But God knows the names that are and will be for all of us, and I will pray and He will hear my prayer.

Cairo nodded. He placed his hand lightly on the beggar's shoulder and held it there, then turned and entered the bazaar, now raucously coming to life amidst the cries of merchants and thieves hawking their endless goods and trickeries.

But there was yet another secret in that house in the Armenian compound next to the cathedral of St James, unknown even to Father Zeno, a secret Joe had discovered some years after seeking refuge there in 1921, when the old priest had given him the rooftop home where he had learned to dream his Jerusalem dreams.

Early in the nineteenth century, it seemed, a young beggar had turned up at the house one blustery winter night, asking for shelter. The beggar was entirely naked, lacking even a loincloth. He had pretended to be an Armenian although the priest who received him knew he was not. He was given clothes and a blanket and shown to a room.

The next morning the beggar made a proposition. If he were allowed to live in the cellar of the house for the rest of the winter, he would carry out slops and do other menial tasks around the compound. This offer was accepted as an act of charity.

It immediately became apparent the stranger was no ordinary man. Before descending into the cellar that night he explained in a humble yet determined voice that he was under strict self-imposed vows of poverty, celibacy and silence. Save for the omitted vow of obedience, in fact, he might well have been a secret Trappist on some solitary mission.

The priest in the house was skeptical at first, but not when he found the stranger had abandoned the cellar for the even greater deprivation and privacy of a dark basement hole beneath it. Here indeed, then, was one of those anchorites who appeared from time to time in Jerusalem to pursue some personal religious task in isolation.

The anchorite never spoke again to anyone's knowledge. For the next twelve years he lived in his basement hole beneath the cellar of the house, performing his lowly duties around the compound and coming and going on occasion, but spending most of his time alone in his subterranean cell.

Or so it was assumed. Actually the cellar above his basement hole also had a small entrance that opened directly onto an alley outside the compound, so it would have been possible for him to leave without being witnessed by the priests. And in fact there were years when he wasn't seen by any of them for long periods. Because of the extreme austerity of the anchorite's existence, the priests, with affectionate humor, had come to refer to him among themselves as Brother Zeno, after the founder of Stoicism.

Then in 1836, or when the anchorite appeared to be about thirty, he walked out of the compound one morning with his open hand raised in the sign of peace, turned south at the gate without a word, and was never seen again.

His abrupt disappearance caused the priests in the compound to ponder the significance of this enigmatic man who had lived near the cathedral for twelve years. Now they spoke of Brother Zeno with awe, rather than mild humor. Where had he gone and why? What new role had he sought for himself?

In the course of the nineteenth century the account gradually acquired the dimensions of a fable around the cathedral of St James. Somehow the priests who later arrived at the Armenian compound found it immensely appealing that an anonymous man of unknown origins, and unknown destiny, had once lived in a basement hole beneath the stones where they walked, oblivious to the strictures of any church yet living the strictest of lives according to the tenets of an unspoken vocation.

The fable was so appealing it became a tradition for the most respected priest in the compound to be assigned as his residence the house that gave access to the basement hole, and to be known thereafter among the other priests as Father Zeno, in memory of that dedicated man who had mysteriously appeared there early in the nineteenth century, and just as mysteriously disappeared a dozen years later.

The present Father Zeno had received this honor in 1914 at the age of seventy-nine.

And I think what most engages our imagination, he had said to Joe, is precisely the puzzle of that man's disappearance. We here have all openly professed the vows of our vocation. Because of them we have taken our respective places in life, and so we continue in orderly lives of service and prayer until our time on earth passes. But him? What was his vocation? What had he sworn to do and where did he go? Are there callings that can never be revealed to others? And then lingering behind the mystery there is always the question of the man's apparent age when he left here, which was Christ's age when He set out on His ministry. Does it have a meaning?

Father Zeno smiled his gentle smile.

A priest may wonder about such things. Here in Jerusalem where we keep watch and bear witness to His sacrifice, we may wonder.

I can understand that, said Joe. It's a strange and haunting tale.

And then putting together everything he had learned about the life of the last of the Skanderbeg Wallensteins, which was more than he had ever admitted to Cairo or anyone else, the dates and disappearances of that pious Albanian Trappist who had left his order and gone into the Sinai to forge the original Bible, Joe leaned forward and asked his question.

What do they say Brother Zeno did in that basement hole for twelve years? Is it known?

It's assumed he was in prayer, but other than that, no. Out of respect for his privacy none of the priests ever visited him down there.

Yes of course. And did he ever have someone from outside the compound visit him?

Father Zeno looked surprised.

Why do you ask that?

No reason really. I just wondered.

Well that's odd because he did, as it happens. A minor fact but recorded, I suppose, because the visits were so rare. About once a year, according to tradition. And also because the priests at that time wondered what could possibly have gone on during those visits, in view of his vow of silence.

Perhaps he and his visitor didn't need words. Is anything remembered about the other man?

The comment's vague. He's described only as very old.

An Arab?

Now Father Zeno looked shocked.

Yes, he whispered.

The man's dress, is anything said about it?

There's one obscure reference that he wore a faded yellow cloak. Why? Does it mean anything? You can't imagine how much this interests all of us here. If we only knew more. If only I knew more.

Father Zeno clasped his hands. He lowered his eyes.

Forgive me, that was uncalled for. I didn't mean to act like a child with his first puzzle. There's much we don't know in this world and much we can never know, and it's the same for all of us. For you, for me, for all of us.

Thus Father Zeno had lowered his eyes in humility, and in humility he had laid aside the questions whose answers seemed unknowable. And Joe had learned that among the people Haj Harun visited on his yearly rounds in the Holy City, along with the nameless cobbler near Damascus Gate whose cubbyhole Haj Harun could never find, along with the nameless muttering man who ceaselessly paced back and forth on the steps to the crypt in the Church of the Holy Sepulchre, along with them there had once been a pious linguistic genius with whom Haj Harun had conversed in Aramaic, the language spoken in Palestine two and three thousand years ago.

The last of the Skanderbeg Wallensteins perfecting his skills for twelve years in a basement hole in Jerusalem, teaching himself to write with both hands because he knew the task facing him in a Sinai cave would otherwise surpass any man's endurance. Preparing himself for the creation to come, the most spectacular forgery in history.

So here beneath the rooftop home where Joe had learned to dream his Jerusalem dreams, right here in a basement hole below, lay buried the original manuscript Wallenstein had brought back from the Sinai after completing his forgery of it, that fabulous creation that had been sought by so many, a document that was unchronicled and circular and calmly contradictory, suggesting infinity, the real Sinai Bible.

Behind him his pigeons were trilling quietly as they fell asleep one after the other. Lying flat on his stomach under the stars, on the little stone bridge that led to his rooftop, Joe held his breath and peeked over the edge of the bridge, down at the narrow courtyard where a single lamp was burning. Father Zeno was at his potter's wheel and in front of him in the soft yellow light, sitting on the ground, watching, was Theresa.

Father, she whispered, it's coming again.

Watch the wheel, my child. Watch it turn.

But I'm frightened. I'm always so frightened when it comes.

Keep your eyes here, my child. We're almost finished and then we'll go in and pray together and all will be well.

Joe rolled silently over on his back and gazed up at the sky, listening to the rub and the squeak of the potter's wheel raising its vessel, the echoless rising whirl of the wheel.

Bless our little Theresa, he thought, little one that she is.

A night seemingly like so many others. Father Zeno tending his wheel and Theresa her sainthood, and above them on the rooftops, Joe, a silent witness with his sleeping pigeons, minding the dreams of new stars over Jerusalem.

Signal night, he thought, quiet place for sure. Demanding night up here beneath the murmurs of heaven.

14

Stern

And if God turns out to be a
gunrunner crossing the desert
in a balloon in 1914?

*C*hristmas Eve, 1933.

Joe sat in a filthy Arab coffee shop near Damascus Gate, slumped over an empty glass of Arab cognac. Wisps of snow blew across the windows and the wind groaned in the alleys. Only one other customer was there at that hour, an Arab laborer asleep at a front table with a newspaper over his face.

The door opened and a large shapeless man came in. He stood for a moment with his back to the door and then came shuffling heavily across the room. Joe stood up and put out his hand.

Hello, Stern.

The Arab under the newspaper stirred briefly and began to snore again. A clock on the wall clicked in the stillness. The unshaven proprietor, moving unevenly from the effects of hashish, brought the cognacs and coffee Stern had ordered. After greeting each other the two men sat for a time watching the snow dance across the windows. Joe was the first to speak.

Snow. Just like the last time. And the same night and the same place, only now it's twelve years later. You know way back then, Stern, I was telling you I was going to become the undercover King of Jerusalem. Power, that's what I wanted. And my father made just such a prophecy on a June night in 1914. Just slipped out of him it did. He had no idea what he was saying, or why, but he said it and he was right so far as what could have been. You know that, Stern? I could have been if I'd wanted to be, but I didn't want it enough. That's a funny thing about prophecy. Even when it's infallible you still have to want it to come true.

Yes.

Yes and just look at this brown oil in our glasses. They're still using it to fuel the lamps like the last time. Before you came in our staggering host there was going around filling the lamps with his wretched cognac, cheaper than kerosene I suppose and works just as well as he prepares this wreck of a place for Christmas, although why a Moslem should be preparing for Christmas is information that eludes me. Make any sense to you?

Stern smiled.

You're looking a lot older, Joe.

Me? Go on with you, not a particle of truth in it. You mean just because my beard's going white and my eyes look like a flock of pigeons have been doing a jig around them these last dozen years? No I don't believe it, but if it were true I'd say it's the rarefied air that's done it, up here on top of the holy mountain and all. A few people get younger in Jerusalem, most age. Over time this place has a way of opening up the guts of a man and laying them out for heavenly inspection. Listen, there's something I've been wanting to tell you. I'm sorry what I said to you in Smyrna in '22. That was a bad time for me and I had things mixed up, had them wrong. It's been a while, can we forget it? It was just that I wasn't doing what I wanted to be doing.

Nobody was, Joe.

Saints preserve us, that's the truth. Well I'm sorry, that's all, and I wanted to tell you so. It wasn't right, but as you say, nothing was. You still carry those awful Arab cigarettes?

Stern offered the packet.

I'm glad you got in touch, Stern, I really am. And not just so I could say I was sorry, although there's that too. My God but I was young then and didn't know much, nothing in fact, plain zero. Since then I've learned a little. You do playing poker in Jerusalem for twelve years.

Stern took a cigarette and Joe lit it for him. He watched Stern's eyes.

Hey, you all right?

What do you mean, Joe?

Nothing.

No, what is it?

The light's not too good in here for Christmas Eve, that's what it is, but what can you expect when they fuel the lamps with the same liquid shit they serve their customers. Bloody Christmas Eves, I never did like them. New Year's Eve either, they're all the same. Bloody expectations and then *boom*, you come crashing down into the truth. Eve, is that the problem? The myth was right after all and we should blame her for all our troubles?

What were you going to say before, Joe?

Can't remember. But listen, why don't you tell an old friend how your work's going? It's been a long time and I need some catching up. You've been all over the place and I've just been here, just been doing not much in Jerusalem. Well?

Look, we were there together. What is it?

Nothing.

Nothing. You want me to ask you about Theresa, Joe? She was there too. And tell you about Sivi? He was there too. He finally died two months ago, a blessing. So what was it?

All right then. It was your eyes, Stern.

What about them?

The match. When I lit the match.

Joe stopped and rubbed his head. A match here, a match in Normandy. He saw a match striking in Normandy, in a tool shed with the smell of kerosene and the stink of rotting wood. Wouldn't there ever be an end to Smyrna? Did it always have to lead you back to other things? That afternoon and evening and night in Smyrna with Stern. With Sivi and Theresa and Haj Harun. Couldn't you escape that ever?

Joe sighed.

Listen, Stern. You're not into the heavy stuff are you? I mean, you know there's only one way out of that.

Stern smiled. He pushed back his hair.

There's only one way out anyway, he said.

Joe nodded. He's big, he thought, never realized how big he really is. Bulky and substantial, just large and there and kind of shapeless but there, reassuring in a way, it's strange. And me small and slight, not much to me now or then, now or maybe ever. Just not much there. Just a poor fisherman's son who's learned to play a little poker in the Old City.

Joe?

Well Christ man I know it, know it full well. It's no easy game you're playing what with the fucking Arabs and Jews at each other's throats all the time and you being both of them and trying to make that work, and coming from where you did besides. The Yemen, what a place to grow up. And why didn't you ever tell me Strongbow was your father? I always had him down for a myth.

He was a myth, said Stern quietly.

I know it and you had to live with it. Have to live with it. Too bloody much.

How'd you find out he was my father, Joe?

Cairo Martyr. We play poker together, remember?

Oh yes, the inscrutable mummy dust dealer. But how did he find out?

From the man who adopted him when he was a child, another nineteenth-century myth who went by the name of Menelik Ziwar.

Ziwar? But that was before Strongbow retired to the Yemen. Long before I was born.

Sure, but then they got together again just before they both died. Weren't you aware of that?

No, of course I wasn't. Where was it? In the Yemen?

Not a bit of it. Old Menelik's arthritis was acting up and the best he could do was limp upstream a yard or two. It was in Egypt, in Cairo. At that same filthy restaurant beside the Nile where the two of them had had their forty-year conversation.

I don't believe it.

All true, all the same.

But I never even knew Strongbow ever left the Yemen. He'd sworn he'd never set foot west of the Red Sea again.

I guess he decided to break his promise in order to see old Menelik. And it wasn't for long, just one Sunday afternoon for lunch. It seems they were catching up on the past.

But that's astounding. When was it?

Maybe 1913? Strongbow wrote that since they were both due to go the other way before long, being in their nineties, they ought to have a last toot in their old haunt and fill up on wine and talk and spiced lamb, and then do a final repeat of their famous jump into the river at the end of the afternoon to clear their heads, so to speak, before they passed on. So that's what the two old gents did, seventy-five years after the first time. Swilled the wine and munched the lamb and raved on in general treating themselves to a scandalous Sunday afternoon, then did their leap into the Nile and went home sober, more or less. Anyway, Cairo Martyr grew up dreaming about Strongbow and all his exploits because of the things old Menelik had told him. Dreams, don't you see. Dreams. Your father gave them to an orphaned black boy growing up beside the Nile, he gave them to Haj Harun too.

He did?

Sure. What about a genie in the desert in the last century? Haj Harun on his annual haj and suddenly finding the sky strangely dark in northern Arabia, so darkly strange he knew there had to be something unusual going on of a heavenly nature. Could it be so? History making one of its moves with the help of a comet? Sound a chime of time, does it?

Joe winked.

That's right, Stern. A genie in the desert, a genie and his doings and Haj Harun a witness to it. And thereafter for Haj Harun, mysteries to dream to.

Stern leaned back and smiled. Strongbow's Comet. It had been one of his father's favorite stories. How he had discovered a comet in northern Arabia, and how a frightened Arab had stumbled upon him while he was taking measurements, and how he had explained the comet to the frightened man.

Yes indeed, said Joe. Haj Harun told me all about the experience and I repeated it to Cairo once and it matched exactly with the account of Strongbow's Comet that he had heard from old Menelik as a boy. So that's how we identified the genie Haj Harun had met out there in the desert so long ago, the very giant and worker of miracles in question. Dreams for sure, you see. Strongbow the genie just leaving them everywhere.

Stern clasped his hands tightly together on top of the table. He was staring at them, frowning, drifting away. Joe took out a thick envelope and pushed it under Stern's arm. He started for the toilet at the back of the shop.

What's that? asked Stern without looking up.

Nothing. Just put it away and forget about it.

Joe walked away. Of course Stern knew what it was. It was money, a lot of money, much more than Stern would ever have guessed. Everyone knew Stern never had any himself. Always spending what little he had on his hopeless dream of a vast Levantine homeland for Arabs and Christians and Jews together, the peoples of his heritage, Stern's mother a Yemeni Jew and his father an English lord who'd become an Arab.

That kind of homeland? That kind of dream? Hopeless. It could never happen.

But Joe wanted to give him the money all the same. Maybe he'd spend a small part of it on himself. My God it was Christmas Eve after all, at least Stern could treat himself to a new pair of shoes. The ones he was wearing looked like the same pair he'd had on in Smyrna that night on the quay, that awful September night in '22. Joe remembered those shoes, he'd never forget them. He'd been looking at them when the knife came clattering down on the cobblestones beside him, the knife that was covered with blood. Lying on his side on the cobblestones with a broken arm and down came that terrible knife beside those shoes. Worn shoes, cheap shoes, not wearing well even then. He'd have liked to have told Stern that's what the money was for tonight, the whole thick wad of bills just to buy one new pair of shoes, so they both wouldn't have to look at the old ones anymore. But of course he couldn't say that, couldn't say anything about it. You didn't talk to a man about his shoes when you hadn't seen him in over eleven years.

Worn, cheap, walking where? Why? Stumbling to what?

Hopeless, thought Joe. Bloody ideals will ruin a man every time, that's what. Kingdom come, that's what. Hopeless in this world.

He came back to the table. The envelope was where he had left it.

Joe?

Never mind now, just put it away so we can forget about it. Bloody snow won't let up, will it? Just goes right on blurring the view in this land of milk and honey that isn't. And don't get gloomy on me this Christmas Eve, I know what was bothering you just now. You were thinking how your father used to get mistaken for some marvel of a genie while you're just a gunrunner sliding downhill with a morphine habit or whatever it is you use to get you over the bumps. But let me tell you that's not all there is to it. There's another side to the tale by God, and a remarkable one it is. Makes a man's hair stand on end and maybe even have faith in the wonder of it all. Did you ever know Haj Harun recognized you the minute he laid eyes on you up there in Smyrna?

He couldn't have. We'd never met.

Oh yes you had. You'd met all right, only you were someone else then. And not just a genie out in the desert playing with his comet, nothing so minor as that. Not just a giant magician slapping a certain hue across the sky so the common folk would know a new prophet was on his way up from the wastes. More than just a Strongbow for sure. In fact you'd be surprised who you were.

Stern smiled.

Who was I?

Well I'll tell you then. The very article, that's who you were. Himself.

Who's that?

God. Now how's that for a case of mistaken identity? It beats Strongbow by more than a little and as I've often said, we have to give Haj Harun credit, we do. When he limps out there into the desert to find his way to Mecca, he sees the sights. Well this sight, and none can match it, occurred at dawn. You were up in your balloon running guns and when you came down at dawn to hide out you nearly landed right on top of Haj Harun, who naturally thought you were God coming down to reward him for his three thousand years of trying to defend the Holy City, always on the losing side. It must have been around

1914, remember it now? A broken-down old Arab in the desert at dawn tottering on spindly legs? His eyes permanently feverish with dreams from the *Thousand and One Nights*? And you coming down in your balloon and him prostrating himself and asking you if you would tell him your name? Remember?

Yes, I do now.

Well how about that then?

Stern smiled sadly. He stared down at his fists and said nothing.

Well?

It's not funny, whispered Stern after a moment. To be rewarded by a petty gunrunner in a balloon. It's not funny. Not when you have faith the way Haj Harun does.

Hold on there, said Joe, you're getting it all wrong. Not rewarded by you, rewarded by God. Listen, you've never seen eyes on this earth shine like Haj Harun's when he talks about meeting Stern in the desert at dawn. *Stern,* he murmurs, and his whole face glows with strength enough to defend the Holy City, always losing of course, for another three thousand years. *Stern,* he says, God manifesting Himself at dawn in the desert for me. And I told Him, he says, that I knew God has many names and that each one we learn brings us closer to Him, and I asked Him His name that day in the desert at dawn and He deigned to tell me, finding some virtue in my mission, even though I've always failed. *Stern,* he murmurs, and he's ready for anything, and nothing can stop him now or ever. And I tell you that's the way he saw it out there so that's the way it was, and you're the one who did it, Stern. Eyes that shine like that, it's enough to make a man cry. So you've got to let him have his due, Stern. He worked hard for that moment to come, and it finally did come, and he deserved it. And if God turns out to be a gunrunner crossing the desert in a balloon in 1914? Well what can we say about that. If that's the way it is, then you and me, we just have to accept it. We might prefer another vision of God but that's the one that came to the man who deserved a vision of God. Me, I've always known Haj Harun sees more than the rest of us. You wouldn't argue with that, would you?

No.

Of course you wouldn't. Because we're stuck in a time and a place and he isn't. We try to believe but he *does* believe, and that's the whole difference. We're sitting in Jerusalem but he really *is* up there in the

Holy City on the mountaintop. And you're not going to slouch in that chair and tell me that one of us has a better perspective on things than he does, now are you? Balloon or not? Petty gunrunning or not? Poker here or poker there, what does it matter? Not when we're using wretched lamp fuel to light our bellies on Christmas Eve. You wouldn't dare tell me any such thing and I know it. True or not?

True.

Right. Then Haj Harun saw what he saw, he learned what he learned, and that's that. One of God's secret names is Stern and there we are. Haj Harun heard it spoken to him once, and hearing it once is hearing it forever. You just can't undo the past and you just can't argue with the facts in this world and that was a fact for him, therefore is. In all his long life, the old man says, he will always cherish that moment above all others. *Stern.* One of God's secret names.

Stern looked up from the table. He opened his hands and shrugged, smiled, this time without any sadness in his face.

Joe nodded and laughed. Even though it was only a small step, he was relieved. But he also knew they still had a long way to go that night, eleven years and three months after that other night in Smyrna.

An evening for reminiscing all right, said Joe, drumming his fingers on the table. What with the alleys outside deserted under the snow and this dreadful Arab excuse for a pub doing no business at all but our meager own, not what you'd call exactly a haven of holiday cheer. Tell me now, what do you know about this formerly talking mummy named Menelik? This Ziwar of antiquity who Cairo's always going on about. Did you meet him? You must have.

Of course.

Well?

Among other things, Strongbow left him all his correspondence when he went into the desert to become a holy man.

Joe made a face.

Correspondence, you say? Yellowing letters? I don't know how awakening and arresting that is on a quiet snowy night in Jerusalem near the end of the year. Maybe we should go back to the time when I was smuggling arms for you in Haj Harun's giant hollow stone scarab. Now that was heavy lifting, I can tell you. And hard on the back with very little assistance from the resident companion sorcerer, I can tell you that too.

But this was an unusual correspondence, continued Stern. About twelve thousand letters and all from one man, the White Monk of Timbuktu.

Joe slapped the table. He whooped.

Hold it. Hold it right there. This may be something I've been looking for. The article in question, the said monastic gent in Timbuktu, he didn't also go by the name of Father Yakouba by any chance?

Yes, the same.

And when his nine hundredth child was born your father sent him a pipe of Calvados in honor of the occasion? Say about seven hundred bottles marching right down to Timbuktu, for which the extraordinary item heretofore mentioned sent your father a thank-you note dated Midsummer night, 1840? Said note thanking your father for this most welcome gift of one hundred and fifty gallons of juice? Timbuktu being as dry as dry with little to relieve the thirst except banana beer?

Stern laughed.

I hadn't heard of that letter, he said. But there was only one White Monk of the Sahara, and he and Strongbow were great friends.

Joe slapped the table again.

My God man, there we have it. Once a long time ago when I first arrived here, Haj Harun turned up with that thank-you note, the way he does you know, being a former antiquities dealer. Well the numbers involved knocked me over they did, since I was still accustomed to thinking of priests as something quite different from what this White Monk was obviously up to down there in Timbuktu. And ever since, I've been eaten with curiosity to know how that White Monk became what he did, where he did. Would you be knowing that?

Stern laughed. He nodded.

You do? Ah and ah, now that's just the job for a Christmas Eve. Just the thing to brighten up this sorry excuse for a village pub on a cold snowy night. Quickly I'll alert our host to bring us a whole bottle of his delicious fuel so we can flame at will. Now then, Stern. Who was this great skin down there in Timbuktu? And moreover, why?

286

He started out as a missionary in Tripoli, said Stern, a member of the White Father order. Originally he was from Normandy, a peasant, and he had a taste for Calvados. Well a cardinal came down to Tripoli from Paris, an art collector who was also epileptic. The cardinal was there to smuggle out some valuable mosaics, but while there he thought he should also deliver a sermon for the sake of appearances. He decided to deliver it in the desert outside of Tripoli, because he'd never seen a desert.

Joe held up his hands to interrupt.

Wait. They chose the Calvados peasant-priest's congregation for the event? It came to pass in the desert under a palm tree for shade? The cardinal got underway and had a bloody seizure?

Yes. The congregation was black and the peasant-priest was facing them, doing the interpreting, with the cardinal standing behind him. I forgot to mention that the peasant-priest was a dwarf.

Joe interrupted again.

Wait, I think I'm beginning to see it now. It's bloody hot out there and the cardinal has his fit and begins swinging his arms to keep his balance, and the Calvados peasant-priest's head is fast becoming a kind of lectern. Down rain the blows, just pounding and pounding away on your man's head, and before long he's being battered something terrible. Like this, is it?

Joe stood up and swung his arms, pounding the table.

Do I have it right? Just swinging away at this head beneath him, for Christ's sake, and then the cardinal goes into the final writhing snatch of his seizure and screams something holy? Maybe that the flesh of the lamb is good to eat? And this last blow of his is so holy and determined, has so much passionate religious conviction behind it, it bangs your man right down into the dust, just lays the dwarf flat out in the dust? True or not?

Have you heard this story, Joe?

I have not, not a word of it, but tales have a way of running true to course and so far this one's holding together as such things should. Now if I'm not wrong, I'd suspect the cardinal collapses in his sedan chair at this point and is wafted away to a cool palace in Tripoli where he can have a glass of wine and a bath and a relaxing snooze. In other words he's finished. He's done what he came to do in the story and now we can forget about him. Yes or no?

Yes.

Still on course then. Still in line and back we go to our hero, our dwarf peasant-priest, who is lying in the dust, flat out and thoroughly dazed, his head singing from the blows of higher authority, trying as best he can to recover from this very holy beating. And his black congregation is staring at him, naturally, and he's staring back at them, and nobody knows what to make of it all. I mean this appears to be a frightful way to spend a morning. True?

Yes.

And those poor blacks sitting there in the dust are starving. Any one of them would be more than happy to have a bite of lamb if they could, just as the cardinal suggested, but they know there's no hope of them ever getting their hands on a morsel, not even the tiniest. Right?

Yes.

And now we find this very same scene, utterly static, a tableau if you like, continuing on through an endless hot afternoon in the shimmering heat under that palm tree, no one moving and nothing but mirages on the horizon, not a cloud in the sky, the black congregation staring at the dwarf priest from Normandy and the dwarf peasant-priest staring at this starving congregation, just on and on as the sun slips lower and lower crushing what shade there had been and burning everyone, until there is no shade, just this hopeless heat and blistering dust, suffocating it is, and that continues for about five thousand hours or until the sun bloody well sets. Is that how it went, Stern?

Yes.

Joe sucked in his coffee and poured more cognac.

All right. Sunset. Here we are then. The sun is gone and now that it's getting dark the people under this palm tree rise like ghosts from the dust, the two sides of them, the dwarf priest on the one side, the starving blacks on the other, nobody having said a thing all day, nobody having moved a muscle all day, and the two sides go their separate ways in the shadows of the night. Correct?

Yes.

Yes, you say? Then I'm beginning to see it clearly now. Well what happens that night is that the peasant dwarf-priest locks himself in his room, lonely as he can be, just lonely as lonely, and breaks out a bottle of Calvados and says to himself, What's going on here? What was all that about? Why is an epileptic cardinal from Paris beating me senseless into the dust? Why is my head being used as a lectern by anyone anyway? Why am I spending an endless afternoon flat out in the shimmering heat, nothing but mirages around me and not a single cloud overhead, while my poor black congregation stares at me and I stare at them? Is there anything Christian about that? says the peasant-priest to himself, pouring another healthy slug of Calvados. Be that the case at hand?

Yes.

Still running to course then. So the next morning we find your man, who's done some thoughtful thinking over his bottle of Calvados in the course of a long lonely night, thinking ahead for sure and ruminating on a more amenable future for himself, we find him respectfully approaching his White Father superiors with a modest proposal. Why don't you send me to Timbuktu as a one-man missionary team, he says, and I'll convert the heathens there. Fact?

Yes.

Good, a fact. Although of course it's also true there's no French army within a thousand miles of Timbuktu, which means converting anyone there is out of the question. But his superiors decide to grant the request anyway, because losing a dwarf peasant-priest from Normandy doesn't mean anything to them, and also because a show of missionary effort so far away to the south would certainly be pleasing news to their cardinal back in Paris, who didn't find their stolen mosaics as valuable as he'd thought they'd be. Still true?

Yes.

All right. Off goes the dwarf peasant-priest, and after adventures that would take hours to recount he finally reaches Timbuktu. There he sets himself up in a dusty courtyard and begins to preach an exceptionally mild message of love that's all-encompassing. Love thy neighbor, sure, that's for certain. But don't stop there. Love strangers and non-neighbors, in fact love everyone you ever meet. Is that it?

Yes.

Do a certain amount of honest labor, but after that and before that and in between times, love anyone you happen to find on the premises?

Yes.

Joe jumped to his feet. He pushed back his chair and climbed up on it. The snow was falling faster outside. The Arab who had been asleep at the front of the shop belched and scratched his groin and belched again, staring in disbelief at Joe standing on his chair, his arms outstretched, dressed in the baking priest's shabby uniform from the Crimean War.

And it is especially important, intoned Joe, caressing the fetid air with his hands, that no one should ever find himself sitting alone in the dust on a hot afternoon staring at a group of people. Nor should a group of people sit and stare at a poor lonely person, even a dwarf, who happens to find himself alone across the way. Instead both sides should rise at once and mix in the love of God. In short, *make love* for God's sake. Don't just sit and stare, make love, now and quickly and all together. Was that the ultra-Christian message, Stern, that was heard down there in Timbuktu?

Stern nodded, smiling up at Joe.

Well then, said Joe, that must be a true account of how a former peasant-priest from Normandy came to establish a huge polysexual commune on the far side of the Sahara in the nineteenth century. And by this manner of activity one Father Yakouba, a dwarf more generally known as the White Monk of the Sahara, became the father in time of nine hundred children. On which occasion the legendary explorer Strongbow, your said father, sent to his old friend the said dwarf in Timbuktu, by way of most sincere and congratulatory sentiments, a pipe of the priest's most favored beverage, Calvados, which by a less prodigious man's measurements would be some seven hundred regular bottles of the stuff. Am I still free from error?

Yes.

Joe dropped his arms. He jumped to the floor, coughing, and sat down. He drank and lit a cigarette.

Wretched drink, this lamp fuel, saints preserve us. But it's cold tonight and we need it. Cairo told me all that by the way. He had it from Menelik, who of course picked it up in his forty-year conversation with Strongbow. But my God what a giant of a dwarf, the White Monk of the Sahara. You know what I wish sometimes? I wish I'd known just one of those characters from the last century. Old Menelik, the White Monk, Strongbow the genie, just one of them.

290

Joe tried to laugh but he coughed instead.

I know, he said, when the coughing subsided, why am I always talking about the past? Bad habit, I'll have to get over it someday. Have to get over all my habits someday. And maybe you'll be wanting to talk to me about Maudie now that you've met her. How she tried to trace Sivi after the massacre in Smyrna and couldn't, and only found out years later that he was living in Istanbul, if you could call it living after what Smyrna had done to him. Poor old Sivi. Christ she must have been shocked finding him like that, living in a tiny squalid room by the Bosporus and working as a laborer in a hospital for incurables, forgetting even to feed himself half the time. And I can understand why she moved there to take care of him, loving him as she did and trying to have that link with the past at least, until he died and she went back to Athens. Sivi would have been that for her even then, giving her life some meaning. Ah the wreckage in this world, what can you say about it? How can you ever explain it to yourself? And Sivi of all people. From what I've heard just about the kindest, gentlest man who ever lived. Always helping everybody and he ended like that. So what's to say? Nothing, that's what.

How'd you know all that about Maud?

Munk. She and Munk have been friends since after the war, you know.

I didn't, but I should have guessed. Through Sivi of course.

Yes. And I've tried to help her, Stern. I gave Munk money to give to her, saying it was a gift or a loan or anything from him, not me, but she wouldn't take it. She must have known it was coming from me and couldn't bring herself to accept it after the way she left me. Munk's tried to help her too but she always refuses, still thinking it's coming from me, I suppose.

But, Joe, why haven't you ever gone to see her?

I didn't think it would help. You can't go back, Stern, you just can't. I know that. I'll never love another woman the way I loved her, but still you can't go back. It's just too long ago and I've put it behind me as best I can. You have to do that, you just have to.

Well what about your son?

Joe smiled.

Bernini. That's a lovely name she gave the lad. I'm going to be seeing him soon, but I won't be seeing Maudie and I don't want her to know, it's better that way. She's got some kind of balance worked out in her life and I don't want to upset it, especially with Sivi just dying. He was her family after all. Brother, father, everything. All she ever had. And I know she must still have some painful memories about me. Time, it takes. So someday maybe. Another time, another place. But listen, I've got a favor to ask you. If she ever needs money, I mean if you can see she really needs it, I'd like you to let me know, write to me, so I can send it to you. She'd accept it from you if she didn't know we knew each other, which she doesn't. I never told her who I was running guns for back when we had that house in Jericho. So will you not tell her? Will you do that for me? So I can get money to her through you, if she needs it?

Stern nodded.

Of course.

Thanks, I appreciate it. Now let me pass on my stirring local news. Cairo and me, we're ending the poker game in a few days. Munk doesn't know it but it's all over at last.

You're leaving Jerusalem?

By the stars, Stern, by the stars.

Where to?

Me? The New World, where else. Ever since I met Maudie and she told me about her Cheyenne grandmother, I've been fascinated by the American Indians. I want to see them. Maybe even try living with them for a while.

Stern smiled.

And Cairo?

He'll be heading back to Africa. You haven't met him, have you?

No.

More's the loss. A fine article, that, totally fine. Holds in trust what you tell him, then hears what you don't tell him and holds that in trust too. Whoever old Menelik was, he should be canonized, bringing up Cairo the way he did. Who was he, Stern?

Strongbow's best friend.

That's a lot.

Yes.

But you shouldn't go on lingering under that burden, Stern. Shouldn't do it. No man can.

I suppose.

Wretched stuff, fuel for lamps. Burns your wick but burns it down and out too.

Joe? What about Haj Harun?

I know, I've thought about that. Munk'll just have to watch out for him. If he wants this bloody place he'll just have to take on the responsibilities.

It'll be all right?

My God how do I know, I guess it'll have to be. Nearly three thousand years he survived here before I met him. Why not now without me?

Because things are changing, Joe.

So they are, so they always are. Changing in Jerusalem, changes in the Old City. How about you. You're going to carry on with what you're doing?

Yes.

No offense, but you know by now it can't work.

Maybe.

Not maybe. You know. The point is you're going to continue doing it anyway?

I have no choice.

Joe leaned forward and placed his hands flat on the table. He gazed at the bulging veins that hadn't shown a few years ago.

No choice, Stern? *No* choice?

Stern nodded slowly.

Yes. It seems it's that way sometimes.

Joe closed his eyes and shook his head. Stern was speaking very quietly.

Joe? That time in Smyrna?

I hear you.

The smoke and the fires, you remember?

We had to get to it, didn't we. Shared it and had to get to it. Yes, I remember.

And Sivi going mad.

Going all right, going and never coming back. A September Sunday in 1922.

And Theresa beating her head on the floor and screaming *Who is that?*

I hear it. I've heard it more than once since then and I hear it now, poor little one.

And Haj Harun?

Yes, trailing his great long bloody sword up there in the garden, weeping and wandering around and around lost in the flowers, lost in the smoke and the flames, just lost, that old blessed sack of bones. Tears my heart it does, him and his tattered yellow cloak and his rusty Crusader's helmet, standing there in the garden holding up his sword, preparing to charge the Turkish soldier who found us hiding there. Been dead before he took a step of course, the rifle aimed straight at his middle, but there he was ready to defend the innocent, defending his Holy City of life in terrible Smyrna with an old sword, awful it was, that moment, I died for him a dozen times before I got the pistol up and shot that soldier in the head. And you know what he's been asking me recently? If we shouldn't arm ourselves because of the way the Arabs and the Jews are going at each other here. The two of us I mean, imagine that. The two of us standing up together to defend Jerusalem. What do you say to something like that? It's daft and all too real.

And the other thing, Joe. The other thing up there.

Joe rubbed his eyes. He emptied his glass.

Yes that too. All right, we've got to do that too. The little Armenian girl on the quay that night dressed in her Sunday best, her Sunday black, because it was a Sunday. Maybe eight years old and raped and bloodied within a breath of her life, lying out there all alone in that hell of screams and smoke and dying. Dying, that's all, the fires on one side and the harbor on the other and no place to go, no place to take her, just dying in unbearable pain. And what you did, Stern, was what I should have done, and I wish I had done it so it wouldn't be tormenting you now. *Please,* she said in Armenian, and you told me what it meant but I didn't do anything so you did, and I should have done it but I was too angry at you and Maudie and the whole fucking bloody world. Mad at myself I mean, let's keep it honest. So after all, Stern, what did you do but end a dying child's pain? Ended the torture.

There was no way she could have lived through that night.

Joe?

I tell you Haj Harun did the same thing and that's why he was weeping in the garden. It happened outside the garden. There was an old Armenian man who'd had his eyes torn out and he was walking into the flames, finished. Strands of bloody tissue hanging from his empty eye sockets. Tears of blood, Stern. Immovable tears. *For the love of God*, he was screaming, *kill me before I burn*. And Haj Harun did. Gentle harmless old soul that he is, he raised his sword and swung it and after that I had to take him by the hand and lead him back to the garden or he never would have found it, he was crying so hard. And Stern, he's been on the losing side for three thousand years defending the Holy City, everybody's Holy City. You're always on the losing side in such a game but he goes on. Always. Losing is all. So what did you do that was so bad?

Stern's hands were shaking. He reached out and gripped Joe's arm.

I'll tell you what I did. I took a knife. *I slit her throat.*

Oh Christ man, screamed Joe, *it wasn't your fault.*

Stern's chair went crashing backward onto the floor. He lurched to his feet and stared at Joe with wild eyes, backing away from the table. Backing away and stumbling clumsily across the room.

Wait, called Joe, you can't just go on running. We'll talk. *Don't go on running.*

Stern stared, a trapped animal backing away, big and hunched and shapeless. He knocked over a chair and kept on backing away, hit a table and backed into the door, frantically groping for the door handle behind him, trapped, trying to escape.

Stern, for Christ's sake. *Wait.*

The door banged open. An empty frame of darkness, snow swirling across it. Joe felt the blast of cold air all the way at the back of the room. He sat there looking at the night and the snow in the empty doorway.

Don't go on running. Once, in this very room, Stern had said the same thing to him. A dozen years ago that was, before Smyrna. Strange, thought Joe, how the words that were meant to help were always the same. Someone said them to you when you were sinking, trying to help, and then a dozen years later you were saying the same words to them. Saying and saying, going around, it never ended. But you just couldn't help running sometimes, just couldn't, you ran away from yourself, just had to, trying to survive in the cold and the darkness. Everyone a victim now or then, everyone, trying to survive.

How long could Stern manage with his morphine? Taking morphine and living with his hopeless dream of a homeland that could never be, Arabs and Christians and Jews together, trying to believe. How long? Running.

The door banged closed. Wind gusting in the alleys and sucking it closed, sealing the light from the darkness, the warmth from the cold, swirling snow in the land of milk and honey.

He was vulnerable, Stern, and that's why people loved him. Bulky and shapeless and going down yet trying to believe, and that's why people loved him. Everybody longed to believe and wanted to reach out to the man who tried to. But everybody didn't make it. Everybody couldn't. How long for Stern?

Running.

The Arab at the front of the shop was snoring again under his newspaper. Joe pushed back his chair and dragged himself wearily to his feet. He'd tried, but it hadn't worked out. A small step at first, then nothing. But maybe someday Stern would recall that small step, maybe sometime it would help him just a little as he sank and sank with morphine in his hopeless dream.

Yes, *Stern.* That too was one of God's secret names.

The proprietor of the shop looked dazed as he staggered over to the table. He managed an oily smile.

Why not? thought Joe. Time for him to collect a tip if he can. More important to him now than the snow and the silence, the darkness, has his troubles like everybody else making a living, making a life. Best he can do. Eyes out of focus and teeth rotting in his head, on the limp and looking to ingratiate himself, best he can do.

Want a woman, sir?

No thanks.

A boy?

No thanks either.

Someone else? It's cold tonight.

I know it.

Snowing, cold. Not a night to be alone out there.

I know it.

Hashish?

No.

So what do you want?

Nothing, nothing at all. Here. Keep it.

The Arab looked down at the handful of bills. His smile spread.

You Jewish?

No.

Christian?

Born that way, yes.

Merry Christmas then.

Right. Thanks.

15
Sheik Ibrahim ibn Harun

What is this game we've been playing, Cairo?
And where did it really start?

Christmas day and Cairo had brought buckets of lobsters and champagne to the little roof in the Armenian Quarter where Joe lived with his pigeons. The weather was cold and raw, the sky overcast, but they set up a table outside so they could have the city spread out in front of them while they celebrated, their time in Jerusalem almost over now.

Here we are in overcoats again, mused Joe, just like that first day of the game twelve years ago when we sat down on the floor in the back of Haj Harun's shop. Funny how things come around and come together. Speaking of which, Cairo, I'm glad you came. I wouldn't have thought of anything so fine as lobster.

I know you wouldn't have. You'd have been inside crouched over your turf fire nursing some dreadful stew.

True enough, and that would have been all right too, but this is much better. The kind of occasion a man can look back to when he's finishing up and getting ready to go the other way, no doubt off in some bloody unknown corner of the world by then, tottering around on useless legs and creaking in every joint and cursing the day he was born, certainly cursing another Christmas to be faced, for what's the sense of celebrating something and trying to be happy when it's all over and behind you and there's no more to come? And probably in his cups as usual on Christmas because that's a black day in Ireland, which is to say the pubs are closed, and alone at home in a dark mood shaking his head and muttering cross thoughts like the malcontent he is at the end of life, having seen what he thinks he's seen although most of it was a blur, when all at once he stays that glass on its way to his lips and peers down into it, right down into that muddy well of his soul, and takes a good look and says to himself, Hold on there you villainous trickster, what do you mean forgetting that beautiful Christmas years and decades ago when you were sitting on a rooftop in Jerusalem with your feet up, you and a friend feasting like lords with the Holy City itself spread out at your feet? Right there in front of you, you grumbling ingrate. And your man will have to admit it then. He'll have to stop cursing everything in sight and throw a smile back into his glass. Dhrink I may, he'll say then, but I've known those moments, I have, those beautiful rare moments and it's all been worth it because of them, all worth it and more because of those sweet rare moments, ah just the sweetest. Sure, that's what he's going to have to say in the end, coming around to the truth at last after a wicked and dissolute life. So will you raise a glass to that, Cairo lad? To this very moment and none other?

Cairo laughed. He uncorked another bottle of champagne and the pigeons took flight. The two of them watched the pigeons fly away and slowly return, swooping in ever narrower circles.

By God they're getting little enough rest today with all these champagne shots going off. But it's nice to see them circling overhead all the same, knowing their home and coming back to it.

Who's going to feed them after you leave?

Don't know, but I'll find some unemployed beggar or pious fanatic to do the trick, no shortage of hands like that in Jerusalem. Say Cairo, I was just thinking. Why'd you really suggest we let Munk win all our money?

Why not? Isn't it appropriate? The three of us began the game and we're dropping out, so he should be the winner.

That's fine with me as I said, but I still have this feeling.

What feeling?

That there's something more. Another reason. Let's admit it, Cairo lad, you're shamelessly sentimental. So what's the other reason?

Cairo tipped his head. He smiled.

Family. That's the other reason.

Joe nodded. He cracked a lobster tail. Juice squirted over his face and he dabbed at it, licking his finger.

Do you tell me that?

Yes. Munk and I are cousins.

Joe waved the lobster tail toward the city.

Hear that, Jerusalem? You just see how it goes around here?

He turned to Cairo and grinned.

Now hold on there, go slow with me today. I'm feasting on a Christmas banquet and not thinking too clearly. Not making a little joke are you?

No.

Cousins, you say? You and the Munk are cousins?

Yes.

Well you wouldn't look to be cousins, that much I'm sure of. But if you say you are, you are. Some years ago I learned it's best not to disbelieve anything you hear around here. So all right then. How do you and Munk come to be cousins?

We had the same great-grandfather.

Joe whistled softly.

And why not, I say. I've always wondered why you had blue eyes. Well he must have been a wandering man. A fair-skinned Sudanese then? Or a dark-skinned Hungarian?

Cairo laughed.

Neither. He was Swiss.

Ah, of course he was, I should have guessed. Traditional neutrality and so forth, not wanting either of you to think he was favored over the other. Clever man he must have been too, keeping his options open in the manner he did, not about to limit his familial future by way of race or continent either. But who was this wandering ancestor with tendencies to father sons in lands as disparate as Hungary and the Sudan?

Albania was another.

300

Also a son in Albania, you say? I don't think I like that. The only Albanians I've ever heard of are the Wallensteins. Now you're not going to be telling me that nasty little Nubar Wallenstein is also kin to the two of you. Not so much, are you? Tell me it's not the case.

Cairo smiled.

I'm afraid it is.

It is? Then I'm afraid I just went overboard at sea in rough weather with nothing to hold on to. Or maybe what's worse, lost my bearings in a vast bog with the evening light sinking and me having no idea which way is out. Take pity, Cairo, which way *is* out? Who was this wandering Swiss?

His name was Johann Luigi Szondi. Born in Basle in 1784.

Why do you mention Basle?

Because that's where Strongbow's study was published and burned nearly a century later.

Stop it, Cairo, we'll just leave Strongbow out of this. Go back to this Luigi fellow. Who was he?

A highly gifted linguist with a passion for details.

Details? I believe it. He left enough of them scattered around. So he's born highly gifted, what next?

In 1802, as a student, Johann Luigi made a walking tour to the Levant and asked for lodging one night in an Albanian castle. The master of the castle was away at war, the master's young wife was alone and friendly. Check an Albanian cousin. Later Johann Luigi became a doctor in Budapest and married Munk's great-grandmother, Sarah the First. Check a Hungarian cousin. Later still he traveled through the Middle East and Africa in disguise, and met my great-grandmother in a village on the fringe of the Nubian desert. Check a Sudanese cousin.

Check, said Joe, I'm suddenly tired. All this moving around and fathering sons at the beginning of the last century is exhausting. Before you tell me any more, can't we just sit still for a moment and contemplate the view?

Of course we can. In fact that's exactly what I was going to suggest.

You were?

Yes. Now let's allow about a hundred years to go by and position ourselves in front of a villa beside the Bosporus.

Why would we want to do that?

To contemplate the view, and also to consider a remarkable event.

Tell me, how do you imagine it's known that young Johann Luigi made a walking tour to the Levant in 1802?

I think Luigi might have told his wife about it later when he married her, Sarah the First. She could have passed the information on down and thus Munk would have the fact tucked away today.

Correct. And the night on that walking tour when Johann Luigi stayed in an Albanian castle? Entertained by a young and friendly wife whose husband was away at war?

I think maybe Luigi didn't bother to mention that one to Sarah the First. No reason to alarm her after the fact, marriage being sacred and all. Merely an indiscretion in his youth, and only one night of it at that.

Cairo gazed out over the city.

Hey wait, said Joe, sitting up. Only one night in the Wallenstein castle and then on his way? How did Luigi know he'd made the wife in the castle pregnant?

Cairo flashed his smile.

That's right. How indeed?

Well he couldn't have known. So there's no way he could have passed on that information to anyone. That information could only have come from the young and friendly wife in the Wallenstein castle.

Correct.

So where are we?

As I said, we're standing in front of a villa beside the Bosporus about a century later, contemplating the view. The year is 1911, to be exact. As we gaze at the last of the sunset over Europe we notice that a carriage is approaching the villa, its curtains drawn.

Which curtains? Carriage or villa?

Both.

Ah.

Now. The gate to the villa is situated in such a way that visitors can draw up to the entrance without being seen by observers such as us, who are seemingly standing beside the Bosporus gazing at sunsets. Naturally, considering the nature of the business often conducted by the person or persons unknown who reside in this villa.

Nefarious business, said Joe, that's what. I can see it coming. All manner of pranks, did you say, going on in this villa?

Perhaps. Now the two of us aren't everyday observers, we both know that, and with our superior vision we're able to see this particular visitor who has just alighted from the curtained carriage to enter the curtained villa. And we do so even though the sun has set and the villa is cloaked in impenetrable shadows.

Shadows, muttered Joe, pouring more champagne. I sense a rendezvous in the works that can't bear the light of day. Definitely a clandestine affair. Of course I already suspected that when I took careful note of the curtains over all and sundry.

Correct, said Cairo. Now can you make out the visitor who is emerging from the carriage in the shadows?

I'm peering. I honestly am. My eyes are sharply narrowed and I'm using my best night vision.

And?

And all I see is an indistinct figure.

A very small figure? asked Cairo.

Yes. Most unusually small.

A woman?

How did you know my suspicions were running in that direction? Well just wait a minute, let me check the gait and the movements. Yes, a woman all right. No question about it.

Dressed entirely in black?

Black as the hour of night. But she's not about to fool me even in those impenetrable shadows.

Is she wearing a black veil?

That she is, said Joe. Hiding her face of course. A clever and cautious woman from beginning to end.

What's that you see sticking through a hole in her veil?

How about that. A cigarette maybe? Must be a heavy smoker if she can't even wait until she gets inside to light up.

You're sure it's a cigarette?

To be frank, I'm not. It's hard to make it out from this distance, 1911 being some time ago and all. I was only eleven then and not thinking much about cigarettes.

I think it looks too long for a cigarette, said Cairo.

Precisely my thoughts.

But it could be a long thin cigar. A cheroot maybe.

Has to be a cheroot, said Joe. I was just going to say so.

Some sort of special Turkish cheroot she has made to order?

Makes sense, murmured Joe. After all we are in Turkey.

Exactly. Careful now, is that the door of the villa opening?

It is, and not making a sound in doing so. Wouldn't you just know it? Well-oiled hinges in the curtained villa in keeping with nefarious practices.

Is that a man stepping out to greet the tiny woman dressed entirely in black?

None other. A man and just as cautious and clever as the tiny woman he's greeting. Skulduggery's afoot and a romantic assignation seems a highly likely possibility.

Is the man wearing a uniform? asked Cairo.

No mistaking a uniform, said Joe. I often wear one myself and you can't fool me there.

And this host cuts a dashing figure in his uniform?

Decidedly dashing. Women along the Bosporus probably make fools of themselves when faced with that dashing figure. Although why my own uniform never has that effect I can't imagine.

Would you say he's a young man? asked Cairo.

That he is, unexpectedly so.

Do you recognize the uniform?

I'm trying, but again this distance of twenty-two years is making things less clear than they should be.

Could it be the uniform of a cavalry officer?

Joe turned and looked at Cairo.

Yes.

Dragoons?

Joe stared at Cairo.

Yes.

A lieutenant colonel of dragoons in the Austro-Hungarian Imperial Army?

Joe whistled softly.

My God, how about that. We're spying on Munk as a young man.

And his visitor, the tiny woman in black? You still don't recognize her?

No, I don't. In fact I'm pretty sure I've never seen her before.

You haven't, said Cairo emphatically. And I've never seen her either. At this point in time, 1911, there are only a handful of people in the world who would recognize her, and most of them peasants, because she has lived such a reclusive life in her little corner of the world. Only a year or two ago she emerged from strict seclusion after mourning the death of her common-law husband. And before that, and for many decades, she lived so modestly and said so little while doing so, she was generally referred to as the Unspoken. But just give her a few more years, I tell you, and she's going to become notorious. Men in high positions all over the world will know this tiny woman as *the Black Hand*.

Joe whistled very softly.

Sophia? Is it really Sophia coming to call on Munk?

Cairo smiled.

After emerging from mourning, Sophia has toyed with lignite mines in Albania and decided to look into oil. She's been studying the oil situation in the Middle East and has become convinced that substantial reserves are to be found along the Tigris. She wants to put a syndicate together to exploit this oil, but to do so she first needs a charter from the Ottoman government, which is in a state of terminal decay and is hopelessly corrupt. Who should she approach with bribes? The routes are multiple and devious. It is absolutely essential that she get confidential information from a disinterested observer, someone outside the government, who is both knowledgeable and thoroughly trustworthy. She has made numerous inquiries in Constantinople and the answers coincide. It appears the person to see is the brilliant young Austro-Hungarian military attaché in the capital. It's true that he's astonishingly young to be in such a position, but everyone agrees he is fully cognizant of the intrigues within the Ottoman menagerie. Furthermore, he happens to be a scion of the most powerful financial family in central Europe, the revered House of Szondi.

That decides Sophia. The House of Szondi is run exclusively by women and therefore she trusts it. Therefore she will go to the scion even though he is astonishingly young.

Secretly Sophia contacts the young lieutenant colonel and a meeting is arranged at his villa, just after sunset for purposes of security, a few weeks hence. The young lieutenant colonel, meanwhile, checks into Sophia's background and finds she is the head of the important Wallenstein clan in Albania. The political situation in the Balkans, never more unstable than now, is of great interest to the Austro-Hungarian Empire, therefore to its military attaché in Constantinople. Mightn't this head of an important Albanian clan have much to tell him? Mightn't this even be an assignment of the highest priority?

Duty calls. Obviously more could come from this meeting if it were not just a dull business conference in a dull business setting. And so we find certain preparations being made in the villa.

For one, the formal dining room has been rejected in favor of a cozy alcove at one end of the paneled library. Here an array of delicacies have been laid out by the servants, who have then been given the night off. Candles cast a soft glow in the villa. An inviting fire crackles in the library fireplace, in front of which sit two deep leather lounging chairs and a soft deep leather sofa. Joe? Are you all right?

Joe's eyes were wide. Cairo smiled broadly.

Now then, said Cairo. What obviously lies before us is a leisurely dinner for two in a secluded villa beside the Bosporus, a sparkling evening over champagne in a cozy setting. Strictly out of duty, mind you, our young military attaché intends to carry out his mission in a most relaxed atmosphere, bringing all his considerable charm to bear.

Joe broke out of his trance. He pounded the table and began leaping around the rooftop, singing, doing a kind of dance.

Our very own Munk, *ho ho ho.* Turning on the charm for Sophia, *ho ho ho.*

Suddenly he stopped in front of the table.

Sophia? Wait a minute. Sophia still the Unspoken? My God, how old was she then?

Sixty-nine, said Cairo dryly. Munk was twenty-one.

Joe roared with laughter and slapped the table. He sat down, only to jump to his feet again.

This is stunning, simply stunning. Here I thought there was going to be a way out of this lurid Luigi bog before nightfall and instead I'm sinking deeper all the time. Candlelight and champagne in Constantinople, you say? Dashing young Munk in his dashing cavalry uniform just leisurely doing his duty at a private sumptuous dinner for two in a villa beside the Bosporus? Fires crackling invitingly and candles casting glows? Soft deep leather lounging chairs and sofas? Delicacies in a cozy alcove? On with it, for God's sake, before I have a liver attack.

Cairo cleared his throat.

It may be you haven't had experience in these matters.

My God of course I haven't, you know that. Just don't ease off now, get on with it.

Yes. Well, you see, when I worked as a dragoman in Egypt back before the war I found there were occasions, not as infrequent as you might think, when an older woman, even a much older woman, could be strongly attracted to a much younger man. Now if she were a wise woman, as Sophia obviously is, she had no illusions about it. She knew perfectly well what was happening and why, but that didn't mean she couldn't enjoy herself.

Oh help, saints preserve us. You don't mean to say the dinner is going to progress from private to intimate?

I do. That's precisely what I mean.

Then here's another quick shot of champagne for both of us. You may not need it but I do. And don't stop. Keep this amazing news churning.

Well, in short, we find the evening taking a vivid course. Dishes are tasted, corks pop, there are pleasantries and laughter. Sophia happens to recall several off-color anecdotes, having to do with itinerant Armenian rug dealers, that have been passed down from mother to daughter in her family for a couple of centuries. Munk, for his part, is able to repeat a number of naughty insinuations currently making the rounds in Constantinople's demimonde. And all the while Sophia is well aware that in return for the attentive favors of this handsome young lieutenant colonel of dragoons, information useful to him is expected. Political and economic information concerning the Balkans.

No, shouted Joe, jumping up and sitting down again. Not another bloody word about the Balkans. Quickly back to the candlelight dinner and tell me what happened next. I know what you're going to say. What happened next?

They made love, said Cairo quietly.

Joe banged the table. He shrieked.

Ha. I knew it. I just knew you were going to say that. All that cozy candlelight beside the Bosporus, it'll get you every time. But my God, is this true? Did Munk really do that?

Yes, a thoroughly friendly matter. Even so, it took some time to bring off.

307

What?

Well when a woman gets into her late sixties, you see.

No. Hold it right there, Cairo. I don't see and that's not information I need at the moment, it's not a problem I'm facing. When the time comes, forty years from now if it does, I'll write you a letter and you can fill me in. But will you just imagine Munk up to something like that? And you too when you were back in Egypt, you shameless dragoman-ex. Where's it come from anyway, this scandalous behavior? Did you both inherit something from this Luigi fellow?

Cairo smiled. Joe was chain-smoking and puffing furiously.

Now just let me calm myself, he said, blowing smoke everywhere. And before we get mixed up with this Luigi fellow again, give me a hint of how the evening in the villa ended. How did it end?

Not until the following morning. The night was a busy one and no one got any sleep. Fortunately the servants weren't due back until noon the next day.

And?

And after some final activities that accompanied the sunrise, Munk fell asleep in his bed. He woke up toward the middle of the morning, hearing water running.

Water?

Sophia was drawing a bath for him.

Ah and ah. What else?

Delicious smells were coming from the kitchen. Munk noticed that his uniform, newly pressed, had been laid out over a chair. His boots, newly polished, stood beside the chair. There was also a bouquet of flowers, freshly picked from the garden, on the night table. Sophia had evidently been bustling about while Munk caught his few hours of sleep. When he finished his bath Sophia appeared with a tray and served him breakfast in bed.

What?

As I recall, freshly squeezed orange juice, eggs and a steak, a pot of strong coffee laced with cognac, and a mountain of hot rolls straight from the oven. Extremely light, he said. Mere fluffs of ambrosia.

Fluffs, yes. Ambrosia. Then?

Then the tiny old woman smiled in the doorway, threw him a wink and was gone. Altogether a singular performance, said Munk. A singular evening, a singular night, a singular morning after. It was his opinion that a woman fifty years younger couldn't have possibly equaled it. There was only one problem.

There was? What?

His back. His back was absolutely covered with long deep scratches. Fingernails, you see. Uncontrollable passion.

I see.

But of course he was more than ready to suffer that because of what had gone with it.

Of course.

And he also had great difficulty walking. His legs, he said, were like jelly.

Jelly, yes.

And he couldn't really straighten up, and he'd never been so sore. Every muscle in his body ached from the experience, although naturally that was fine too.

Joe sagged in his chair.

I'm limp, he said, I can't move. That's all, I hope.

Not quite. Apparently the heavy scent of Sophia's cheroots lingered in the bedroom for days. Munk said he used to go in there and find himself immediately lost in a reverie. He said it was several weeks before he could pull himself together and get back to working in a proper manner.

Proper? cried Joe. What's proper about any of these goings-on? It's all outrageous, that's what, and should never have been repeated to a sober Christian like myself. Mere fluffs of ambrosia indeed. A scandal.

Cairo laughed.

Now in the course of that very long night Sophia talked about a number of things, including the man she'd loved all her life, the last of the Skanderbeg Wallensteins. Her mother had been a servant in the Wallenstein castle in 1802, when that young and friendly Wallenstein wife had taken a Swiss stranger to her bed, and had been so excited by it she had to tell some of her female servants about it the next day, after the stranger had gone on his way. Thus Sophia was able to describe the Swiss stranger who'd been the father of her beloved Skanderbeg, the young Swiss student with a passion for details who'd been on a walking tour to the Levant that year. I mean she described his appearance exactly, down to a quite specific and intimate fact.

What fact? asked Joe.

Cairo cleared his throat.

It seems the Hungarian Szondi men all inherited a certain peculiarity from Johann Luigi.

What peculiarity?

A physical one that proved exceptionally pleasurable to the Szondi women.

Move on, Cairo, what specific fact?

It has to do with size, with dimension.

Oh.

And with a change in direction.

Oh?

Highly unusual. About halfway along, it seems, matters take an abrupt turn. Thus movement is going on in many directions at once, so that the love the Szondi man is expressing is being expressed in a whole host of different manners at one and the same time. Apparently you can't speak of thrust in such a case. And in and out is simply out of the question. Apparently there's only one word for the sensation the woman feels inside her in such a case.

Which is?

An explosion. A vast explosion of continuing duration as long as he's inside her. That change of direction, you see, simply strikes everywhere. Apparently it feels as if something about the size of a baby's head is in there, humming and singing and shouting for joy.

Explosions, muttered Joe. These revelations are exhausting me. Back to Munk and Sophia at once.

Yes. Well when Sophia described the young Swiss student who had impregnated the young and friendly Wallenstein wife in 1802, Munk recognized at once that this student was none other than his own great-grandfather, the tireless Johann Luigi Szondi.

Tireless Luigi, said Joe. That's him all right. But hold on there. What about this male Szondi peculiarity you were speaking of?

What about it?

Well Sophia had just spent the night with Munk.

Yes.

And so?

Oh you mean didn't she recognize the similarity, the connection, between Munk and that Swiss student of the early nineteenth century? Of course she did. No woman could mistake that explosion. In fact

310

Munk speculates that was the real reason, once they'd got into bed, that Sophia was so taken with him. He's modest about it and doesn't put it down to his charm. No, he thinks Sophia must have found the idea of it immensely appealing. Erotic to the outer limits, in other words, making love with the great-grandson of the man who'd fathered her beloved Skanderbeg.

I'll never understand the Balkans, said Joe. Go on.

Well Sophia also told Munk how her Skanderbeg, formerly a Trappist by the way, had discovered the original Bible in the Holy Land, been shocked by its chaos and gone on to forge an acceptable version. A new original.

Discovered what? whispered Joe. The wind up here's playing tricks with my head.

The original Bible, repeated Cairo slowly. You know, the Sinai Bible.

Joe choked. He reached for his handkerchief but didn't get it up to his mouth in time. A slug of dark brown phlegm shot out of his throat and landed in his champagne glass. Joe gazed absentmindedly at the glass for a moment and fished in it with a spoon.

You're smoking too much, said Cairo.

Joe nodded vaguely.

I believe it. What I don't believe is this business about the Sinai Bible, Munk knowing about it all these years. Why didn't he ever mention it to me?

Did you ever mention it to him?

No.

Well?

I see. But wasn't he interested in finding it?

Munk's not religious, said Cairo. You know that.

I do. But I'm not religious either.

So?

Joe shook his head. He seemed dazed.

All right, Cairo, so the bog's all around me and I'm sinking fast. Give me a hand and pull me out before my head goes under. In other words, when did you learn all this from Munk? About this Luigi fellow who was your common great-grandfather and what he'd been up to one night in Albania? No I don't mean that, I mean about the Sinai Bible. When did you learn about the Sinai Bible?

When I met Munk.

What? All the way back at the beginning of the poker game?

Yes.

How'd it happen? I'm about to go under for the last time.

I asked Munk about his name. Menelik Ziwar had told me my great-grandfather's real name was Szondi.

He did? Old Menelik the mummy? On his back in the bottom of his sarcophagus conjuring up the past again? Well I thought I was going under for the last time but it seems you can sink forever in this bog. I mean, how did old Menelik know that? I always thought he was ferreting out tombs along the Nile, not spending time down in villages on the fringe of the Nubian desert soliciting accounts of Swiss wanderers who had passed that way in disguise some years before he was born.

Menelik had known my great-grandmother when he was young, when they were both slaves in the delta. She told him about the father of her child, who'd been a well-known expert in Islamic law in his day. Later Menelik was able to trace this expert back to Aleppo, where he discovered his real identity. Aleppo, you see, was where Johann Luigi had lived for several years, perfecting his Arabic, before assuming his disguise and setting out on his wanderings.

Ah sure, someone's real identity. So tell me now in the end when it's almost over, what is this game we've been playing, Cairo? And where did it really start?

Cairo laughed. Any one of those places we've mentioned?

Yes I suppose. And when. When did it start?

Any one of those times we've mentioned?

I believe it, I do. All these years I've been circling around like my pigeons up there. Well why not pop another song of time so we can see the scheme of things over the Old City?

Cairo opened another bottle of champagne and the pigeons scattered in the air. The two men watched them swoop back and slowly begin to circle.

Ah that's better, that's nicely reassuring. For a moment there all this was unsettling my mind. Here I'd been thinking about finding the Sinai Bible these last dozen years and more, thinking no one in the game knew the great secret of its existence but me, and what do I discover all of a sudden? You and Munk both knew about it, that's what. And you, Cairo. Just a couple of months ago we spent a long night up here talking together, deciding to end the game, and you let me run on about the Sinai Bible as if you'd never heard of it. Guilty or not?

Cairo smiled.

No, I never did anything like that.

You didn't? Is my mind adrift and afloat in the manner of Haj Harun? I certainly thought you did.

No. I simply asked you how you'd heard about it. And more important, what it meant to you.

Is that all?

Yes.

And I just ran on and on after that? Well I do that, I know. But why didn't you interrupt me and say you already bloody well knew about the Sinai Bible? That everyone in the game knew about it? Of course, what else, since it's just about the oldest piece of goods in Jerusalem.

About three thousand years old? said Cairo, smiling.

Joe groaned.

Oh all right, so I was running on and you were just being a good listener. But tell me this, Cairo. After you'd heard about the Sinai Bible, why weren't you ever interested in finding it? Why wasn't Munk?

I guess we had our own goals in the game.

And so you did. And so in the end, all we know is where the game ends. Jerusalem naturally. Jerusalem of course. Saith ending of endings end. Jerusalem as it was and will be. And here we are with you and Munk and that nasty little Nubar all cousins today, friends and foes alike related, and where does that leave me? Don't I get to be related to someone?

I would think so. In fact since you were the youngest of thirty-three brothers, I would think you must have quite a few nieces and nephews, not to mention their children.

True, I must. Quite a few. Even though seventeen of my brothers were killed fighting in the Great War, that still leaves room for a number of nieces and nephews and their children.

Where are the rest of your brothers?

America mostly, scattered around something called the Bronx. I'll have to look them up someday. But you and Munk and little Nubar all second cousins a century after the fact. That was some job for one great-grandfather, this tireless young Luigi. Whatever became of him?

He died of dysentery at St Catherine's monastery in 1817. Do you know anything about St Catherine's?

Just that it's quiet and remote. I tramped in there once to have a turn around and climb the mountain. Wanted to know what it felt like to stand up there, but of course no one spoke to me or gave me any tablets.

A lobster tail cracked in Joe's hands.

Oh my God, wait, you're not going to tell me that's where Skanderbeg Wallenstein found the Sinai Bible?

Of course.

Where else, of course, naturally that was the place. Anything more?

That's also where he did his forgery. In a cave just below the summit.

Joe whistled softly.

Full circle, no stop. St Catherine's it is on all counts, all points touched and none left out, the miracle of the mountain and why not. Luigi fathers everyone and then dies there, having been a Christian and a Jew and a Moslem at one time or another, and then one of his sons finds the original Bible there and forges a new original there. And then one of his great-grandsons, our very own Munk of course, finds his cause there, through the intervention of a Japanese baron of course, just as you'd expect, and soon this said Munk will proceed to win the Great Jerusalem Poker Game, of course and of course. It's the nature of the game assuredly and it's all clear to me now, now that it's behind me. That rogue Luigi has brought it all together, and nicely so. But he must have been a mischievous one, that's what he must have been, carrying on and about the way he did and ordering and disordering things a century later. Ah yes. And tell me, Cairo, speaking of nasty little Nubar, what do you hear about him these days?

He's in Venice and doesn't seem to be faring too well. There could be drastic news soon.

Can't say I wouldn't be ready for that. Never did like the way he tried to tinker with our game. To my mind you either sit down and play or you don't.

And lastly, said Cairo, there's the name Johann Luigi used when he was traveling in disguise.

Do you tell me that? I was just hoping there might be one last tiny item tucked away somewhere. What name could it have been?

Sheik Ibrahim ibn Harun.

Was it now. Well well well. I think he deserves a toast for that as well as everything else. Let's hoist a glass to Sheik Luigi and his particular names. I like the idea of him calling himself Abraham, the son of Harun. Who's to say after all? On his way down from Aleppo, when he began his wanderings, he just might have stopped in Jerusalem and met a remarkable gent by the name of Harun, and decided that if he was going to wander in these parts it would be best to become the adopted son of that remarkable elderly gent, honoring the old man too that way and also maybe picking up a little of the old sorcerer's magic by association, just in case a miracle became necessary, which it seems to me his wanderings certainly were. Yes indeed, a striking possibility and worth a toast to cap our Christmas celebration.

They got to their feet beside the table heaped with lobster shells and bottles. Joe was wearing mittens, Cairo had put on his gloves. The weather had grown colder as the afternoon wore on. The sky was dark and it looked like snow again. They stood with mufflers wrapped around their ears, gazing out over the Old City.

To Sheik Luigi, said Joe. Without him there never would have been the longest poker game in the back room of Haj Harun's former antiquities shop.

They drank, then went inside the little hut and threw their glasses into the small grate where a turf fire was slumbering.

A Christmas and was it not, Cairo?

A time, Joe. A good time for all of us.

Joe lowered his eyes. He looked down at the floor.

Ah God willing, for some of us anyway. Peace to seek.

16

Venice
1933

*And it was here beneath the Grand Canal
that he would secretly plan the
destruction of the Great Jerusalem
Poker Swindle and decree the ruin of
its three criminal founders.*

O n a cold December day in 1933, Nubar lay shivering in bed
watching the thick winter fog roll up against the windows of
his palazzo in Venice. Sophia was now sending him cables almost every
day inquiring about his health, asking him what his plans were,
wondering how his short holiday in Venice had inexplicably stretched
into a stay of nearly a year.

WHAT ARE YOU DOING THERE, NUBAR?

It was terrible. He couldn't possibly tell Sophia what he was doing.

TO BE FRANK, I'M IN HIDING. I HAD TO ESCAPE FROM ALBANIA
BECAUSE OF AN INCIDENT IN A FISHING VILLAGE AND I CAN'T COME
BACK RIGHT NOW BECAUSE OF THE LIES THAT MIGHT BE TOLD ABOUT

ME. PEOPLE WILL DO THAT, JUST LIE AND LIE. BUT NO MATTER HOW OUTRAGEOUSLY I'M SLANDERED, BUBBA, I'LL TRIUMPH IN THE END, I PROMISE YOU.

And he could even imagine exactly what her response would be.

PROMISES, NUBAR? SPARE ME, DON'T PROMISE ME ANYTHING. JUST TELL ME HOW YOU SPEND YOUR DAYS. ARE YOU GETTING OUT OF THE HOUSE ENOUGH AND ARE YOU DRESSING WARMLY?

And another statement of fact.

WELL TO BE FRANK AGAIN, BUBBA, I DON'T DRESS AT ALL DURING THE DAY BECAUSE I NEVER GET OUT OF BED. DAYLIGHT FRIGHTENS ME. SO I LIE IN BED ALL DAY SWILLING MULBERRY RAKI, WHICH IS ABSOLUTELY FOUL, THE WORST THING IN THE WORLD FOR A STOMACH AS GASEOUS AS MINE. BUT YOU SEE I FEEL A NEED TO DRINK AND A COMPULSIVE NEED TO DRINK ONLY THAT. AND WHILE SPENDING THESE LISTLESS DAYS IN BED, AS I'VE DONE FOR MONTHS, I CONTINUE TO WORK ON MY JOURNALS, WHICH ARE TITLED THE BOY.

And another imagined response.

SPARE ME, NUBAR, I KNOW HOW YOU ATE WHEN YOU WERE A BOY. POORLY. NOW PLEASE DON'T MAKE ME DRAG EVERYTHING OUT OF YOU. ARE YOU EATING PROPERLY OR NOT?

And a statement of fact again, and a response, and on and on.

I'M EATING A SINGLE BAKED CHICKEN WING TWICE A DAY, BUBBA, ONE AROUND NOON AND ANOTHER IN THE EVENING, AND THAT'S ALL I EAT. I ADMIT IT DOESN'T SOUND LIKE MUCH, BUT AGAIN I SEEM TO HAVE A COMPULSIVE NEED TO EAT NO MORE THAN THAT, AND TO EAT ONLY THAT. IT'S ODD, I AGREE. OBVIOUSLY I'M STARVING MYSELF TO DEATH.
. . .
PLEASE, NUBAR, SPARE ME YOUR LURID FANTASIES AND TELL ME HOW YOU SPEND YOUR EVENINGS. ARE YOU WRITING POETRY AGAIN?
. . .

317

NO, BUBBA, I'D HARDLY CALL MY EVENINGS POETRY. I CONTINUE SWILLING MULBERRY RAKÍ AFTER SUNDOWN, BUT THEN I DO SO FROM A WOODEN CANTEEN THAT I CARRY WITH ME TO THE PIAZZA IN FRONT OF SAN MARCO'S, WHERE, IN THE RAIN AND THE DRIZZLE, I HAUNT THE VAST FOG-BOUND EXPANSES SEARCHING IN VAIN FOR SOMEONE, ANYONE, TO GIVE ONE OF MY JOURNALS TO.

· · ·

DO YOU WEAR A HAT, NUBAR? AND PLEASE REMEMBER TO TAKE ALONG A SCARF EVEN IF YOU KEEP IT IN YOUR POCKET.

· · ·

OR NOT EVEN THAT, BUBBA, THEY DON'T EVEN HAVE TO TAKE ONE OF THE JOURNALS. I'D SETTLE FOR VERY LITTLE NOW. IN FACT I'D BE QUITE HAPPY IF SOMEONE, ANYONE, JUST ALLOWED ME TO READ A BRIEF EXCERPT FROM ONE OF THE JOURNALS TO HIM OR HER.

· · ·

GOOD, NUBAR. I'M GLAD YOU'RE TAKING A SCARF WITH YOU WHEN YOU GO OUT IN THE EVENING.

· · ·

AND IS THAT TOO MUCH TO EXPECT, BUBBA? TO ASK SOMEONE TO STOP FOR JUST A MINUTE TO HEAR THE WHOLE TRUTH ABOUT GRONK? AND THE WHOLE TRUTH AS WELL ABOUT THE DESTRUCTIVE THINGS THAT WERE DONE THERE BY A VILE AND UTTERLY SELFISH AFGHAN, A MAN SO CONTEMPTIBLE HE WAS OFFICIALLY DESCRIBED IN AN ALBANIAN COURT OF LAW AS THAT FILTHY FOREIGNER?

· · ·

PLEASE DON'T BE SO IMPATIENT WITH FOREIGNERS, NUBAR. I'VE ONLY KNOWN ONE PERSON FROM AFGHANISTAN, THE PRINCESS WHO VISITED US YEARS AGO, AND SHE WAS AS LOVELY AS ANYONE COULD BE.

· · ·

NO, YOU WOULDN'T THINK SO, BUBBA, BUT APPARENTLY IT IS TOO MUCH TO EXPECT. APPARENTLY THERE'S NOT ONE PERSON ON THIS EARTH WHO'S WILLING TO LISTEN TO THE WHOLE TRUTH ABOUT THE AA.

· · ·

IS THAT A WORD, NUBAR? WAS THE TRANSMISSION FAULTY OR HAVE I MISSED SOMETHING?

· · ·

THEY'RE INITIALS, BUBBA, AND THERE ARE SOME DEMENTED PEOPLE WHO MIGHT EVEN CLAIM THEY STOOD FOR THE ALBANIAN-AFGHAN SACRED BAND, A TOTAL LIE. FROM ITS INCEPTION THAT NOTORIOUS

318

ORGANIZATION WAS ACTUALLY THE ALL-AFGHANISTAN SACRED
BAND, A FOREIGN MADNESS AND A FOREIGN CONSPIRACY BENT ON
DUPING INNOCENT ALBANIAN FARM BOYS INTO PERFORMING FOUL
AFGHAN ACTS. YOU'VE HEARD THE AFGHAN SAYING ABOUT WOMEN
AND BOYS AND GOATS, IN THAT ASCENDING ORDER?

. . .

PLEASE, NUBAR, NO MORE CONSPIRACIES.

. . .

BUT DON'T YOU SEE WHAT I'M GETTING AT, BUBBA? WHEN I VENTURE
INTO THE RAIN AND FOG OF THAT HUGE PIAZZA IN THE EVENING,
AND CONTINUE GOING AROUND AND AROUND IT ALL NIGHT, I'M
SHAMEFULLY IGNORED AND EVEN SHUNNED, AS IF I WERE SOME
LOATHSOME CREATURE. AND I'M STARVING AND MY VISION IS
BEGINNING TO BLUR AND ON TOP OF EVERYTHING ELSE I STILL HAVE
ALL MY OLD SYMPTOMS OF MERCURY POISONING. SO YOU SEE MY LIFE
HAS ALMOST BEEN RUINED BECAUSE OF A FILTHY FOREIGNER WHO
WAS RESPONSIBLE FOR EVERYTHING, AND THAT'S THE WHOLE TRUTH.
MY JOURNALS EXPLAIN IT CLEARLY AND SUCCINCTLY.

. . .

TAKE A HOT BATH, NUBAR. GET A GOOD NIGHT'S SLEEP AND
TOMORROW THINGS WILL LOOK BETTER.

To be frank with Sophia? It was out of the question. There was no
way he could tell her what he was really doing in Venice. He could
only go on making up imaginary activities and receiving Sophia's
worried responses. The exchange seemed endless.

I'M VISITING PALACES, BUBBA, STUDYING THE WORKS OF VERONESE.

. . .

ARE YOU SURE, NUBAR? I NEVER KNEW YOU WERE INTERESTED IN
ART. WHAT HAPPENED TO MERCURY?

. . .

AND I'M ALSO VISITING MUSEUMS, BUBBA, MAKING A STUDY OF THE
RISE AND FALL OF MARITIME POWER IN THE MEDITERRANEAN.

. . .

MARITIME POWER IS FINE, NUBAR, BUT ARE YOU DRINKING MINERAL
WATER FOR YOUR GAS?

. . .

MINERAL WATER SUPERB, BUBBA. GAS UNDER CONTROL.

. . .

I'M SO GLAD, NUBAR. AND YOU PROMISE YOU'RE EATING PROPERLY?

A NICE PIECE OF FISH OR VEAL AT LEAST ONCE A DAY? NOT JUST RAW VEGETABLES AND THAT DREADFUL WHOLE-WHEAT BREAD OF YOURS?

. . .

WITH ALL THESE ITALIAN DELICACIES BEFORE ME, BUBBA, I HAVEN'T TOUCHED WHOLE WHEAT IN MONTHS, AND YOU CAN BE SURE OF THAT.

. . .

ARE YOU SURE, NUBAR?

. . .

ABSOLUTELY. BESIDES, BUBBA, WILD BOAR HAS JUST COME INTO SEASON AND I MUST HAVE GAINED TWENTY POUNDS ALREADY.

. . .

WONDERFUL, NUBAR, KEEP IT UP.

. . .

I WILL, BUBBA, I CERTAINLY WILL. I'M FAT AND SLEEK AND EVERYTHING'S PERFECT, SO I GUESS THAT'S IT FOR NOW. CHEERIO.

. . .

NOW DON'T GET ANGRY, NUBAR, BUT WILD BOAR IS VERY RICH AND I SIMPLY MUST KNOW. ARE YOU REGULAR? JUST CABLE YES OR NO.

. . .

YES.

. . .

MARVELOUS. HAVE A NICE WEEKEND.

But when the weekend came there were more worried cables from Sophia. Of course she would have stopped sending them if Nubar had told her that he had married upon his arrival in Venice and fathered a son. But then Sophia would have rushed to Venice to meet his wife and see his son, and she would have discovered that his alarmed wife hadn't set eyes on him since the evening of their wedding, when Nubar, thoroughly distraught over the recent events he had fled in Albania, had suddenly begun to harrangue his new wife with one of the interminable *AA* speeches he had been accustomed to delivering in Gronk, ranting on inappropriately about *AA* rituals and truncheons and discipline, even going so far as to describe in considerable detail the uniforms he had designed for the *AA*, whereupon the horrified young woman had abandoned him on the spot, screaming that she would never speak to him again, and returned at once to her home in the Armenian community of Venice, where their son Mecklenburg had been born when the time came.

So naturally Nubar didn't dare to tell Sophia anything about his marriage or his son. Nor could he admit that he had been dangerously deteriorating ever since his arrival in Venice, especially since he had bought his gloomy palazzo on the Grand Canal.

Slowly starving in his palazzo, in fact, amidst a large unruly staff of slovenly servants who added more of their relatives to the payroll each week in order to rob him. Who had gone from stealing simple items such as paintings and silverware to cleaning out whole rooms in the most unscrupulous manner, until finally the entire palazzo had been stripped bare save for a few pieces of furniture left in his own bedroom.

Intolerable behavior on the part of his thieving servants, who found him so preoccupied with his compulsive fantasies they had recently become so bold as to begin ripping out walls to get at the wiring and the copper tubing and the plumbing, anything at all that they could sell for scrap on the mainland.

No plumbing. Not even that. For a month now Nubar had been forced to steal flowerpots at night from the cafés he haunted and smuggle them back to his bedroom closet so he could have something to use as a toilet the next morning.

Fog. The penetrating cold damp fog of a Venetian winter, Nubar adrift in a dream city floating out to sea, lost in the rain and the drizzle on the tides of a landless dream, hiding in bed in his empty palazzo, shivering in a fetal position on a damp December morning.

Nubar jumped. One of the tall bedroom windows was cracking, shattering, cascading down on him, the window frame having apparently been loosened during the night when a gang of his servants had chiseled away a valuable cornice on that side of the palazzo.

Nubar shuddered as the glass splintered noisily and came showering down on the bed. When it was over he peeked out from under the covers. Clouds of dense fog were billowing in through the jagged gaping hole, filling the room with an icy dampness.

Fog, fetal. Nubar felt dizzy. His winter dreams were becoming a nightmare. Soon the fog in the bedroom would be so thick he wouldn't be able to make out the fireplace in the far wall. He had to escape from his bedroom while there was still time, before the fog billowing in through the window swallowed up everything and trapped him in bed for the rest of the winter. With an enormous effort he threw back the covers.

Naked. He hadn't realized that. No wonder he was so cold. He groped his way over to where the chest of drawers was supposed to be.

Gone. The servants must have carried it away during the night so they could sell his shirts and socks. He felt his way along the wall to the closet.

Empty. Nothing but piles of festering flowerpots. They'd taken his suits and shoes and coats to sell as well. He got down on his hands and knees, hoping to find the clothes he'd taken off when he returned at dawn, but after crawling only a few feet he cut his thumb. He popped the bleeding thumb into his mouth. Glass everywhere from the broken window. He'd have to find clothes elsewhere.

Thus toward the middle of the morning on December 21, 1933, a naked Nubar Wallenstein, sole heir to the largest oil fortune in the Middle East, sucking his thumb and shivering violently in a swirling fog, left his fetal position in the master bedroom of his spacious Venetian palazzo and wandered into the corridor on the second floor, in search of clothes to wear on what would be the longest day of his life, under his arm a stack of incoherent journals, bewilderingly contradictory, titled *The Boy*.

It was dark in the corridor, the chandeliers having all been removed months ago. Nubar sucked his thumb and worked his way along the wall. Behind him the fog from his bedroom billowed out into the corridor in impressive clouds.

Fog. Ahead to the left a feeble yellow glow came from what had once been the music room. Nubar tiptoed over and peeked in.

A gang of about a dozen servants and their relatives were milling around the room with torches and heavy crowbars, arguing loudly about who should hold the torches and who wield the crowbars to pry up the marble flooring.

One of the women had left a battered old pair of brown galoshes outside the door. Nubar stepped into them. They were torn and cracked and much too large for him, about twice the size of his small feet, but at least walking on rubber would be better than going barefoot on the cold marble floors.

Nubar shuffled forward, slowly moving away from the weak yellow glow that already seemed dimmer. Behind him the demolition crew in the music room erupted into passionate Italian curses as they bumped into one another and knocked each other down, suddenly unable to see what they were doing because of the thick fog rolling into the room from the corridor.

Somewhere back there a voice screamed, followed by a different scream and a third. Crowbars were striking something solid with heavy thuds. Heads being broken? A falling-out over loot? Why not, the thieves deserved it. Nubar sucked his thumb and giggled. He skated over to the top of the grand staircase, where a torch had been jammed into a hole in the wall.

He removed the torch and examined his finger. It was still bleeding slightly. He put the thumb back in his mouth and waddled down the staircase toward the grand entrance-hall on the ground floor, the volumes of *The Boy* pressed tightly against his sunken chest.

Disorder on every side. Holes in the walls, craters in the floors. Here and there flickering corners heaped with chunks of rotting bread and gnawed bones and the glittering skeletons of chickens picked clean, stinking salami wrappers and twisted olive-oil tins and mounds of rigid tangled pasta, the debris his servants had left around the makeshift cooking fires they had hastily set up and abandoned on their destructive migrations through the palazzo.

Rampaging Visigoths, thought Nubar. Marauding Ostrogoths. The fools. Didn't they realize that when they pillaged him they were pillaging the very foundations of Western civilization? Idiots. When would they ever learn?

Nubar picked his way carefully around the smoldering campfires toward the lofty devastated space that had once been the salon, through the desolate wasted savanna that had once been the library.

Mad savages, he muttered as he shuffled forward, his destination a small room behind the kitchen where the cooks had once changed into their uniforms before coming on duty, months ago when that was still done. He thought there might be some clothes there but when he finally reached the small room, now a murky cave with assorted shards and bones scattered around the entrance, he found only some underwear hanging on a hook, women's underwear, monstrously large even by Italian working-class standards.

Women's underwear. Monstrous. Nubar poked through the huge

damp articles and found mold everywhere. They must have been hanging there for months, at least since the rains of the previous spring. Still, he had to have something to wear.

An enormous pair of thick brown stockings, too big for him to use as stockings. A scarf? Nubar wound the stockings around and around his neck, making a thick scarf for himself.

Enormous brown bloomers. Nubar stepped into them and found that the waistband came all the way up to his armpits. He wound the bloomers around the top of his chest, tying knots, three or four times around his chest and dozens of knots before the bloomers would stay up. He sucked his thumb and studied the next article.

An immense brown canvas corset, boned. The corset was also big enough to go around him three or four times. Nubar looped the corset ties over his shoulders and knotted them under his armpits. The corset reached down below his knees and was pleasantly warm. Because it restricted his legs he found he had to take small mincing steps, but no matter. He had to take small mincing steps anyway because he couldn't lift the large brown galoshes off the floor, only push them forward a little bit at a time.

A brown canvas brassiere, each cup large enough to hold a man's head.

Nubar giggled.

Why not? His ears were aching from the damp cold of the fog that had followed him down the main staircase from his bedroom. Impenetrable fog. Soon it would become so thick it would obscure all the rooms on the first floor as well.

Nubar pulled one of the brassiere cups over his head and fitted it snugly around his ears, tying the strap under his chin. With half of the brassiere now a warm skullcap enclosing his head, the other half hung on his back shaped like a roomy rucksack.

Why not? thought Nubar. He tied the strap from the lower half of the brassiere to an eyelet in the corset, so the rucksack could be steady and not dump out its contents when he moved.

Steady. Nubar floated into the pantry and removed the wooden canteen he kept hidden there behind a broken wagon wheel. Then he filled the canteen with mulberry raki from a demijohn he kept hidden under the decomposing carcass of a sheep that looked as if it had been slaughtered for ritualistic purposes.

324

Barbarians. You couldn't be too careful. Anything of value had to be hidden from these pillaging hordes.

Steady. Voices approaching. Perhaps a patrol?

Nubar pressed himself against the wall in the pantry and held his breath as a wrecking crew of servants trooped through the kitchen shouting loudly to each other, apparently coming from the direction of the main dining room with something long and heavy, perhaps a beam, going toward the back door. The noisy gang passed no more than a few yards away but Nubar, dull brown and immobile, was able to escape detection in the thick fog.

He dropped the canteen into his rucksack and entered the scullery, there to make his most spectacular find of the morning, a long greasy housecoat propped up on a pole, like an animal skin, beside the dead embers of a campfire, no doubt left behind by some woman vandalizing another wing of the palazzo. Nubar pulled it down and found that the housecoat was a fine garment in faded violet with a large floppy collar, the collar very soft to the touch after years of being nibbled and chewed. The greasy violet housecoat had a deep pocket on each hip and a smaller pocket on the chest.

Long and warm and greasy, what could be better on a cold winter day? Nubar went through the pockets to see what might turn up.

A large brownish rag, stiff with what looked like dried blood. Nubar closed his eyes and sniffed.

Raw horsemeat, there was no mistaking the smell. Raw horsemeat had been wrapped in this rag. Probably it had been carried under the saddle of a Tartar horseman as he came wildly galloping out of the steppes of central Asia, the heavy sweat of the animal and the weight of the rider tending to cure the raw meat so the horseman could rip off a digestible hunk at the end of the day for his meal. Barbarians. Disgusting.

A nearly full packet of Macedonian Extras with a box of matches.

A tube of lipstick and a tin of rouge.

A single earring made for a pierced ear, with a dangling spherical stone of fake lapis lazuli.

Three one-lira pieces.

A medallion stamped with Mussolini's face on one side and the Blessed Virgin Mary's on the other.

Barbarians. Savage plunder. Nubar put everything back into the pockets of the housecoat except the stiff bloodied rag, which he sniffed again. He blew his nose on the rag and dropped it into his rucksack for easy access. Then he put on the housecoat and found it truly magnificent, a stately garment that swept out behind him and trailed along the floor in the manner of a bride's gown, or even a queen's at her coronation.

Nubar giggled. He made several formal turns around the kitchen, smiling haughtily down at his admiring, imaginary subjects. At the door he stopped and uncorked his canteen, taking a long drink of the fiery raki that immediately infused him with strength. His eyes narrowed slyly as he peered into the foggy darkness of the corridor off the kitchen.

A descent into the underworld? Had the time come for *the whole truth?*

Yes it had, and Nubar was ready. Civilization was going to survive despite the worst efforts of the barbarians.

The idea had come to him while he was putting on his huge brown brassiere, precisely at the moment he had pulled the cup down over his head and made a thinking cap out of it. A brilliant plan for reversing the failures of the last months, those abject and futile efforts to peddle *The Boy,* at night and alone, to sneering strangers in the rain and the fog in the piazza in front of San Marco's.

For nearly a year now the reports of the Uranist Intelligence Agency had been accumulating in the subcellar of his palazzo, sent regularly from the Middle East and stored according to his standing instructions. Nubar had been too busy trying to peddle *The Boy* to visit the subcellar in the last year, but he knew that in those reports there would be a complete account of the poker game in Jerusalem over the last year.

And more important, there would be detailed descriptions of the activities of those three master criminal degenerates, Martyr and Szondi and O'Sullivan Beare, who were trying to gain control of Jerusalem in order to keep him from the inheritance that was rightfully his, the original Sinai Bible discovered by his grandfather a century ago and buried by him in Jerusalem, the philosopher's stone that would guarantee Nubar immortality when it came into his possession.

What evil new designs, what fiendish plots had those three sinister figures been using against him?

Nubar intended to find out. And then he would issue the order that would end their diabolical twelve-year game and eliminate the three of them for all time.

Order at last, unwavering discipline and correct toilet training, absolute authority. The final solution.

No longer to be obsessed by Gronk dreams and memories, by desperate attempts to have someone, anyone, take *The Boy* seriously. All of that was behind him now. By an act of will he would do what had to be done in the winter fog of Venice. He would do what was necessary to end the Great Jerusalem Poker Swindle. He would bring them total war and then the fools would see what disobedience led to and learn the meaning of *the whole truth*, his rule that would last a thousand years.

Nubar's smile twisted into a smirk. He raised his torch in front of a mirror in the kitchen and squinted at himself approvingly.

Corset and brassiere and bloomers and stockings, a greasy warm housecoat, all oversized and substantial. A massive study in brown gently overlaid with faded purple.

Still smirking crookedly, the journals of *The Boy* tucked under his arm, he floated forward and drifted silently down the corridor to the door that led to the cellar.

Twenty steps to the cellar. Nubar opened the door at the bottom of the stairs that led to the subcellar and descended the thirty steep steps to the landing halfway down. A faint light rose from the depths. He changed direction, watching carefully, and started down the last steep stretch of forty steps.

He was almost at the bottom before he could make out the figure. A man in livery was digging with a pickax and shovel, one of his footmen muttering in a maritime Genovese accent about the secret treasures rich foreigners always buried in their deepest cellars.

Peasant swine, thought Nubar. The barbarian had no idea that the treasures here weren't to be found in the ground but in the reports of the Uranist Intelligence Agency.

The footman had removed a section of the cobblestones that paved the subcellar floor and had dug a hole about four feet square. He was now standing in the hole up to his waist, vigorously hacking away at the clay with his pickax. Beside the hole lay the footman's blue satin swallowtail coat. A candle that stood in the clay was dripping wax on the gold braid of the coat, and Nubar was immediately infuriated to see gold braid being treated with so little respect. He stamped his feet and shouted defiantly, his anger directed toward the defilers of civilization everywhere, his voice weirdly distorted by the confines of the subcellar.

Out, peasant swine. Out, you evil creature.

The footman whirled. He stared. Nubar was moving slowly up and down inside his huge stationary galoshes, his long greasy housecoat shaking in rage, the brassiere encasing his head quivering with indignation.

The footman screamed and leapt from the hole in horror. He bolted up the stairs to the kitchen where he threw himself through a casement window and went crashing down into the dark water beside the palazzo, there to be entangled in a sluggish flow of sewerage that was moving out into the Grand Canal under the impenetrable cover of fog.

Nubar, meanwhile, paused by the bottom of the stairs to get his bearings, and what he saw astonished him. The entire subcellar was packed with stacks and stacks of neatly piled papers, dossiers and card files and loose-leaf folders, the unread reports of the Uranist Intelligence Agency over the last eleven months.

Extraordinary, thought Nubar as he gazed out over the thousands and thousands of reports, the towering collections of amassed data, realizing for the first time just how productive his intelligence agency really was.

Nubar shuffled over to the hole the footman had dug and stuck his torch in the clay. He knocked over several tall stacks of reports and made a couch for himself out of the paper. The footman's coat, folded, served as an armrest. He took a drink of mulberry raki from his canteen, accidentally biting off some of the wooden spout in his eagerness to begin, not noticing there was wood in his mouth so great was his concentration, chewing the wood and swallowing it along with the mulberry raki. Then he arranged himself comfortably on his paper couch, tucked the tails of the greasy housecoat snugly around his legs and lit a Macedonian Extra, inhaling deeply.

A drop of water fell on his nose. He licked it away.

Salt water?

Nubar looked up at the ceiling. He estimated the height of the subcellar staircase with its two directions to the north and east, the height of the regular cellar staircase with its third northerly direction. He recalled the location of the cellar door in the palazzo and calculated its distance from the landing in front of the palazzo.

Nubar smiled. There was no doubt about it.

The archives of the Uranist Intelligence Agency lay directly beneath the Grand Canal. And it was here beneath the Grand Canal that he would secretly plan the destruction of the Great Jerusalem Poker Swindle and decree the ruin of its three criminal founders.

Nubar's eyes narrowed.

Jerusalem the Holy City on the heights, above the wastes and the deserts? The eternal city secure on its mountaintop? Well they wouldn't get away with it, those barbaric criminals. Order and alignment and *the whole truth* would triumph, he would liberate Jerusalem and take what was his.

Nubar licked another drop of salt water off his nose. He picked up a report at random and began to read.

Perhaps it was only the lack of air in that subaqueous cellar, but to Nubar the report in front of him seemed unusually interesting, far above the normal quality of UIA material.

In the beginning, indeed, it was impossible to imagine just what the subject of the report would turn out to be.

It had been submitted by Dead Sea Control, which was responsible for the Jerusalem district, located at a distance from Jerusalem, for security reasons, amidst the sulphur and salt deposits on the south shore of the Dead Sea. The station was housed in a cluster of tin huts that had been erected by a now defunct mining enterprise. Although nicely hidden away behind the huge columns of salt common to the area, the tin huts were unbearably hot most of the year, which perhaps explained the incoherency of many of the station's reports.

Originally Jericho had been considered as a likely location for the reporting center of the Jerusalem district, but Nubar had personally intervened in favor of the sulphur site on the Dead Sea, despite the heat. It pleased him to know the UIA's most important field station was nestled in the lowest spot on earth, within those grotesque geological formations that were generally accepted to be the natural ruins of Sodom.

Dead Sea Control had evaluated the report as POTENTIAL URINE, which meant it had been written by an informer who had shown enough initiative to be considered a potential *Uranist intelligence* employee. Beneath the formal title was a descriptive caption, uncommonly cryptic by UIA standards.

Submitted as background material only, to illustrate the difficulties faced by Dead Sea Control in collecting relevant information about Jerusalem, in view of the mythical nature of that city up there on the mountain. And especially in view of the view from down here on the shores of what has been referred to, in an important piece of literature, as the dried cunt of the world.

(That very long novel, still banned in most countries as obscene, deals exclusively with a single day, June 16, 1904. Amazing, don't you think? Of course we have a lot of time to read long novels down here.)

Nubar snorted. Did his agents think they were getting paid to read long novels? He made a mental note to fire off a cable to Dead Sea Control as soon as he had finished reading the report.

ARE YOU MAD? NO MORE REFERENCES TO CUNTS AND NO MORE OBSCURE LITERARY ALLUSIONS. STICK TO THE TRUTH FROM NOW ON OR YOU CAN EXPECT IMMEDIATE DISCIPLINARY ACTION.

NUBAR

SUPREME LEADER

He read on.

Submitted, secondly, to illustrate the difficulties faced in separating interesting, relevant information on Jerusalem from the mass of uninteresting, irrelevant details in which it is invariably encased.

And lastly, submitted because the report does have some legitimate curiosity value when read with an open mind.

An open mind? Nubar had an open mind and the idea of reading something with curiosity value intrigued him after all these months of lying in bed all day and sneaking around in the rain all night trying to get someone to take *The Boy* seriously.

He turned the page.

EYES ONLY *Jerusalem to Dead Sea Control.*

DATE *when information was acquired: August 1933.*

DATE *when information was forwarded to Control: Halloween 1933. (Delay due to time required to write up report.)*

TIME *when information was elicited: Several hours on a very hot afternoon in August 1933.*

PLACE *where information was elicited: The Moslem Quarter, the Old City, Jerusalem.*

PERSON *from whom information was elicited: Name, race and nationality unknown. A man on a pilgrimage to Jerusalem. (They're always coming and going by the thousands, these pilgrims, aren't they, and there's certainly no way to know who most of them are. Now this one happens to remain anonymous throughout the report, on the face of it simply because I was never able to find out who he was. But mightn't there be some larger design beyond that? Could it just be, perhaps, that he was meant to be anonymous in order for him to assume the role of the archetypal pilgrim? One single part in the narrative, thereby, put forward to represent all the seekers who have sought Jerusalem over the millennia?*

Not so farfetched, it seems to me, once you get into the entanglements that are coming.)

PERIOD *covered by information in this report: From 930 B.C. to August 1933.*

WHAT *follows initially: Unclassified records (public).*

WHAT *follows in the middle: Top Secret speculations (private).*

AND FINALLY WHAT *follows in the all-important end. (A note to agents filling out this form. You have now arrived at the meat of your report and you are warned, here above all, to be brief and to the point. Your ability to describe your meat succinctly is the only reason anybody will ever read your report, if anybody ever does, which is in no way guaranteed by the hierarchy of the UIA. So summarize ruthlessly, in one sentence, making your case in plain language accessible to all. Extravagant attitudes may be allowed elsewhere, but not here. And the same goes for dabbling in fanciful notions or toying with idle speculations, with taking side trips down curious byways or pausing to explore obscure corners, all of the above and more, in fact any device whatsoever that may creep into your reports elsewhere. That's one thing but this is another, and we repeat, it must not happen here. Your meat of the matter, that's what is wanted now.*

All right then, we're there, this is it and good luck. State your end product, what valuable contribution you have today to this crazy business we're all in. Go.):

True identities of all major figures who have operated clandestinely in Jerusalem during the period covered by this report (930 B.C. to August 1933).

The first records Nubar came to were copies of documents from a Jerusalem tax office, dated from 1921 to 1933. But there was no indication what significance the records might have, or what was being taxed.

Next there were Jerusalem telephone bills and water bills for the same years, evidently purloined, followed by bills of lading for a cheap but sturdy juice squeezer of Czech origin, the squeezer's lever and cup and strainer all detachable for packing and cleaning purposes.

The bills of lading were dated 1921 and traced the juice squeezer from a factory in Prague, by rail, to an outlet on the Black Sea. By Bulgarian lugger, in a load of general cargo, to Constantinople. By cart, overland to Beirut, and by Greek caïque down the coast to Jaffa. Whence by rail up to Jerusalem, the ultimate destination of the juice squeezer.

Nubar put his finger on the last bill of lading and gazed into the dark corners of his subcellar.

Jerusalem. A pattern was beginning to emerge.

He tightened the stockings around his neck against the chill, scratched himself thoughtfully and went back to the report. He had finished with the records.

The next page showed a floor plan of what appeared to be a tiny room. The walls were irregular. There was a door and one window, a counter and two chairs. At the end of the counter next to the door was the emblem of the UIA, ⛢ , also the symbol of the planet Uranus. Outside the door in a space marked *alley* was the number *18* and an arrow with an *N* at the tip. A scale beside the arrow listed *foot* and *yard.*

Nubar measured the room with his thumb and found it to be about eight feet long and five feet wide, narrowing to only three feet at the back.

He turned over the diagram. Now the pages began to be numbered for security reasons.

Page 1 of 407 pages, a report on the Great Jerusalem Poker Swindle.

1. The preceding diagram shows a fruit juice stand. Mine. I squeeze fresh juice by the glass, on order, and customers generally drink it on the premises. Shops in the Old City are often small and oddly shaped.
2. N indicates north.
3. 18 indicates the street number my shop might have if it were on a street and had a number, which it isn't and doesn't, being situated in a narrow alley and cul-de-sac near the bazaar in the Moslem Quarter, the rent there being about as cheap as can be found inside the walls built around the Old City by Suleiman I in 1542.

Good, thought Nubar. *Completeness and unerring accuracy* was the motto he had adopted for the UIA way back in 1921 when he had first begun hiring literary agents to steal all the known works of the great doctor and master alchemist, Paracelsus, real name Bombastus von Hohenheim.

4. Trade is reasonably brisk in the summer, almost nonexistent in the winter and more or less half and half at other times.
5. To the east of my shop at a distance of a dozen yards or less, occupying the end of this dead-end alley, stands the entrance to two vaulted rooms owned by an elderly man who claims he was formerly an antiquities dealer. This elderly

man wears a faded yellow cloak and a rusty Crusader's helmet, goes barefoot, and calls himself Haj Harun.

Nubar instantly sucked in what was left of his cigarette, inhaling so forcefully it burned both his fingers and his lips. He licked his lips and gasped.

Haj Harun's shop? The actual site of the vicious poker game for the last twelve years? Nubar closed his eyes to concentrate. He took a deep breath, then read on.

6. My clientele comes almost exclusively from the lower classes, but without regard to race, religion or creed. Members of other classes, however, have patronized my shop on occasion, generally because they were lost in the Old City and seeking a way out, as we shall soon see below.

Indeed we will, thought Nubar suspiciously.

7. The constant stream of visitors, many wealthy, who frequent Haj Harun's murky premises at all hours of the day and night, for purposes of poker, never enter my shop. On their way into Haj Harun's they often remark disdainfully that my shop is much too dirty for their patronage. But on their way out, penniless and dazed, stripped of all they own, they just as often sag on my counter and beg for credit. Please? A mere glass of juice? Just a sip? Just a lick of the strainer? No, I answer firmly, cash on the counter having always been my policy.

Excellent, thought Nubar. Sound and businesslike. Why take pity on anyone? It could only lead to disruptions in the social order, and order was all-important.

In fact Nubar was beginning to like this informer and his thoroughly straightforward approach to a problem. No wonder Dead Sea Control had seen fit to evaluate him as POTENTIAL URINE. He was indeed. Nubar thought of another cable that should be sent as soon as he finished the report.

FLASH PRIORITY. BRAVO TO ALL HANDS. OUR MAN AT THE FRUIT JUICE STAND IN THE OLD CITY IS THE BEST POTENTIAL URINE WE'VE HAD IN YEARS. YOU ARE HEREBY AUTHORIZED TO PROMOTE HIM

BY ORDER OF

NUBAR

LEADER,

FIELD MARSHAL,

SUPREME GENERALISSIMO COMMANDING

Nubar smiled. He liked that. Good. He read on.

*8. I have no phone. The phone-bill records apply to the phone in a nearby
coffee shop where I have made all my personal and business calls over the last
twelve years, or since I arrived in Jerusalem.*
*9. I have paid no taxes over the last twelve years because my cash flow is
meager and I have been able to bribe the tax clerk in charge of my alley with
free pomegranate juice. Therefore I have included the tax records for this same
coffee shop, and also its water bills, because completeness and unerring accuracy
are everything to an informer for the UIA.*

Perfect, thought Nubar. Maybe the enormous sums of money
consumed by the UIA weren't being entirely squandered after all.

*10. During the twelve years that I have operated this fruit juice stand,
pomegranate juice has outsold orange juice, although not by much. Before
coming to Jerusalem I worked briefly in Damascus and for a longer period in
Baghdad. In both cities I was a self-employed technician in sputum analysis.*
*11. The symbol of the UIA, seen on the counter in the diagram of my shop,
marks the exact location of my imported juice squeezer.*

A fine grasp of detail, thought Nubar, reaching the end of the page.
He paused to tug his skullcap more tightly around his ears as protection
against the cold drafts sweeping fitfully through the cellar. Time to take
a break for a little refreshment? Why not?

He took his canteen out of his rucksack and drank, feeling new
warmth from the mulberry raki, at the same time absentmindedly
nibbling off what was left of the wooden spout of the canteen, totally
absorbed with the methodical reasoning of this informer. The report

was unfolding with undeniable logic, and he could see that the informer was determined to do his duty, to tell the whole truth.

Nubar chewed and swallowed the wood.

> 12.   May I just state here that I have always considered it the greatest of honors to serve as an informer for the UIA, which I firmly believe is all that stands between Jerusalem and utter chaos. Without the UIA, Jerusalem today might well be at the mercy of those three notorious villains who call themselves Martyr, Szondi, and O'Sullivan Beare or Fox, depending on his mood and also on how much he's had to drink, and how long it was since the last drink, and how long it may be to the next.
>
> 13.   Jerusalem must be saved from the barbarians.
>
> 14.   Only the UIA, and its Supreme Leader, can do it.
>
> 15.   Despair and defeat to our enemies.
>
> 16.   I pledge myself anew to selfless service for the UIA, and above all for its Supreme Leader.
>
> 17.   Conclusion of the foregoing.
>
> 18.   The narrative form is herewith adopted for purposes of clarity.

Nubar read on, thoroughly captivated.

The informer was Persian, he said, and an adherent of the Zoroastrian faith, which he admitted one didn't seem to hear much about anymore. He had grown up in a remote hill tribe in Persia and he considered himself lucky to have been born at all, since the tribe had almost been wiped out by a cholera epidemic in the first half of the nineteenth century.

Living in those remote hills at the time was a young foreign lord who had fallen in love with a girl from the tribe. The epidemic had broken out only a few weeks after he met her and the girl had abruptly died. Thereafter the young man had patiently nursed the sick without regard to his own welfare.

This legendary foreign lord was said to have been seven and a half feet tall. He had used a huge magnifying glass to examine his patients, so large his unblinking eye had been two inches wide behind it. After making a diagnosis he would then prescribe medicine according to the hours he read on his portable sundial, a monstrously heavy bronze piece which he wore on his hip. The foreign lord's knowledge of herbal remedies was unsurpassed, and without him no one in the tribe would have survived.

Nubar stirred uneasily. He had the sensation of being here, or somewhere, before.

When the epidemic subsided, continued the informer, the young foreign lord took his leave, never to be seen in those remote hills of Persia again. Quite naturally the thankful survivors in the tribe had come to revere this gentle and merciful giant as Ahura Mazda, chief of the gods of goodness in the ancient Zoroastrian pantheon, who had seen fit to sojourn in their hills in order to deliver them from the forces of darkness and death.

As a result, ever since, everyone in the tribe had been a profound believer in Zoroastrianism.

The informer was including this information, he said, to explain his unusual religious beliefs, which might otherwise be viewed as anachronistic and suspect in this day and age, and thereby bring into question his suitability as an officer-in-training for the UIA, said training to be concluded at the end of this report when he would qualify as a professional UIA officer on duty in a danger zone, Jerusalem, which would entitle him to receive special hazardous-duty pay, in addition to an officer's regular salary and full medical and retirement benefits.

Nubar grinned. He shook his head.

What was this brazenly self-serving attitude? Did this nonentity, this Zoroastrian squeezer of juice, really think he could promote himself in one short paragraph from a petty informer to a full-fledged officer's position in the UIA? Did he really imagine Nubar could be fooled so easily, even here in a cold damp cellar beneath the Grand Canal?

Nubar snorted. No, it hadn't quite come to that yet. Routinely, in his head, he dashed off another cable to Dead Sea Control.

ARE YOU MAD? HAS THE SUN DOWN THERE IN THAT DRIED CUNT OF THE WORLD BEEN GETTING TO YOUR BRAINS? NO, REPEAT NO, PROMOTION FOR THIS ZOROASTRIAN CHARLATAN. MEDICAL AND RETIREMENT BENEFITS OUT OF THE QUESTION AND NO HAZARDOUS-DUTY PAY FOR THIS SHIRKER. FOR ALL I CARE HE CAN GO THE WAY

OF THE LOST GREEK AND THE TWO OF THEM CAN RELIVE THE
PERSIAN CAMPAIGNS AGAINST GREECE AND THE GREEK CAMPAIGNS
AGAINST PERSIA. I ABSOLUTELY REFUSE TO BE DUPED.

NUBAR

SUPREME LEADER AND FIELD MARSHAL,
GENERALISSIMO COMMANDING EVERYTHING

That was better. Much better. He knew he couldn't be too careful.
His control had to be absolute, discipline simply couldn't be relaxed for
a moment. One instance of even the lowliest lackey promoting himself
and everyone in the organization would see it as a sign of weakness on
his part, at the top. Then all of them would begin promoting
themselves and plucking grandiose new titles out of the air.

This dangerous tendency had to be stopped before it gathered
momentum. A follow-up cable to Dead Sea Control was in order.

PRIORITY FROM THE VERY TOP. FREEZE, DOWN THERE. ALL
PROMOTIONS BARRED UNTIL FURTHER NOTICE. DID YOU REALLY
THINK YOU WERE GOING TO GET AWAY WITH SOMETHING? WELL
YOU'RE NOT. SIT RIGHT WHERE YOU ARE UNTIL YOU HEAR FROM
ME. IT MAY BE A HARDSHIP POST BUT IT'S THE ONLY ONE ANY OF YOU
ARE GOING TO SEE FOR A WHILE AND YOU CAN COUNT ON THAT. NO
ANSWER NECESSARY AND NO EXCUSES TOLERATED.

NUBAR

LEADER AT THE VERY TOP
AND CHIEF OF ALL FORCES.

Suddenly Nubar frowned. Something the informer had said was
troubling him, working at the back of his brain.

Yes, he remembered it now. He pursed his lips to whistle in surprise
but of course he couldn't whistle. It was all coming back from those
early historical reports, the background material on the poker game that
had been sent to him when the UIA first began to operate in the
Middle East.

A huge magnifying glass with an unblinking eye two inches wide
behind it?

Menelik Ziwar, the unknown black Copt and foster father of Cairo Martyr, had allegedly used just such a glass when he was lying on his back in retirement in the sarcophagus of Cheops' mother.

But the magnifying glass hadn't originally belonged to Ziwar. It had been a gift from his dearest friend, an unnamed giant of a man who had worn a massive greasy black turban and a shaggy short black coat made from unwashed and uncombed goats' hair, both said to have been gifts from a remote hill tribe in Persia. This friend, mysteriously, had appeared from nowhere on Sunday afternoons to continue a forty-year conversation he was having with Ziwar over drunken lunches in a filthy Arab restaurant beside the Nile, the lunches ending toward sundown when both men jumped over the railing into the river for a swim.

A portable bronze sundial, monstrously heavy?

The one the giant explorer Strongbow had worn on his hip in the nineteenth century? The same sundial that was now on the wall of the former antiquities shop in Jerusalem where the poker game was being played? Chimes attached to it that sounded erratically, confusing time?

A giant in both cases. *A giant.* An elusive figure who may have secretly owned the entire Middle East at the turn of the century.

Nubar gripped his throat. He was having difficulty breathing. Being so small, he couldn't help but be terrified by the specter of a man seven and a half feet tall.

Or was he a man? Perhaps much more? Did that explain his height and his odd behavior, the sudden appearances and disappearances in a filthy restaurant beside the Nile? In a remote hill tribe in Persia in time of need?

Ahura Mazda, chief of the gods of goodness?

Nubar fell back limply on his paper couch. His unfocused eyes roamed the ceiling.

He had now arrived at the main body of the juice squeezer's report. The direction of the narrative was vague, a tortuous route through the Old City with no hint of its destination. To Nubar under the Grand

Canal, mythical Jerusalem seemed to be growing ever more indistinct on its faraway mountaintop.

The informer's account began with the anonymous pilgrim, mentioned at the very beginning, whose name and race and nationality were all unknown.

One hot afternoon in August this pilgrim had lost his way in Jerusalem. He was trying to find a gate out of the Old City, any gate would do, but the maze of alleys had confused him. He wandered into the cul-de-sac where the informer's fruit juice stand was located and collapsed in the doorway. After numerous glasses of pomegranate juice the pilgrim eventually revived. As he did he began to talk about the cause of his near-total disorientation.

The first stop on the pilgrim's itinerary that morning had also been his last, St Savior's Convent, the Franciscan enclave in the Old City that was practically a city in itself. He had arrived in time to join a scheduled tour, but soon after the tour started he became enamored with a statue in an alcove and found himself detached from the group.

The pilgrim opened the nearest door and discovered he had chanced upon the convent bakery, his first serious mistake of the day.

At this point in the narrative, wrote the informer, the pilgrim had begun to twitch violently. He laughed loudly until tears came to his eyes, then all at once stopped laughing and moaned as if in great pain. The informer thought the man was suffering from sunstroke or perhaps some hysterical disorder. In any case it was only after gulping down several more glasses of pomegranate juice, newly squeezed, that the pilgrim was able to resume his account.

Somberly Nubar chewed his lip. A cable had come to mind. Imprecise language could be dangerous, because it might very quickly lead people to make false conclusions.

MY FRIENDS. LET ME MAKE ONE THING PERFECTLY CLEAR.

IT IS ESSENTIAL TO OUR NATIONAL SECURITY, AND TO OUR SURVIVAL AS A FREEDOM-LOVING PEOPLE LIVING UNDER GOD, THAT THE JUICE SQUEEZER BE WARNED NOT TO USE EXAGGERATED TERMS FOR CONCEPTS HE DOESN'T UNDERSTAND.

WHAT I MEAN TO SAY IS JUST THIS. STRICTLY SPEAKING, THERE IS NO SUCH THING AS AN HYSTERICAL DISORDER. THERE IS ONLY DISORDER

OF A GENERALLY LAWLESS NATURE, WHICH IS TO SAY LAWLESSNESS IN
GENERAL, AND THAT CAN ALWAYS BE CONTROLLED BY DISCIPLINE AT
THE TOP, IF IT IS IRON DISCIPLINE.

SO, MY FRIENDS, LET ME SHARE THESE THOUGHTS WITH YOU. TELL
OUR GOOD FRIEND THE FRUIT JUICE SQUEEZER TO SIT UP STRAIGHT
AND CONCENTRATE, AND TO BE READY. HE TOO WILL HAVE HIS
ORDERS, NO LESS THAN YOU DO, FOR THERE IS A PLACE FOR
EVERYONE BENEATH ME.

AND SO LET ME SUBMIT AGAIN FOR YOUR CONSIDERATION THE
SIMPLE YET VITAL PROPOSITION THAT WE CANNOT HOPE TO SURVIVE
AS A FREEDOM-LOVING PEOPLE UNDER GOD IF WE ALLOW SELF-
DELUDED CITIZENS AND SELF-APPOINTED ZEALOTS, NO MATTER HOW
WELL-INTENTIONED THEY ARE, AND I PERSONALLY KNOW THEY ARE
OFTEN WELL-INTENTIONED, STILL WE CANNOT ALLOW THEM TO RUN
AROUND THE STREETS OF JERUSALEM, OR AROUND THE DEAD SEA
FOR THAT MATTER, EVEN IF IT IS THE DRIED CUNT OF THE WORLD,
SHOUTING WHATEVER COMES INTO THEIR HEADS.

BECAUSE, MY FRIENDS, IT JUST WON'T WORK.

NUBAR

THE GENTLE AND UNDERSTANDING,
YET NONETHELESS, BY NECESSITY,
IRON FIST AT THE TOP.

Nubar smiled benignly. He tucked his housecoat more tightly
around his legs and read on.

The anonymous pilgrim, wrote the informer, now found himself
standing in the doorway of the convent bakery. Inside the bakery a very
old priest was doing a jig in front of the oven, while removing loaves of
freshly baked bread. All the bread seemed to have been baked in one of
four distinct shapes. The pilgrim remarked upon this, upon saying hello,
and the old priest readily agreed.

Exactly four, said the old priest merrily, right as right you are. And
those four shapes are none other than the Cross and Ireland, and
Jerusalem and the Crimea, and what do you think of that?

Here the pilgrim made his second serious mistake of the day. He didn't slam the door and run. Instead he stood there, and shook his head, and said he didn't know what to think of it.

Well the Cross for obvious reasons, said the old priest, still doing his jig, and Jerusalem for equally obvious reasons. And Ireland not only because I was born there but because it's the most beautiful land there is so far as lands in this world go. And the Crimea because I was in a war there once and survived a disastrous cavalry charge there, and as a result of surviving that folly I saw the light and found my vocation in the Church, God's orders being vastly superior to man's at all times but especially so when you've seen service in the Light Brigade. So that's all of it and for the last seventy years I've been serving God soberly here where you see me, in front of this very oven turning out delicious loaves of bread shaped in the four concerns of my life. And after seventy years of such service, I suppose it's not surprising that I should be known to all who know me as the baking priest.

Nubar's head jerked back.

The baking priest. The man who had rescued O'Sullivan Beare when he first arrived in Jerusalem as a fugitive. The mysterious priest whom Nubar's agents had never been able to trace or identify. Was he real or had O'Sullivan Beare made him up?

Nubar had never known until this moment. And with that secret now out in the open, who could imagine what else might follow?

Nubar giggled happily. He congratulated himself.

At last it was all coming together.

In his excitement Nubar snatched up his canteen. He gargled with a mouthful of fiery mulberry raki, chewed some wood off the canteen, lit a soggy Macedonian Extra. He knew success would be his in the end. He'd always known it.

The informer in Jerusalem, meanwhile, was continuing his leisurely account of the conversation between an anonymous pilgrim and an elderly Franciscan known as the baking priest.

Since it was August, the bakery was hot.

Frightfully hot? asked the baking priest. He then said that although he was naturally accustomed to the oven's heat, he could well understand how it might be uncomfortable to others. For this reason he suggested the pilgrim should feel perfectly free, if he wished, to take off his clothes and hang them on the hook by the door.

And here was the pilgrim's third serious mistake of the day, and by far the most disastrous.

He should have realized, as he later told the informer at the fruit juice stand, that the bakery was so unbearably hot his sanity couldn't survive there for long. There was no question that he should have bolted at once, realizing the folly of listening to a man who was nearly a hundred years old, who had been merrily dancing in front of an oven in Jerusalem for seven decades, baking the same four loaves of bread.

But the unfortunate pilgrim, sweating heavily and already dazed, did as he was invited to do. He took off all his clothes and hung them on the hook by the door.

Naked then, he promptly collapsed beside a large water jar, too weak to do anything but splash an occasional handful of water over his burning head, utterly defenseless against any fancy the Franciscan might choose to conjure up as he capered around the room, distributing loaves of bread to its four corners.

On a pilgrimage, are you? sang the old priest. Well let me tell you there be odd events here, odd events within and about our Holy City, and none stranger than the epic tale of a long-term resident of Jerusalem who saw a genie in the last century and God in this one. Know about him? Probably not, but my source is unimpeachable, being the former terror of the Black and Tans in County Cork, and with such noble service behind him we can do nothing but believe him down to the last syllable.

The old priest fixed the helpless naked pilgrim with a maniacal stare. Maniacal, yes. There was no other word for it. After seventy years in front of that hot oven, the old priest's eyes glowed with a disturbing and unmistakable luster.

Are you ready then? said the old priest to the pilgrim. What's that, you are? Good. Well here's how this oddest of odd epics goes when properly told. But before we begin I suppose we should give it a name for itself and that would have to be *God and the Genie*. And then when you consider the man who saw them both, whose very own epic it is, you just might want to ruminate further and let your imagination go and sense that we have a Holy Trinity on our hands. Just might, I say.

No one would want to go all the way with such a thing and claim it for sure. All right then. Our headlong charge is coming up, so hold on now. Tighten your reins, lad, sit tight and smartly. We're about to cover some ground in a breathtaking breakneck gallop as daring as any the world has heard since the plains at Balaklava thundered to the gallant hoofbeats of hopeless heroes. Ho, I say. *Ho-o-o-o-o-o-o.*

But before I report on what came next, wrote the informer, I think I should mention a funeral that was held in the spring in Haj Harun's back room. It was for Cairo Martyr's little pet, the albino monkey with the bright aquamarine genitals who was in the habit of curling up on Martyr's shoulder and pretending to be asleep, until his name was spoken.

The pet died of old age, in its sleep, and the funeral was quite an event. Szondi and O'Sullivan Beare and Haj Harun joined Martyr as pallbearers, since it seems they all had great affection for the little fellow and sadly mourned his passing. In fact the poker game was closed down for two weeks in tribute to the pet, whose grave is known only to the four of them, the burial party having set out with great stealth one dark moonless night, carefully on the lookout to see that they weren't being followed.

I include this information, wrote the informer, because it may have some significance I don't understand.

Bongo, screamed Nubar.

And immediately regretted it, for the syllables somehow seemed to feel at home in the confines of that subcellar and the echoes twanged around and around Nubar's head even after he had clapped his hands over his ears, *bongobongobongo.*

If the report went on like this Nubar knew he was going to get upset, possibly even angry. A quick cable to the fruit juice stand in Jerusalem was needed.

FLASH FROM HERE. ARE YOU MAD? HALT ALL FUTURE REFERENCES TO ALBINO MONKEYS. COLOR OF GENITALS UNIMPORTANT. I NEVER

LIKED THE IDEA OF THAT FREAKISH BEAST FROM THE JUNGLE. UP UNTIL THIS POINT YOU WERE DOING WELL BUT NOW YOU'RE BEGINNING TO SLIP. GET BACK TO THE EPIC TALE AND NOT ANOTHER WORD ABOUT THINGS THAT DON'T MATTER.

NUBAR

TOP BONGO.

No. Wrong. Was his mercury poisoning causing his brain to substitute words inadvertently? Or had that loathsome name jumped into the cable because it was echoing around his head?

Either way it was dangerous. He had to be careful. Using the wrong words could lead to confusion in the ranks, even chaos. His absolute authority might come into question. In his mind he crossed out the last line of the cable and wrote TOP LEADER instead.

But that seemed too brief. He pondered the problem for a moment and decided on a longer ending.

GET BACK TO THE EPIC TALE AND NOT ANOTHER WORD ABOUT THINGS THAT DON'T MATTER.

NUBAR

THE TOP ALL RIGHT AND ALSO JUST PLAIN NUMBER ONE, SO YOU BETTER GET USED TO THE IDEA FAST.

Nubar scratched himself and turned pages.

The man referred to as a long-term resident of Jerusalem, the witness to the events in the epic, was described by the baking priest in such a way that the informer knew it had to be his neighbor in the alley, Haj Harun. No one else in Jerusalem wore a faded yellow cloak and a rusty Crusader's helmet tied under the chin with two green ribbons.

Both of the unusual occurrences in the epic, sang the baking priest, seeing a genie in the last century and God in this one, took place while this long-term resident, an elderly item, was making his annual haj.

Here the informer interrupted his narrative to make a personal observation. There was no way of knowing, he wrote, whether Haj Harun went to Mecca every spring, as he claimed. He also disappeared at other times, saying he was off exploring imaginary caverns of the past beneath the Old City, something he claimed he had been doing for the last three thousand years. The informer then added a comment on that.

> What is one to make of these extravagant claims that seem to pop up every time Haj Harun is mentioned? Can the old man be believed or is he suffering from terminal amnesia? Or perhaps from advanced dementia brought on by acute senility?

> If you want my opinion, it's the latter. That's exactly what I think. This Haj Harun is definitely a strange one. And furthermore, I question the legality of anyone skulking around beneath Jerusalem for the last three thousand years. Isn't that against the law? Wouldn't it be a clear and present breach of some existing statute, perhaps the sanitation code, for example?

Nubar snorted furiously. They weren't going to get away with this. Immediately he made a mental note for another cable to Dead Sea Control.

ARE YOU MAD? WHY ARE YOU LETTING THIS INFORMER THINK? I WANT FACTS, NOT SPECULATIONS, AND I DON'T WANT TO HEAR ANYTHING MORE ABOUT SANITATION CODES OR LEGALITY IN GENERAL, OR IDLE OPINIONS ABOUT WHAT'S LEGAL AND WHAT ISN'T. I AM THE SANITATION CODE AND WHATEVER I DO IS LEGAL BY DEFINITION, REMEMBER THAT. ANYTHING SAID TO THE CONTRARY IS A SUBVERSIVE CRIME THAT AIDS AND ABETS THE ENEMY, AND THAT CRIME WILL BE DEALT WITH AS IT DESERVES TO BE, WITH UTTER RUTHLESSNESS.

THAT IS TO SAY, WITH CRIPPLING FINES AND PURLOINED MAIL FOLLOWED BY CONSTANT SURVEILLANCE, BY OFFICIAL VERBAL ABUSE AND BREAK-INS AND SHOOT-OUTS AND OPPRESSIVE HARASSMENT BY ALL AGENCIES, BY PERJURY AND BLACKMAIL AND INSINUATIONS OF SINISTER FORCES AT WORK, BY SECRET PHYSICAL BEATINGS WHERE POSSIBLE AND UNRELIEVED THUGGERY ALL AROUND.

AND LET ME MAKE ANOTHER THING PERFECTLY CLEAR. NO ONE IS
GOING TO GET AWAY WITH AIDING THE ENEMY. I REPEAT, WHAT I
DO IS LEGAL AND IF ANYONE ELSE DOES ANYTHING I DON'T LIKE,
ESPECIALLY ANYTHING THAT IS IN THE LEAST WAY THREATENING TO
ME, I'LL GRONK THEM AND GRONK THEM GOOD. AND YOU CAN BET
YOUR SWEET ASS ON THAT YOU SHITHEAD ASSKISSING CUNTLICKING
ASSSUCKING CHICKENSHIT COCKSUCKING FUCKOFF ASSHOLES.

THAT'S RIGHT, YOU'RE IN TROUBLE NOW, BOY. AND IF I WERE YOU
I'D STAND UP AT ATTENTION AND START SHOUTING HAIL TO THE
CHIEF AND I'D SHOUT IT AS LOUD AS I COULD AND I'D KEEP ON
SHOUTING IT UNTIL THE CHIEF TOLD ME OTHERWISE.

YEAH. YOU'RE NOT GOING TO HAVE ME TO KICK AROUND ANYMORE,
YOU BUNGHOLE COCKSUCKING ASSHOLES. BUT I MAY JUST DECIDE TO
DO A LITTLE ASSKICKING MYSELF AND HOW'D YOU LIKE THAT, YOU
CHICKENSHIT SANITATION FARTS?

YEAH, SO WATCH OUT, BOY. BIG NUMBER ONE MAY JUST TAKE OFF
THE GLOVES AND COME DOWN THERE AND GIVE YOU DEAD SEA SHITS
THE KIND OF REAM YOU DESERVE.

YEAH. ASSHOLES.

> NUBAR
>
> FUCK SUCK KILL.
> ULTIMATE LEADER AND SUPREME
> AUTHORITY AT THE
> TOP OF THE HEAP AND ALONE
> THERE FOR ALL TIME.

Nubar felt a little better after that, but it only showed you could
never relax your authority. They were all ready to go over to the
enemy if you showed the slightest weakness, the slightest deviation from
absolute iron-fisted control.

He brushed away something that seemed to be nibbling at his ear, an
imaginary bat perhaps, then returned to the report.

Now the narrative was back in the Franciscan bakery, the pilgrim
sprawled naked on the floor with his head on fire, the baking priest

dancing around through the fierce heat bearing fresh loaves of bread in all directions.

Off to Mecca he was all right, sang the baking priest, just as sure as the wind will blow he was going to reach his Mecca, this elderly article on his annual haj in the first half of the nineteenth century. Well he gets himself well down into the desert that spring, well down into Araby and away from the customary tracks as is his custom when on a haj, when what does he find going on down there all of a sudden in Araby? What, you say? He finds the sky turning strangely dark one morning, that's what, darkly strange I say. And all alarmed he is and why not, since he's in the middle of nowhere where no man should be, and what happens then but he stumbles across an apparition of a man who's all of seven and a half feet tall, and what's this striking figure doing but sighting through some complicated astronomical instruments, by way of measuring heavenly bodies. Like it so far?

Nubar groaned. He closed his eyes.

Seven and a half feet tall. Surely not Ahura Mazda again?

He took a long drink of mulberry raki, coughed weakly and read on.

Well, sang the baking priest, clapping his hands and slapping his sandals on the floor, well and then *well*. It's not exactly what an honest traveler would expect to run into out there, and with this apparition looming up in front of him with heavenly instruments and the sky so dark and all, well your man is just suddenly very frightened.

Why, you say? Because he knows a thing or two about the world and one thing he knows for sure is that this has to be a genie he's dealing with. But luckily for him this genie is a good genie who takes pity on him and decides straightaway to make things better, not worse. So the genie tells him right off why it's dark out there. It's dark, says the genie, because a comet is passing overhead. But no one knows about the comet except him, the genie, because of course a genie can have his very own comet if he wants one, and it seems this genie did. And now this genie was out there in the desert plotting his comet's cycle of six hundred and sixteen years, taking roundabout measurements of this heavenly plaything of his, so to speak. All this the giant good genie quickly relates to your man the elderly item.

The baking priest did a quick turn in front of the oven. His cassock twirled and he came up with an armful of bread before resuming his tale.

Well that's certainly something now, but although it explains the darkness of the sky out there, it also tends to mystify your man.

Exactly six hundred and sixteen years? he asks the genie, in a humble whisper of course, showing the greatest respect. Why exactly that period of time?

For a good reason, answers the giant good genie, who then goes on to demystify the situation at once. It seems, you see, that this comet he has discovered and made his own is related to certain unexplained events in the lives of Moses and Nebuchadnezzar and Christ and Mohammed, along with a few lesser known passages from the *Thousand and One Nights* and an obscure reference or two from the Zohar, those literary matters thrown in for balance and good measure.

That is to say, those events in those lives *would* be unexplained if it weren't for this comet the genie had discovered, which had come over at the proper time in those lives to do the job required of it, said job being to provide heavenly evidence that something important was going on in the lives just mentioned.

Do you follow me? The giant good genie's comet was up there to explain the inexplicable, although no one else knew it, and the genie was down there in the desert using his astronomical instruments to keep our heavenly historical affairs on course, as he always does when his comet comes over every six hundred and sixteen years, no more and no less and will you just imagine that? Will you now?

A case of genuine celestial evidence, the baking priest had added. Makes you think, doesn't it. And since then the man who told me all this has learned the name of the giant good genie in question. Strongbow is his name. And so that heavenly body up there that explains the inexplicable and lets us know that important events are happening in important lives, said celestial evidence has to be known of course as Strongbow's Comet.

Celestial evidence? Nubar didn't like that at all. Who were these people and what did they think they were doing over there in Jerusalem, in Araby, inventing this nonsense? His grandfather had discovered the original Bible and now it was rightfully his, the philosopher's stone belonged to him. It was as simple as that. Decisive action was needed.

SPEEDIEST FLASH. ARE YOU MAD? GENIES DON'T EXIST AND THERE-
FORE I ABSOLUTELY FORBID A COMET BEING OWNED BY ONE. MAKE
THIS EPIC TELL THE TRUTH OR FACE SEVERE REPRISALS, PRODUCE OR
GET OUT. THIS IS MY FINAL WARNING, YOU DEAD SEA FARTS, AND IF
YOU DON'T BELIEVE ME JUST TRY ME.

NUBAR

THE TOP

The top, yes, but he had to be careful all the same. Treachery was everywhere. Betrayal was everywhere. And of course he knew exactly what they were trying to do with their comets and genies and maniacally dancing priests. It was a savage onslaught by the barbarians again with their primitive ideas and their instincts out of control, their profoundly ignorant belief in the superstitions of the heavens and giants to be met in the desert and swaying shamans seen illuminated in a cave, the shadowy figures of primitive brains trying to assault a rational mind. But they wouldn't get away with it, and if they continued to try to delude him they would soon see where it led.

A page from the report in his lap floated loose and rose slowly in the air. Up up and away. Nubar watched it disappear somewhere up there in the gloom.

Drafts. Icy drafts. It was cold in the cellar and getting colder. He needed more light to be able to see in this damp cave beneath the Grand Canal. He needed some heat.

The pit dug by the footman was at his feet. Despite their savagery even the barbarians had known what to do at the end of the day. A fire surely. A blazing roaring fire to warm the fierce horsemen and cheer them after another day of relentless butchery on the way to Europe. There were thousands of UIA reports here, more than he could ever use. Burn some, why not. Nubar pushed a pile of them into the pit and tossed in a match.

Light, heat, the flames shot up. This was much better. He pushed in more reports and settled back comfortably beside the crackling pit, able to see more clearly now, able to think more clearly because he didn't have to worry about the icy drafts.

Mulberry raki, strong and nourishing. He took a second gulp and thoughtfully chewed some of the wooden canteen.

A Macedonian Extra, just right. They thought they could wear him down with their lunatic antics but never had a gang of madmen been more mistaken. The barbarians believed in their primitive magic but Nubar knew better. He could handle it all and he was prepared to do just that.

He smiled shrewdly, not concealing his contempt, and picked up another page.

And now, sang the baking priest, having seen our genie in the last century, we'll be on with this epic tale and skip right up into our century, to just before the Great War. Once again your man the elderly item is off on his annual haj, resolutely making his way through Araby, through the wilderness and wastes and wearing his rusty Crusader's helmet as he does at all times against contingencies, steadfastly trudging through the desert to reach his Mecca, his faded threadbare yellow cloak flaring into a sail now and then to give him a push, a tug, the nudges he so badly needs if he's going to continue to make headway against the vicissitudes.

The baking priest pulled open the oven door and peered in. The blast of hot air struck the pilgrim on the floor and flattened him out a little more, if that was still possible. The oven door clanged shut.

Right we are, all's well. Now where were we? Oh yes, down in Araby of course and your man has just finished walking all night, and just before dawn, being tired naturally enough, he ducks under a rock to catch a nap, to catch forty nods as they say, his spindly legs protruding out from under the rock and looking like nothing so much as two ancient and exhausted lizards intent on dying. When all at once he hears a noise, a most unusual noise for way out there, a kind of *whooshing* sound as if something big were moving in the air, and he pokes out his head from under the rock. What might that be? he wonders.

The baking priest began to spin in front of his oven. Cassock twirling, sandals flapping, around and around he whirled.

What might that be? Well I'll tell you what that might be. That just might be the happiest moment of his very long life. It just might be ecstasy for him, that's what. Because who's coming down in that place that any other man would call Godforsaken? Any man except him, that is, with his centuries and centuries of faithful service. Who's descending right there on top of this tattered and battered soul, this starving and exhausted and tottering elderly item? Who's just dropping in for a look in that remote corner of the desert formerly and normally forsaken?

Himself, that's Who, do you follow me? Our Lord God and Creator.

The baking priest had stopped spinning when he said that. He stopped and crossed himself solemnly and gazed down at the pilgrim naked on the floor.

And his face was grave as was only to be expected, and the tone of his voice most reverent. Yet the pilgrim saw a twinkle in the priest's eye even then, even then when he was referring to his Maker. Caused by seven decades in front of an oven in Jerusalem, no doubt, enough to bake anybody's brains.

The pilgrim didn't move. He couldn't move. He lay speechless, naked on the floor.

Are you still with me? sang the baking priest as he scooped a load of hot loaves out of the oven and went dancing across the room.

At this point in his account, wrote the informer, the naked pilgrim on the bakery floor had finally succumbed to heat prostration and begun hallucinating.

It was impossible to make any sense out of what the pilgrim later that afternoon, between glasses of pomegranate juice at the informer's fruit juice stand, claimed the baking priest had said after that. Or rather, sung after that. The larger part was incomprehensible gibberish, the remainder incoherent hearsay.

Nevertheless, for purposes of completeness in UIA reporting, a summary of the rest of the epic was being included.

Summarized, the subsequent events in the baking priest's epic tale were these.

Page 17 of 407 pages, a report relating to the Great Jerusalem Poker Swindle.

    A. *Conclusion of the foregoing.*
    B. *The narrative form is hereby temporarily suspended, for purposes of clarity, in favor of itemized notes.*

1. The man the baking priest has been referring to throughout as that elderly item or article, obviously Haj Harun, prostrated himself in the desert at dawn the moment he poked his head out from under the rock and saw God above him.
2. God was riding in a balloon.
3. The balloon descended and came to rest beside the rock where Haj Harun, as still as a lizard, had been about to catch forty nods after walking all night. Needless to say, Haj Harun was now alert and not thinking about forty nods, having waited three thousand years for this moment.
4. God stepped out of His balloon and saw that Haj Harun was terrified as well as ecstatic. God immediately offered Haj Harun food and water from a supply He was carrying in His balloon.
5. Haj Harun refused in the humblest of whispers.
6. God then offered to give Haj Harun a ride in His balloon to the nearest oasis, if Haj Harun were too weak to walk, as seemed likely.
7. Haj Harun again refused in the humblest of whispers.
8. God asked Haj Harun if there were anything He could do for him out there in the desert. Haj Harun finally had the courage to rise to his knees, as God had been begging him to do, and speak.
9. Haj Harun said that he knew this world was a desert compared to God's kingdom. He said he also knew that God has many names, and that every name we learn brings us closer to Him. He said that he was a pathetic creature who had spent the last three thousand years futilely defending Jerusalem, always on the losing side, as was the case when you were trying to defend everybody's Holy City. So he had forever failed in his mission, yet he had never given up hope. In fact he was still trying.
10. Haj Harun admitted it was a sorry effort that deserved to go unrewarded. Yet if God could find any merit in his failure, and would be so gracious as to tell him His name that day, then it would be a blessing to Haj Harun that

would make up for all his suffering over the last three thousand years in the cause of Jerusalem.

11. Apparently God did find merit in Haj Harun's futile efforts, for He decided to grant the request. He said His name that day was Stern.

Nubar stopped reading. He was appalled. Stern? *Stern?* He knew who that was, the name had turned up years ago in a report, and after that several other times. Stern was a petty gunrunner of no importance whatsoever. Moreover, he was a morphine addict. At the time Nubar had immediately dismissed him as inconsequential.

No, not even that. Dismissed him as nothing, a nonentity. The kind of shuffling forgotten wreckage you could expect to find anywhere in the world. No money, no power, some ideals maybe and a friend or two but going nowhere, just stumbling downhill with his morphine habit. A cipher, nothing, to be dismissed and forgotten.

So what was he doing turning up here being mistaken for God?

Ridiculous. Utterly ridiculous. This simply couldn't be allowed to go on for another minute. A cable was in order, succinct yet all-inclusive.

FLASH FROM THE TOP. YOU'RE ALL MAD. GOD ISN'T STERN, STERN IS A PETTY GUNRUNNER WITH A MORPHINE HABIT. WOULD GOD BE LIKELY TO BE RUNNING GUNS ACROSS THE DESERT IN A BALLOON? WOULD GOD BE LIKELY TO BE A MORPHINE ADDICT? NOW WOULD HE? WOULD HE?

NUBAR

GOD AS HE SHOULD BE.

Nubar rubbed his eyes wearily. Another page of the report was floating away in the gloom. He reached out and grabbed it as it tried to escape. He was getting tired of this. Why not be done with it once and for all?

FINAL FLASH FROM THE TOP. YOU'RE ALL FIRED, EFFECTIVE LAST MONTH. NO SEVERANCE PAY, NO RETIREMENT BENEFITS, NO MORE UIA, NO MORE NOTHING. DIE DOWN THERE ON THE DEAD SEA FOR ALL I CARE, AND DON'T SAY I DIDN'T WARN YOU. MY PATIENCE IS GONE, YOU DROVE ME TO THE LIMIT ON THIS ONE.

ONE OF GOD'S SECRET NAMES IS STERN? IF YOU CAN BELIEVE THAT
YOU CAN BELIEVE ANYTHING. ASSHOLES.

NUBAR

ALONE AS ALWAYS.

That made him feel better. He decided to read a few more pages before he went upstairs and fired all his servants as well. He didn't know what time it was but it must be getting on toward the hour for a baked chicken wing. Ah yes, here he was.

12. *While talking to God, Haj Harun had noticed something about His eyes that reminded him of the giant good genie, seven and a half feet tall, whom he had met in this same desert while on a haj in the nineteenth century.*

13. *Thus Haj Harun understood at that moment that God and the genie were father and son.*

14. *Haj Harun thanked God profusely for telling him His name that day and wept with joy. He backed away from God on his knees and continued in this manner for the rest of the morning, until God and His balloon were no longer visible beyond the sea of sand.*

15. *Nearly a decade later Haj Harun met God again, this time in Smyrna during the fires and massacres in 1922. To defend the innocent and protect God's children, Haj Harun had transformed himself into the Holy Ghost and carried a sword, in a smoky burning garden, God's children at the time being named Theresa, Sivi, and O'Sullivan Beare.*

16. *Before the massacre in Smyrna, Haj Harun had already survived the sacking of the Holy City by Assyrians and Babylonians, Persians and Greeks and Romans and Crusaders, Arabs and Turks, encouraging the citizenry as best he could.*

17. *(As you can see, there was a good reason back at the beginning of this report for indicating that the number of my fruit juice stand would be 18, if the shop had a number which it hasn't, being located in a dead-end alley too small for numbers.*

   It should also be noted here, if the UIA hierarchy is unaware of it, that 18 means life in Hebrew.)

18, then. *In addition to everything else, Haj Harun claims he witnessed the original Bible being written in his youth, say around 930 B.C.*

The primary author of the Bible was a blind storyteller who recited tales in the dusty waysides of Canaan in exchange for a few copper coins from those who tarried to hear him. During the recitals these tales were recorded by a friendly imbecile scribe, who was the blind man's traveling companion.

However, what the blind storyteller didn't know was that he wasn't the sole author of those Holy Scriptures. The imbecile, being friendly, had also wanted to play a part in the production.

Haj Harun, as a little boy, had peeked over the scribe's shoulder.

And yes, sure enough, the imbecile scribe was happily adding a few thoughts of his own to the pages.

Nubar lay on his makeshift couch with his hand on his heart as water dripped down on him from the Grand Canal. His heart was palpitating and he felt dizzy. An unfocused pain moved back and forth behind his eyes. He had barely begun the report in his lap but he knew he was far too weak to go on with it.

He tossed the report into the fire.

Weak, yes. As weak as a flower, a frail Albanian flower withering away in an icy subcellar underneath Venice, driven there by marauding hordes of barbarians bent on destruction and chaos, once there repeatedly and savagely assaulted by the ravings of primitive minds insanely out of control in Jerusalem. Weak from hunger, close to starvation. Was there anything left in his canteen?

He reached into his rucksack and pulled out what was left of the canteen itself, now about the size of a small drinking cup, holding perhaps half a cup of mulberry raki. He drank the raki and chewed the little cup around the edges, nibbling in nervous bites, gnawing his way to the bottom of this last relic from Gronk, the kind of canteen used by peasant boys when they were out working in the fields.

Nubar gazed at the fire. Barbarians were surging forward on every side threatening civilization, yet still there was no reason to fear what he had just read, none whatsoever. It was all meaningless fantasy, a web of buffoonish tales having nothing to do with reality.

A Zoroastrian operator of a fruit juice stand in the Old City? A naked anonymous pilgrim sprawled on the floor of a convent bakery? A maniacal baking priest piling up bread in four shapes?

Ludicrous.

Then too, the time span was considerable. From a hot August day in Jerusalem in 1933 to Smyrna in 1922, from God in His balloon just before the Great War to a genie-astrologer in Arabia in the first half of the nineteenth century. Finally all the way back to the dusty waysides of Canaan in 930 B.C.

Absurd.

And the ultimate source of all this, none other than Haj Harun. His epic tale weaving up and down the alleys of Jerusalem over the millennia, passing from beggar to beggar in the bazaars with new variations added each time it was retold by another thieving layabout, another shifty-eyed Arab or unscrupulous Jew or hallucinating Christian in that unreal city on the mountaintop where the real Sinai Bible lay buried.

Nubar squeezed his fists in a frenzy.

Lies. All lies.

God in the twentieth century, Stern? The genie in the nineteenth century, Strongbow? The two of them having something about the eyes that showed they were father and son?

And worst of all, that vision of Haj Harun in 930 B.C. Haj Harun as a little boy, peeking over the shoulder of an imbecile scribe and noting that the scribe was happily adding a few thoughts of his own to the original Bible.

Nubar clenched his fists and exploded. He staggered to his feet, shrieking.

Lies and more lies. They think they'll get me but they won't. I'll get them.

In a fury he hurled more reports into the fire that was raging in the pit at his feet. The smoke swirled around him and he fell back weakly on the couch.

So weak after fighting everybody for years, especially those three evil criminals who had set up the Great Jerusalem Poker Swindle to deprive him of immortality. Why had there been that disaster in Gronk simply because he liked to dress up a little? Those three depraved criminals in Jerusalem dressed up, he had read about it in reports long ago. They all dressed up and had their fun, so why had it been wrong when he wanted to wear a uniform? And why did he have to fight everybody in life? Fight endlessly?

Nubar's roving fingers found the tin of rouge and the tube of lipstick in the pocket of his housecoat. He took them out and began to play with them idly, applying a little bit here and there, wondering what Paracelsus would have done in this damp murky cellar on an evening such as this. Ignored the icy drafts and the water dripping on him and gone on to repeat his mercury experiment a thousand times in search of the unique set of circumstances? Two thousand times? Three thousand times?

Breathing those heavy mercury vapors anew on a gloomy winter evening in Venice? Yet again inhaling his beloved fumes beneath the Grand Canal? At last dreaming his way into the philosopher's stone of immortality?

Nubar's gaze fell on a crate that had surfaced from under the stacks of reports he had dumped into the fire, a crate with a vaguely familiar shape. He crawled over and opened it.

Cinnabar. Mercury ore.

A whole crate of cinnabar from his alchemist's workshop in the castle tower room in Albania. Left over from the days when he had performed mercury experiments, shipped here as part of the UIA archives. Odd that it should happen to turn up in front of him now, just when he was thinking about mercury.

Alchemy in the steps of the master. Six years ago, only that?

Happy days and nights then, he remembered them well. Long hours spent alone at his workbench in his castle tower room, communing over mercury with the master, Bombastus Vonheim the Celsus of Parahohen.

Was that right or was it Bombastus von Ho von Heim?

Parabombast? Paravon? Paraheim and Paraho?

No no, it was Parastein of course, Nubar Wallencelsus Parastein. The incomparable Parastein. What had happened to him in six short years? Where had he gone?

Nubar pushed the crate of cinnabar over to the pit and watched it tumble into the roaring fire. Smoke, fog, dreams. Mercury vapors. Swirling new fumes in the subaqueous archives of the Uranist Intelligence Agency.

Nubar found the medallion depicting Mussolini and the Virgin Mary in his housecoat and turned it over and over, looking for a similarity between the two faces. He found the three one-lira coins and put them into his mouth to suck. He pushed more reports into the fire.

Something was missing. In order to see clearly in the billowing smoke and mercury fumes he needed the third eye of occultism. But where was his small obsidian sphere, the precious ball of black volcanic glass, his primitive third eye?

Lost. He'd never find it now. His fingers touched something round in the pocket of his housecoat. He held it up.

The single earring, fake lapis lazuli, the color of the sky. It looked like a robin's egg.

Nubar attached the hook of the earring to his skullcap so the robin's egg would rest on his forehead. Yes, that was better. His head was expanding, his supernatural powers of perception were beginning to return. He could feel his brain growing, swelling like an egg to encompass all of life.

Ultimate thoughts now in the underworld, the time had come. His left eye, the eye that had bothered Wallenstein men for three centuries in times of stress, automatically sealed itself shut as Nubar considered the ultimate enemies arrayed against him.

Ahura Mazda, chief of the gods of goodness, the secret owner of the Middle East who had also been known as Strongbow, a giant genie who was implacably pursuing him from the nineteenth century. Why? Why had he, Nubar, been singled out for persecution by the giant good genie?

God his son, father of the genie, Himself, in the twentieth century disguised as a petty gunrunner and morphine addict named Stern. Years ago Nubar had dismissed Stern as too insignificant to bother with.

And lastly, *Haj Harun,* that timeless ghostly figure who had witnessed everything, even the writing of the original Bible.

Nubar smiled and his right eye also sealed itself shut. With both eyes closed in the smoke, in the billowing mercury fumes rising from the pit, he could at last see the universe as it was through his mystical third eye.

And? Was it going to turn out the way that maniacally prancing baking priest had suggested at the beginning of his epic tale? Were the ultimate enemies arrayed against him the Holy Trinity? The Father and the Son and the Holy Ghost?

An idea came to him. Even though the Holy Trinity was arrayed against him, that still left the Virgin Mary, and where was the Virgin Mary? Was he the Virgin Mary in disguise? It was true, after all, that in some parts of Greece there was the belief that when Christ was born again He would be born of a man, which was why the men there all wore trousers with a large sack in the seat, to catch the Savior when He appeared.

Extraordinary. A fascinating new possibility with limitless ramifications, not only for him but for the world. As he turned over the medallion in his hand the black volcanic eye in his forehead stared blindly at the roaring fire in the pit, oblivious to the smoke and the flames and the fumes in the cave.

A move to Greece at once? The sun and the sea, lucidity and the Savior?

Nubar grinned and the grin froze.

The astounding event that was the talk of Venice that winter occurred precisely at twelve o'clock noon on December 22. Some claimed it had to do with the fact that the previous night had been the longest night of the year. Others, calling this mere superstition, argued that darkness and night had played no part, rather high noon and broad daylight had.

In any case, whether one or the other, Nubar would never have been found without it, his strange fate never known.

The heavy fog that had hung over Venice for days began to clear toward the middle of that morning, December 22. Tourists eager to see the wonders of the city were quick to take advantage, and by eleven-thirty a modest but steady traffic of gondolas was plying the Grand Canal.

In one of the gondolas was a party of Argentines, of German descent and strongly in favor of Mussolini's Fascist policies, the only actual witnesses to the event.

What made it seem so eerie, they said later, was that the stately palazzo had collapsed without a sound.

One moment they were admiring its beautiful lines as they passed through the water, an ornate and dignified structure on the Venetian skyline that was typical of what they had always imagined a palazzo on the Grand Canal would look like, and the next moment it was simply gone, no longer there, having silently disappeared before their very eyes in a puff of smoke.

They blinked. They couldn't believe it. There was nothing but sky where the palazzo had been, sky and a mysterious puff of smoke that was already wafting away on the wind.

The clocks in the church towers all over Venice were striking noon. The palazzo had disappeared as if it were an empty dream.

The experience was uncanny, said the Argentines. For several minutes they sat dumbly in their gondola, too stunned to speak, staring into that patch of newly empty sky.

Of course the palazzo had made some noise collapsing, but not enough to be heard above the loud pealing of the city's church bells, which engineers later speculated might have upset the palazzo's delicate balance with their combined vibrations. And there was a perfectly reasonable explanation for the smoke, although it would take twenty-four hours to discover it.

While the stunned Argentines sat immobile in their gondola, other parties of tourists began to arrive on the scene from up and down the Grand Canal. The gondoliers landed and what they found astonished them, just as it astonished the police who arrived some minutes later.

For it seemed the Argentines' strange impression had not been wrong at all, rather it was based on airy fact. The floors and interior walls of the palazzo had all been removed, indeed, its insides in their entirety. There had been absolutely nothing at all left in there.

The palazzo *had been* an empty dream before it collapsed.

It didn't take the police long to find out what had happened. When they went to question the servants who had worked in the palazzo, they found them all living in richly decorated villas far beyond their means, as were many of their relatives. One servant after another broke down and confessed.

The pillage, they admitted, had been going on since the beginning of their employment there. It had progressed from single objects to stripping whole rooms, to ripping out the plumbing and wiring, then to the marble in the floors and the wood and stonework in the walls.

The previous night they had finally made an end to the job by carrying away what was left of the floors and interior walls, leaving an empty shell behind.

By the evening of December 22, the scandal had taken on enormous proportions, particularly because the palazzo had been owned by a foreigner. The ability of the Fascist government to maintain law and order was being held up to ridicule, and tourists were leaving by train for Switzerland and by ship for Patras, outraged that a foreigner in Italy could be treated in such a manner. The police had to act immediately or the situation would have become intolerable.

Thus by ten o'clock that night seventeen former servants and several hundred of their relatives, screaming and weeping and shouting, had been dragged before judges and arraigned for a multitude of offenses ranging from unpremeditated theft and similar crimes of passion, to the systematic defacement of a national landmark, which an urgent cable from Rome, received just after dark, indicated the palazzo had secretly been for about the last one hundred years, unknown to anyone in Venice.

Meanwhile the search went on for the victim of this terrible conspiracy, who was described by the former servants as an Albanian millionaire, about twenty-seven years old, of extremely eccentric habits.

By gondoliers who for months had been carrying the little millionaire back to the palazzo just before dawn, he was identified as that bizarre figure who had been haunting the piazza in front of San Marco's through the hours of darkness for almost a year, dressed in evening clothes and a top hat and an opera cape and thoroughly drunk from some powerful alcoholic beverage, which he carried in a wooden canteen slung over his shoulder.

As for his activities at night in the piazza, thousands of witnesses were ready to testify that they had seen the little millionaire sneaking up behind tourists in cafés and annoying them in the most flagrant manner by whispering on endlessly about something called *Gronk*, as if this single word, unrecognizable to anyone, not only conveyed a whole host of meanings but also implied unlimited possibilities of an unknown nature. And always he had carried in his arms a stack of journals titled *The Boy*, which he had tried to give away but never could, it apparently being the little millionaire's destiny to go on carrying *The Boy* around with him forever.

These furtive nightly performances were known to thousands in Venice, but other than that the police could learn only one other fact concerning the little millionaire's public life. Several restaurant owners stated that he had been in the habit of dropping in around midnight to order a single baked chicken wing, which he then carried off into the darkness in a paper bag.

Yet even though he hadn't come to the piazza in front of San Marco's on the night before his palazzo collapsed, the servants reported that he definitely wasn't to be seen in the empty dream when they had carried out the last supporting beam. Nor had a body been found in the ruins.

WHERE IS THE MAD NIGHTLY PEDDLER OF GRONK? screamed the headlines in the newspapers.

The police intensified their search on the morning of December 23. Lists were checked and it was found that a footman from the palazzo was not among those arrested. The footman hadn't returned home and had last been seen by other servants on the morning before the collapse, dressed in blue satin livery and carrying a pickax and shovel in the vicinity of the kitchen.

The police put out an alarm for the man and before noon they were led to a Communist laborer in a cheap café on the mainland, drunk on grappa, who was wearing blue satin knee breeches. At first the laborer sullenly denied any knowledge of his satin breeches, saying they would never exist in a Communist state. But under threat of a sound beating from the Fascist police crowding around him, he soon admitted he had taken the breeches off a delirious man who had washed up on the shore two days ago, thinking they would add a little color to his life. After hiding the breeches under his shirt he had hailed a passing group of mendicant monks, who had carried the delirious man back to their monastery to care for him.

The monks were traced and the footman was found lying in a corner of the monastery garage, just emerging from a coma caused by excessive ingestion of Grand Canal water. The police slapped him to bring him around and the footman told a confused tale.

One morning, he said, days or weeks or months ago, he had no idea when the catastrophe had befallen him and how long he had been in a coma, he had been carrying out his normal duties in the subcellar of the palazzo when he had met an apparition of womanhood so horrifying, so unnatural, that he had run upstairs in terror and jumped through a casement window to swim for his life. But the sewerage had been sluggish that morning around the palazzo. As he swam out into the Grand Canal the fumes overwhelmed him, he lost consciousness and didn't know anything after that.

But he did remember that terrible, ghastly apparition he had seen in the subcellar by torchlight.

And never before that moment, swore the footman, crossing himself again and again and shaking violently as putrid bubbles popped out of his mouth, could I have imagined such a female figure existed on this earth, Hail Mary, mother of God.

A subcellar beneath the palazzo? The policemen were amazed, but not so one of the learned mendicant monks who had been listening with them in the monastery garage.

Yes indeed, observed the monk. That palazzo was once shared by Byron and his favorite pimp and catamite, Tito the gondolier, which I happen to know about because Tito was a granduncle on my mother's side. Well to escape the hordes of women and boys who were always besieging Byron in his living quarters, he had a secret subcellar built where he could retire late at night and write his poetry. Undoubtedly that's why the palazzo was a secret national landmark that none of us knew about until yesterday evening. Some of Byron's greatest poetry must have been written down there.

The police rushed back to their launch and quickly roared away from the mainland, sirens howling, making for the Grand Canal. With little difficulty they found the entrance to the cellar in the palazzo ruins. Twenty steps down stood the entrance to the subcellar, a low narrow door hidden behind a blanket, exactly as described by the footman. They pushed it open.

Immediately mountainous clouds of thick acrid smoke belched from that gloomy cave and went swirling up over the city, obscuring the sun, Nubar having burned the entire archives of the Uranist Intelligence Agency in his mercury pit, to keep warm, during the cold damp night of the winter solstice.

Firemen arrived with masks and emergency equipment. They found Nubar stretched out beside his smoldering mercury fire, alive but unconscious, and carried him up to the surface where curious crowds had gathered. The canal in front of the ruined palazzo was now thronged with the bobbing boats of eager sightseers from all over the world.

Somberly the Fascist firemen brought Nubar forward on a stretcher and laid him out on a high platform they had erected beside the water, in full view of everyone, not only because their countrymen loved a spectacle but also, in this case, to impress the masses of foreign tourists with the Fascist efficiency of their rescue operations.

The sightseers sighed and were silent. Waves lapped gently against the assembled boats and gondolas. Respiratory and other equipment quietly wheezed beside the raised platform, which had been hung with bunting and Fascist banners for the occasion.

Then the Fascist mayor, the Fascist chief of police and the Fascist chief of the fire department took turns announcing in loud voices what they saw before them, shouting the facts up and down the Grand Canal and describing in considerable detail the thick layers of rouge and lipstick, the various large brown garments and the even larger purple one, the single blue earring resting on Nubar's forehead and the three one-lira coins resting on his tongue, in one hand the medallion depicting Mussolini and the Blessed Virgin Mary, and in the other hand the most curious object of all, a Jerusalem water bill, paid, dated 1921, on which he had scribbled some words before losing consciousness, *poker* and *Jerusalem* and *Haj Harun*, *Paracelsus* and *Bombastus* and *immortality*, *Ahura Mazda* and *Stern*, *genie* and *God*, *the Sinai Bible.*

The presence of the coins in Nubar's mouth suggested that he might have been swallowing foreign objects while in the subcellar. A stomach pump was therefore immediately wheeled into position, but all it brought up was a large amount of chewed wood impregnated with alcohol.

This mysterious piece of information proved too much for one of the spectators, a French thief and former dealer in stolen ikons who had arrived in Venice not so long ago after an extended stay in the Holy Land.

It was true that he had been accosted by Nubar more than once in the piazza in front of San Marco's late at night, which he had found insulting enough in itself. But the real cause of that Frenchman's passionate dislike for Nubar was a period he had once spent in purgatory, after being hired by the UIA to infiltrate the Great Jerusalem Poker Game. The Frenchman had entered the game as ordered and had lost disastrously to an American Indian chief, who resented his trafficking in stolen Christian artifacts. Part of his loss included being assigned to slave in front of a hot oven in the Old City, his purgatory, with a man known as the baking priest serving as his parole officer.

A very hot oven. The Frenchman remembered every dripping minute he had spent in that fierce heat baking bread in the same four shapes, as directed by his ancient parole officer who all the while had danced back and forth in a merry way, which had only infuriated him more.

All those horrible experiences he blamed on Nubar for getting him into the game in the first place. So it was with unrestrained glee that the high-pitched French cry came floating down the Grand Canal.

Shit my God. He ate his canteen.

On the last day of the year Nubar regained consciousness in the hospital and it was apparent he would never be normal again. His frozen grin was directed toward the ceiling, his stony stare fixed on some invisible quarry. Every twelve minutes or so he stirred and softly whispered parts of the words he had scribbled on the Jerusalem water bill, paid, dated 1921.

And those were the only syllables Nubar ever uttered again, rearranging them endlessly in senseless mercurial anagrams that were somehow pleasing to him, *Parabastus Bombhaj* and *Sinaisalem Bombpoker, Ahurahaj Paramazda* and *Sternpoker Bibletality, Jerugenie* and *Immorharun, Hajstern, Jerupoker.*

Jumbled private words that seemed to soothe him in the airless stillness of the eternal dimensionless rock encasing his head, a secret and solitary philosopher's stone that no one would ever penetrate.

For Nubar, safety at last, peace at last, immortality at last. All his enemies defeated and Stern dismissed, Ahura Mazda dispelled and Haj Harun forgotten in the dream of stone he had finally entered.

17

Crypt, Cobbler

The whole point, is that all? Well of
course I was getting around to it. I was just
sort of sizing up the countryside along
the way. What's the point of taking a
trip if you don't see the sights?

*T*he last night in December, 1933. Twelve years to the day since
the three of them had met by chance in a cheap Arab coffee shop
in the Old City, seemingly by chance then, the three of them escaping
the wind on a blustery afternoon that had been cold and heavily
overcast with snow definitely in the air. And now they sat around the
poker table in Haj Harun's back room, one or the other of them
shuffling the cards for a while before passing the pack along.

An ambling affair, said Joe. Just one of those quiet rambling evenings
that comes along sometimes. I mean it is the last day of the year so it's
only natural a man might want to take a moment to look back a bit,
just to see how things went maybe, insofar as they did.

Sure, said Joe, shuffling the cards. And that's some news all right
about the end of our little Nubar. Losing his head like that under the
Grand Canal and finding a stone to put in its place. With him out of
the way I guess we could go on playing poker forever, if we wanted to.

Yes, well I can't say I'm sorry for him. Always was a nasty little piece of goods by any account. But I'll tell you something else. I do feel sorry for Sophia, even though I've never met her. From all you hear she sounds right to me, and I imagine she must be taking it hard.

Yes, said Munk. But she also knows she indulged him too much from the beginning.

Habit both good and bad, murmured Joe. Can run both ways, indulging a man, depends on the man, like most things. Hey there, Munk. Not recalling a breakfast in bed beside the Bosporus, are you? Dashing young officer of dragoons being served steak and eggs and a pot of strong coffee laced with cognac? Not to mention a mountain of hot rolls straight from the oven and light as light? Ah yes, mere fluffs of ambrosia, no less, in your wicked youth. And your uniform pressed and your boots polished and a bath drawn? Never crossed your mind once, you say, in all these years?

Munk smiled.

I talked to her yesterday, he said.

My God, you what? How's that? You talked to Sophia?

On the telephone, yes. I thought I should call her as one old friend to another. It was over twenty years ago, and only one night at that, but all the same.

Of course all the same. Well quick man, out with it. What'd she say?

She was in Venice. We didn't talk about Nubar, mostly about his baby son. There was one, it seems, and Sophia had just found out about it. She was excited about that and also happy about the baby's mother, who happens to be Armenian. So perhaps the good news has made up for the bad. She plans to take them both back to Albania with her.

And you? What'd she say about you?

She asked me to come pay her a visit at the castle in the spring. I said I would.

Joe hooted. He reached over and slammed down the pack of cards in front of Munk.

Your turn to shuffle, and did you catch that, Cairo? Catch our former dashing young officer of dragoons still in action? The lady in question's over ninety, so what's he going to do about it? Pay a friendly visit for old times' sake, that's what, console the old dear because of the memories. Now is that what ambrosia does for you or isn't it? One taste and you can't ever forget? Just never? Ah but that's fine, truly fine, I love the whole idea of it. And you do a little reminiscing with her, Munk, you do that. A woman her age, she'd like that for sure.

Munk smiled as he shuffled the cards.

Business isn't going well for her, he said. The syndicate's breaking up, not that she cares much about that sort of thing anymore. It was setting it up that was a challenge to her, not making money once it was going. So yes, I'll journey up and see her, and she can straighten me out on the situation in the Balkans, and I'll have another chance to smell those cheroots I remember from my younger days.

Forget the Balkans, said Joe, I never could understand what they were. But the rest of it is marvelous, just marvelous, I love it. You do that and let us know. By God, isn't it true we can get lucky now and then and time doesn't pass at all? Or rather it passes all right, it just doesn't take all the good things with it. Now and then only, but it's comforting to know it can happen at least. And speaking of your younger days, Munk, what news from *the Sarahs* lately in their various outposts in the New World, mostly Brazil?

They're getting along, back on their feet in business.

Sure, we all knew that would happen. And the all-male Szondi baroque ensembles? Are they getting back on their feet and into their chairs after a decade or two in the discount dry goods trade?

They seem to be.

Well then, Munk, it seems you're just situated here for good and ready to get on with your affairs, building a homeland and so forth, a sober matter certainly after the spew of cards we've had here for the last twelve years. Trading in futures from the beginning, you were, just dealing away like a madman in the market. Hey, where're you going, Cairo?

Cairo had gotten to his feet. He went swaying into the front room in his stately robes and came back with a stone box, which he placed on the table. He smiled and held out his hand. Munk gave him the cards and Cairo began to shuffle.

What's that? asked Joe.

A box, said Cairo.

A man can see that. Why stone?

They made them that way so they'd last. Menelik gave it to me once. He'd found it in a royal tomb he'd excavated.

Well what's in it then?

Ashes.

From what?

From a forty-year conversation beside the Nile. Long Sunday afternoons over wine and spiced lamb in a filthy open-air restaurant on the banks of the Nile, with placid ducks paddling in circles and squawking peacocks getting ready to mate and scurrilous evidence richly woven under the trellises of leafy vines and flowers, and waiters who got so high on their flying carpets over the years they simply didn't move anymore, couldn't move anymore, couldn't imagine why anyone would want to move anymore. Long Sunday afternoons that always ended with drunken plunges into the cooling water.

Sure, said Joe, we know about that. But what are the ashes?

The ashes of two friends who met in an Egyptian bazaar early in the nineteenth century, both young then, both just starting out on their separate paths. One a black slave, the other an English lord.

Joe whistled softly.

You've got the ashes of old Menelik and Strongbow in there?

I have.

Where did you get them?

I just went and got them.

And what are you going to do with them?

Cairo smiled.

Early in the spring when Munk goes to pay his call on Sophia, I'm going to take this box down to Egypt. I'll choose a Sunday that pleases me and go back to that filthy restaurant beside the Nile where they had their forty-year conversation, or if it's gone, to one like it. Then I'll order wine and spiced lamb and stuff myself, and lean back and while away the afternoon listening to Menelik and Strongbow carry on the way they used to. I'll listen to them tell the story again of the incredible White Monk of the Sahara and his nine hundred children, and the Numa Stone that scandalized Europe after Strongbow planted it in the temple at Karnak, and I'll pound the table and order more wine and roar with laughter with them at all the old tales, all the wonderful tales. Menelik smuggling Strongbow's study into Egypt in the bowels of a giant hollow stone scarab, and Strongbow striding off to the Hindu Kush and returning to stride off to Timbuktu, and Menelik building a spacious retreat for himself in the top of Cheops' pyramid and finding he was afraid of heights, and retiring instead to the sarcophagus of

Cheops' mother with Strongbow's magnifying glass in hand. And Strongbow finally finding peace on a hillside in the Yemen, in the simple tent of a Jewish shepherd's daughter. Empires bought and empires sold and an unknown scholar who was the wisest of his century, a former slave so brilliant he spoke a language that's been extinct for eleven hundred years, a young explorer who began his haj by shouting that he had once loved well in Persia. And all the rest of it, all the wonderful old tales they shared. And that final reunion when they both came back for one last Sunday afternoon together in their filthy haunt beside the Nile. Both in their nineties then and knowing they'd go soon, which they did, within a few months of each other just before the Great War. Just all of it. With all the wine and the food and the stories that never stopped, because they could never get enough of them.

Cairo paused. He looked down at the table and shuffled the cards slowly.

And then? asked Munk after a few moments.

And then a time will come toward the end of the afternoon to jump over the railing into the river, the way they did. And I'll go over the railing with them for a last plunge, a last swim at the end of the afternoon to clear my head or perhaps just to celebrate life. And when I come out I'll no longer have the box. The Nile will.

Cairo nodded solemnly.

Once I thought I wanted to carry something quite different back to Africa. The black meteorite that's in the Kaaba in Mecca, the Holy of Holies. I wanted to bury it in rich black African soil as payment for the slaves the Arabs took out of Africa. But this box is what I'll carry back, and I'll give it to the Nile. The two of them would have liked that, I know it. As for me, it's the right thing to do.

Cairo finished shuffling the cards. He smiled and placed them in front of Joe. Joe looked at him, then whistled very softly.

Now if that isn't something. And all because the two of them taught you to dream when you were a little boy. Only that, nothing more. Well, Cairo, I'm glad for you and I'm glad for them. It's good you know where you're going and why, and when we have to look back it's better this way than the other. Better to be going to the river and giving it your gift, rather than burying something.

Joe turned toward the door.

Here now, what's this?

They listened to the chimes attached to the sundial in the front room strike the hour. While they were striking Haj Harun wandered in and began roaming around in distraction.

Twelve times, said Joe when the chimes stopped. Just right for nine in the evening. Hey wait.

The chimes had begun to strike again. They tolled twelve more times, creaked and repeated it, creaked and repeated it.

Four times in all, said Joe, once for everybody. By God that portable sundial hasn't missed a trick in the years we've been playing cards here. It's the business all right. Daft time out of control as usual in the eternal city. Haj Harun?

The old man stopped pacing.

Prester John?

I was just thinking the three of us wanderers here ought to have one friendly little hand tonight by way of welcoming out the old year. How would you like to take your place on top of the safe and bear witness as Clerk of the Acts?

The old man smiled shyly.

If that's what you want.

We do, we certainly do. Can't have a proper friendly little hand without our guardian knight in his place.

The old man nodded and slowly climbed up the ladder to the top of the tall antique Turkish safe. He sat down and straightened his faded yellow cloak, adjusted his rusty Crusader's helmet, retied the two green ribbons under his chin. Then he turned and peered into the nonexistent mirror in the wall.

Wanderers of the era, he announced. Travelers and countrymen and fellow Jerusalemites, I am ready.

Fine, said Joe, just fine. Well then, gents, I might as well do the honors since I find the cards sitting in front of me. Let's see, how does straight five-card poker strike you? Nothing wild and nothing stray, the customary three to draw. Only one hand now, so look smartly and here they come.

Joe dealt the cards and he and Munk fell to studying their hands. Cairo, as usual, left his cards face down on the table, untouched. After a moment of deliberation, he selected the first and the third and the fifth for discard.

Hold on, he said suddenly to Joe. You didn't announce an ante.

No reason to, that's why, just a friendly game tonight. Symbolic and nothing more on New Year's Eve. No need for any money to change hands.

No good, said Cairo firmly. I can't play poker that way. If you won't ante, I will.

You will? What is it then?

The goats in the Moslem Quarter, said Cairo.

The two men looked at him.

Those used for sodomy, he added solemnly. Joe whooped and Munk broke into laughter.

Do you tell us that, Cairo lad. Well now, why didn't you say before you were thinking along such lines? If that's the kind of friendly hand we're playing then I'll be glad to make a friendly ante of my own. Sure, let's see. I'll throw in the goats in the Christian Quarter. Meat. Which leaves you shy, Munk. Don't you have something to sweeten the pot? Or can't you contain yourself long enough to say.

Munk was still laughing, wiping the tears from his eyes.

The goats in the Jewish Quarter, he managed to gasp at last. Milk.

Good, said Joe, even better than good. This is the way to start a hand off for sure. Beats playing with silly money when you're sitting at a poker table in the eternal city. What use can money be anyway, in such a place? None's the answer, contradiction in terms. No need for money in eternity. On the other hand there's always a need for real goods and services, which is why Haj Harun has spent so much of his long life in the service trades. A Holy City needs them more than most places and that's a fact, what with pilgrims and conquering armies and the just plain curious forever trooping up the mountain to have a look around and catch the sights.

Joe glanced slyly across the table.

You're not supposed to do this, gents, it's against all rules and I know it. But for once I'm going to drop my poker face at this table and come right out and say it, straight fact. You better both be careful in the next few minutes. What I mean is, watch it. Don't be foolish, keep a steady rein on, don't get carried away. Why, you say? Well I'll tell you why. Because I think I'm going to win. I've got this feeling coming over me, a suspicion amounting to a conviction, that fate is casting a lascivious glance in my direction. So that's all, you're warned. How many new cards then?

He pushed aside the discards.

Three to you, Cairo, although you don't know what you're holding or what you threw away. And here are your three new beauties, Munk, and lastly three for the dealer. And are they?

Ha, shouted Joe. Didn't I warn you? That lascivious glance has opened into a smile and the smile has burst into a grin that's holding nothing back. In other words I made it and you can both drop out right now. Fold up your tents and save your strength for another day. Fate's got me in her embrace and that's that. Good night to the both of you.

Cairo cleared his throat.

I haven't looked at my cards yet, but then I never look at my cards until the betting's over. There's been no need to before and there's no need to tonight. I'll win anyway.

Joe snorted.

By God, is that mad arrogance or not. Do you hear that, Munk? And after I just warned him too. What do you make of it? Doesn't he deserve to lose with that kind of attitude? Reminds me of that colonel out of central Europe a few years back, the one with the double monocles and the blond wig who liked to play with the joker wild and would throw anything away to get his hands on an ace. He was mad arrogant too.

Munk nodded. He smiled slightly and said nothing. When he had picked up his new cards a quizzical expression had come over his face. Now he was frowning, gently rubbing his chin, lost somewhere in thought.

Mad arrogance, muttered Joe, that's what. Well the bet's to you, Cairo, yours for starters. What manner of real goods and services are you going to wager for openers?

No openers, said Cairo. Not this time. I have no intention of wasting time tonight trying to inch the stakes up. I'll start at the top and the two of you can play or not, as you choose. Now I think you'll both agree that through my various illicit enterprises, I control the Moslem Quarter in this city.

The mummy dust king is about to strike, muttered Joe.

Well do I or don't I?

You do. Agreed.

Correct. Now then, that's my bet. Control of the Moslem Quarter. I'm putting the Moslem Quarter on the table. If either of you wins, which you won't, it belongs to you.

Joe whistled softly.

That's arrogance and then some. You mean the *whole* Moslem Quarter?

That's right. Down to the last sun-baked brick.

People? asked Munk, shaking himself out of his trance.

Down to the last unborn babe asleep in its mum's belly, not knowing what it's in for when it has to wake up.

Fair enough, said Munk, gesturing extravagantly. If that's the way it is I'm betting the Jewish Quarter.

Jaysus all right, shouted O'Sullivan Beare, all right I say. If that's what you're up to I'll put down the Christian Quarter. And it goes without saying the Armenian Quarter automatically goes to the reckless devil here who owns the best cards. In other words it's finally a case of winner take all in the eternal city, is that it? Jerusalem is on the table and one of us is going to pick it up in the next few minutes? Is that what we're doing?

Munk smiled, he nodded. Cairo nodded and frowned.

Well then it's time, said Joe. By God if the moment hasn't sneaked right up on us, just sneaked in out of the night when no one was looking on this last day of the year. Now I hate to disappoint you both but you shouldn't have done that, shouldn't have gone so far by half. Here. Just look at this lineup I'm holding.

Joe turned over his cards. Four jacks and a queen. He touched each one of them lightly with his forefinger.

Like it? Isn't that something? Heaven laboring once again for a beleaguered Irishman? Yes I do believe it, just look at that regal party. The crown prince has come to inherit the kingdom for sure and the queen is along to ease the transition, to let all of us know all affairs are ongoing and cordial in the royal palace now that the heir apparent is to receive the land and the jewels. Not bad I say, just as it should be, and I'm ready for the succession and the ascent. So Cairo lad, do I take you or no?

One at a time, Cairo slowly turned over his cards.

A king. A queen. A king and a king and a king.

He looked up and smiled at Joe, who sighed.

Well my God I do not take you, do not even begin to. It seems the crown prince can't succeed to the throne after all, because it's still occupied by the incumbent. Bloody outrage, that's what. Regicide would have been in order but it's too late for that now. And I've only myself to blame. I should have suspected just such a scheme on your part, considering how you've been hawking pharaohs for years by the pinch and the snort. Undone, as simple as that. The king keeps his kingdom and the crown prince will have to go begging for a realm. The king also keeps his queen and will allow no ascent on that score either. So then, Munk, it's to you now. Time. Reverse and relate.

Munk stared at the two of them for almost a minute. Finally he turned over his cards and spread them out on the table.

Joe whistled very softly.

Do you tell us that now. It seems, Cairo, there may be higher powers at work in Jerusalem. It seems our Munk has called on them to intervene and they've done just that. It seems even royalty is powerless in the presence of a higher cause such as Munk's. *Four aces,* would you believe it. Aces, some kind of unit above the human plane. Yet even so Munk puts a queen with them for reproductive purposes, so his aces can take the form of a swan or a bull or a zephyr or God knows what in the Eastern Mediterranean manner, and impregnate the queen with the heroes of future generations. It's just beyond our scope and ability, Cairo, and there we are with our legacies gone, our ambitions dashed, twelve years of honest labor and dishonest endeavor simply finished. It's back to the bazaars for us. Munk takes Jerusalem and we're forced by events to make our way elsewhere.

Cairo nodded pensively. Joe scratched his beard.

Hey Munk, he said, could you take out your special watch for a moment?

Why?

Oh you know, in case we have to find out in a hurry whether time is slow or fast or nonexistent tonight. Nothing really, that's all.

Munk took out his watch.

Now then, said Joe, shouldn't we hear it officially from the top of the safe? The final judgment on this table where three men have striven mightily in their purposes? Hello up there, Haj Harun?

Yes?

Fate is upon us and must be spoken, and the best cause wins. That was the last hand the three of us will ever play here. And so after twelve busy years, if you would, the ultimate pronouncement.

Haj Harun straightened his helmet.

From the top of the safe, he said, I see that the man holding the watch with three levels is the winner.

Just like that, murmured Cairo.

Game of chance, added Joe. Sometimes it comes and sometimes it goes and it seems it's come for our partner here, our very own Munk. Seems he's just up and taken it all. Ah well, somebody has to win in the end. Isn't it so, Cairo?

Yes.

Munk pushed back his chair. He began walking around the room.

What's this about it being our last hand? The two of you aren't serious, are you?

By God we are, of course we are. Was anybody ever more serious than Cairo and me?

But what's going on? I don't think I see it.

What's to see? Game of chance and you won it.

That's right, Munk. That's all there is.

All the same, said Joe, it's frightening to drop over a million pounds like that. I'll never see that kind of money again but of course it all started with a fraud, fishes in the shape of what? Perfectly dreadful thing to be doing in the Holy City and I don't deny it. The baking priest went along with me out of the kindness of his heart, casting a blessing here and another there, saying there was no harm to it, but I wasn't really representing the early Christians.

Haj Harun stirred and looked down at Joe.

What's this? asked the old man. You're not doubting yourself, are you? Questioning what you've done here?

To be frank, I am.

But you've helped defend Jerusalem.

Joe moved uneasily in his chair.

Don't know that I have. Can't say I've done that particularly.

But it's true, *I* know you have. You've believed in the miracle of Jerusalem. You've had faith.

Well you're more forgiving than most. But listen, what would you say if I told you I were going on a trip.

And not coming back?

Yes.

The old man shook his head sadly on top of the safe, his spindly legs dangling. His helmet went awry and a shower of rust fell into his eyes. He began to weep quietly.

I'd miss you, Prester John. But I've always known you'd have to leave someday, to return to your lost kingdom in the east.

Ah yes, my lost kingdom, I almost forgot. But if I were to leave, and Cairo here too, wouldn't you still have someone to talk to?

Haj Harun looked down at Munk. He smiled.

Of course, there'd still be Bar Cocheba. He'd understand.

Yes, said Joe, I'm sure he would. So will you do that for us, Munk? Will you?

Munk stopped circling the table. He stood still, gazing at the two men at the table.

So that's it, that's what you meant. You were serious, this was the last hand. You're both leaving Jerusalem?

Yes we're off, Cairo and me. I've been here long enough. After all I only came by accident because a freighter in Cork happened to be carrying some nuns to the Holy Land on a pilgrimage, and I just happened to be a nun at the time.

And you, Cairo?

After I spend my Sunday afternoon beside the Nile I'm going back to the Sudan. I'll find a village on the edge of the Nubian desert, like the one where Johann Luigi Szondi met my great-grandmother. After all I'm a good deal older than the two of you. I'm fifty-three and if I'm going to have a family, it's time to start.

Joe?

Oh I'll just go ambling one way or another looking for Prester John's lost kingdom. The old country first I think, I'd like to dig up the musketoon I buried long ago in an abandoned churchyard. Then the New World I think, like *the Sarahs*. Out west maybe, you know how I've always wondered about the Indians. Childish isn't it. Amazing how a man can grow older and still have the child inside him, but there you are. And so too with the Sinai Bible that I wanted to find so much for so long, because of its treasure maps don't you know.

Joe smiled.

Amazing isn't it. Treasure maps? That was the child inside again. But I've got a confession to be making to you now, and it's just this. I know exactly where that Bible is, I've known for some time. And I won't tell you right now how I found out, but I will ask you to keep that information to yourselves. You see I've decided it should stay where it is for a while, until the right moment comes. Then I'll ask Haj Harun to go and get it for me.

And when will be the right moment? asked Cairo.

Ha, said Joe. Can't say, can I. Don't know, do I. Not now I don't but when that moment comes it may well have to do with family. You're not the only one at this table, Cairo, who's thinking along those lines.

And the treasure maps you wanted so much? asked Munk.

Sure, said Joe, and there are such things, they do exist. But they're not to be found in books, I've learned that. Time it took me, being such a young and innocent one and all, you Munk having ten years on me and you Cairo having twenty, and Haj Harun, well just plain close to three thousand. But I did learn the truth of the matter finally, and it's that the treasure maps around here are to be found in Haj Harun's head, right behind those shining eyes, naturally so, it's the only safe place for articles so precious, so rare. And they've been there for a long time, ever since way back then when Melchizedek, the primary priest of antiquity, was the first and last King of Salem, City of Peace, reigning on this mountain long before Abraham journeyed out of the dawn of the east with his flock and came to seek him out and receive his blessing and father the sons called Ishmael and Isaac in this land, long before Arabs and Jews ever existed with their troubles or even had names like that to divide them, long before then Melchizedek had already dreamed his gentle dream here on the mountain, Haj Harun's dream, and in so doing given it life forever, without father, without mother, without descent, having neither beginning of days nor end of life.

On top of the antique Turkish safe, Haj Harun smiled shyly.

I told you that, he whispered. Those were my words. We were sitting out on a hillside east of the city one evening, watching the sunset.

That's what we were doing, said Joe, and it was only this spring, and you pointed at the city as the sun went down and said that. And you said *you* were Melchizedek, because you both had and have the same dream, and I couldn't understand any of that at first and I said you were all mixed up, mixing up time again. But you weren't. You were right. Time works your way and not the other, and it took me a while to get used to the idea, to really know it, but now I have and do. Now I've learned the truth of it, the truth of the treasure maps too. Peace is the treasure, peace to seek, Melchizedek's gentle dream on the mountain. So a time will come for the Sinai Bible, gents, but it's not here and now. Here and now is for you to pick up your winnings, Munk, and let me tell you we've made it perfectly respectable for you, just very tidy and respectable.

Respectable?

Yes, your winnings. For my part, I knew you wouldn't want to be caught handling those dreadful religious articles I peddle on the side, so I've arranged to sell the concession to that shifty-eyed Frenchman who used to come to the game sometimes. All proceeds from the sale to go to you, to be paid in full over the next year. And what's more, he'll be working out of Beirut so you won't even have to look at him around here. I convinced him it was a more reliable business than dealing in stolen ikons, safer too, and he said he didn't want to live in Jerusalem anyway. Bad memories, he said. Especially that time back in '29 when Chief Sipping Bear wiped him out at this very table and sentenced him to work at an oven in purgatory, with the baking priest as his parole officer. Didn't much care for that apparently, did not, said the Frenchman with the shifty eyes.

As for pharaonic mummy dust, murmured Cairo.

Munk smiled.

Yes?

I knew you wouldn't want to be involved with that either. For philosophical reasons of course. It does speak of a distant past, after all, and what you're looking to is a future, the more immediate the better. So you won't have to deal with the pharaohs, Munk, neither in their powdered nor their mastic form. I've found a man who is buying all my mummies, and the mummy operation in its entirety, for a very handsome price. And he'll be headquartered in Alexandria, so you won't have to see him around here either.

Have I also met this man by chance?

By chance, you have. He was in the game the same evening when the Frenchman fared so poorly against Chief Sipping Bear. An elderly Egyptian landowner, cotton-fat, spastic when excited, said to be impotent if his favorite hunting falcon, hooded, isn't perched on the mirror that runs the length of his bed.

I remember him, said Munk. The black English judge found him guilty of having made a fortune by exploiting his workers. As I recall, the judge took away his cotton crop for the next ten years.

Precisely. Well now he's suddenly come up with the money to buy the entire mummy dust trade in the Middle East. And although spastic at times, he does have a keen business mind. And although elderly, he does have a large brood of what he calls nephews, who could and should be put to work. The falcon problem, it seems, was merely an eccentricity of his later years.

I see.

And there we have it, said Joe. We seem to be right all around, Munk, with no questionable affairs for you to worry about. You just take this money you've won at honest poker and use it to build those irrigation ditches you like so much. How Cairo and I come by the money has to do with us and a spastic elderly item in Alexandria and a shifty-eyed item in Beirut. Sure. And now the money will go to dig irrigation ditches in the wastes, so the wastes can be crops, and the truth is that's a nice way for money to go when it's going somewhere. So what's left but our rounds?

Rounds? asked Munk.

Right. It's New Year's Eve, isn't it? And one thing I've discovered along with everything else here, is that making the rounds on New Year's Eve is a regular ritual. So tonight we might as well all do it together, all four of us.

Cairo smiled. Munk looked mystified.

What rounds?

Haj Harun's annual inspection tour. Tell him, Aaron.

I will, said the wizened old man from the top of the safe. On the last night of the year I always go around the Old City to pay my respects to the elders of Jerusalem and see how the past year has fared for them.

That's all?

Yes, said Joe, but it might be more of a task than you'd suspect at first. Even though there are only two stops.

Only two? asked Munk.

Sounds minor, doesn't it. And so it does sound that way, but it's not. Far from it.

The first place we go, said Joe, is the Church of the Holy Sepulchre, to the top of the steps that lead down to the crypt. There's a man there on top of the steps who paces back and forth muttering to himself. He's been doing that for two thousand years, according to Haj Harun, and he's the first one we want to talk to.

What about? asked Munk.

Nothing, as it turns out.

No, I mean what does he say?

That's just it, he doesn't say anything. Nothing at all. He's so mysterious he doesn't even see us when we come up to him. Just goes right on pacing and muttering, in his own world altogether, some kind of holy vocation, don't you see. Now the other stop is a cubbyhole not far from Damascus Gate. A cobbler works in that cubbyhole, and according to Haj Harun he's been here much longer than the man on the top of the stairs, ever since the beginning in fact. He was already a man when Haj Harun was still a boy, and that dates him certainly. So he has a great deal to say. But the odd thing is, we can never find him.

Why? asked Munk.

Because Haj Harun can never remember where his cubbyhole is. It's near Damascus Gate, but exactly where he can't recall. Of course the configurations of the alleys have changed a bit since then. The last time

Haj Harun did find the cobbler on a New Year's Eve, you see, was just before the Captivity. But the cobbler's here all right. Has to be. It's his home. So we keep looking.

Joe smiled. He drummed his fingers on the table.

That's right, Munk. A case of the crypt and the cobbler. Now this cobbler, as Haj Harun remembers, is just about the most talkative fellow you'll ever meet. He talks and talks and brings the events of a year up to date in minutes. And why not, dealing with soles the way he does? Having been around since the beginning the way he has? To him the world's a shoe just walking and walking and never standing still, what else does he see? No solitary silent crypt for him, not hardly. He's out there in the turmoil with the shouts and the cries of the hawkers, out there amidst the peddlers of commerce and empires, right out there where the crowds never cease to pass, sitting in his cubbyhole not far from Damascus Gate, a witness to it all.

While that other fellow, Munk, the one with the mysteries, he just mutters and paces in the gloom on top of the stairs in the church, going no place to outward appearances but guarding his crypt all the same. Pondering the darkness down there, I suppose. So what's that make them, do you think, opposites in the game? Partners therefore?

I've asked myself that question, Munk, and when I did, quick came the answer. Joe you unsteady bogman, said this voice inside me, listen to your own unsteady conscience. The reason you have the one is because you have the other. No way to do it without both, not if you're going to have an eternal city. A mysterious crypt, you say, and a man devoted to it? Just dandy, all fine and good. But what about everyday people and their everyday chores and concerns? That's the world too and the truth of it.

Granted, I say. Assuredly. And then the voice comes back and says to me, all right then, and what's the view from the opposite side of the bog? If the world were nothing but turmoil and cries and shouts, nothing but commerce and peddlers and emperors and so forth, just walking and walking around, would that do us? Would it really now?

Well no, I answer at once. In all truth, it wouldn't.

And so? says this voice inside me, this person thinking his and her thoughts. And so?

And so you've got me, I answer. Just walking around won't do. We have to have this other fellow who minds the crypt. Or mines it or whatever. It's all the same with a dark silent crypt containing mysterious secrets, mining it or minding it, who can say. And if all this sounds to you like a bloody convoluted description of the situation, Munk, I can only say it is. But no more convoluted than the situation itself, which is those alleys near Damascus Gate where Haj Harun has been on the lookout for his cobbler friend these last two thousand five hundred years. When you're dealing with an eternal city, in other words, you've got to know its basic professions, cobbler and crypt minder-miner.

Makes you dizzy does it, Munk, the simplicity of these professions? It does me, I can tell you that, it makes me dizzy up here on top of the mountain. Of course it'd be different if I were like Haj Harun up there on his safe and could take the long view the way he does, but I wonder if I'd want to? Seems to me one Babylonian invasion is enough. Seems to me watching the Crusaders clank around with their bloody awful swords, just once, would be more than enough. Me, I don't want to go back on the run in the hills of southern Ireland. Don't want to crawl onto that terrible quay in Smyrna again and see Stern pick up a knife and slit a little girl's throat out of kindness. I just can't manage it. I'm a bogman and I'm down there and this mountain is too high for me. I can't really climb it, can't ever reach the top. I don't have the cause that would allow me to do that. You've got a cause all right but I've just been a visitor here, and the visit's up and now I'm leaving.

Munk had been gazing thoughtfully at Joe. All at once Cairo burst out laughing. Joe looked at him and pretended to scowl.

By God what's this, laughing at such tender sentiments right to a man's face? You mummy thief and obvious blackguard, everyone knows you've stolen as much time here as I have with your mummy dust traffic through the ages. So what's so funny about what I just said?

Cairo laughed even harder. Joe threw his hands in the air.

Hear that, Munk? No respect at all for a man's inner feelings, just none. Just hoots and howls like an emperor looking down on the lesser folk. Well out with it, you Nilotic ghoul, what's so funny? Try to get hold of yourself. We're waiting.

Cairo's laughter finally subsided. He rubbed his chest, smiling broadly.

Waiting, that's right, we all are. In another moment poor Munk is going to think you're the cobbler in question.

Me? Why would he ever think such a thing?

Because of the way you've been carrying on, just talking and talking. You tell him we have to accompany Haj Harun tonight, but you don't even tell him why, the whole point of the thing.

Oh, said Joe, pretending to make another face. The whole point, is that all? Well of course I was getting around to it. I was just sort of sizing up the countryside along the way. What's the point of taking a trip if you don't see the sights? What's the point of sitting down to a stew if you don't sniff it and savor the aroma and sip it slowly around the edges first to get a hint of all the flavors? What would you have me do? Boil down the stew and reduce the trip to one word?

Haj Harun does, said Cairo, beginning to laugh again.

Well of course he does but that's because he takes the long view, as I was saying, unlike you and me. Now Munk here's different from us, he's got his cause to take him up the mountain. And sure there it is coming right on, I can see the future now. Haj Harun and Bar Cocheba together again fending off the Roman hordes and their monstrous siege machines, rolling and rumbling machines, simply monstrous. The two of them manning the ramparts against the enemy and racing along the walls and jogging around and around through the alleys of the Old City, resolutely so, keeping on the move for sure because a moving target is harder to hit than a stationary one, I can see it now for sure. And here come the Romans hurling their monstrous boulders and insults at the city, I can see that too.

Joe, hold on there. Where are you going this time?

Me? No place. Who ever suggested such a thing? You mummy ghoul, how can you say that when you know I'm just sitting here as sober as can be. It's just that I don't like to see an era ending, that's all. I enjoyed this poker game.

Munk laughed.

That's enough from the two of you. What's the one word? Why are we going out with Haj Harun tonight?

Joe sighed.

I guess it's the same with you both, nothing but facts and down to business, straight and dry facts and nothing else. Won't allow a man to properly savor his stew. Well anyway, Munk, you know the one word already but just to make it official, just to sum it all up at the end of twelve years of poker, we'll have it formally proclaimed by the source. An official announcement that the game at this table is officially over. Haj Harun, guardian of the past and the future?

Yes?

You're sitting up there on top of the safe with a better view than the rest of us. What's the one word that sums up Jerusalem?

Haj Harun straightened his faded yellow cloak, his spindly legs dangling. He adjusted his rusty Crusader's helmet and gazed at the nonexistent mirror in the crumbling plaster of the wall.

Dreams, he said happily.

Yes, sighed Joe, and so it is. And the reason we're going out with Haj Harun tonight, to look up these two senior citizens, is because it just so happens they secretly keep this city on the mountaintop going. The pacing muttering man at the top of the stairs to the crypt and his partner in time, the garrulous cobbler? The one unspoken and the other unfound? Well you see, Munk, tonight they have a dream, a special dream, and we have to wish them well with it. Tonight they dream there *is* a Jerusalem. And because they do, it will be here when we wake up tomorrow, dreamed into existence for another year. So there you have our task on New Year's Eve, if you want it in a word.

Munk nodded. Haj Harun stirred on top of the safe.

Prester John? You mentioned earlier that I haven't been able to locate the cobbler's cubbyhole for some time, but tonight I have a curious feeling I just may find it. In fact I think there's a very good chance I'll remember where it is tonight.

Well of course there is. I never believed anything else.

And you'll like him, the cobbler, you'll all like him. He has amusing stories to tell and he's much better on dates than I am, and also he goes back much further, having already been a man when I was still a boy.

I know we will. Certainly we will.

Haj Harun smiled distantly.

Well I think I'll come down now. I think it's time we began our rounds.

Truly, yes do that. According to the once portable sundial in the front room, it's almost o'clock.

18

Bernini

*They'll all tell you that, straight
off and no question about it. We go
right on in the lives of others and
there's no end to it for sure.*

On a late winter morning so brilliant it could only be found in
Attica, the flat white sunlight hard on the glittering sea, a
small dark man made his way slowly down a beach near Piraeus to the
spot where a small dark boy stood scaling stones out over the water.
About five yards away the man sat down on the sand and shaded his
eyes.

Hello there.

Hello yourself.

Good day for that. The sea's just right.

That's what it is.

What's your record then?

Nine so far but I'll get up to eleven or twelve, I always do. Say,
what's that funny old uniform you're wearing?

Officer of light cavalry, acquired in the wars.

Must have been a long time ago to look that old and ragged and have so many patches on it.

It was. I was just thinking so myself as I was walking down the beach.

And the uniform doesn't even fit you. It's too big in the chest and you've had to roll up the sleeves.

I know it. Maybe I was bigger once.

You mean you've shrunk?

Well as a matter of fact it wouldn't surprise me at all to hear that I've shrunk or grown, one or the other perhaps, but both is far more likely. After all, genies do that so why shouldn't we? They go from being great huge giants striding across the earth from Timbuktu to the Hindu Kush, talking to everyone along the way more or less, to being so small and quiet they can spend seven full years in a tiny Sinai cave, speaking only once in all that time and then only to a mole. Sure, that's what they do.

The boy laughed. He scaled another stone out over the water and held his breath. He clapped his hands.

See that? Eleven, what'd I tell you.

A good one all right. You're getting there.

That's a funny accent you have. Is that from the wars too?

Sometimes I think it is, one war or another. Seems likely don't you know.

Do you always talk like that?

How?

Kind of around and around.

Don't know that I do, can't say that I don't. Must be that I circle things sometimes, because it's hard to get your hands on them. Tell me now, would you happen to be knowing the woman who lives in that small house up there on the edge of the beach? Maud's her name.

Of course I know her, she's my mum. You work in town with her or something?

No, I knew her a long time ago. In Jerusalem it was. Yes that's right, lad. I'm your father.

Bernini's hand held a scaling stone in the air. He smiled and there was nothing but joy in his face.

Are you really Father?

I am, lad. The very one.

Bernini shouted and laughed. He lunged toward Joe who swept him up in his arms and swung him around. They fell together on the sand, laughing and breathless.

I knew you'd be coming soon. I didn't say anything about it but I knew.

Of course you knew it, lad. What else would I be doing?

Were you famous in the wars? Is that where you've been?

Nothing of the sort. When I was fighting, back before I met your mother, nobody knew my name or even knew I had one. I wore a flat red hat then, and a green jacket, and shoes that had buckles on them, and I stayed up in the hills of southern Ireland with my old musketoon, talking to no man, hiding during the day and on the run through all the hours of darkness. And because of that, you see, they thought I was one of the *little people* when they chanced to catch the barest glimpse of me far far away in the distance at dusk or dawn, and because I was at least getting on toward being the size of a man, as I still am, they came to call me *the biggest of the little people*. The *little people* have no names, you see, and the farmers didn't know who it was up there in those hills who was helping them out by arching bullets into the air from a great distance, in the manner of a howitzer, so that the bullets came down to strike the enemy from above, thereby putting the very fear of heaven in the hearts of the enemy, maybe even the fear of God if they believed in one. No, the farmers didn't know who it was, but they certainly liked what that unseen presence was doing, so they paid me a great compliment and called me that.

But who are the *little people* really, Father? Are they elves?

Well they wouldn't take kindly to being called merely that, because they're so much finer and grander and cleverer than any elf could ever be. Who are they then? They're wondrous beings and spirits with the most mysterious of manners. And besides that, behind and beneath it all, they really run the land and the country.

Any country?

Joe looked thoughtful.

I'm not so sure about that. I wouldn't say all that much, I don't believe. But they do run the land and the country where your forebears on my side came from. Secretly of course. I don't have to tell you that.

Why secretly?

Because that's the way of the world, lad. Isn't it always so?

I don't know. I thought kings and parliaments and presidents ran countries.

So it seems from afar, but that's only for the sake of appearances, only on the surface of things. In actual fact the *little people* are in charge, always have been and always will be. But you don't ever see them, so much as experience them. When you're out in the woods you hear them whispering and dancing and playing their games, but you daren't go investigate the event right then, because they wouldn't like it. They don't take kindly to people peeking in on their revels and games, that just won't do. So you tiptoe away and come back the next day to have a look around in that glen or dell, and one glance is enough, one glance tells all, you know immediately they've been there. You can see that all right, but of course you haven't seen *them*. And so it goes, and that's the way it always goes. Never in your whole life do you actually see them, but that doesn't mean they're not always out there, just out of sight, whispering and humming and singing and carrying on in general, playing away and mischievously passing the ages the way their kind does, feasting and dancing and holding their hurling matches brazenly on the strand, at night of course, in the soft moonlight, when you're at home in bed falling asleep and can't catch them at it. And they're not alone out there. There are pookas and banshees and the whole lot of them, all of them passing the ages in the ways that amuse them. But tell me something frankly, lad. Before I ever mentioned them, didn't you already know about them?

Bernini smiled.

Why do you say that?

Just wondering, just guessing. Well?

I've never told anyone, whispered Bernini seriously.

Of course you haven't.

It was a secret.

And it's a good one. Well?

Bernini nodded. He smiled.

You're right, I did know they were there. I didn't know that's what they were called, and I didn't know what they wore, but I knew about *them*.

Well it's a pretty outfit, isn't it. Just right for ones so fine and grand

and clever, so mysteriously watching over us in their pursuits. Although it's also true the ones *you* know may wear quite a different costume. There's no limit, of course, to how they can carry on.

Bernini was smiling rapturously now.

Will you tell me all about them, Father? About the games they play and the dancing and the singing and all of it?

I will, lad. From beginning to end we'll discuss their sly mischievous ways, always off where they can't be seen having their fun and winking at the sky as they tip their heads so gaily and set their feet to flying in a whirling whirligig so fine, so grand, the very sunshine itself flutters and laughs.

Bernini clapped his hands.

Oh yes, just whirling and whirling in their flying shoes with buckles. But what's *this* uniform then? This queer old one you're wearing?

Ah, lad, another whole place and time. We'll get to that too. The man who owned this one before me is known as the baking priest, as fine an item as ever walked in the streets of the Holy City. Saved my life, he did, when I was on the run and arrived in Jerusalem starving and penniless, a fugitive from injustice and the youngest by far of the Poor Clares who were making that dreadfully shocking pilgrimage that year.

What's a Poor Clare?

A nun, lad, a nun from the strictest of orders. That's why the pilgrimage was so shocking. Because normally Poor Clares can't even leave their convents, not ever, let alone travel to a place like Jerusalem with its unlimited sights and sounds and smells. Anyway, I went to the Holy Land as a nun.

But a man can't be a nun, can he?

That's right, he can't. He simply cannot. But apparently Himself decided to make an exception that year so I could escape from the city of Cork and be transported to the Holy Land in order to fulfill a prophecy made by my father.

Who's himself?

God. Chose to intervene, He did, the baking priest told me all about it when he made me a hero of the Crimean War and awarded me the first Victoria Cross ever given, which until then had been his own. Here you see it. A Victoria Cross for defending Ireland against the English.

So you're a great rich man now?

Not at all, none of it. I'm just a poor fisherman's son from the Aran Islands who's been adrift and afloat in our Holy City for fourteen long years. Just one O'Sullivan Beare who found himself in Jerusalem by chance, although it's also true we're known as the O'Sullivan Foxes on occasion, for what reason I can't imagine. But with a name like Bernini now, with a fine name like that, you'll be going on someday to build fountains and stairways to heaven and beautiful colonnades for the pope. Good lad. If it had been up to me I might have called you Donal Cam, and that's not half so ringing.

Who was Donal Cam?

The famous bear and fox among your ancestors on my side, known in his time as *the* O'Sullivan Beare. Some centuries ago he walked a thousand of his people out of the south of Ireland to the north, in the dead of winter and fighting all the way, escaping the English and starving too, just as I was doing three hundred years later as a nun. Well he limped and he fought and he led his people, and after two weeks they arrived where they were going. And they were safe now, the thirty-five who had survived out of the thousand. So he was a hero because of what he did. But for all that, I still like Bernini better as a name.

Your name's Joe.

That's what it is, that's mine, as simple as can be. And after that the names of half a dozen other saints, same as my father who had the gift.

What gift?

Prophecy. To see the world as it was and shall be. He was the seventh son of a seventh son, you see, and when you are you have the gift. While me, I was just the thirty-third son and last.

Bernini's eyes shined when he heard the numbers. Joe gazed into them and saw something. A shadow flickered across Joe's face.

Good with figures are you, lad? Quick, what's five plus eight?

Eleven or twelve, said Bernini.

Is it now. And how's that? How can it be both?

Because some days I scale a stone eleven times and some days twelve. I know Mother says that's not the way you're supposed to do arithmetic, but that's the way I do it. At different times, to me, different numbers answer better. When I have a feeling about one, I use it. But then if I don't have a special feeling, a number turns up anyway. Do you know what I mean?

Joe gazed at his son and his frown slowly changed to a smile.

Do you tell me so. Is it always that way with you? In other things besides arithmetic?

Yes, I'm afraid it is. Does it make you angry?

Nothing of the sort, lad. I'm here to love you and accept you as you are. And it strikes me you just might be a poet, did you ever think of that? In poetry all things slip and slide, just as they do when you're hearing the whispers of the *little people,* and knowing they're there behind the wall all right, but not seeing them.

Well I don't think I'm a poet, most of the time I don't seem to be anything. Do you know? Most of the time I'm just here by the sea. And even when I'm not, I still am really, down here looking at the sea and listening. Do you know where it goes?

Sometimes. And sometimes I'm also just like you. I just sit and look at it and listen. I used to do that a lot down on the coast of the Sinai, in a little oasis on the Gulf of Aqaba. I used to fly my Camel down there and sit for days listening and watching, just keeping watch through the hours of light and dark.

Bernini laughed.

You flew a camel? The same way they have flying carpets in the stories?

Does sound strange, doesn't it. But that's also the name of an airplane, you see, a Sopwith Camel it's properly called. Now tell me, do you like that looking and listening more than anything else?

Yes.

Joe knelt on the sand and put his arms around Bernini's waist.

Well lad, then I'm surely glad I found you here. Right here on this very spot by the sea.

Bernini put his fingers in his father's beard.

I'm glad too, for a special reason. I knew you'd be coming soon but not just today, and that's a wonderful surprise. Today I mean. It's my birthday.

I know it is, lad, that's why I'm here. Thirteen years ago you were born on this very day in Jericho, a place of sunshine and flowers near the River Jordan, another kind of oasis it is. And our little house was near the Jordan, on a path to it, we weren't far away from it at all. So close it was then, that river of miracles, so close it seemed, nearly at our feet it seemed. Ah it's true what the old man says. The years, they just slip away and slide together.

Why are you crying, Father?

Not crying really. Just happy to have found you, here by the sea. Just happy. That's all.

Who were you talking about who says that?

The old man? Someone like no other. A friend I had in Jerusalem. He showed me the world and showed me what it's all about. Haj Harun is his name. So gentle and frail, you wonder how he's ever done it.

Done what?

Lived three thousand years in Jerusalem. He *has* done that, you see. It may be hard to imagine over here, away from that holy mountain, but it's true. Do you believe me when I tell you so?

Yes. Haj Harun. The man who's lived for three thousand years in Jerusalem.

Joe smiled. Bernini smiled.

Maybe when you grow up, lad, you'll be like him. What do you think?

I don't know. Maybe I will.

Joe sighed.

A wonder, that's what.

Father?

Yes.

Are you going to stay here with us now?

Well as it happens, lad, I'm not. When a time comes it comes, you see, and that's what it's done for me. So I'm off to look at new places, the New World probably, which is to say America. I'm going to find out about it and then when I do, you and I will discuss it. In the meantime you've got your mum and she's a wonderful woman, God never made better.

I love her.

I know you do, and in my way, so do I.

Then why are you leaving?

Ah you are a clever little piece of goods, on the foxy side of the O'Sullivans, I'd say. But the answer is straightforward. It's that I must. Having been born a fisherman's son, I'm bound for the desert.

You may not understand that now, but someday you will.

Oh no, I understand it now.

You do? How's that?

A man named Stern told me. He's a new friend of Mother's.

Did he now? What'd he say?

Well he was leaving here once and I asked him the same thing, and he said that sometimes a man has travels to make.

Well well, it's true I guess. Not that your mother doesn't have her own to make, she does. But aren't you a smart one to be knowing all that at your age.

Bernini hung his head.

I'm not smart, he whispered.

Why do you say that?

Because I'm not.

Bernini hesitated, staring at the sand.

What is it? said Joe quickly. You mean your not being able to read? I already know about that.

Bernini nodded.

That and the other things, he whispered. Not being able to do arithmetic the way you're supposed to.

Here here, said Joe in a soft voice, stop hanging your head like that and take a look out to sea. There are all kinds of ways of being smart, we both know that. Take Haj Harun. Most of the time he doesn't even know what century he's in. You go for a walk with him through the streets of Jerusalem and he may be back somewhere a couple of thousand years ago, rambling through alleys no one else is smart enough to recognize. All lost it would appear, but he's not, not really. It's just that he sees things we don't. The rest of us, we see what's around us, he sees more. So you can't say what's smart and what isn't, there are all kinds of different ways. A lot of people would say Haj Harun isn't smart, and he wouldn't be if it came to selling vegetables by the pound or cloth by the yard. Hopeless, he'd be, there'd be no profit ever. But if you want to know who the holy men were and what they thought, or better than that, what they felt in their hearts, or even the unholy Assyrians or anybody else, then you take a wander with him through the streets of Jerusalem and you'll find out, you'll know. Our gentle knight he is, watching over the eternal city.

Bernini looked up. He smiled.

You talk as if Jerusalem wasn't a place.

Oh it is all right, it's just that it's more as well. Something you carry with you, inside of you, wherever you go. And as for those travels we mentioned, you'll be having your very own someday.

I hope so.

You will, I know it. When I was your age I was just bursting with the dream of them. Just dying to get out in the world and try my hand.

And you did.

Yes I did, I tried. Funny thing is, that's still what I'm doing.

A shadow suddenly came across Bernini's face. He was gazing up the beach toward the little house. Joe looked quickly away and back again. There was pain in his eyes.

Say it, he whispered.

Bernini shook his head, his mouth set.

No say it, lad, whispered Joe. You know it's always best to say things. People hear them anyway. What is it?

Well all I meant was, she'll be home at five or six.

Yes.

Well aren't you even going to come and see her?

Joe took a deep breath.

No.

Not even for a few minutes?

No.

But we're going to have a birthday party and there's a beautiful cake. I saw it on the shelf.

No. I can't, lad.

Just for a few minutes? To have a piece of cake?

Ah, a few minutes or a lifetime. It seems there's no difference.

But then you're not going to see her at all?

Not this time. A time will come, but it's not now.

But why? Won't you tell me why? She's my mother and you're my father. Why?

I'll try to tell you, it's hard to explain. You see she has a life of her own now and I'm not in it. You are, and old friends like Munk, and new friends like Stern, and the people she works with and others, they make up her life now. Especially you. But I'm somewhere else. I mean I've been somewhere else so long, I'm somewhere else now.

But she'd like to see you.

I don't think so.

Are you afraid to see her?

Not afraid, no, I just don't think it would be for the best at the moment. Someday, but not now. Your mother and I haven't seen each other in thirteen years, and some things are too recent. Scars take time to heal. You have to treat the past gently.

What's too recent?

Sivi's death, for one.

But he was such a sad old man. He almost never talked and he never smiled, not even once. He just sat and stared at walls, at nothing. It made me uncomfortable to be in the same room with him.

That was when you knew him, lad, but it wasn't always so. Things change. There was a time when Munk knew him long ago, and your mother and Stern, when he was always smiling and laughing and telling stories, amusing everybody and making things better than they had been before. I didn't know him myself then, but they say there was never anyone, never anyone who enjoyed life more. Just accepted everything and everyone and put people at ease right away, and made them laugh and was kind and generous, and was always saying funny things. But then the fires of Smyrna got in the way, and the slaughter and the screams, and soldiers beat him with rifles and he was never the same after that. What I'm saying is that he was a good man, and that he and your mother go back a long way, long before I ever met her, and it can hurt terribly when someone like that is taken from you. When they die. It just seems then that nothing is right in the world, just nothing at all, and you feel that nothing will ever be right again. It takes time to get over that. And you know how she spent these last years taking care of him.

Bernini nodded.

Yes you do, you saw it. Without her he wouldn't have had much of anything these last years. And before that it was the other way around. Before that he helped her, along with all the others. Sivi was her link to the past, to bad days as well as good, but a link in any case, giving life some continuity, a dimension, a meaning. After all he'd been the brother of her husband, the one who died in the war before your mother and I met, and later he took her in when she left Jericho with you just after you were born. Just so many things he did for her, just so many memories she shared with him. So his going is more than it seems, more than you can imagine. When you lose someone like that, someone who's been so much a part of your life for so long, it's as if all those years have suddenly been taken away from you. Your own past, taken away from you. You feel cheated and robbed, it's just terrible to go through. Son?

Yes?

I've gone on about this because I think you should understand it. There's no way you could know it yourself, from what you saw of Sivi. No way you could realize what his death must mean to her. So that's enough of the past for her to deal with right now. She doesn't need me walking in.

Bernini nodded. He looked out to sea.

Why did she leave Jericho with me?

Well that's a direct question, isn't it. She'd have to give you her answer, but I guess mine would be that I didn't know enough. I'd had no experience with a woman, you see. Only twenty when I met her and we were together less than a year, and I didn't know what things meant. I just didn't know what people were doing when they did them. So I got things mixed up, got them wrong. I did that with your mother.

Did what?

Didn't understand the silences, the anger. I was so dumb I thought it was something I'd done. We do that when we're young. We think that anything that happens, happens because of us. So I thought I'd done something and she didn't love me anymore. Of course it was just the opposite. She did love me but she was afraid, because love had always hurt her before. So she pulled away from me and I didn't know why. Leaving me because she loved me. Terrible pain for the both of us coming out of the love we had for each other. Life can be like that, it can do that. Just turn on itself. It's the strangest thing. You have to be so careful with someone you love. People are fragile when you get that close to them. Living alone is easier by far in this world, or even living with someone but keeping yourself alone all the same. There aren't any risks then, but you're always the poorer for it. The riches are in the risks and that's the truth, you'll find them nowhere else. Not ever, as I well know.

I still don't see what you got wrong.

Joe smiled.

You don't now? Well nothing more than myself of course. That's always it. Whatever you do or don't do, you're the one who's done it. Did you know the O'Sullivan Beare clan used to have a lovely legend?

What's that?

A saying, a motto. *Love, the forgiving hand to victory.* That's the legend and none was ever better. It says everything that has to be said. Well I've always known the words, but when I was younger I didn't really understand them. I took people for what they said and did, and that's not enough in this world. You also have to take people for what they don't say and don't do. Sounds simple, but it's not until you learn it.

I think I've already begun to learn it.

Bernini's face was serious, intent. Joe nodded.

How's that, lad?

Well I don't listen to people's words so much. I listen to what's inside.

What's that now? What you call *inside?*

Bernini put his hand in the sand. He pushed it back and forth, making a trough. All at once he seemed faraway.

What's inside, lad?

Have you ever seen the fishermen throwing those little octopuses against the rocks by the harbor after they catch them?

I have.

The octopuses are so small, you wouldn't think they could be that tough. But they have to keep smashing them against the rocks over and over before they're ready to be hung up to dry. But then later when they're grilled over charcoal and cut in little pieces with olive oil over them, aren't they the best thing in the world?

They are, the very best. A feast in themselves.

Yes, said Bernini, beginning another trough in the sand. Joe watched the trough grow.

But now I think I've missed your meaning, lad. What was it you were telling me about what's inside?

Just that. That's all. That even though the octopuses are small, someone has to work very hard to make them good to eat. But when they do, they're the best thing in the world.

Joe smiled. He drew a line in the sand and capped it with a shorter line, then made a loop at the top.

Know it?

A cross with a circle on top of it?

Well it's not quite a cross, is it, not quite a circle either. It's an old mark, called an ankh. In ancient Egypt it was the sign for life, or maybe the sun, same thing. My friend Cairo told me about it, and he had it from a living mummy called old Menelik.

Are there really living mummies?

It seems so. Why?

Because I've always wanted to think so.

Have you now. And why is that?

I like the idea of people not dying.

Do you? Then I think you're going to like the story of my friend Cairo being brought up by his foster father, who was in fact a living mummy.

Wait a minute. Cairo's a city, not a person.

Things can be different for different people. For me, Cairo will never be a city but a man, a great huge black man who's so strong and friendly he lifts you right up off the ground when he greets you. Puts his arms around you and hugs you, and all of a sudden you find you're up there dangling in the air. It's his way of shaking hands, of saying hello.

Really?

Yes. Anyway, this living mummy, old Menelik, brought up Cairo with a grin as dry as dry while lying at the bottom of a sarcophagus where he'd been residing through the ages beside the Nile, endlessly talking away to Cairo and telling him all there was to know about secret tombs and temples and what went on inside of pyramids, not to mention his friend the genie, Strongbow by name, who had a comet of his own as an eternal plaything.

Bernini clapped his hands.

Old Menelik? The genie Strongbow?

Exactly, lad. The stuff of dreams, that's what they are. Men have fallen by the wayside trying to keep up with the likes of them. There's magic in those tales that flies, that leaps across time with its sparkling visions, the magic that comes at one and the same time from the songs of long ago and the lovely tunes yet to be sung.

Bernini got up and began to walk around in a circle, looking for stones to scale. He stopped for a moment and raised his head.

Is that really the way it is?

How's that, lad?

It never ends?

Oh no blessed be, it never does. Just keeps right on going. I'll tell you that and so will Haj Harun and the baking priest, and the potting priest and all the rest of them. Stern and Munk whom you know, and Cairo whom you don't know, and a cobbler in Jerusalem whom I don't even know myself although we went looking for him last New Year's Eve, looked hard and didn't find him that time, but there'll be another time because Haj Harun has never forgotten him, hasn't and won't. So yes indeed, just ask any one of them and the answer will always be the same. They'll all tell you that, straight off and no question about it. We go right on in the lives of others and there's no end to it for sure.

Why?

Ah, now you're getting to it and I can see why you like to spend your time down here on the shore, just watching and listening until you have it all. And the sea will whisper the answers, lad, it will do that for you. Gently, don't you see. Quietly, don't you know. Whispering away just for you. Because it's here for no other reason.

Bernini smiled.

Aren't you going to choose a stone, Father? Aren't you going to scale even one?

I am. That's why I'm here. To see you on your birthday and scale a stone across the water. Like to hear something else while I'm looking for a stone?

Sure.

You've got a brother or a sister in Jerusalem.

Bernini smiled.

No I haven't.

Yes it's true. Of course the child is only a half-brother or a half-sister.

Well which is it?

I don't know.

How old?

Almost eleven. Do you like the idea of it though?

Sure. But why all the mystery?

It just seems that's the way it is sometimes. It just seems some things are always a mystery.

Well who's the mother?

402

A saint. That's why I can't see her anymore and don't know anything about the child. She's a saint and she lives with God.

Bernini frowned. He laughed.

I don't think I should believe everything you say.

Don't you now? Can't imagine why you'd tell me that. Although of course the world is full of facts, and we're all free to choose the ones we want to believe.

Bernini went on laughing.

Father, haven't you even found a stone yet? They're all over the place.

I know they are and I'm looking. I'm looking. Now here's a possibility and here's another, but I want to take my time, I want to find one that's just right for now. Mind you, it's not always the same one that's wanted. It depends on the shape of the waves and the cast of the wind and the slant of the sunlight as well. Sometimes a skimmer will do the job, light and fast, and sometimes one with more weight to it is in order. There's no way of knowing beforehand. You just have to dream.

You're talking in riddles again, Father.

Am I now. Just jokes and riddles and scraps of rhymes? But you see a life without dreams is no life at all, a loss for sure and sadly so. Or as Haj Harun used to like to say, *time is*. And always said in a very ethereal manner, it was.

What's it supposed to mean?

Oh I don't know, that we're here by the sea together? That we're sharing the sun and the sea and finding our stones to scale over the water? It's not much, what we're doing. On the other hand, it's everything. Scaling stones is the tale.

What tale?

Haj Harun's tale, I guess. And the baking priest's and the potting priest's, and Cairo's and Munk's and Stern's, and your mother's, and my own and yours. All of them about to be told, when I find the stone I'm looking for.

Sometimes you have a queer way of talking, Father.

I do, it's true. It comes from those times when I was a boy straining so hard to hear the whispers of the *little people*, trying so hard to catch the sounds of their singing and dancing, even though I knew I'd never see them. Whispers, that's right. Whispers, that's all. But once you hear those whispers, lad, you never forget them and you're never the same. Because they remind you of birds soaring free in the sun and sea gulls gliding in your wake, and a fine strong tide running you home in your little boat after a night at sea, running you home to the new flowers smiling in the green green grass. And then home you are at last on your little island and it's dancing you think of and singing and making your feet fly in the sun, and maybe later, when the moon has risen softly, even holding your hurling matches brazenly on the strand. And feasting through the ages, even that. Ah yes you do, that's what you think of. And you strain so hard to hear those whispers as the years go by. You want so much to hear them again and you do try, just try and try, you do that even though the whispers are dimmer, are farther away this year than last, last than the year before. And yes, it's true, even though you know the wonders of their world are beyond you, always were and always will be. You'll just never see them, just never, never have and never will, but still you go on believing in them and trying to hear the tunes of their dancing and the songs sung at their feasts, mysterious whispers in the sparkling sunlight, the whispers you heard when you were a child so long ago. So long ago.

Bernini saw the tears in Joe's eyes again. He was going to run over and hug him but suddenly it was all right. Suddenly Joe was jumping up and down and laughing, running on the sand and laughing, the man his mother had told him about, the magical Irishman she had once met in Jerusalem.

Well no, not told him. Not in those words. But he had heard it anyway.

What is it, Father? What did you find?

Joe whooped. He leapt in the air and held up a stone.

Do you see it, lad? Flat and thin and just right for the asking? A wafer to fly and fly for sure. Now how many times would you say it's going to skim on the sunlight out there before we no longer see it? Before it slips beneath the waves and speeds away as fast as a fish swimming from one end of the world to the other? Just going and going where the sea goes. How many times, Bernini?

Nine times?

Nine times easy. Eleven and twelve times easy. And then after that, one more time in honor of this special day. Watch it and you'll see I'm right, lad, and it will always be so, skimming on the sunlight, swimming and swimming from here where we stand by the sea as you've learned to do, looking and listening now thirteen times easy on your birthday, as Haj Harun has done these three thousand years in Jerusalem, as the baking priest said right there in the Holy City while leavening the four concerns of his life, the four winds and the four corners of his holy kingdom. Yes, *our* holy kingdom. Made for us if we'd only believe it. So watch this hand of mine fly now. Watch it, Bernini lad. And watch this precious stone skip for us in the sunlight to the very ends of the earth.

It can't go that far, Father.

Oh yes it can and much more. Twice that, to tell all. In fact it will go so far it will circle the world and come back to us. That's right, that's what it will do. And if you look hard tomorrow you'll find this very same precious stone right here on the beach, right here by the sea where you watch and listen, its long journey made and a long list of marvels witnessed for sure. So watch now. Here flies our dream on the sun.

An Editorial Relationship

Many years ago when I was a young assistant editor at a New York publishing house, a stroke of fortune led me into an editorial relationship that was to last a long time, until after the writer's death. Our entanglement, like many between writers and editors, was muddied by friendship on the one hand and by the desire to publish on the other.

The relationship began when the editor-in-chief, Tom Wallace, who was leaving the house for another, handed me the file of an author named Edward P. Whittemore.

He was called Ted. He had gone to school with Tom in the 1950s, they were old buddies from Yale, and there the resemblance ended. Tom was a classic Yale type—sentimental yet incapable of expressing emotion, good-hearted and highly principled, and completely stuck in his ways. Ted, by contrast, was completely out of the loop. He defied the loop. Ted had lived all around the world, been in the CIA (in fact, nobody knew for sure if he was really out of the CIA), written several crazy novels that were sort of about espionage and sort of about the mammoth course of history, its large brutish atrocities and the small moments of goodness, books that were compared to Fuentes and Pynchon and Nabokov.

Tom described the books by saying they were really all about poker.

Ted was famous to about six thousand people who thought he was a genius; nobody else had ever heard of him at all. He had two marriages that hadn't worked out, and a girlfriend he was breaking up with, and a strong Maine accent. He was a recovering alcoholic who once had been the kind of drinker who wanted to crawl inside the fifth to lick it completely clean, and a chain-smoker, and he lived on the East side of town.

As it turned out, of all the places he could have lived in the city of New York, he lived on Third Avenue and 24th Street, while I lived on 24th Street and Sixth Avenue. This is the kind of magical coincidence that populates the novels of Edward Whittemore and it seemed strangely appropriate that our domestic routines were performed in locations that were exactly parallel, yet existed a precise and unbreachable distance apart, as though we were two matching magnets with the contrary ends facing one another.

In 1981, I was handed the manuscript of Nile Shadows, which was third in a projected quartet of Jerusalem novels. This quartet followed his first, and possibly his splashiest novel, Quin's Shanghai Circus, which we had published seven years earlier.

Ted had also written several that we did not publish. I was told both that Ted was a genius and that it was possible that the manuscript was not publishable or needed a great deal of cutting. I knew almost nothing about editing fiction; I had never worked on anything remotely this serious, which meant that I was going to have to concentrate very hard. Once I opened it and began there was no question but that this was what they call the real thing. For me, how terrifying and how thrilling.

The first time I read it slowly, almost without thinking, submitting to it, letting it sink in. The book was both domestic and fantastic, its settings shabby and arcane, and doom was everywhere. Ted understood the big and how it depended on the little. Centuries of conspiracy pivoted on a chance encounter. Friendship was everything, and utterly ephemeral. A shaft of light illuminated horror, then a sweet timeless calm, then slapstick. Words kept it going, words and talk and more talk: chatter, letters writ in stone, a scream in an emergency, a late afternoon's long slow story, a coded telegram.

The editor's job was to be inside it and yet float above it, to see where it wasn't true to its own internal logic, to love the characters and expect them to be themselves, to applaud every song—but to mark the slightly flat note—to be sure the plot had all its small signals straight. The second time I read it I tried to remember every word, every gesture, every motion.

My editorial letter advised—but most of all it paid attention. It is not so much the comments made by a careful editor that help a writer revise, I think, but the simpler fact that these comments show the writer that he is being watched. He is being watched intently by someone who tells him, in as many ways as possible, that this matters. And so he thinks harder, he reaches in all directions — plot, character, gesture, sequence, tone, echo — and, so doing, activates the deeper and shadowed part of the brain where music and feeling are stashed. The place where stories begin.

Ted lived in a tiny apartment very high up above Third Avenue. He had a big window and a dark-floored single room, a small kitchen—the refrigerator contained only a pint container of milk and a plastic tub of tofu—and a bathroom with a towel. In his room were a double bed, a desk, a writing chair, a second chair, a television, and an ashtray. Just the setting for a former spy.

I went over there on my way home from the office several times, to drop off the edited manuscript, to look at his changes, to explain the copy editing. I gave Ted more personal attention because the novel demanded it, and also, although without saying a word, somehow Ted expected it. The desk was occupied by his typewriter and a few completely neat stacks of typing paper and previous drafts, so instead of interrupting his work space, I laid the box of manuscript on the bed, cracking it open and leafing through the pages, tracing the progress of one detail or another, the intricate traces of his threads. We bent over the manuscript together.

The revisions took place in the winter, so when I stopped by it was always dark out. I was working long hours, partly to get over a disappointment with a man that had happened at the time; work was a secure place for me in the middle of this unhappiness. One night it snowed and we went to the window to marvel. The snow flew in specks outside the window, tiny furry points of light in the darkness, cold dusty sisters to the lights flickering on Third Avenue below and the many apartments winking on the other side of the canyon. We stood next to the glass and watched the snow swirl, high in the heavens of New York, so far away, it seemed, from the rest of my life.

As we stood there looking at the snow in that night sky, that winter night in New York, Ted Whittemore, quite unexpectedly, ran his hand lightly down my back. Tentatively. I did not move, and he did not touch me a second time.

We went back to being an editor and a writer.

Ted left the country after the manuscript went through copy-editing, but before we published the book. He took a freighter to Jerusalem. Ted said that it was a bad idea to fly to the Middle East, because you were traveling through so much time that it should take a long time to make the journey. Also a freighter was cheaper than flying, and Ted never had any money.

He read his galleys in Jerusalem, where he lived in an apartment in the courtyard of the Ethiopian Church. In the early mornings, on one side of the courtyard wall, a flock of French Nuns sang their devotions. All day, around the circular Ethiopian Church, a school of monks walked and murmured their prayers. And Ted read his galleys in July and we published in the Fall.

When I pitched the book at sales conference, I got applause, which usually doesn't happen at a sales conference, certainly not for a novel that will advance fewer than seven thousand copies. But the sales reps, those cynical hard eggs, put their hands together, not so much for my performance as for what Ted meant to the house as a whole. His books were the books we published that proved to us that publishing could be about good writing and fearless imagination and vision.

Before he moved from New York, Ted sent me a note. "I'm glad you're part of the Quartet," he wrote. And so I became connected to Ted Whittemore, connected forever.

*

The book, as it turned out, did not sell well. It had some good reviews, but the machine of publishing did not kick in for Whittemore. The reps applauded at sales conference, but the machine did not kick in.

Great fiction is hard to sell. What happens to a person who reads a book—if it's any good—is a profoundly private and irrational process, and the more distinctive the novel, the more private and irrational the process. That's where the trouble with publishing begins.

*

Two and a half years later, I left the industry. I was frustrated by the limitations of the business end and I had fallen in love, this time, I thought, for keeps, to a man who lived in Western Massachusetts who had three kids and joint custody and who was very persuasive. Love to me was more important than work, so I moved to Massachusetts and married. But I discovered that I was not as nice, not as accommodating, as I had thought I was. Even though I had always believed that I was able to make anything succeed if I just worked hard enough at it, I was not able to respond to my husband's demands, and he was very far from being able to help me mend my unhappiness. We were soon miserable.

After two years we divorced. Although the marriage had been horrible, still divorce was like suddenly falling into nothing.

The summer after, I got a call from Ted. I had heard from him from time to time. He had heard about my romance and my departure from New York, and now he'd heard about my divorce.

At my end, over the years, I'd also had reports of Ted back from Tom, who visited Ted in Jerusalem. Ted was with a wonderful woman, a painter named Helen, Tom reported. A year or two after that news, Tom told me that Ted had broken up with Helen, abruptly. Without so much as a day's notice, said Tom, Ted had packed up and left Helen and left Jerusalem. Tom said Helen was heart-broken. Tom disapproved and so did I.

Although I disapproved I was still glad to hear Ted's voice. He was back in the country and writing, up at the family home in Dorset, Vermont for the season. Would I come up to see him?

I did, twice. Dorset is beautiful in the summer, green and leafy and a good ten degrees cooler than Western Massachusetts. Ted showed me everything and how much he loved it and how much he wanted me to love it, too. We talked a little about the book he was working on, but mostly we didn't. The Whittemore family home was big and rambling; late afternoon we sat on white Adirondack chairs on the great lawn, sloping into a meadow, and watched the young girls from the dancing school down the road mince like birds into the middle of town, to buy their sweets. Beyond, the mountains misted with blue, and flowers of all shapes and colors and sizes waved in the breeze.

We swam in the Dorset Quarry. The Dorset Quarry is a writer's dream, because when you swim in the Dorset Quarry you are swimming in the space left by the stone that now is the New York Public Library, the great lion library at 42nd Street. The quarry's stone walls rise high and flat, gray streaked with white. Boys in baggy bathing suits jump off the high walls screaming. Women paddle quietly. Children sit on low ledges and dip in their feet. At the far end is an island of stone; birch trees rise skinny and white from its nooks.

After we had spent some time in the water, Ted got out, but I stayed in. He threw me my swimming goggles and I went exploring around the shallower end of the quarry. Looking for what kind of gunk grew down there, where the New York Public Library used to be.

I saw something green. I went to the surface, got a big gasp of air, dove down and swam, down and down and down. I reached for the green and headed back up.

It was a twenty-dollar bill. I swam over to Ted and gave it to him. We were both amazed. "Are you coming out?" he asked.

"In a little," I replied. I went back to see what else was down there. Again, I took a big gasp of air, dove down and swam, down and down and down. Something green. I grabbed it and headed back up.

"Ted," I said. I waved the bill. Ten dollars.

The next time down, I found a five. And that was it. I looked, but nothing else was down there. I shook the water out of my hair and we spent the money on dinner.

It was not surprising to me that magic like this would happen around Ted. It seemed almost predictable. Ted Whittemore was a magician, not only of words, but of moments. He marveled, and any sensation, of light or sound or character or scent, was ratcheted up another notch. We walked past swaying meadows and through the graveyard where all the Whittemores are buried. We drove down roads, looked at the cows, stopped the car near a stream and took off our shoes and hopped from rock to rock and stood in the running water, listening to the leaves rustle and the water bubble, smelling the good air.

Ted put his arms around me and kissed me. I kissed him back, but then I said no.

He could not imagine why I would not grasp this good thing. He could see it so clearly, something between the two of us, he could see it and he wanted it. The world is full of possibilities, he said. I could see it, too, when he talked about it, because Ted always made me see whatever he saw, but I still said no.

I came back, however, the next weekend, and I told him I would sleep with him, but only one time, and then it would be over and he had to understand that this was the only way it would happen.

I told myself this was because I was a woman who recently had been hurt, and that Ted was, after all, the man who had left Helen, but my true motives weren't so attractive. Ted's proposal appealed to me a lot—I had a particular weakness for writers (the man who had broken my heart that long-ago winter and the ex-husband were both writers)—but I had no intention of getting tangled up with Whittemore. Like a spoiled child, I wanted to play out this flattering scenario but without accepting responsibility for what would follow. Crazily enough, Ted agreed to my counter-proposition, and so, only once it was.

Afterwards, back in Massachusetts, I spoke to Ted occasionally, but finally, I stopped returning his calls, his persistent, baffled, loving, persuasive, tempting calls.

*

That was 1988. In February of 1994, I was planning on visiting friends in New York (from Washington, DC, where I had moved four years earlier), and so I called Tom Wallace to see if he wanted to have lunch. Tom had become a literary agent, but he was the same Tom, solid as a rock. He gave you a sense that the important things still mattered and that history counted for something. It was a good thing I had called.

"By the way," he said, "I meant to phone you and ask—have you talked to Ted Whittemore lately? You might want to give him a ring. He's back in New York. Ted's had some tough times, I'm afraid, and now there's bad news. He's very sick."

Ted had been diagnosed with a very lethal, inoperable prostate cancer. He was working on a new book and living with a woman named Annie, who had a brownstone on the upper West side, right off the park in the 90's.

Whittemore was completely happy to hear my voice. Yes, he was well; how was I doing? We arranged to meet at Tom's office at 2:30 on Friday, if I could manage to get Tom back by then. We agreed that Tom could talk a person's ear off and lunch was bound to go on forever.

I hadn't seen Ted for so long. Tom's receptionist buzzed him in and he walked into the reception area and took off his knit cap, holding it in both hands, twisting it slightly. His face was puffier than before, but his smile was the same, a smile of such colossal affection that I practically fell down looking at him. He turned his head slightly to the side when he smiled, and the edges of his thin, wide mouth turned up in delighted mystification and complete charm.

He put out his arms; I fell into them. We hugged, hard.

It was snowy and cold. Ted and I walked through Central Park, ice crunching beneath our feet, the same way we had walked down the dusty roads of Vermont, talking, talking, talking. We stopped at a food stand for tea and sat on a patio, in a corner protected from the wind, looking out across an oval frozen pond. Although his attention seemed to be entirely on the beauty of the day, the moment, and the happiness of being together again, Ted still managed to read the notes and overhear the conversation of the man sitting next to him. Once a spook, always a spook. As we headed up the hill away from the tea shop, he told me the man had been writing poetry. Bad poetry, he said, but not as bad as it might be.

That first long walk, he never mentioned his illness. I saw him again the next afternoon and we walked in the blistering cold wind over by the Hudson. He still didn't talk about it. We just walked, often with our arms around one another, to be close and to keep from slipping on the ice, trooping down the streets that became Ted's because of what he saw. "See that fellow at the corner, in front of the shop?" he'd say, giving a friendly salute to a rangy, beaten-up, leather-faced man. "Been here for years. Turkish, you know." And then he'd explain how the junk in the guy's store told you everything you needed to know to understand some invasion in the seventeenth century, and it would all make perfect sense.

He didn't talk about his illness, but we did agree that I would read his novel when it was done. He was very pleased. And so we fell back into the role of editor and writer, but of course we were something else, too, after all of this time. Time makes friendship in a way that no single action possibly can. That, after all, is what Ted's novels are about—time, friendship, and history, the real history.

At one point, but only once, Ted asked me about the events in Dorset, and afterwards, and how I had stopped being in touch. I didn't have much to say about it.

"Bad timing," I said. He nodded.

That summer Ted and Annie went to Italy, and I saw Ted again in the Fall. I had dinner with him and Annie, but before, he and I took a walk. That's when he told me.

He sat me down on a park bench, over by the wading pool where children sail their boats. It was November and getting cold. We were warm enough, though, in hats and scarves and gloves. He had something to tell me, and spoke very clearly and simply and straight. He had cancer and it could not be cured or permanently halted. He was in remission thanks to heavy doses of hormones; they had left him impotent, but that was better than being dead.

"The trouble is, that I can go out of remission at any time," Ted told me. "And the docs say that if that happens, I can go in as fast as three weeks." He paused. "It changes how you view things. Some things, like politics and what's in the newspaper, become utterly unimportant. And things like friends, family, especially friends, become the most important things in the world."

Ted looked at me. He reached for my hand, and held it fast. "So you see, having you come back into my life, now, all of a sudden, well it couldn't make me happier."

I wrapped myself around him. My arms and also one leg hooked over his lap — actually we probably looked fairly ludicrous there on the bench—but it was a moment where it didn't matter how we looked or what we were doing with our bodies. Ted held on tight. Nothing could change what was, the bad or the good. I said I loved him and then we said no more, just held on.

As we walked back to the house, and Annie, and dinner, we talked. He wanted very much to finish the draft of the novel, the last book he would ever write. I wanted very much to read it.

*

When Ted was still in remission, it seemed to me there were some things going on that were suspicious. Ted had always had a bad back, but it had gotten worse, why he wasn't sure. My assumption was that this was the cancer, he just didn't want to dignify it with the name. That would be giving it too much ground.

I called him one Sunday, from my apartment in Washington. Annie said he was out and she didn't know why he hadn't returned. Several hours later, Ted called and told me the story.

"The most amazing thing happened," he said.

He had gone to a hotel to meet a man who was going to do his taxes; the place was way over west on 58th Street, practically in the river. He walked down the hall to meet the man and heard some music coming out from behind a door; the hotel rented larger halls as well as rooms for people who had business to transact. After getting the tax stuff taken care of, he passed by the door again.

This time it was open. And he could hear the music more clearly. It was gospel. There was plenty of gospel, Ted had explained to me, in the book he was working on, but he had never actually been to a live service. A woman standing by the door saw his interest, and pulled him in. He sat in the rear.

"The music was wonderful," he said, "just what I'd imagined. So full of feeling and passion and emotion and all the good things of being human. The sound just rolled over me. Everyone was singing and the sound was immense." It went on for a long time, and then there was quiet. A small woman came to the front of the room Several people stood up, in no apparent pattern.

Ted's back was hurting him, so he stood up, too.

He hadn't understood. All of the people who had stood up were brought to the front of the room.

The woman prayed over them. She prayed for strength and

health. Calls of reassurance and encouragement came from all corners of the room. She prayed in front of Ted. And then she knocked him down.

"I could see what was going to happen, because it happened with the other people," Ted told me. "She stood in front of you, and behind you stood this immense black guy, and she knocked you down, and you had to fall right back. Where the man would catch you. You had to trust her, you see. You had to let yourself go, just completely."

"And did you?" I asked.

"I did," said Ted. "I can't tell you how marvelous I feel."

*

Ted finished the novel in March 1995. I was working for the federal government at the time. It arrived in my office on Monday and I took the day off on Thursday and edited it and had it back to him on Saturday.

"Don't rush," he had said, wanting not to inconvenience me. "Take your time."

But I knew we had no time. I read it once, all the way through. I could see the shape. The first time through, I began to understand who the people were. I read it again, slowly, and edited it, page by page, I listened to its sounds, word by word.

I was not young, not then. I was no longer a confused and anxious assistant editor at a New York publishing house. I was no longer a damaged woman who did not know her own heart. I had no questions about who Ted Whittemore was to me; I understood in many ways what was important about his work. I concentrated.

This book was not about espionage. It was about a healer. Ted began the book three months before he got his diagnosis, but still the book was about a healer. And, also, for the first time, Whittemore's main character was female. Her name was Sister Sally and she was unlike any of his other characters; the man with whom she has a brief love affair, Billy the Kid, however, resembled characters in the earlier books and also resembled Ted.

I wrote that I was going to push him very hard. "I think you have a bit further to travel with Sally and Billy. So let's go." I started by telling him that I didn't think the verb in his first sentence was in the right tense. This was a brutal and ridiculous way to start an editorial letter, but I had no choice. I had to be thorough. I told my dear friend what my thoughts were as I read. I tried to remember where everything was and to see when things worked together and when they did not. I commented, I queried words, I flirted with him, I reminded him of old successes and other moments we'd both loved in other Whittemore books, I cheered, I wondered out loud about the characters so he would see how they appeared to someone else, I suggested, I doubted, I applauded, I reflected, I pushed and pushed and pushed.

Ted told me the letter was helpful. Very helpful. He was excited about getting back to work. I sent a copy of the editorial letter to Tom, who had become Ted's agent. Tom called me up. He thought my comments were good.

And, in his old-fashioned manner, Tom said, "You know, the letter you wrote—it's a love letter, in a way."

A real writer puts his heart and soul and all his intelligence on the page. Any book can be the last one. Every one of the writer's words, every small motive, counts. The editor must attend as though nothing else matters.

*

Ted went out of remission a few weeks after he completed the draft. Although his levels of pain increased and increased in the weeks and months that followed, he was able to do some revisions.

I told him that his revisions were more than I could have hoped for. I came to New York from Washington several times, working on the pages and leaving notes with him, telling him every doubt, but most of all I told him how wonderful the book was, and how each revision made me more convinced that the book was complete and perfect inside of him and our only task was to ask the right questions and bring it all to light.

I called Ted every other day, sometimes every day, until that became too difficult. He told me things about himself, so that in those last months I was allowed to understand more about him and how he'd lived his life.

Combined with my love for Ted was a certain brutality which I tried to keep in check. I tried not to push him too hard. I tried not to let my disappointment show on the phone when he said he was just too tired from the pain, too sick from the drugs, to be able to write.

There was one section in the book that I really wanted him to revise. It was the scene where Sally and Billy fall in love. The woman in this novel was nothing like the women he'd written about before, who quite frankly had always struck me as a little pale. Sally was a real powerhouse, a force, a tragic mess. One day he called me at the office and told me he'd spent three hours writing the day before, and he felt like hell but he'd revised that scene, which was central to the love story, the scene I was sure he had inside him. He told me—but I did not see the pages. I did not see the fix.

Of course, it is dangerous when an editor has a favorite fix. It's not your book.

Because there was so little time, however, I let myself want it. In part, I just wanted what I wanted, and used the drama of death to cover up my presumptuousness and greed—but in part, I felt unconsciously that my desire for the fix would encourage Ted to fight harder, to slow down the illness for the sake of the writing.

Underneath this I must have believed that writing was more important to Ted than everything else, that he had no more powerful motive for staying alive. Was I crazy?

Meanwhile, he was in and out of the hospital. Annie left to go to Italy, alone, to get some time away from cancer, on a holiday Ted told her she needed to take. Carol came to take care of Ted.

Years back, Carol had been with Ted, longer than anyone else. She had ridden motorcycles all around Crete with Ted. She had been with him the day when, discouraged about ever writing anything worthwhile, he spotted a scarab in a dusty British glass case in the British Museum and the whole idea of the Quartet was born. Carol showed up when things took a turn for the worse. From early until late, she moved hospital beds and nurses in and out of Annie's house, not sleeping much if at all.

One night, when I hadn't been able to talk to Ted for ten days—I had been out of the country—I called him from my younger brother's house, where I was visiting.

Ted told me that he felt, suddenly, he had enough energy to really finish the book. Carol would read it, too, and Ted would mark places to cut, which I would then execute, leaving him the time to write the revisions he wanted to do.

My brother came into his bedroom where I was using the phone. So did my sister-in-law, so I moved out to the unfinished porch out their bedroom, carrying the portable phone, which was taped together with gaffer's tape from the results of abuse by children. As my brother and his wife lay together, sleeping, preparing for another day of work and family, I stood on the deck in the black night and schemed with Ted.

"Yes," I said. "Yes you can do it. Yes," I said. "We've had some great breaks already. You finished the draft before you went out of remission. Remember? Now we have another big break."

The night was wide. "This is what you can fix," I said. "With the time left. I'll come to New York. We'll talk about the cuts."

"Isn't it marvelous," said Ted to Carol, "that just when we need her, just like magic, Miss Judy appears. I hadn't heard from her. Wondered where she was. And here she appears. Stage Left. Enter Miss Judy."

"Yes," agreed Carol, wanly. "It's a good sign." I could hear the humoring in her tone, although I did not know, I could not see what she could see.

Instead, I egged him on. One more piece of luck, I said. One more good break. When so much has gone badly, one more piece of good luck. It's a wonder I didn't ask him to sit down at the desk then and there and write me a scene.

I never knew whether I was important to him for anything but the books. And I never knew if he would have been important to me if it weren't for the books. That was where we connected.

Ted had his own brutality. He had his ambition, which resulted in modest living and ruthlessness. He told me once that women were simply more generous than men, that they were better people, and although I never doubted that Ted had deeply loved the women in his life, and made them feel deeply loved, I wondered if that was an excuse for his bad behavior. He had two daughters, who didn't speak to him for years, although they visited him during his final illness. He said he had been a very bad husband, and a very selfish man. He knew what he was and he knew that as a result of how he had behaved, he had lost his daughters. But he had written his books. Ted had two granddaughters; one is named after his sister, as though his family got his children, but he didn't.

*

Six days after I returned from my brother's house to Washington, at 6:20 on a Sunday morning, my phone rang.

"Judy. It's Ted. Listen," he said, speaking urgently, "I'm in terrible trouble and you have to help me."

"Okay," I said. "Tell me what's wrong."

"I don't know where I am. And you have to come and find me."

"Of course," I replied. I paused.

Ted didn't know where he was, but I knew. He was lying in a hospital bed in his bedroom. He was too sick to be anywhere else. He was there, he just didn't know he was there. So I had to get him to bring himself back.

Suddenly my bedroom seemed very big and empty and the telephone cord a slender tie to the voice at the other end.

"Can you tell me where you might be, Ted?" I asked. "Can you tell me where you think you are?"

"Certainly," said Ted, practical, sure of himself. "I seem to be somewhere near Annie's. So you can start looking there."

We talked for a while, and got into a conversation about other things that were going on where he was. Some things confused him, like the workmen who were lifting big sections of pipe onto the roof of a nearby building (they might have been there or might not have been there). When we talked about it, he thought of some reasons why they were there and seemed to grow easier in his mind. And so we said goodbye.

One or two minutes later, the phone rang again.

"Judy, it's Ted." He seemed in a hurry. Or anxious. It was hard to tell.

"I just looked at the clock. It's six thirty in the morning. You must think I'm crazy." He sounded a little frightened.

"No," I answered honestly. "I don't think you're crazy. I just think you're on a lot of drugs, Ted. You're probably on a lot of morphine. That can mess you up. Besides," I added, looking out at the pale summer morning sky, "it's already light here. You probably looked out the window and saw how light it was and figured it was okay to call. Is it light where you are?"

Ted was reassured, and again we talked for a few minutes before he became tired and distracted. I couldn't go back to sleep after we hung up the phone, so I made some coffee and tried to read the Sunday papers. But he was much on my mind.

That evening, I came home around nine thirty or ten from a family picnic at the house of one of my older brothers, in Baltimore. I was afraid for the blinking light on my answering machine. My machine tells callers to wait for the famous beep. Ted had waited and left this message. I listened.

"Judy. It's Ted." He spoke very fast, slurring one or two words. "Calling on your famous number that you can't make a call since you're waiting for my beep.

"Judy. I've got some great news from you today. For you today. With you today. And the news is: is that I'm no longer mad! And don't you think that it would be nice to know that Ted Whittemore is no longer mad? Wouldn't that be fun! I hope it would be! Nice for a change anyway.

"Your number is still the change. Change. Still hasn't changed. My number hasn't either. What changed is that I'm no longer crazy!

"So listen. If you could call me sometime. At that number you know all about. And we could talk on that number.

"There are a lot of things . . . that are going to become clear — which never were!"

At this moment, Ted's voice, rising in excitement and joy, is abruptly cut off As though he simply went spinning off the face of the world. I think I knew then that I would never talk to him again, never hear his voice again.

Of course he did not go, spinning. It was not that simple, that easy, or that much fun. He continued for another month, increasingly disoriented, consumed by pain, pumped with drugs. He soon had nurses around the clock at home, he went in and out of the hospital, and finally went into a hospice. Several years earlier, I had helped to care for someone through the end of a terminal illness, so when my phone calls to New York were not returned by family and by the two women who, at different times, had shared his life and now had the honor and burden of seeing him through his final passage, I knew what this meant. They had too much on their hands to bother calling back concerned but peripheral friends. They were doing the hard work, and the least I could do was stay out of the way.

When it was all over, I knew, I would be handed the manuscript, for Tom was one of the literary executors and he would vouch for me. I would see if Ted had revised that love scene. I would make sure that all the changes in his hand were faithfully entered. I would see if any of the cuts we'd discussed were possible, but be cautious in my acts, just cleaning things up.

Then I would pass the pages to Tom and he would try to sell the story. Tom, however, never was able to make that sale. The novel felt unfinished.

*

The family held a memorial service in Dorset on August 12th. I flew to Hartford, rented a car, and drove north.

The day alternated between brilliant sun and showers. Dorset, in rain or shine, was as beautiful as ever. Tom spoke at the service. He said that Ted had compartmentalized his life, that different parts of Ted's life didn't touch. The parts that were represented in Dorset—his family, his true and good friends from Yale, who had supported him during his illness, who spoke of the powerful love they had felt from Ted during that time—were strangers to me.

After the service we were all invited back to the house. It had been renovated, but some parts of it were as I remembered. It was strange to stand there and see those same rooms. Time passed and the house emptied of visitors. Even the family disappeared, for a family meeting that may or may not have had to do with Ted; maybe they were burying him in the old graveyard with the other family members. The house was empty, except for a woman who went from room to room, clearing away food and drink.

I sat in a rocker on the back veranda and had a glass of wine. The rain came and went, yet again, spattering the tall meadow grasses behind the house. And then the sun shone bright. I took my empty glass to the kitchen and then I went to an upstairs bathroom, put on my bathing suit, and headed to the Dorset Quarry.

It was as ever. Young men went screaming over the high cliffs, cannon balling into the water. Two women paddled at the shallower end, near where I had found all the money. Children dabbled their feet, sitting on the ledge.

The water was cool. The birches tossed their leafy arms in the sky. Life contains these perfect afternoons. I swam from one end of the quarry to the other. And then I put on my goggles and dove down, deep.

The rain had left the depths murky, however, so there was nothing I could see.

Judy Karasik
Silver Spring, Maryland and Vitolini, Italy, 2002

Edward Whittemore (1933-1995) attended Yale University before serving as a Marine officer in Japan and spending ten years as a CIA operative in the Far East, Europe, and the Middle East. Among his other occupations, he managed a newspaper in Greece, was employed by a shoe company in Italy, and worked in New York City's narcotics control office during the Lindsay administration.